PRAISE FOR *UNSTRUNG*

"In Spinella's wrenching tale of love and loss, one woman must come to terms with her past and the decisions that have shaped her life. Spinella has filled her incredibly emotional novel with multifaceted characters, and nothing is as simple as it seems in this true page-turner."

—*Publishers Weekly*, Starred Review

"Every character is a work in progress, which makes this tale extremely realistic."

—*RT Book Reviews*

"In *Unstrung*, Laura Spinella orchestrates a brilliant, multilayered story about family expectations, forgiveness, and whether we can truly love ourselves and others just as we are . . . an honest and raw exploration of one woman's journey as she learns to embrace her talents and the goodness life has to offer."

—Kerry Lonsdale, author of the #1 Kindle bestselling novel
Everything We Keep

"A darkly quirky tale in which nothing is quite as it seems, *Unstrung* is about family legacies, dark secrets, one volatile violinist who sees her gift as a curse, and three men who are about to define her future. It will punch you in the gut and melt your heart."

—Barbara Claypole White, bestselling author of
The Perfect Son and *The Promise Between Us*

D0862647

PRAISE FOR *GHOST GIFTS*

"An engaging writing voice, realistic characters, and a compelling mystery make this a must-read! Aubrey and Levi are compelling and likable, both individually and as a team, and the way their stories intersect increases the appeal. Just the right blend of emotion and humor combine with captivating suspense for a paranormal mystery that is sure to delight fans. The flashbacks heighten the tension and deepen the poignancy, and the romantic angle has a great slow-burn passion."

—*RT Book Reviews*, 4.5 stars

"A wild adventure of a mystery, brimming with layers, secrets, and more than one person who should feel guilty . . . paranormal mystery/romance fans will find a gem of a story in Laura Spinella's *Ghost Gifts*."

—*Fresh Fiction*

"*Ghost Gifts* transcends labels like 'murder mystery' or 'love story' or 'ghost tale,' giving readers a masterful plot that weaves effortlessly between past and present, sharply pivoting whenever you think you've put your finger on it. The characters and setting come to life so vividly that you forget you're reading a book. Laura Spinella's *Ghost Gifts* is an absolute treasure."

—David Ellis, #1 *New York Times* bestselling author

FORE
TOLD

ALSO BY LAURA SPINELLA

Ghost Gifts Novels

Ghost Gifts

Other Titles

Unstrung

Perfect Timing

Beautiful Disaster

Writing as L.J. Wilson

Clairmont Series Novels

Ruby Ink

The Mission

FORE TOLD

LAURA SPINELLA

Montlake
Romance

Published by Montlake Romance, Seattle

www.apub.com

Amazon, the Amazon logo, and Montlake Romance are trademarks of Amazon.com, Inc., or its affiliates.

ISBN-13: 9781542046749
ISBN-10: 1542046742

Cover design by Faceout Studios

Printed in the United States of America

For Grant, because he understands "You're only given a little spark of madness. You mustn't lose it."

PROLOGUE

New Paltz, New York
Carnival Days

Aubrey Ellis was five the first time life turned upside over, like a somersault in deep seas. Her parents were dead, and she was sent to live with her grandmother—Charlotte Antonia Pickford Ellis Heinz Bodette, carnival mistress deluxe. The woman's hodgepodge troupe and a traveling life were Charley's soul, though Aubrey quickly became her heart. Despite the odds, or the odd environment—the certainty of falling asleep in Piscataway only to wake in Poughkeepsie, the loneliness that lingered in carnival crowds—Aubrey prevailed. She had to. Her life's other demand required all her wit and will, because Aubrey's second somersault was the inexplicable ability to speak to the dead.

At twenty-one, Aubrey found that the freakish yet fascinating phenomenon of her childhood was never far from her thoughts. To her surprise, it was Zeke Dublin who had managed to soothe the most calamitous memories, peppering Aubrey's life with security and happiness. In the heat of the current summer, those emotions had become Aubrey's focus, perhaps a driving force, and she didn't want the feelings to end. She'd imagined Zeke would want the same. How could he not? But as fantasies so often went, reality had muscled its way into this evening.

She was alone now, in a camper nicknamed Mule, stretched across rumpled sheets and a mattress that was the entire bedroom. Nearly an hour had passed since Zeke had abruptly exited. Beside her lay a thin gold chain. She picked it up, watching metal and moonbeams intertwine. Aubrey blinked and dropped the bauble, a gift from Zeke.

Her expectation hadn't been without cause. Zeke had filled the voids in Aubrey's life, first with friendship, then with a deeper sense of family. And now, for better or worse—a love story. The chain tangled around her fingers again, and Aubrey swiped at the tear running from her cheek to her ear. Zeke didn't do "See you next season . . ." presents.

Common sense said to focus on facts: Tomorrow, carnival season would come to a close. Aubrey would return to the University of New Mexico. Like every other year, Zeke would head somewhere else. She sat upright and peered through a curtain of gauzy gold fabric. A campfire burned like a small sun. At its edge sat Zeke. One hand gripped the neck of a Coors Light bottle; in his other, a cigarette smoldered defiantly. Because she'd asked him to quit, Zeke had done just that back on opening day. Aubrey glanced at the unlikely gift, the necklace, and laughed. "He probably didn't even buy the damn thing. He probably won it in a craps game at the Renaissance fair three counties over."

She simpered at rings of smoke, which did not move, like a halo over Zeke's head. He downed another mouthful of beer, perhaps drowning the prickly words he and Aubrey had exchanged. He was backlit by distant carnival lights, twinkling round globes that decorated the setting but were there for safety. The grounds were vacant; shutdown and cleanup had long passed. It had to be after two in the morning. The Heinz-Bodette carnival was doing the thing it did least: sleeping.

Aubrey scooted off the end of the mattress and placed the necklace on a shelf. Tugging a pair of denim shorts over her long legs, she then slipped a UNM Lobos T-shirt over her head. Exiting the tiny bedroom, she inched through the dark, narrow interior. In the cramped forward bunk, where Nora usually slept, Aubrey reached between the wall and the mattress and came up with a spare pack of Camels. Hidden contraband—it was the smallest act of loyalty Zeke's sister would demonstrate, even if it did end up killing him. The camper door squeaked as Aubrey opened it, and nothing moved but cool September air. She wrapped her arms around herself. "Coming back in?" she asked. Zeke shook his head, his frown evident even when lit by a small sun. She pivoted on the camper's steps.

"Fire's warm if you want to sit."

She turned toward his voice and came down the creaky metal steps. He snuffed out the cigarette and pulled a low beach chair closer. She knew he couldn't do it—go back inside. The tension between them made the confines of the camper too tight, too real for Zeke, who'd run away from life so long ago.

Tentatively, she circled the ring of fire. While the flames were warm, the air was not, and goose bumps rose as she lowered herself into a chair. They even dotted the deep scars on Aubrey's arm—an unpleasant keepsake from age seventeen, a physical ghost gift she did not want. Zeke's gaze moved from her face to her arm. Most people would see the scars; Zeke saw that she was cold.

He shrugged off a worn green flannel shirt. "Here. Just put it on." She accepted the peace offering, such as it was. The garment was laced with the scent of Zeke—a lusty combination of wandering and lure. She buttoned a few buttons and crossed her arms, her fingers gripping into the sleeves of the soft fabric. Zeke's dark gaze settled on her face, and he reached out, grazing his thumb over the scar on her chin. "Guess we all have things we don't like to talk about. Things that could set off an argument."

"True. But mine won't keep us apart."

Zeke picked up his beer and drew it to his mouth, lowering it before taking a sip. "Hell, Aubrey. You're twenty-one. Anything could happen by the time you graduate next May." He snorted a laugh. "For one, you might find the right guy."

Aubrey narrowed her eyes.

"We agreed," he said. "I might be your other half, but I'm not *that* half." He traded the beer bottle for a small branch, snapped a piece off, and tossed it onto the fire. "Not a forever half."

She didn't argue; it wasn't about romantic ideals or ideal romance.

"That guy, he's out there." Zeke pointed the remaining stick like a wand toward the future. "He just doesn't know it yet. I'd like to meet him someday." He raised a dark eyebrow. "'Course, that's not to say I won't hate the son of a bitch. But I'd still like to get a good look."

"When I find him, I'll be sure to tell him all about you on our first date."

Zeke dropped the slip of wood. "I don't want to talk about this anymore."

"Why? Because our relationship doesn't fit into *your* off-season?"

"No. Because I'll never fit into Aubrey Ellis's life. Not really. Be realistic. There's a kind of guy who wins the girl. He isn't me." Zeke grinned. "Damn. He might even be better looking too."

Aubrey bit down on a smile. Physically, you couldn't define Zeke at a glance; he required the double take. Dark locks of hair, the kind never meant for scissors, outlined salient bone structure, all of him complemented by a sinewy frame. Above his left eye was a zigzag scar, a flaw that Aubrey guessed was also scored to his soul.

"Ah hell, forget the other guy." He drank the beer. "You might skip over him altogether and find a life in Los Angeles or Paris. Last I checked, carnivals weren't much for stops in Paris."

"I know. Future addresses. It's what started the argument. Remember?" She sighed. "I'm not coming back, Zeke. I love my grand-mother. You know how much Charley means to me." Her blue-gray gaze took in a small army of RVs and more distant tractor-trailers, the permanent fixtures in ever-changing scenery. "I love a lot of the people in this place. Some days I even love *the place*, but . . ." Aubrey was abso-lute in her decision. "I'm done. I don't want this."

"Right. I got it. Your entire life turned out to be nothing but a summer job."

"That's not fair. I never chose this, and I'm ready to move on. Earlier, I was only suggesting—"

"I heard you. You were suggesting that wherever you land, I could come hover, like some flesh-and-blood ghost."

"Not funny," Aubrey said, though the imagery was. Zeke was one of a few people who viewed Aubrey and her ethereal gift as . . . *seamless.* "And my suggestion includes Nora. You know that, right? This honestly can't be what you want for your sister."

"Wow. Wouldn't your grandmother love to hear that?" His Adam's apple bobbed with a longer swig of beer. "Imagine Charlotte's reaction."

"She gets it, Zeke. This is her life—not mine. I'm grateful for everything she's done. The roofs over my head, a life where ghosts aren't the most curious thing I encounter in a day." The scar above Zeke's eye vanished into a deep groove. "Even so . . ." She slammed herself into the chair. "I didn't think wanting one zip code, instead of a dozen post office boxes, was so crazy."

"Can't speak for Nora, but I don't need any zip code. The last one we had didn't work out so good. I don't know what you want my response to be."

"That you'll think about it. That you realize how smart you are, that surviving shouldn't be your life."

He looked toward shadowy traveling carnival props, the most stationary things in his life. Envy fluttered; Aubrey wanted to be the stationary thing. "Look, if Nora wants to go to college or ends up with a two-car-garage life . . ." He pointed to the small Heinz-Bodette camper. "Hell, she'd like that, more than bunkin' in a tin can or under a bridge." He hesitated. "So would our parents."

It startled Aubrey. Zeke so seldom spoke of his dead parents. Years before, when he and Nora first turned up in Yellow Springs, Ohio, the siblings were hungry and dirty and pickpocketing thieves. Nora's gaunt appearance drew concerned citizens as she feigned a spot-on fainting spell. Why not? The sun was hot, the crowds thick. Adults had rushed to Nora's aid, leaving backpacks and purses abandoned. It was elementary pilfering for Zeke until Carmine nabbed him by the shirt collar. Charley had intended to call the police. Zeke's stomach stopped her. It growled so loudly that Aubrey heard it from the alcove of the Winnebago where she hid, eavesdropping.

As a teenage Zeke awaited his fate, the lilt of a brogue seeped into Aubrey's head. *"Ailish . . . ,"* Aubrey whispered. Present among them was a woman, her spirit cloaked in motherly light. She belonged to the hungry boy. Warding off her presence, Aubrey forced her diviner senses onto the physical scene before her.

It wasn't that difficult.

Zeke was a shrewd talker—a skill that might have been effective on a social worker, a law-enforcement officer, even a judge. But with Heinz-Bodette's seasoned carnival owner, it was useless subterfuge. Charley paused her inquisition to tempt the gangly teenager with her lunch. Zeke pounced on a cold grilled cheese sandwich. Between massive bites, the boy explained that the Heinz-Bodette troupe had thwarted his honest means of obtaining a meal. Workers had emptied trash bins of discarded funnel cakes and half-eaten hot dogs before he could scavenge through. Zeke proudly admitted to tracking the carnival through six stops before *they'd* been caught.

Charley immediately wanted to know about the "they." One boy might be a lone drifter; two were most likely trouble. She'd suggested Zeke's partner in crime might be in greater peril if she were to call the police. Young Zeke had swiped his dirty sleeve across his mouth, reassessing.

He went on to talk about his life the way you might let a suspenseful story seep out, each morsel detailing an existence that made carnival life sound mundane. Zeke's tale of rootlessness wove on, peaking as he admitted to his grandest act of thievery: stealing his sister from foster home number four. When Charley asked why, Zeke was clear: "We'd done okay until then. But on the last placement, we got separated." The gusto with which he'd eaten the sandwich petered out to no appetite. "The home where Nora got put, there was an older boy . . ." Zeke was quiet, and discomfort settled over the room. "We couldn't do any worse after what happened to Nora—or what happened to land us in foster care in the first place."

Aubrey was surprised that Charley didn't ask about Zeke and Nora's parents. They were apparent to her—the mother, Ailish, and the equally Irish father, who had also passed. She stifled a gasp. A violent passing, she surmised, hearing a gun fire over and over. *Red . . . a flood of red . . .* The startling taste of blood swamped her mouth, overtaking the Sour Patch candy she'd eaten. The parents hovered distantly, and this told Aubrey something: they wanted Zeke and Nora where they were.

From her hiding spot, Aubrey recalled something else. A few days earlier, Charley had been in an ill-tempered mood. A vivid dream had woken her; it involved a double-talking teenage boy and a wispy girl close to Aubrey's age. It was one of countless curiosities associated with Aubrey's psychic gift. Often, her grandmother would dream of a live person connected to a dead soul Aubrey would soon encounter.

That day, Zeke's story was all Charley needed to hear; it was all Aubrey remembered, except for the fact that when the Heinz-Bodette troupe left Yellow Springs, Ohio, it had two new hands with it. Aubrey finished out the season thinking the brother and sister would blend in like she had—one of the few permanent fixtures in a traveling life.

It wasn't to be.

That summer, on the morning of their last stop, Zeke and Nora had vanished. No explanation, no note. Charley, who understood itinerants, took the news far better than Aubrey. Not unlike her own parents' abrupt abandonment, Zeke and Nora's desertion haunted her. Maybe this was the reason Aubrey felt that something lost was found when Zeke and Nora turned up in Boonsboro, Maryland, the following year. A number of seasons would come and go before her friendship with Zeke blossomed, bursting like a bright flower on a winding, waiting vine.

The current summer had grown intense, with Aubrey entertaining fantasies about changing the wandering aspects of Zeke. Earlier, she'd tested the theory; the conversation hadn't gone well. The two of them stared into the campfire now, one of hundreds they'd shared. Zeke nudged her arm with the beer bottle. She took it, finishing the beer and, in turn, agreeing to a truce. "You're right," she said. "After I graduate . . . after next May, that's a long way off. Who knows what I'll want? Maybe I will take a job in Paris. Such an old city—imagine the spirit population lying in wait."

Zeke stole a glance. "Don't reverse psychology me, Miss Magna Cum, whatever sash UNM hangs around you. Like Marie Antoinette's ghost would interest you."

"I won't deny that it's a rare and interesting thing when a well-known spirit shows up. I still swear it was Edgar Allan Poe in Havre de Grace last summer."

"And I still say that's what I get for teaching you to drink." Zeke pulled his lanky frame out of his chair and straddled Aubrey in hers; his knees sank into the sandy surround of the fire pit. "And so you know. If you did go to Paris, I might turn up." He kissed her, and Aubrey felt warmer than the fire in front of them. "Let it go," he said. "Just pretend it's any other year. Nora and me, we've stayed longer than usual. Can't it be enough? Wear the necklace and think of me. Leave it like that—just the way it's been."

Aubrey put down the beer bottle and wrapped her arms around his shoulders. "On one condition."

"What's that?"

"Tell me where you'll go this off-season."

"Can't tell you what I don't know." He smiled; she softened.

"A hint?" she asked. He kissed her again, his hands sliding beneath the green flannel. "A direction, at least, north . . . south?"

"Sorry, sweetheart. Depends on the wind. We'll find a way to make a buck and not get ourselves labeled grifters." He stood, pulling Aubrey to her feet. "Let's go back inside. You can write down the directions to the desert Southwest. Maybe come Christmas we'll show up, surprise you."

And that was the thing about Zeke Dublin—you never knew when or where he might turn up.

◆　◆　◆

Zeke stood in front of Charlotte's desk, his belongings packed in a duffel bag beside him. He waited for her to initiate conversation.

"That was a first," Charlotte said. "Aubrey leaving before you and Nora."

"If she's as smart as I think she is, she'll keep going. She won't come back because of me."

"Nor me." Charlotte leaned back and looked out the window of the Winnebago as if she might catch of glimpse of her granddaughter, who'd boarded a flight over an hour ago. "But of course we're both old carnie liars," she said. "Of course we both want her to."

Zeke grinned, a charm that he knew had greater effect on Aubrey than her grandmother. "I just want her to be happy. We both do."

Charlotte tapped red-painted fingernails on the ledger in front of her. "And you're positive that equation doesn't include you?"

"Only to the extent that I'll be there should she ever need me." He hesitated, taking his own glance out the window. "Come on, Charlotte. Nobody needs a grifter in their life—not permanently."

She didn't argue, jowls bobbing in what looked like agreement. "So where are you and Nora headed? As always, you're welcome to visit New Mexico, maybe for the holidays?"

It was a good offer. A few times, for Nora's sake, he'd considered it. He couldn't do it; Zeke couldn't call any place home. Not after the horrifying one they'd left behind when he and Nora were Dunnes, not Dublins. "We didn't do so bad with Indian gaming venues last year, picked up some work. New Orleans riverboat before that."

"I gathered as much when the two of you showed up in a car this season, not desperate for a meal or a paycheck."

"Right. Anyway, not sure where this winter will take us. Not just yet . . ." He spoke while trying not to eye the safe behind her. The door was closed. But the lever pointed to three o'clock, indicating it wasn't locked—this wasn't Zeke's first carnival. "Whatever direction, we really need to get moving."

"Of course. Carmine made the bank run this morning. Cash isn't how I'd like to make payroll, but it's what carnies prefer."

"True." Zeke cocked his chin toward the safe, which seemed appropriate considering the conversation. The fuzzy buzz of a walkie-talkie cut in, Joe's voice crackling through.

"Hey, Charlotte, you busy?"

"Just settling the books with Zeke. What's going on?"

"I got no idea how this happened, but it looks like some hooligan dumped a liter of Coke into the motor of the Whip."

"You're joking?"

"Wish I were. We did have a rowdy band of teenage boys roll through here right before closing. Do you want to call the cops?"

Charlotte sighed, shaking her head at Zeke. "This is why people have jobs in the real world."

"So they don't have to put up with stuff like that?"

"No. So they can take a vacation and visit a carnival." She clicked on the talk button. "Let me come take a look." She guffawed at Zeke while talking to Joe. "I'm not sure if it's worth the bother. I can't remember the last time local law enforcement was inclined to take our side on vandalism. *Not in our town,*" she said mockingly. Charlotte talked, and

Zeke drew a pack of Camels from his shirt pocket. He dropped them on the desk as she made the cumbersome rise. Zeke rose too and darted ahead, holding open the door of the Winnebago. "Be back shortly," Charlotte said. "And don't smoke in here!"

"Yes, ma'am." He waited, not ducking back inside until Charlotte rounded the corner near the Skee-Ball and other games of chance. The Whip was located on the far side of the carnival setup; she'd be gone at least twenty minutes. He was sorry about the liter of Coke; the repair would be costly. He'd leave a few extra hundred dollars behind. Zeke moved through the air-conditioned motor home, the space dedicated to the business side of the Heinz-Bodette carnival. Passing by the desk, he absently grabbed the pack of Camels and tucked them into his shirt pocket; his line of vision honed in on the Heinz-Bodette safe.

Seconds later, he knelt before the cool metal box like it was an altar. Zeke wiggled his fingers and hesitated. Then he gripped the iron handle and pulled. His heart hammered as if the Holy Grail were stored inside. "It's not stealing," he assured himself. "Not that kind, anyway." Zeke plunged his hand into the heavy Hamilton safe, past money he could smell. Stored behind the cash was the thing for which he had come.

Locked inside Charlotte's safe was a leather-clad box. Inside the box were her son's—Peter Ellis's—ghost gifts, just bits of paper, really. But unlike Aubrey's ghost gifts, which were more like mementos that connected to the past, these ghost gifts were all about the future, or so Zeke had learned.

Without them, last winter would have been a survivor's challenge. And it wasn't as if Zeke were taking them for himself. Hell, he could get by on a park bench as long as he picked a warm enough climate. He was doing this for Nora. Nora, who didn't have her brother's survival instincts, who shouldn't spend any nights on a bench or under a bridge. Nora, who'd already spent nights in worse places.

By the time Zeke pumped the pep talk through his head, he was sitting at Charlotte's desk. In front of him was the rectangular box. It was an curious thing that attracted the eye and had a cover like a book. But the interior was hollow: the perfect place to store scraps of paper. So many that no one would ever notice if a few were missing. The box's double knot told him Charlotte hadn't opened it either, not since Zeke hunted through its contents last September.

He undid the leather tie, pausing to rub clammy hands on denim-covered thighs. "Quit being such a fucking pussy. It's not like Peter Ellis is gonna haunt you for swiping a few of his ghost gifts." At least he didn't think so, and he boldly flipped open the cover. He stared at the papers, which came in every shape, color, and purpose. Anything you could think of to write on: napkins, business cards, the corner of a menu, ticket stubs, letterhead, matchbooks, construction paper, sheets ripped out of notebooks and legal pads. Each piece of paper, no matter its format, contained a prediction.

Zeke glanced out the window before refocusing on the box and his quest for a slice of guaranteed future: places, names, dates—there were hundreds, maybe a thousand. Many made no sense. Most read like omens. His hand hovered over a business card, print side up. He remembered the red lettering from last year. *Watt's Fertilizer. We Spread Miracles. Noble, Oklahoma.*

Fertilizer?

It was the kind of card nobody but a farmer, maybe a crop duster, would look at twice. Zeke turned it over and forced a wad of spit down his throat. On the back, Peter Ellis had written the word "Murrah." The next words he read aloud: "April massacre . . ." Recent facts slammed into his head. The Murrah Federal Building in Oklahoma City. A horrific bomb blast crystallized, one where hundreds of people had perished, and a tragedy Peter Ellis had predicted. It proved the depth and validity of his ghost gifts. It had to; the man died years before the terrorist act occurred.

An ill feeling wove through Zeke, and he dropped the card back in the box like it was on fire. It was too much prophecy, the kind no person would want to be responsible for. In the icebox hollow of the Winnie, Zeke wiped a bead of sweat from his lip. Less ill-omened writings passed through his fingers, clearer predictions that had long passed. They included World Series winners and prizefight champions. On plain white paper were a sketch of an apple and the words "Lisa project." He didn't know what it meant. Zeke stared at the contents, which also included numerous predictions that only bore numbers—maybe twenty or thirty of them. He shrugged, unable to put rhyme or reason to those predictions either.

Finally, Zeke found what he was looking for, information he could use. These scraps of paper were similar to the ones he'd taken last summer. They'd read: "Thunder Gulch . . . Derby winner . . . long shot . . ." along with the year, and "Tyson, knockout, eighty-nine seconds . . ." Both prophecies had turned into big paydays—enough to feed him and Nora and to buy a car to bring them back to the carnival this summer. It sure as hell beat dish washing and hitchhiking.

Now Zeke dealt himself a fresh hand of ghost gifts. As he closed the lid, a paper bearing a crayon-drawn cowboy hat and three large *X*s caught his eye. The exhilaration of future pay dirt pumped through him, sure of how the Dallas Cowboys would fare in Super Bowl XXX. He added it to the papers he'd already taken. Hell, horse racing was legal and so were Vegas wagers. Zeke glanced back at the safe. It wasn't like taking piles of money that didn't belong to him. These were random scraps of paper that no one was using for anything. How much harm could it do, guaranteeing what was to come? What was so wrong, Zeke thought, in helping himself and Nora to a little bit of a future?

CHAPTER ONE

Boston, Massachusetts
Present Day

"One more time, Miss Ellis, from the top." FBI agent Jack Hanlin leaned muscular arms into the table, his face coming closer to hers than in previous rounds of questioning. "Explain to me again how it is you had prior knowledge of today's Prudential Tower explosion."

Aubrey's legs felt like bags of sand, her brain having washed out to sea hours ago. "I don't know how many ways I can say it." She shifted in the chair. Did her lie gain or lose credibility with each repetition? "I overheard some men talking outside the Grind Café on Huntington Ave. When I got the gist of their conversation, I went straight to the nearest security guard." The rhetoric had been her hardline stance since the midmorning explosion. The blast had left a gaping hole on the lower level of the iconic Boston venue. It was an explosion that Aubrey had been forewarned about by a surprising but accurate ghostly prediction.

Hanlin glared at his suspect, then turned tightly in the gray cement space. Wiggle room was in short supply—so was his patience, she guessed. During the inquiry, Aubrey had made a thorough assessment of Agent Hanlin—a tough, but not without compassion, by-the-book man. If the situation weren't so ridiculously dreadful, it might be comical. His demeanor reminded her of Levi's—Aubrey's significant other for the past dozen years. Well, a dozen years less five months. *Levi . . .* She sucked in a breath and focused on the disaster at hand.

At the end of hour one, the agent had removed his branded FBI jacket; just past hour two, he'd turned up his starched white shirtsleeves with succinct movements. His forearm bore a tattoo. Via an ethereal nudge, Aubrey recognized it: Navy SEAL. A probing spirit was clearly attached to it, and she'd wisely pushed it away. Hour three had segued into a round of good cop, bad cop. Agent Hanlin exited and an Agent Kirkpatrick entered the tomb-like room. While his breath and disposition were harsher than Hanlin's, Aubrey didn't waver—not without earthly backup, which she thought might have arrived by now.

Fortunately, iron will was among her assets, and Aubrey tuned out Kirkpatrick like she would an ardent specter. In answer to his questions, she only reiterated hers: Would they please contact Deputy Chief Sullivan? Aubrey felt certain her own FBI contact would be her best advocate. But by the end of hour four, hope had dwindled. She thought future high points might include a custody transfer, landing her in the sort of place where terrorist types were never heard from again. Kirkpatrick left, knocking over a chair, spewing threats that sounded like an episode of *Law & Order*.

Daylight had to be fading, though it was hard to tell in the windowless room. With Levi and their son, Pete, no longer living at home, no one would wonder where she was. Aubrey swallowed down that reality as Agent Hanlin returned. She was strangely glad to see him. She wanted to ask the time, but something about him had changed. His mood was evident by the way he yanked up the chair, jamming it into the table. The force was enough to shove the opposite side into Aubrey. Her captor had an envelope and an iPad with him. Agent Hanlin laid the iPad on the table and held on to the envelope.

Grimly, he enlightened Aubrey with facts she did not know. Facts connected to the explosion that Aubrey had warned a security guard about twenty minutes before it occurred. As she listened, her mood shifted too, from distress to concern to guilt. She closed her eyes, a swell in her throat rising. In spite of her preemptive warning, which had prompted a complex-wide evacuation, Aubrey had been too late. Hanlin informed her that two civilians were dead, the result of a basement blast that could not be prevented.

"Damn it." Aubrey pressed her hands flat onto the cool tabletop.

Opening the envelope, the agent placed two photocopied driver's licenses in front of Aubrey—Patricia Lawrence from Madison, Wisconsin, and Anthony Revere from Swampscott, Massachusetts. Jack Hanlin drew her attention. "They were cousins, Miss Ellis—just ordinary folks, spending the day in Boston. Mrs. Lawrence was visiting with her husband and four children. Thank God only she and Mr. Revere went to use the restroom located on the lower level. He was nice enough to escort the family into the city, do the tourist thing with them. I highly doubt either cousin figured they'd end up dead today."

Aubrey's stomach knotted. She touched the photocopy image of Anthony Revere and his cousin Patricia, who now had four motherless children. A wave of obligation rode her, the impersonal driver's licenses taking on the look of treasured family photos. In the face of Anthony Revere, she saw something familiar, a resemblance. She stretched her fingers, making contact with the printed pages. Heat emanated, and a voice filtered through. It was the same specter she'd communicated with right before the deadly blast.

"Madame, do not be melancholy . . . Messages can be challenging to deliver . . . let my own hurried attempt to forewarn be a reference . . . My sincerest regrets if they remove you to the sponging house . . ."

"What the hell is a sponging house?"

"What?" Hanlin said.

"Uh, nothing." The specter's voice was gone, and Aubrey wondered if the nineteenth century had its own version of waterboarding. "I told you . . ." She sat taller and reverted to what she assumed was the safest explanation. "I was supposed to meet a friend—"

Agent Hanlin flipped through several pages of notes. "Right, a Zeke Dublin. Last known address, a post office box in Las Vegas. Not terribly reassuring, Miss Ellis. What little info we could obtain, the guy's like a ghost, a grifter for sure. Dublin's background is—"

"Oh my God. How many times do I have to say it? I've known Zeke since I was a girl. He's always moved around a lot. That doesn't make him a terrorist."

"And during your last phone conversation, tell me again what you talked about."

She answered through gritted teeth. "Zeke called weeks ago. He said he might be taking a trip east." She splayed her hands wide and clenched her fists, which landed in her lap. "It was a business trip. It had nothing to do with what happened today. I never even saw him." She paused. "Look, do . . . do you know if anyone's heard from Deputy Chief Sullivan? Piper Sullivan." He shook his head, and Aubrey was unable to decipher whether it was a reply or disgust.

"I want you to look at something." Agent Hanlin tapped on the iPad. "Here's the security feed from outside the Grind." He spun the device toward her. "Would you agree this is you, seated there this morning?"

It was grainy, but it would be difficult to argue with the time-stamped security camera footage: Aubrey dressed in the same distinct houndstooth jumper and black tights she currently wore. It was a wardrobe choice that was not specter friendly, apparitions being partial to bright colors. Clearly, today it hadn't mattered. That morning she had ventured into Boston—partly in need of a distraction, partly enticed by Zeke's text. The two were supposed to meet near the waterfall wall inside the Prudential Tower. The train schedule choices meant Aubrey could be an hour early or a half hour late. She'd chosen early.

In the security footage, she sat alone at an outdoor table a half block away from the southwest entrance to the massive tower complex. The emptiness of the surrounding tables had made for a lonely setting, enhancing a sense of foreboding. Obviously, Agent Hanlin saw the scene differently, her story vanishing like any good ghost: there were no men in the footage, no conversation to be overheard. Aubrey continued to watch her lie unravel. The initial images revealed nothing but a woman drinking a cup of tea on a sunny Friday morning. Her disposition, she thought, was readable: introspective, maybe sad. In truth, Aubrey's focus had been on Levi and twelve-year-old Pete. How much their lives had changed in recent months.

In one giant step, Hanlin was on her side of the table. Aubrey felt his breath in her ear as he peered over her shoulder. "I'm a good judge of demeanor, Miss Ellis. I'd say that's the look of a woman with a lot on her mind."

"I don't get much quiet time." She glanced back at him. "I was thinking about my son. My . . ." Aubrey stopped. She and Levi—Aubrey wasn't sure about the label anymore.

She refocused on the Huntington Ave footage, where a breeze picked up and a stray newspaper page took flight. A coffee cup rolled out of view, and prefall leaves skirted across the pavement. Aubrey's dark hair blew back. Not visible to the camera was the taste of chai tea, which had turned metallic. She watched herself swallow, making a sour face. Aubrey appeared blind to scattering debris, deaf to whipping wind. The sudden presence of an epic entity had caught her off guard.

You never knew what Boston would unearth; few places offered such a rich array of history and the dead. On the grainy feed, Aubrey looked across the table. Her back pulled stiff as history sat down across from her, a man who'd been dead for more than two hundred years.

Sitting in the interrogation room now, Aubrey resumed the tense position. Jack Hanlin sighed. On the screen, she reached across the wrought iron table, gripping something—the way a carnie might finesse a sleight of hand. The specter had handed her the usual offering—a token ghost gift. Of course, it's not what Agent Hanlin would see. The low-grade video made the object difficult to decipher. Aubrey tipped her chin upward. She'd never watched herself communicate with a spirit. Of course, to the average eye she appeared to be carrying on a conversation with no one.

"Did you dump the earpiece?" Hanlin asked. "We've checked every receptacle you passed, but maybe you tossed it in a sewer drain."

"What?" Aubrey's attention was rapt on the empty café chair as she dropped the spirit's ghost gift in her Burberry bag. The one they'd confiscated the moment she was taken into custody.

"An earpiece. Clearly you're wearing a communication device of some sort, talking to your contact."

"Oh my God. No!" She wove her fingers through her hair, gripping tightly at the crown. Naturally, that would be the agent's perception, and any mention of a ghost gift would sound like lunacy. Short of Piper coming to her rescue, Aubrey was out of ways to convince him. "That's absurd. I'm talking to . . ." Lowering her hand, she squeezed her eyes shut and fabricated yet another lie. "I was, um . . . I was rehearsing a pseudo-conversation with my son. We've been having some trouble with him lately."

"Ma'am, that's quite a rehearsal."

Aubrey's videotaped reaction grew more animated, an obvious exchange of dialogue. Take your pick: unstable individual or anti-American, maybe a good dose of both. With a gaping hole in the lower level of the Prudential Tower, she guessed either accusation would hold up in court.

Agent Hanlin darted back around the table. The military emblem on his forearm caught Aubrey's eye. "Personally," he said, "I might buy a pseudo-conversation. Maybe even a pep talk with yourself—but this?"

He tipped the iPad toward her. Aubrey's recorded expression shifted once more, now radiating panic. Seconds later, she lurched from the café chair and hurried toward the nearest tower entrance, exiting the camera's frame.

Hanlin sat. They'd arrived at a crossroads. Aubrey's gaze dipped, and she focused on his decorated arm. She went for a long shot and the heavy-duty ghostly presence connected to the former Navy SEAL since he'd hustled her into the room. The entity had been circling, wanting in each time the interrogation hit a lull. Maybe a little shock therapy would alter Hanlin's take and give Aubrey a chance to confide the truth. She eyeballed Hanlin and granted the specter access; the ghost's response was immediate. "Shaun says hel—" She stopped. He was a fast talker. "No, he says, *'Hola, Lead Dog.'*"

And just like that, the tables turned.

"What the fuck did you say?"

"Shaun . . . Ramirez . . . wait. You call him . . . the, um . . . *'the Irish spic.'*" Aubrey stared at the agent's arm. "He says, *'SEAL Team Six on deck.'*" Jack Hanlin yanked back his inked arm, like the tattoo contained a coded bio. "He, uh . . ." Aubrey briefly closed her eyes. Granted, the upset of the circumstance was not making for the most fluid pathway. Her nose filled with the scent of spent ammunition, dirt . . . blood. She heard the heartbeats of ten . . . twelve men, cautionary silence, then bedlam. A dog barked sharply in her ear; crystal clear, she saw a German shepherd pace.

Like all Navy SEALs, Shaun Ramirez was determined. He followed his training and acted on opportunity the second Aubrey allowed it. She tipped her head, separating expletives from content. "Shaun said to stop with the effing nightmares already—that you would have done the same thing." Hanlin stood, wide-eyed, his mouth gaping. It struck Aubrey as his first unrehearsed expression. "Our meeting isn't under pleasant circumstances," she said. "But I can see that you're a dedicated, loyal kind of man, Agent Hanlin." Aubrey honed in on his live emotions, which now provided a solid connection to his dead SEAL team member. "The

IED—Shaun says Cairo sniffed it out first, too fast. He followed Cairo, and the device exploded. They're glad they took the brunt of the blast for the team. *'Zero regrets . . . ,"* she quoted. "And, um . . ." Aubrey rolled her eyes. *"Woof,"* she said dully. "Afghanistan, was it?"

The agent's startled look dropped like a fallen solider. "All kinds of soldiers are well trained, Miss Ellis—particularly covert ones. Speaking of teams, there must be a formidable one behind you. You must have profiled every agent on this detail, come prepared to encounter any one of us. We're done with the 'good cop' portion of the program."

Shaun Ramirez's presence vanished like desert dust, and Aubrey's heart began to pound like those twelve men's. Maybe an ethereal approach wasn't the best idea. Hanlin's fists curled; it was no longer the tattoo that stuck out but the veins in his forearms.

"Let me be perfectly clear. Director Kirkpatrick has no issue with the use of physical force in a situation like this. Man, woman . . ." He shrugged. "Makes no difference to him. Personally, I don't condone it." Aubrey blinked at his cement-like pose and the locked door. "But if you don't start saying something of value, I will have no choice but to take a coffee break that you will regret. I'm part of what we call 'the greeting card team.' Be assured, there are agents who would have abandoned my friendlier approach hours ago."

Aubrey was out of subterfuge and viable explanations for a warning about the Prudential Tower explosion. An explosion conveyed by Boston's own Paul Revere. *Paul Revere.* She imagined how absurd it would sound. A knock at the door interrupted her borderline panic. Agent Hanlin exchanged a few hushed words with another man. The door opened wider. He turned to Aubrey. "Seems your Deputy Chief Sullivan has arrived."

"Oh, thank God." Aubrey lurched from the seat as a woman in a tan overcoat rushed into the room.

"Sit down!" Agent Hanlin barked, and Aubrey followed the order. "Aubrey, are you all right?"

The peril and upset sank in. Her chin quivered, and her hand moved across her mouth, feeling the half-moon scar on her chin. It'd taken decades, but today Aubrey had managed to end up in a moment almost as frightening as the one that had caused the scar.

"Aubrey?" the woman asked again.

"And beyond Deputy Chief Sullivan, you would be . . . ?" Agent Hanlin asked.

"Assigned to a special government task force, based in the New England region. Your superiors have my full credentials."

Hanlin looked Piper over, and Aubrey could see his usual spot-on assessment hit a wall. Piper was like that—external Southern sweetness, like she should be saying *"Bless your heart"* while pouring you a glass of iced tea.

In reality, any iced tea recipients would quickly find themselves hog-tied and at her mercy. Piper had been among the first female Army Rangers and, like Hanlin, now made the most of her repurposed skill set. "I've worked with Miss Ellis in the past," Piper said. "She's been most beneficial, aiding us with a number of cases."

"Okay, you must have checked out, or you wouldn't be in here. But we did a thorough search of Miss Ellis's background. She might have a decade-old bestseller to her name, but she has nothing to do with law enforcement."

"Did you miss the special task force part? Surely you're aware that not everything in government can be found in a file." She glanced at Aubrey. "Cut from a Levi kind of cloth, isn't he?"

"He's a show-me kind of guy, for sure." Aubrey thudded back in her seat.

Piper turned back to Agent Hanlin. "Miss Ellis works with us in a civilian capacity, on a case-by-case basis. My task force works with the Center for Missing and Exploited Children."

"Good for you." Hanlin looked her over. "But that has nothing to do with this morning, when she rushed into the Prudential Tower and forewarned a security guard about an explosion. An explosion that occurred twenty minutes later. It took two lives, Miss Sullivan."

"Deputy Chief Sullivan," she corrected.

"I believe the Federal Bureau of Investigation and terrorist activity will trump any credentials you can offer, *Chief*."

"I can vouch for Aubrey's good standing. I assure you, she's in no way mixed up in any terrorist plot."

"Really? Do you have a better explanation for her curious café exchange with what had to be an earpiece counterpart?"

"I've seen the footage." He looked surprised. "Be assured, Agent Hanlin, my resources rival yours." She smiled, a crooked thing that was hard to read. "Aubrey, on the other hand, has resources that make ours rather pedestrian. While I understand your concern, what you need to know is that you're wasting your time here. Whoever is responsible for today's tragedy gets further away every moment you spend interrogating her."

Another knock interrupted. "We may need to move this to a larger venue." Agent Hanlin opened the door, and two more jacket-wearing FBI personnel walked through, carrying a clipboard of papers and Aubrey's empty purse, the bagged and tagged items taken from it. "Gentlemen?"

A muscular man who looked like he could split wood with his teeth spoke first. "The team's completed its initial testing of the blast area."

"And?" Hanlin glanced at Aubrey and Piper, appearing surprised that the conversation was taking place in front of them.

"No trace of explosive devices was found. Apparently there was a maintenance crew here a few months back. They replaced a hydraulic valve on a large generator. The manufacturer contacted us when they heard about the explosion."

The second agent, boasting a numbers-kind-of-guy look, pushed spectacles higher on his nose. "Seems a pressure regulator on the newly installed valve was found to have a faulty connector. It's a defect the manufacturer just discovered. They were in the process of tracking down sites where those regulators were installed. Unfortunately, they hadn't gotten to this one. If the faulty connector were triggered, the manufacturer stated the pressure could build to a deadly level."

"A deadly level . . . hydraulic valves. What are you saying?" Agent Hanlin asked.

"The explosion was an accident." The numbers guy adjusted his glasses again. "The manufacturer is taking full responsibility. They're making a statement right now. Considering present-day terrorist concerns, they felt it their duty to come forward immediately." Hanlin didn't budge physically, probably not mentally either, as the reporting agent continued his update. "Kirkpatrick's been informed of everything. He's spoken with all parties involved. Our team and Kirkpatrick, they're concurring with the valve manufacturer." The agents glanced at Aubrey and Piper, who was now seated, holding Aubrey's hand. "She's not involved. Kirkpatrick said to cut her loose."

Hanlin pointed to Aubrey. "Then how the fuck do you explain her warning to the security guard?"

The bulkier agent shrugged. "We interviewed the guard again, told him about the accident. Says now that he's thought about it, maybe the woman wasn't so specific. He said maybe it was more of a hunch on his part, a bad feeling. And lucky for most of the building that he went with it. Without that early warning, who knows how many people would have been injured or worse in a panic."

"I see." Agent Hanlin shook his head. "Good to be the hero who saves a couple of thousand lives. Especially when the blast turns out to be a mechanical malfunction." The irritation in Agent Hanlin's voice didn't ease. "And so that's it?"

"As far as she's concerned." The eyeglass-wearing agent looked at Aubrey. "Believe me, Director Kirkpatrick's wholly relieved it was no more than an accident on his watch."

"I'm sure that's true." Hanlin pointed a finger at Aubrey. "But it doesn't explain how she could have possibly . . ." He slapped his arm against his side. "Great. That's just great. Thanks for the update." The exiting agents handed Hanlin the bagged items taken from Aubrey's purse, along with the brand-new Burberry accessory. It looked like it'd spent a week on the luggage carousel at Logan.

"Satisfied, Agent Hanlin?" Piper said. "I told you, Aubrey Ellis's only connection to law enforcement is a positive one. I'd like her released as quickly as possible. If you have follow-up questions, I'm sure you have her Surrey address on file, if not staked out."

Jack Hanlin glanced at Aubrey's purse and placed the plastic bag of her personal items on top. "Not so fast. Accident or not, none of it explains the story she's been peddling since security nabbed her. Two people are still dead. I don't care what caused that explosion; nothing explains her obvious prior knowledge."

"To be honest," Aubrey said, "I was thinking the exact same thing." She looked at Piper. "It wasn't a past event, Piper. It wasn't a simple ghost gift or a filter of information that solved a decades-old crime or a recent one. It wasn't a connection that led me to the resolution of a cold case. It was a statement about future events."

Piper tucked a length of curly blonde hair behind her ear. "And that's different?"

"You know it is."

"What the hell are the two of you babbling about?" Hanlin asked.

The women traded a glance, and Piper held up her hand. In a drawl that drew you in like a campfire tale, Deputy Chief Sullivan spent the next thirty minutes filling in Jack Hanlin's blanks. With each story, his skepticism didn't shift, though he appeared to grow more curious.

In the meantime, all Aubrey could think was that Agent Hanlin's reaction would have been Levi's reaction had she spilled everything about herself at their first meeting. She pushed away old memories of the *Surrey City Press* and focused on Piper's explanation. How for the past decade, in a rather covert fashion, she'd offered her psychic services in at least a dozen cold cases, all of them involving missing children. Nearly every case Aubrey worked on was now archived under "solved."

"And in January of this year," Piper said, drawing to a close, "Aubrey was able to lead my team to a barn outside Lexington—a property authorities had gone over with a fine-tooth comb. Under a classic 1954 Edsel was a hidden trapdoor. Inside a dirt cellar was Lily North, a nine-year-old girl who'd been abducted from a mall in Braintree."

"I know the story," Hanlin said. "She was presumed dead. Solid detective work finally broke the case."

"Aubrey broke the case. Months before we found the girl, Edith Pope died. She was the mother of Errol Pope."

"The creep who took the girl."

"Exactly."

"But what does that have to do with solving the case . . . or her?" He pointed at Aubrey again.

"Seems Edith went to her grave carrying a good bit of guilt and information. Eventually, via Aubrey's spiritual guide and Edith—"

"Via what?"

"Trust me," Piper said. "It's all in the sealed file. By way of Aubrey's gift and with Edith's cooperation, she led us to the barn and the Edsel."

"That's insane."

"That's why we don't broadcast it on the evening news."

Agent Hanlin cleared his throat. "So what you're telling me . . ."

"Oh my God, yes!" Aubrey slapped her hands on the table. "I see dead people! Get over it!" She gathered her composure. "Look. I'll show you. Would you, um . . . could I have my purse and the plastic bag?"

"Aubrey?" Piper said tentatively.

He obliged, handing over the freshly trampled handbag and her personal items. From the tagged plastic bag, she withdrew a thimble—about the size of a high-tech earpiece. "I'm going to take a chance here. Otherwise, if you like, you could surely have me arrested for stealing historical treasures." She held out the thimble, closed end up. Engraved on the tip was a tiny cursive *R*. "This is a piece of silver given to me this morning by its maker." She smiled at Agent Hanlin. "It will be a smart addition to my collection."

"Of silver?" he asked.

"Of ghost gifts."

"Ghost . . . ?"

"Gifts."

Jack Hanlin blinked at her and ran his hand over the tattoo on his forearm. "You, um . . . before . . . earlier." His color had turned pasty pale. "You talked about Shaun . . . Cairo."

"Shaun Ramirez has been waiting some time to communicate with you. It was everything I told you—believe it or don't."

"He's been dead for eight years."

"And he's quite pissed off that you've been spending your live ones wallowing in guilt. For whatever it's worth, before you so rudely dismissed him, Shaun said, 'Get some therapy, maybe a dog. Cairo's cool with that'—whatever that much means." Aubrey turned back to Piper before Jack Hanlin's voice drew her back.

"The IED." His tone softened. "It wasn't just Shaun. Cairo was my canine. In truth, he was the lead dog. It was Cairo's job to head in first, but Ramirez shouldn't have been behind him. They both bought it, hidden tripwire."

And the disdain filling Aubrey yielded. "I'm sorry, about your friend . . . your dog. But that was the message—from both of them."

Hanlin furrowed his brow and turned away from the women.

In a smaller voice, Aubrey spoke to the deputy chief. "Piper, listen to me." Sullivan's gaze, glued to the back of Hanlin's head, peeled away. "Regardless of why that explosion occurred . . . learning the information in advance of the event, it has *me* spooked. The dead don't show up to predict the future. That's not how it works." She leaned closer. "It's not something I get to say very often, but believe me when I tell you: nothing like this has ever happened to me before."

CHAPTER
TWO

Biddeford, Maine

Levi debated between rolling up his shirtsleeves and tolerating the flies and heat. He gave in to the elements and turned up the starched fabric. It was a warm day for late September, particularly in Maine. Regardless, a shiver prickled up his spine as he surveyed the scene from his swampy perch. Distracted momentarily, Levi smacked at his bare forearm: a mosquito, not a fly. "I should have brought all-purpose bug repellent," he muttered to himself, imagining what was buzzing around the dead body forty yards in front of him.

As he slogged forward, Levi's shoes sank farther into the marshy land. It hadn't occurred to him to bring waders either. Hell, it wasn't like he owned a fishing pole. His son liked basketball, skateboarding, and miniature models. Both Pete and Levi found fishing to be a big yawn.

Dan Watney, supervisory field agent, had called Levi in. He was a full-time contact and sometimes friend. Dan worked the law enforcement end of crime, while Levi dug in on the reporting side. More than once, the pairing had turned in a slam-dunk crime-solving effort. Earlier that morning, while making Pete's lunch, Levi had spoken to

Dan with his cell phone pinched between his shoulder and chin. That's when Dan dropped his dead-body bombshell, and Levi dropped his phone into the mayonnaise jar. A short time later, after seeing Pete off to school, Levi got in his car and drove north.

He wanted to breathe deep now, but the smell of sun-soaked, putrefying flesh permeated the air. A dead body—one thing that could easily out stink a marsh, a normally robust place where cranes nested and owls navigated endless sky. According to Dan, at first glance it appeared to be an execution-style murder, a body discovered by—who else?—birdwatchers. The rural Maine topography showed off waterfront properties, though really it was home to nothing but repurposed swampland and new money. On his drive in, Levi noted a single secluded housing development—Five Points at Blue Cove. In the distance, from his swampy vantage point, a surround of rocks outlined a jagged inlet. Geology, time, and the ocean provided the blue hue. *Beryl.* Levi noted the color of the stone, unsure when his brain had stored the miscellaneous fact. The classification of rock and color denoted the prime waterfront real estate. A glass house with a red roof stuck out from one point. *And big money.* That thought was strictly an observational detail.

Navigating a winding road on his way in, Levi had located the rural location not by GPS but by spotting Dan's steely gray SUV and a van. It was a good thing; otherwise, he would have blown right past the scene. You couldn't see the estuary, never mind the houses or swamp-like land now filled with a mix of local and federal authorities. High reeds made for good privacy and, apparently, the perfect unmarked grave—no burial required. Better still, no people to find it.

Levi was the only media person on-site. That wouldn't last. As it was, he should have informed his *Ink on Air* producer about Dan's call. But Levi's TV newsmagazine producer only would have insisted on sending a camera crew. Dan's tip was privileged information, and Levi wasn't about to cross that line. Five years into his *Ink on Air* television gig, and Levi still had trouble negotiating professional nuances. So what else was new?

From shin-deep muck, he surveyed an expanse of cattails, gaps of water, and, most notably at the moment, the partially submerged body. He'd waited as the local police cut away enough reeds to reveal the victim, though Levi was at too great a distance to make out much. Turkey buzzards circled, and he forced spit down his dry throat.

Law enforcement snapped photos and gingerly combed the scene, still marking significant areas, perhaps the direction or clues as to how the body entered its final resting place. Alive or dead? It would be a difficult crime scene—no footprints, for one. Unless the killer or killers dropped a business card, evidence would be tough. Finally, a man lumbered toward him. Levi had been watching Dan from the distance, the field agent's coppery hair signaling like a flare. After peeling off latex gloves, he extended his hand to Levi. "Some mess. Poor bastard. I wouldn't wish that resting place on my worst enemy."

"Even then, your worst enemy is something I wouldn't want to be." Levi looked toward the body. "How long?"

Dan shook his head. "Too long. Hard to tell since this particular setting accelerates natural decomposition." Dan brushed an arm over his sweaty brow. "If it'd been winter, we'd have a hell of a lot more to go on. Whoever dumped our DB did it strategically." He glanced around the perimeter. "Serious exposure, plus heat, a variety of feeders."

Levi pressed his hands to the air between them. "I think I've got it."

"Just trying to prepare you, man. Won't be like our live drug dealers in the Keys or the prostitution ring in New Orleans. This is stomach-hurling stuff. Except maybe that one girl, she had the quirky set of—"

"Yeah. I remember." It was hard to forget the curious range of women connected to a politically funded call-girl operation he and Dan had thwarted. "And sorry to say, this won't be my first dead body."

"Won't be a wall full of floating bones either. Not like your famed Missy Flannigan case." They exchanged a nod. "Aside from not pretty, there's no ID—obviously." Dan raised a hand to scenery that, given a different circumstance, would have looked like a Maine tourism brochure. "This marsh runs into a bog." He pointed northeast. "Out to sea from there. Body was faceup, submerged at times with the tide, which factors into its condition. Male is our best guess, but the coroner will have to confirm. Looks like maybe it was dark hair, Caucasian, possibly Latino, but again, speculation. That's about all I can tell you."

"No, it's not." Levi stared at the foreground action. "Your bosses wouldn't have called you, and you wouldn't have called me, if that was all. These aren't your stomping grounds. This homicide doesn't fall to federal jurisdiction, not at a glance."

"Not true. For one, based on our *moist* location, it's not immediately determinable that the crime didn't occur at sea or aboard a ship."

"Dan, I'd appreciate it if you'd avoid the word 'moist' at all costs."

Dan pursed his lips. "To conclude my point, maritime law is assumed until proven otherwise and prompts initial reasoning for calling me in." His expression sobered. "Grislier but relevant, the flesh is so deteriorated with the fatal wound to the head, crack in the skull is exposed. It was close range for sure."

"Hence your execution assumption, possibly organized crime and crossing state lines."

"You are on your game, Levi. And those are enough facts to put this body on my radar."

"Back to that. There's nothing else of interest, nothing that got your attention?"

"Maybe. A tattoo."

"Wouldn't it be stranger to find a body without one nowadays?"

"Point taken."

"And it's intact?"

"Partially. One thing I can tell you, and the ME will agree, no two bodies decompose the same way. Clothing might have preserved parts of our John Doe."

"I'm assuming the tat isn't typical, doesn't say 'Mother' or show off some pride of motorcycle ownership."

"Actually, it's more like a symbol," Dan said. "And that's why it got my attention."

"Cult?"

"Why don't you come see for yourself?"

"I thought you'd never ask," Levi said. "I was beginning to think you'd called me up here for the mezzanine view, sunburn, and teaser content."

"I had to wait for the local Buford T. Justice to bless off on everything."

"And he was fine with you bringing press in?"

"Who said I identified you as press?" The two men trudged into deeper marsh, murky water pooling around Levi's knees. "You'd just better hope our local Joe Friday isn't much for television newsmagazines. Might blow your cover."

The two men approached, and Dan drew a small jar of Vicks VapoRub from his pocket. He handed it to Levi. "Great . . ." Unscrewing the lid, he scooped out a finger full and ran it beneath his nose. "You're the only person I know who rides around with Vicks in his glove compartment. Ever think about that?"

"Yep. Keeps my nose from reminding my brain how many dead bodies I've had to sniff." Dan kept on a steady forward path, and Levi grew more grateful for the Vicks. Even so, he gagged at the stench, his eyes watering. "'Course," Dan said, "I didn't offer any rub to the village Barney Fife crew. Let them run and retch, might get them out of here quicker." He winked and moved a step ahead toward his team.

Dan's job required a certain sort of disconnected wiring, something Levi appreciated but did not possess. That said, he viewed himself as the type of man who did not rattle. Seeing the body, Levi felt a shudder, and he had to borrow a touch of his father's military mind to keep steady. Grisly was an understatement. The combination of decomposition, weather, and feeding wildlife made determining factors, like facial features, impossible. It was worse than any victim he'd seen on a coroner's steel slab; it rivaled photos he'd viewed of other postmortem bodies. Anatomy didn't indicate the victim's sex but clothing did—a dark long-sleeved shirt with buttons on the right side and men's pants, probably jeans. Tufts of brown-black hair protruded from skin-covered portions of the skull. From the specifics he could gauge, which included little more than height and darker hair, Levi could have been looking at himself.

"Here," Dan said. "Guys, can you turn him for me?" Two gloved men from Dan's crew straddled the victim and gently rolled him to his side. Levi cleared his throat as the lower half seemed to separate from the torso. Levi focused on the victim's saturated shirt. Dan leaned over, and with the blue tip of his standard Bic pen, he pushed up the shreds of fabric. While the exposed flesh had eroded to some extent, the angle did show off an unusual tattoo located on the body's forearm.

"I see what you mean," Levi said. "Definitely a Prince-like symbol."

"Yeah. My first thoughts: gang, terrorist cell bond, prison embellishment—none of them holds water." From his swampy stance, he looked at Levi. "No pun intended. And that ink isn't like anything I've encountered. We'll get a forensic artist to take a stab at reproducing it; our databases may tell us more."

Levi took a mental snapshot. The mark, about six inches long, appeared to be a riff on the letter *E*. But it looked more like something a graphic designer would dream up than crude body art. Dan continued with instructions. "And I hope you guys brought the heavy-duty body bags. Let's make sure we get all of him. It'll be like picking an overcooked chicken out of a pot." He shook his head. "Okay, guys. You can put him down."

"Hang on a second." Levi squatted as close to the body as he could and shifted his line of vision from the curious tattoo to the tattered tape on the body's bound wrists. "Huh."

"Huh, what?"

"Can I have that pen?"

Dan offered a screwy look. "You're the writer. Where's yours?"

"Mine hasn't been used to poke a dead body today. I prefer to keep it that way."

Dan complied, handing over the pen. Levi leaned in and breathed through his mouth. He turned his head to the side as a gurgle of vomit surged up his throat.

"Steady there, dogged investigative reporter."

Levi held his crouched position and his breath. "Would you shut the fuck up?" With the pointy blue tip, he scratched at the tape caked in body tissue and swampy debris. A few strokes of the pen's tip and the black film eroded. Levi and Dan eyeballed one another. "Curious."

"Green tape." Dan lowered himself to Levi's side. "And that's not duct tape. Guys, let's get some close-up shots of this."

"No, it isn't. It's narrow compared to standard duct tape. More like electrical tape."

"Unconventional choice for an execution murder." Dan narrowed his eyes. "Generally, murder accessories—tape and blindfolds—are standard issue."

Levi attempted to inch back. Dan leaned even closer, emphasizing Levi's opinion about the field agent's disconnected wiring.

"Good enough," Dan instructed his crew as numerous camera shots clicked off. "You know I would have found the tape at the coroner's office."

"But now you found it that much sooner." Levi stood. "I can't say it's a clue, but how many non-duct-taped body parts have you seen when it comes to . . . *this*?"

"None that I can think of. Great catch, Levi." Both men backed off the body. "Why you're a reporter and not a badge, I'll never figure out."

"I'll introduce you to my father someday. My dislike for other people's rules will be evident. Besides, I like my puzzle-solving point of view. You can execute the legalities."

"Okay, guys. You can bag him—and be careful. Did somebody get me an order to take the body across state lines? I'm no bird-watcher, and I don't want to spend the next two weeks watching it rain in Maine while the local coroner fucks around."

"You're all set, boss. He's headed to Boston," said the lone female team member.

"Thoughts?" Dan asked Levi as they moved toward their vehicles.

"Like you said, not much to go on at this point. I'll be interested to hear what the coroner concludes." Levi was quiet for a moment. "Poor bastard, I wonder what his last thoughts were, final view—the moon, maybe the stars."

"Ah, there's the writer." Dan shook his head. "Fuck the stars and moon. Something smaller and handier might have resulted in a more promising last thought."

"Like what?"

"Like a Glock 26 hidden in his sock."

"Right." Levi looked over his shoulder. The cove and glass house had vanished from his line of vision, like they weren't even there. "Guess we'll see what the ME concludes."

"From that?" Dan thumbed over his shoulder. "Unless the DB's dentist doubles as the coroner and recognizes his work, I wouldn't count on much. It's part of why I called you in. I wouldn't mind your help on this one. The whodunit is going to be mystery number two."

"Because the 'who is he' is going to be a far tougher problem to solve."

"Correct. Can't say it'll make for an Emmy-winning story—could just be a local yokel and corner drug deal gone bad. God knows the New Hampshire heroin train can easily ride this far north. Even so, I'd welcome your input." He smiled at Levi. "In an unofficial capacity, of course."

"Of course." The two men reached the road, where the scent of rotting flesh ebbed, swampy nature backfilling. The scene might have passed for bucolic if not for the body bag sagging between four agents plodding through the marsh. "We do have a good track record," Levi said.

"Listen, you don't have to sell me. Whatever your journalistic intentions, I'm all for making use of your brain in the name of justice."

Levi was half listening, distracted now as he busied himself with a soaking-wet pant leg and shoe. He and Dan had worked enough cases together, and Levi knew the arrangement benefited both men. Removing his dripping sock, Levi couldn't recall if his gym bag was still in the trunk. Even dirty sweats and dry tennis shoes would be preferable. "Trench foot."

"What?" Dan said.

"Trench foot. It's what World War I soldiers ended up with from standing in the mud, not keeping their feet dry."

"It was a couple of hours. I think we're safe. What made you think of that?"

"I'm not sure. I don't even know where that random thought—"

Before Levi could theorize, Dan's phone buzzed with a pure *Dragnet* 1950s ring. He looked at the device. "Huh. Deputy Chief Sullivan?" He raised a brow. "What the fuck would she want?"

Levi glanced up from his bare foot. Piper and Dan were professional acquaintances, but only because of Aubrey and Levi. "Aubrey mentioned something about Piper being on vacation. Aruba, I think."

"Maybe something interesting washed ashore." He answered as Levi removed his other shoe. "Deputy Chief—Field Agent Watney. What can I do for you?"

As Levi was about to check his trunk for dry footwear, a shiny red-and-gold band of paper caught his eye. Instinct drove his next action. From his pocket, he withdrew the multiprong Swiss Army Knife he carried and opened the tweezer end. With it, he picked up the object—a sizable cigar band.

"Say that again." Dan's tone caught his attention. "Reception sucks out here." He plugged a finger to his ear, his gaze shooting to Levi. "No, I didn't know that. This morning? In Boston?" He was quiet. "I've been working a dead body from the middle of a swamp since dawn. What did you say about Aubrey?" Instantly, Levi was hypertuned, tucking the tweezer-pinched band of paper into his shirt pocket. "You're kidding?" Dan's steady voice turned incredulous. He held up a hand to Levi, who now consumed all of the agent's personal space. "So she's okay . . . they're releasing her?" He nodded more deeply. "Uh, yeah. I can definitely get ahold of him. Levi's with me. Yep. I'm sure he'll be on his way ASAP."

Levi took out his phone; there were no missed calls, no texts from Aubrey. "Is Aubrey all right? What happened?"

"Looks like our swamp victim will have to wait." Dan glanced toward the crime scene and back at Levi. "If you can believe it, Aubrey's day has been more eventful than yours."

CHAPTER THREE

Surrey, Massachusetts

A few hours after her release, Aubrey sat in her living room staring at a double shot of tequila—a drink Piper had poured. She drew the glass to her lips but put it down. "Do you think he'll come?"

"Of course he'll come." As she spoke, Piper peeked out the curtained window for the third time. "Levi is stubborn, Aubrey." The women traded a glance. "Okay, jackass stubborn."

Aubrey made a face.

"A, uh . . . a man who stands his ground. Better?"

"With everything that's been going on with Pete, between Levi and me . . . today is the last thing we needed."

"I hear you. But your name never made it to the press. Levi and Pete will only know what you tell them."

"Clearly you've never tried to keep anything from Levi."

Piper raised a brow and moved toward a leather chair, sitting. It was Levi's chair, or it had been until he'd moved out five months before. Two months ago their son had followed, choosing to live with his father. Aubrey blinked back tears, never imagining her personal life slipping to less than square one. Piper shifted her weight in the midcentury modern leather recliner. All Aubrey could see was Levi in the chair, the room full of retro decor that had so suited them both.

Her belly, her body filled with emptiness. She forced a smile in Piper's direction. The two women shared a solid working relationship. At times, it felt like friendship. Right now, it wasn't what Aubrey wanted. It wasn't enough. Car doors slammed, rattling her dark funk. Leather squealed as Piper stood. Aubrey couldn't help but notice the firearm secured at her waist. It was a subtle reminder of the many things she and Piper did not have in common.

"It's your grandmother . . . a woman's with her."

It was typical Piper talk, never conversational, always assessing. "That's Yvette. You remember. You met her at our Christmas party last year. She lives with Charley. Kind of her caregiver slash companion."

"Right. Slipped my mind, sugar." It was opposing imagery: Piper's blonde curls swaying as she turned a vigilant stare back to the window. "Yvette. Married four times. Hails from Arkansas. Third husband was a serious shit." She flashed a smile in Aubrey's direction and returned to the street view. "Kind of man I prefer to deconstruct in an interrogation room while he's handcuffed to a comfy metal chair."

Aubrey offered a disapproving glance.

"If I recall, that's when Yvette took up carnival life." Piper tapped a finger to the windowpane. "Expert with a needle and thread. Likes to yak." While Aubrey viewed Yvette in a somewhat different light, she couldn't disagree. "Your grandma, how's she getting on?"

"Charley's tough," Aubrey said. "I tried to convince her not to come, that everything was fine. Once I told her the whole story, particularly the part about a spirit offering a future prediction. . . well, there was no stopping her. For a woman in her nineties . . ."

Piper glanced at the beamed ceiling and spoke with the seriousness generally reserved for bad guys. "Praise Jesus we all make it that far."

Then she was back to the window. "Newsflash: armor-clad news junkie just pulled up behind them."

"Levi?" Aubrey stood.

"I said he could be a stubborn ass, honey. But I'm not blind; his chiseled looks are only second to his loyalty." Yvette opened the front door. The wheelchair rolled through, and Yvette stopped long enough for Charley to squeeze her granddaughter's hand.

"Just tell me you're fine?"

"I'm okay, Charley. You didn't need to come."

"I think I did."

Their eyes and the warmth of physical touch disengaged as the wheelchair moved past Aubrey. Once the path was clear, she stepped out the front door. An audience was the last thing she wanted. On the neatly painted porch—pillow-lined swing, beautifully potted plants, every inch meticulously maintained—Aubrey folded her arms. She glanced down; near the tip of her big toe was a spot of chipped paint. She shuffled forward, covering it. It read like a marker of Levi's lengthy absence.

He stopped near the integrated ramp at the bottom of the porch steps. "Are you all right?"

Aubrey nodded, her self-comforting grip pulling tighter.

"What the hell happened?"

"I've been asking myself that for the past ten hours."

Levi came up the steps. In her bare feet, Aubrey had to tip her chin upward. Her damp eyes blinked into his.

"You've, um . . . you've gathered quite a crowd. Why don't we go inside? You can tell everyone the whole story."

Aubrey nervously tucked a crow-colored lock of hair behind her ear. "I wasn't sure . . . they took my phone. Piper said she called you. You didn't answer."

"I was on assignment. Crappy service. Dan called this morning. A body was found near Biddeford, Maine."

"Oh? A body?"

"Yeah. Bullet to the head, execution-style murder. Not much more to report—male, Caucasian, we think . . . exposure."

"Sounds dangerous."

"No more so than the drug cartel we busted out of the Keys. Listen, could we . . . ?" He pointed toward the living room. "I'm not the one who found myself linked to the word 'terrorist' today. Forget Dan's case. Until Piper's call, I didn't even know about the Prudential Tower incident. What the hell were you doing there, anyway?"

"A while back . . . weeks. Maybe a month ago, Zeke called. Yesterday, he texted me."

Levi remained in standard investigative mode, awaiting more facts.

"He was in town and asked if I wanted to meet him, catch up. You know Zeke, he tends to turn up out of nowhere."

"Actually, I don't know Zeke at all—aside from one whirlwind visit where he blew into my living room like he owned the place. What was that, four . . . five years ago? Where was he in all of this today?"

"Nowhere." She shrugged. "I never saw him. I warned the security guard about the explosion. From there it was bedlam, with me not-so-nicely escorted to a nearby building, basement room." She turned for the door.

"Wait." He touched her shoulder. "What do you mean you warned a security guard about the explosion?"

"Welcome to my day, Levi. Do you want to hear the story from the top?"

His expression grew befuddled. Aubrey recognized it. He wore the look when she first shared her gift with him—curiosity combined with a large helping of disbelief. *Square one*, she thought, *on so many levels.* Levi headed inside.

Aubrey grabbed his arm. "Where's Pete?"

He turned back. "At home. He doesn't know anything about today. He's staying with the Frasers—condo next door—until I get back."

"Home is here . . . but fine." She hated the fact that her son wasn't playing basketball in the driveway or in the basement working with one of his many miniature models. Worse, Aubrey still could not grasp that neither man in her life would come home to the bedrooms in their house that night. But in this moment, what could she do? She was lucky to have basic freedoms restored, to sleep in her own bed tonight. Aubrey let go of Levi's arm and walked past him.

Inside the house, a hushed conversation between the three women petered out. Levi stopped near his chair, gripping his hands around the back. It was a meaningless action, but Aubrey read it as possessive. The chair—something Levi wanted. Something he missed. She rolled her eyes and sat on the tufted tuxedo sofa. *Wonderful . . . I'm jealous of reproduction furniture . . .*

"So," Levi said, sitting too. "Expand on what you said outside. You had a forewarning about the explosion? I'm a good reporter, Aubrey; I'm not a mind reader. What happened today?"

"To be honest, I have as many questions as you do." She sank further into the bright orange retro sofa. "On one hand, I had an encounter with an entity this morning." Everyone in the room offered a blasé hum. "On the other . . . the spirit was a historical figure, quite famous, really." An uptick of interest rumbled through. "But even that's not the part that got my attention. It's what the ghost told me that's got me spooked."

For the next hour, Aubrey dialed back the day, filling in the finer details of her encounter with Boston's most famous silversmith. "So, while I'd like to tell you," she said to her now-captive audience, "the off-script part was a visit from Paul Revere, that was the least of it. Although . . ." She paused, finally sipping the tequila. "Encounters with the famous and infamous dead are few and far between."

"I remember one," Yvette said. "We'd stopped in Milledgeville, Georgia. You were fifteen, maybe? You *ran into* an author, right?"

"That's right," Charley said. "It was the first time you were more amazed than startled by an entity seeking you out. You were queasy but giddy."

Aubrey smiled. "It's not every day a book lover gets to chat with a favorite author. Well, at least not a dead one. I told you about that, Levi. Remember?"

He nodded. "Flannery O'Connor."

"I had no idea Milledgeville was Miss O'Connor's hometown." She caught Levi's glance, which clearly said *"Get on with it."* "Anyway . . . today, running into Paul Revere might have been the talking point. But the precise, futuristic information he offered, that part was astonishingly different."

"And you're positive it was a foretelling?" Charley queried.

"Yes. Absolutely. I mean, it was a nineteenth-century sort of communiqué. But it was definitely a . . ."

"Prognostication." Charley's tone was filled with as much foreboding as Paul Revere's warning.

"Yes. He sat across from me and said, *'Woman, I come to share news of a monumental eruption, the likes of which might indicate multiple powder kegs.'* Then he pointed to the Prudential Tower." Aubrey picked up the ghost gift, the silver thimble, which she'd placed on the coffee table. "His drifting, parting words were something like, *'Heed my counsel, madame. Move with haste. The patriots inside haven't much time, and neither do you . . . less than an excursion from Lexington to Concord . . .'* Charley?" Aubrey twisted toward her grandmother. "Spirits have never predicted future events. That doesn't happen."

"Not true," Levi said. All eyes turned to him. "Didn't you say Brody saved a boy's life the day he first visited you on Rocky Neck Beach? Didn't my brother's ghost forecast a future event?"

"To an extent," Aubrey said. "But this was different. Yes. Brody prevented a single incident whereby a toddler would have drowned. And you're right—it was a warning about a future event. But this was so much larger. It was also completely detached from me." She was irritated that she had to point out the blood bond between Levi's dead brother and their son. "Brody connects to my life . . . *our life*. Pete is his nephew."

"I see what you mean." He eased back into the chair, sipping the drink he'd fixed.

"But today, if that tower hadn't been calmly evacuated, I can only imagine the pandemonium that would have ensued. Everyone, including me, thought it was a terrorist attack. It might not have been the explosion that killed or injured people, but the guaranteed panic."

"Indeed," Charley said. "So the good news here is that you were able to offer a forewarning, my dear. Hang on to that." In Charley's lap, one swollen, misshapen hand rested over the other; she gripped it tighter. "Your father was never as fortunate."

"My father? What does today have to do with my father?"

"A good bit, or so it would seem." Charley's tired gaze panned the group. "A great deal of time has passed. Years that have turned into decades. My Peter . . ." Her aged eyes looked across the room, taking in second and seventh grade photos of her great-grandson. "He's been gone so long. I thought surely we'd passed a point where your father's gift no longer mattered." She focused on Aubrey. "Your gift . . . I truly had come to believe it would never manifest itself like this."

"Like what, exactly?" Levi said.

Charley raised her wrinkled arm, touching her fingertips to her forehead. She focused on her granddaughter. "My dear, how much longer have you lived than your father? Quite a few years, I believe. If my mind hasn't gone too fuzzy."

She thought for a moment. "Ten years. I'm about ten years older than he lived to be."

"That's what I thought, and much of the reason I felt we were in the clear." Her head bobbed with a telltale tilt. "Let me ask you something: Would you agree our gifts exhibit differently? For me, it's seeing the living connected to the dead in my dreams." On the coffee table, in front of the group, were the photos Piper had provided—the victims from the Prudential Tower explosion. "And when I dreamed of these people, saw their faces, they were very much alive."

"These people," Aubrey said. "The ones who died today?"

"Yes. I recognize their faces. I dreamed about them several nights ago—a family reunion, I believe. There were others, but you're only showing me these photos. I didn't know who they were or how they would connect to a spirit you were likely to encounter. I certainly didn't know they'd end up victims of a tragedy." Staring at the pictures, she raised a wrinkled brow. "An interesting yet no less frustrating amendment to my own gift."

"I don't get it," Yvette said. "How do those people connect to Paul Revere?"

"Anthony Revere." Aubrey touched one of the photos. "From Swampscott, Mass."

"Copy that." Piper had been standing near the edge of the fireplace. She motioned toward the photos. "They're all descendants of the famed midnight rider and Revolutionary War hero."

"Huh," Levi said. "If I recall my history, Revere had two wives and sixteen children. I'd imagine he has a good many descendants."

"About a dozen of whom were in town at a reunion," Piper added.

"Okay . . ." Aubrey ran her fingers through her hair. "That makes the historic Mr. Revere's appearance more understandable. Although it hardly explains his ability to supply me with a forewarning about future events." Her gaze darted between the random photos. "Go back to my father, Charley. You asked if I thought our gifts . . . yours, mine, my father's, they all work differently. But what does today have to do with—"

"Prognostication. That was my Peter's gift. From what you've said, it appears your gift has taken on certain aspects of his. Until now, your gift has always been about spirits seeking you out to bring closure, messages. Or it has been with rare exception."

Absently, Aubrey drew her hand over her pockmarked arm—the result of a less positive ethereal meeting.

"It's different for all of us," Charley said. "When it comes to my great-grandson . . ."

Levi and Aubrey exchanged a look.

"As intense as young Peter's gift appears, he's still figuring it out, isn't he?"

"We're not going down that road," Levi said. "But yes. Pete's gift is different. Part of it centers on his dreams—like Charley. Yet it's far more intense. But like I said . . ."

Aubrey bristled at his stern tone. Their movements seesawed as she picked up the tequila shot and he placed an empty Scotch glass on the coffee table.

"Charley," Levi pushed on. "Tell us more about how you interpret what happened today. How Aubrey's gift suddenly seems like her father's."

"It's alike," Piper said, moving closer to the group. "Today proves that to you, doesn't it, Mrs. Bodette?"

"My granddaughter tells me you're a clever girl." Piper half smiled, clearly absorbing the word "girl." "And a correct one at that."

Aubrey was leery of her conclusion. Most memories of her father were not warm recollections but impressions of a man most people had labeled insane.

Yvette wrapped her arms around herself; Aubrey saw goose bumps rise. "I only met your father a couple of times," she said. "I'd just joined the troupe. He and your mother, they brought you to visit Charlotte—you were just a baby. Peter, he was such a nice man. But . . ."

Aubrey tilted her head; conversations about Peter Ellis were rare.

"Have you ever met anyone who wore worry like a layer of skin? That was Peter. Darkness was never more than a flicker away."

The concern on Charley's face deepened. "Yvette is on point, Aubrey. I've never shared the exact nature of your father's gift because . . . because navigating your own gift was burden enough." Charley made a cumbersome lean toward her granddaughter. "Until your grave forewarning from Mr. Revere, the need to be specific about Peter's gift didn't strike me as necessary."

Aubrey recalled tiny moments from their life in Greece. It was her mother's homeland, and where she'd taken her husband and daughter to live when Aubrey was just a toddler. The move had been her mother's desperate attempt to ease the nightmare of her father's psychic gift. A few memories were crisp: Aubrey's hand in her father's, the two of them walking along rural roads, passing by goat herders and a distant mountain village. Lush scenery gave way to visceral memories: her mother's fears, her father's sad, haunted life. The imagery was beautiful, but Peter Ellis's pain was most vivid in Aubrey's mind, the way his gift had tortured and dominated. "Seems like maybe we've arrived at necessary, Charley. Wouldn't you say?"

Charley nodded stiffly. "The spirits who visited your father, they visited for the sake of prognostication. And I'm afraid, to a large extent, those forewarnings were not good news." Aubrey traded a glance with Levi. "You know how you sometimes draw or write things that are guided by a hand other than your own?"

Aubrey hummed under her breath; Piper answered. "Like the Lily North case. You drew the Edsel . . . well, an old-fashioned car. Then you asked for a permanent marker."

"I kept underlining the car I drew until I put a hole right through the paper."

"The trapdoor beneath the car," Levi said. "It's how Edith Pope finally indicated the girl's location."

"Score one for the psychics and good guys," Piper said. "Before Aubrey intervened, we tore that car apart, thinking it was the key."

Aubrey turned back to her grandmother. "Charley, tell me more about my father's gift."

"That's quite a long story. Much of it is stored in a leather-bound—"

"Letter box." It was just enough to prompt memories of a five-year-old Aubrey. "I remember seeing it at the top of their bedroom closet. There were photo albums my mother kept up there. She'd take the albums down every so often, look through them." She thought for a moment longer. "But never the box; she never took it off the shelf."

"I imagine Ena kept her distance from the letter box. I'm sure your mother associated much of their misery with it, or, more to the point, its contents."

"Why? It was just a box." Aubrey focused on the floor. "It was brown, leather covered, with a piece of strapping tied around it. Or am I imagining that?"

"No, your recollection is quite right," Charley said. "You're also correct about it being a letter box. You'd be lucky to find one on those Internet sites nowadays, letter writing being such a lost art. It belonged to Oscar, my second and fourth husband. He was always mysterious about its origins. But he would never part with it. Perhaps it belonged to his family."

"What, um . . . what do you suppose his family kept in the box?" Piper's tone was poised at DEFCON 1.

"Why, letters, I imagine." As Charley answered, Piper lowered her radar, and Aubrey hid a sliver of a smile. "Back then, years ago, missives were customary correspondence, as were letter boxes to store them. I gave the box to Peter when he was quite young." Her wrinkled brow wove tighter. "I'm not sure why, but I recall an incredible urge for him to have it. It wasn't until then that I knew to worry."

"Charley." Levi shimmied forward in his seat. "What did Peter use the letter box for?"

"Ghost gifts." She looked from Levi to Aubrey. "From the time he was fifteen or so, that's where he kept them."

"But my father's ghost gifts, they weren't about closure." Aubrey's lungs burned; she thought they'd burst from the ambivalent breath she held. It wasn't quite like discovering you possessed a horrid genetic disease. On the other hand, it also wasn't like learning you'd inherited a stunning gift, like the ability to paint or play the violin.

"So Peter's ghost gifts and this letter box," Piper said. "It sounds like the equivalent of parents learning what their kids keep on their laptops nowadays."

"Perhaps, if not for a few distinct differences," Charley said. "My son had no choice about the messages he kept inside. He couldn't unplug them or erase history before it happened. Peter couldn't stop the ghost gifts from bombarding his life, knowing of horrific twists of fate in advance. Nor did he possess any ability to prevent them. The burden that came with his ghost gifts was life altering. And now, with what happened today, receiving such a spectral foretelling . . ." Charley drew a tremulous breath and looked into her granddaughter's eyes. "It seems to me, my dear, that burden has become yours."

CHAPTER
FOUR

An hour passed, really a lifetime for Aubrey—her father's life. Aubrey wanted details, and Charley complied, telling ghost stories, the most literal kind. Peter Ellis had been compelled to write things down, sometimes draw them—the visiting specter haunting him until he submitted. Many messages were tragic, events like a devastating earthquake in Turkey, decades ago, or the seemingly unconnected names of several dead girls from Cape Cod. This disturbing bit of information piqued both Piper's and Levi's attention. Levi noted, "I know that story from the *Hartford Standard Speaker* archives. My mentor at the paper was the lead reporter. It was the 1960s. The Costa serial murders terrified the region. The guy was convicted of three of the killings and suspected of four more."

Charley offered a tiny nod of agreement. She went on, explaining that some predictions were more specific than others. "For instance, the Cape Cod murders—the victims were names Peter scribbled on heart-shaped pieces of paper. He only tied it all together during our New England stops the following summer. Peter read about the murders in the newspaper. He was horrified when he saw that the names matched those he'd written down."

Levi shifted in his seat. "Jesus . . . heart-shaped papers . . ."

"Why is that significant?" Yvette asked.

A swallow rolled through Levi's throat. "Costa—he removed the heart of each victim. Crime theorists compared his methods to Jack the Ripper."

"And so you begin to see my Peter's many dilemmas and demons." Reverently, Charley closed her eyes.

"Lord help him . . . ," Piper said. "If he'd gone to the police or press with that information . . ."

"Precisely." Charley opened her eyes, looking soberly at the group. "Peter would have appeared strongly suspect, if not worse." She pressed her swollen, fisted hands to her mouth. "I don't think it was my son's ghostly encounters that wreaked havoc with his mind. It was more the burden of doom. The Cape Cod murders were particularly hard on him. I believe that event ignited his journey toward madness, the inability to cope.

"And with each passing year, Peter's ghost gifts became more pronounced. At first he tried to navigate the future. For instance, before the earthquake in Turkey, Peter went to the authorities. He was clever enough to approach the prediction from a pseudo-geological standpoint, claiming he'd been doing some seismic testing in the mountains. All the Turkish government did was hand him over to the American embassy. They promptly escorted him to the border."

"But surely," Aubrey said, "at some point he could have proven an overall pattern about his predictions."

"Perhaps. If the various messages had been consistent and specific. The majority were too vague. They alerted Peter to tragedy but only provided enough information to label him a fool or . . ."

"Madman." Piper said it absently, focused on nothing. She blinked at the faces staring into hers. "Apologies. I didn't mean to say that out loud. But being on this side of the law, I can see it. It's what I'd say right now if I hadn't witnessed Aubrey's hand in things like Lily North's rescue."

Charley's cloudy gaze met Piper's. "I understand your position more than I care to. It broke my heart for Peter, to see his life unravel so bizarrely." She looked at her granddaughter. "But your friend is correct, Aubrey. *Madness*. It's how nearly everyone viewed your father. In the end, it might have been the truth."

"Imagine," Levi said, "his point of view. No one will listen, no one believes you. Charley, have you ever considered the endgame, why Peter's gift existed?"

"I'm not sure what you mean."

"I was thinking, if Aubrey's gift is to bring closure, communicate between the dead and living, maybe her father had the same obligation. Maybe because he couldn't do that, it exacerbated his burden."

"That's an interesting assertion. And I've had more than a few decades to ponder the possibilities."

"Charley," Aubrey said, "were my father's messages all tragic?"

"Actually, no. A good number were of a more frivolous nature— horse races, a variety of sporting events." Charley laughed, surprising her audience. "I always thought of those messages as recompense, not that Peter pursued any of them."

"Because?" Piper asked.

"Probably because he was too troubled to consider it. Years ago, Oscar and Truman," she said, referring to two of her three late husbands. "Then Carmine. We tried to interpret the messages, put order to them. Some we did; many appeared to be gibberish. But you should know, among the decipherable predictions, all came to pass—even those dated after Peter's death."

"*After* his death?" Levi said. "The predictions exceeded his life span?"

"By quite a bit." Charley's head bobbed. "Inside the letter box, on bits of red paper, the numbers nine and eleven appear over and over—at least a dozen times. I remember Aubrey's mother calling me, crying into the phone. Apparently, whatever entity compelled Peter to notate those numbers, he found it particularly disturbing."

"Jesus," Piper gulped. "I guess we can all see why."

Levi poked at his glasses, inching to the edge of his chair. "The 9/11 terrorist attacks, that happened years—"

"After my father died," Aubrey said, finishing his thought.

Charley shifted her stiff shoulders. "Another precarious component of my son's *gift*. But until today, what did it matter? Good predictions or bad, I know what they cost Peter. After he and your mother died," Charley said to Aubrey, "I considered burning the box."

"Why didn't you?"

"Because the letter box and messages were such an integral part of the son I'd already lost. Because I feared that destroying it would somehow be a bigger mistake than keeping it."

Aubrey wished Charley had burned the letter box. It might make what was happening a little less real. She rose from the sofa, turning the information over in her head: Was this fateful family history repeating? Her own future, was it destined to be assaulted with tragic insights, events she had little hope of preventing?

Maybe today, at the Prudential Tower, she'd gotten lucky. Aubrey looked out the front windows before glancing over her shoulder. *Luck?* She wanted to laugh. Levi had sunk into the leather recliner, where he ran his hand over a five-o'clock shadow and a brooding expression. She returned to the dark street view. She thought of Pete and the past year, the serious friction that had turned her relationship with Levi into something unrecognizable. Add another layer, she thought, to the things wedging their way in between herself and the man in her living room.

CHAPTER
FIVE

Everyone filed out, and Aubrey shut the door, standing with her back to it. That left Levi alone near the fireplace. She was marginally surprised he hadn't left with the others. His gaze shifted between her and a small sea of framed mantel photos. Over the years, the collection had grown. She knew Levi had been touched when Aubrey included the photo of his brother and himself posed in front of a British naval plane; he'd grumbled a bit when she insisted pictures of his parents be added to the collection. Right now, he seemed focused on photos of their son—a boy who was the mirror image of Levi, except for his eyes. Pete's eyes were all Aubrey's, her father's, and her grandmother's. Given the moment, it seemed like a wildly telling Ellis family feature. Levi shook his head. "Just I when I thought there couldn't possibly be anything more to navigate."

"Pete doesn't have to know anything about this."

He faced her. "Doesn't he? Your grandmother . . ." He pointed at the door. "She just rolled in here and delivered a huge chunk of your father's past that she kept from you. It might have been good to know going into . . . I don't know . . ." He flailed an arm upward. "Your life—such as it is."

"To what point, Levi? So I could add my father's demons to my list of concerns? I think, given the circumstances, Charley did the best she could. Through no fault of his own—and now with a clearer picture as to why—my father didn't provide the best examples for handling afterlife encounters."

Levi shoved his hands into his trouser pockets. It was a rare submissive gesture. "I didn't mean to snap."

She understood. It wasn't the frustration of the day, or what they'd learned about Peter Ellis, but another facet to be factored into the Ellis family gift and what it might mean.

"You're right." His tone was more even. "There's no reason to tell Pete. In fact, it'd probably be a bad idea."

"How is he? I'd like to know."

"Coping some days. Dreaming most." His gaze zeroed in on Aubrey. "Continually confronted by entities unknown."

From the time their son was two, maybe three, it was clear that Peter St John had inherited a version of the Ellis family trait. Unfortunately, it wasn't as clear as eye color or a cleft chin, his gift reading more like a hybrid strand of DNA. "So I take it Pete's theory about himself isn't panning out. Removing me from his life doesn't change who he is."

"Not so much. But you know that was never my suggestion. You know I didn't encourage him to come live with me."

"You didn't discourage him." Aubrey picked up a toss pillow and did just that, heaving it onto the sofa. "I told you both. My mother took my father to live in the country thinking it would change things. Levi, when will you accept that the afterlife is not influenced by an earthbound address?"

In rhythmic frustration, he tapped his fist against the mantel. "Every time I think I have a handle on the peculiarities of our life, things tip the other way."

"Thank you for the insight." Aubrey folded her arms. Levi turned, facing her. "I wasn't sure you still considered it *our* life." He reverted to the mantel view, Aubrey absorbing the conflicted vibe pulsing off him.

"To answer your question about Pete, he's doing okay. There's nothing new . . . nothing significant to report."

"Come on, Levi. He's my son too!"

He turned back. "I think we've established that and then some."

"You can't keep giving me bullshit answers like 'He's coping.' It's not fair."

Levi shifted his wide shoulders. "What do you want me to say, Aubrey? It's about the same as when we both lived here. Last night was unremarkable. He didn't come screaming into my bedroom. But the week before, I spent two nights on the floor of his room." He snickered. "Odd. For some reason I can't convince him there's no monster under the bed."

"That's very helpful, Levi. Smart-ass remarks are just what I was hoping for—particularly after the day I had."

"Sorry." He paused, pursing his lips. "We're managing. We try to focus on normal. Schoolwork, his friends. Irrelevant things, like skateboarding. He misses his models. We get his math homework done, get more takeout than I'd like. It . . . it's all temporary."

"Temporary to what end?" When Pete asked to move out, Aubrey passionately fought it but reluctantly agreed. Despite any issues between herself and Levi, he was an excellent father, and she couldn't deny their son a chance to search for answers or what he regarded as normal. "I didn't think he'd stay away this long." Aubrey plucked a sweater off the back of a chair and tugged it on. A chill, emotional and physical, penetrated.

"He's doing the best he can. He asks about you; we talk about you. Look . . ." Levi strode toward her. "Our son is smart and confused, brilliant in many ways. But sometimes he's just a terrified twelve-year-old boy."

"Who, for as much as he's like me, is also very much like his father."

"Lucky kid." The brooding look returned to Levi's face. "When he's ready, he'll come back. Whether it's to live here or visit, that I don't know. But he misses you, whether he says it out loud or not."

Aubrey nodded, an acknowledgment that this wasn't a typical tug-o-war between estranged parents.

"It's just for now."

"For now, *not* being with his mother feels pretty good to him." Tears that she'd kept in check all day spilled past the rims of her eyes.

"Aubrey, it's not about good or bad. It's just what makes Pete comfortable. He's experimenting. You know how difficult this past year has been for him. We got away with his life for a long time. Our assumption, or wishful thinking, that his gift was more like Charley's."

"Until clearly it wasn't." She knotted her arms, rubbing her hands against the knitted fabric of the sweater. In recent years, Pete's vivid dreams had taken a sharp turn. One night, he'd torn into his parents' bedroom, hysterical, screaming about a wildly vivid dream—one where he believed he woke up to find a ring of people standing at his bedside. For any other boy, in any other house, the child would have been soothed and encouraged to go back to sleep. *It was a nightmare, son. See. There's nothing in your room, your closet. Here's a flashlight in case you get scared; we'll leave the door open . . .* Instead, a stunningly wide-awake Levi had sprung from the bed, asking, "What did they want?" and inspecting his son for physical damage. Aubrey had been too terrified to move. The sound of Levi's voice, in the moment, in their living room, startled her back into the conversation.

"Aubrey? We still agreed on that much. Right?" Levi said. "Pete comes first. Helping him figure this out, handle it."

"So he doesn't end up like my father." A point that had circled in the back of Aubrey's mind landed front and center. She could only imagine what it was doing in Levi's head.

"Or it could be that Pete is more like his uncle, so at a loss to be understood that he can only see one way out." He hesitated. It'd been years since Levi learned the truth about Brody's death, but the reality of it had never eased. "Suicide."

"Levi, don't even." Aubrey closed her eyes. She was surprised his thoughts were about his family and not Aubrey's. Sadly, the reminder wasn't without merit: Brody St John and the desperate choice he'd made to end his suffering. She couldn't imagine her own son reaching a state of such despair.

"I'm trying not to do that. You have no idea how much. I have every hope Pete will work this out, just like you did. He's tough. He has us. But I think it would be unwise to lose sight of what can happen."

Aubrey swallowed down the dark thought. While Levi had moved out months ago, luggage and laptop, it was the physical distance that felt most peculiar. Perhaps more so today. He only stood a body length away, yet it felt like the width of the entire commonwealth.

"So tell me," he said. "What happened today, what you learned about your father—how's that sitting?"

"*Fidgety*" was what she wanted to say, something crawling up her leg, invading her mind. Any other emotion would result in a complete meltdown, and Aubrey stabbed at humor. "Perplexed," she said. "What do I do if Ben Franklin shows up with a key and kite string, warning of an incoming tsunami?"

He laughed. At least levity was hanging in there. "Tough call. But you're not without a point. There isn't much to do besides wait and see if it happens again."

"So while we wait . . . ?"

Levi's gaze turned examining. "While we wait, I'd like to get a closer look at the papers inside that letter box. I want to know more about what's written on them, how it works, what it all means."

"And that's something you're willing to do?"

His cheeks ballooned and he expelled the air. "Why not? Personally . . . obviously, things aren't great between us." They mutually avoided eye contact. "Even so, we've proven to have some solid tag-team mystery-solving skills."

"But to be clear, you'll really be doing it for Pete. I mean, that's understandable, I just want to be honest about . . ."

She didn't finish the thought, and he was quiet. "Not just for Pete. Aubrey, I—" Levi took a step in her direction. "Listen, today was a lot for all of us, but mostly for you. My hard-ass exterior gets that. Do you . . . if you want, I can go get Pete. We can stay the night."

"You mean you can force him to stay the night."

"He's not the only one who's allowed some understanding here."

Every exhausted part of her wanted to scream *"Yes!"* "No," she said. "We agree on that much. I won't force him, and that's what we'd be doing." He didn't argue, and Aubrey sat, finally finishing the hours-old tequila. "I'll be fine." She smiled cagily. "I'll take a hot bath . . ." She held up the glass. "Maybe have another one of these . . . call a friend."

"Which friend?" His question was abrupt, and Aubrey's mouth gaped in reply. "The people you'd talk over today with, as far as I know, that's a short list."

"I could call Piper."

"Really?"

"Or I'll call Yvette, my grandmother."

He glanced at the mantel clock. "My guess is it was an hour past their bedtime when they left here."

"What's your point, Levi?"

"Nothing." He folded his arms. "Maybe something. Look, obviously there are issues." He pushed up his glasses. "But the reasons for our . . . *being apart* are complex. Aside from Pete, it's not like we tired of each other or fought over money, or one of us cheated."

"Good point. Why take typical routes of estrangement when we have so many other options?"

"Aubrey, I won't dismiss everything noted under common causes. Your go-to list of confidants may be short, but there is one of them who happens to be in town: Zeke Dublin. I haven't forgotten what prompted you to go into Boston in the first place."

"And you'd be so opposed to me seeing Zeke that you'd force your son to spend the night?" Aubrey squashed a flicker of surprise. "That's a little knuckle-scraping, particularly for you."

"Just tell me if that's your plan. It's only a question."

"Remind me again of your current address?"

"So it's not my business?"

"Levi, I don't have the energy to go ten rounds about us right now. Zeke's an old friend. Nothing more."

"If you say so." His mouth bent to a frown. "Before today, our life was complicated. That just expounded tenfold." Levi plucked his jacket off the chair. "No matter how old it is, or how innocent you view it, nothing positive will come from Zeke Dublin's presence. Whatever our issues, I'm positive about that much."

CHAPTER
SIX

South Side, Chicago
Fifteen Years Earlier

The light on Jesus's face was different. That was the first thing Zeke noticed as he slid into a pew of Precious Blood Catholic Church. He was alone and purposely early for his sister's wedding rehearsal. Last time he sat in the sanctuary, it was in the front row and more than twenty years ago. Back then, their neighbor, Mrs. Cavatello, had poked Zeke, telling him to sit up straight, pay attention.

Hell, fourteen-year-old Zeke had been paying attention—it was his parents' funeral. What the fuck else would he be doing? Of course, his attention wasn't precisely where Mrs. Cavatello thought it should be: prayer, grief, and reflection. Only if prayer, grief, and reflection were precursors for revenge.

Vengeance was where Zeke's mind had been on that steamy August day and in the years since. He and Jesus exchanged an in-the-moment glance. *I'm on the right path. You know I am . . . an eye for an eye.* "And if You object," he said, speaking aloud, intent on fending off his conscience, "now's a good time for that lightning bolt." He waited.

"Okay, then. And aside from one giant unforeseen complication . . ." Zeke peered to the sides of the pews, decorated for tomorrow's wedding, with knots of blue hydrangeas, white ribbon, and betrothal. He sighed. "I'll take your no comment as a sign that I should keep right on going." Zeke straightened his spine to a position that would meet with Mrs. Cavatello's approval.

Their South Side upstairs neighbor had been a decent woman. After their parents' deaths, she'd even tried to convince her husband, Vitale, to take in the Dunne kids. On funeral day, Zeke stood in the Cavatellos' hall and eavesdropped on Vitale Cavatello's objections: One, they couldn't afford it. Lucina only needed to look around the cramped Chicago project dwelling to realize as much. Two, if they could afford it, Vitale wasn't interested in raising orphaned kids—particularly Micks. Three, the Dunne's deaths were not a murder-suicide like the police had concluded and newspapers reported.

His accented voice, which only seemed to know how to yell, lowered, and young Zeke had had to press his ear to the door: *"No one will dare speak it beyond a whisper, Lucina. But it's whispers all over the neighborhood. Kieran Dunne and his wife are dead because of the people he worked for. No man gets in with Giorgio Serino and keeps their hands clean. Kieran, he crossed Giorgio, snitched on the eldest son. Doesn't matter what the cops say—they're all dirty. Kieran paid; his wife paid. Now you ask me to connect the Dunne bambini to our house . . . it's una pazzia!"*

Zeke traded another memory-refreshing glance with Jesus. After his parents' funeral, Zeke's and his sister's belongings were packed up and moved from the Cavatellos' apartment to temporary housing at the Department of Children and Family Services.

At the time, Zeke didn't know what to believe about his parents. The things Vitale Cavatello said, they couldn't be true. His father was no snitch. Of course, the alternative was even more damning. If his parents' deaths were a murder-suicide, what did that say about Zeke? It would make him the son of a killer. Someone twisted enough to have murdered his own wife, the mother of his children.

In his head, Zeke could still hear Kieran Dunne, who'd emigrated from Dublin, his Irish intonation crisp. *"Just you wait, Ezekiel . . . there's better times ahead for us Dunnes."* Zeke had compelled himself to believe his father's words. It also meant believing Vitale Cavatello was right and that Giorgio Serino was responsible for his parents' deaths.

Zeke squeezed his eyes closed again. To this day, the imagery was a mural on his brain: After nearly getting caught stealing candy at the corner deli, Zeke had discovered his parents' bodies. He'd sprinted up four flights of stairs. Home. Safe. Coming inside, Zeke had leaned against the wall, breathless and with a mischievous grin, positive adrenaline couldn't pump any harder. He'd blinked into the splatter, standing in red puddles of darkness. His pounding pulse all but exploded as the tiny space registered, a room filled with blood and bits of his parents.

His mother had been perforated by bullets; his father's body marred by one clean shot to the head. Even though fights between his parents had been rare, and his father had the whiskey under control that summer, everyone appeared to accept the official conclusion, including Vitale Cavatello, whose true opinion had to be overheard.

Sitting in the pew, Zeke opened his eyes. It didn't help. He was bound to the horrific images, permanent as the Polaroids the police had taken. As the years went on, Zeke had returned to the neighborhood, asked questions, secured more details. Whispers came clearer as time loosened lips, and other damning facts surfaced: It had been more than retribution. The hit had been a lesson for Jude Serino, Giorgio's eldest son, a demonstration in how to handle disloyal employees. Jude had been there; he'd stood by and witnessed cold-blooded murder.

With that information firm in his head, Zeke reviewed his plans once more. While there'd been no obvious objection from Jesus, cloud cover had dimmed the sunlit hues on the Savior's face. "Yeah. I get it. Something to do with vengeance being Yours, not mine. I learned that one at the Whittaker stop in Apple Cove." Zeke recalled the scripture from nightly Bible study at foster home number four. "It's too late; I've come too far. I'm not leaving this world without evening the score."

Rising from the pew, Zeke plodded forward. In his mind's eye, he saw two caskets passing back down the aisle. Mentally, Zeke got a grip on the hot edges of anger. In the moment, he couldn't do a damn thing about revenge. Among his vows was the one about protecting Nora's happiness, which meant watching her marry Ian Montague, half-brother to Jude and Bruno Serino.

Thunder rumbled and the sanctuary's stained glass darkened. The church doors opened, and cheery, tipsy voices rose from the vestibule. One last time, Zeke and Jesus made eye contact. "If You can't root for me, could You just not rain on Nora's wedding day? I'd be obliged."

♦ ♦ ♦

The next morning, Jesus went as far as to provide sunny weather. Everything else, especially Nora's groom, remained a fateful paradox. It all put Zeke closer to the Serinos than he ever imagined. Ian's mother, a Brit, had been briefly married to Giorgio Serino and around only long enough to produce a last spawn. Upon divorcing Giorgio, whom Ian's mother caught with a housemaid a week after Ian was born, she'd returned to England. Ian was raised there, so distanced from his American relatives that he'd taken his mother's surname. He'd come to the States not long ago, seeking his American heritage and finding Nora. Nora, who, because of Ian, appeared truly happy for the first time in their young but troubled lives.

Nora was so head over heels about Ian, she'd sworn Zeke to secrecy. She never wanted Ian to learn about her tragic youth—his bride raped by the boy in the room next to hers and at the hands of the system meant to protect them. She didn't want Ian to know how Zeke and Nora ended up in foster care in the first place. *A tragic car accident,*

Zeke. That's what I've told Ian about Mummy and Daddy. It's all he ever needs to know. He certainly can't know anything about . . . me. Otherwise, Ian might prefer to marry someone else . . ."

Zeke had stared into Nora's teary eyes, a heartbeat away from telling her the truth. He couldn't do it. It would end Nora to know she'd fallen in love with the son of the man who'd murdered her parents. So for different reasons, secrecy was fine with Zeke. It would also keep Nora safe. The last thing Serinos, Jude in particular, needed to know was that Zeke and Nora were Dunnes, not Dublins—the surname Zeke had assumed years ago.

Bells chimed, and in the vestibule of the old church, Zeke focused on his sister. Dee, a longtime carnival friend, fussed with the veil. It would have been Aubrey's job, had she been there. He'd seated Charlotte moments ago, on the bride's side, where their own mother would have sat. Yvette, Carmine, and a few other members of the Heinz-Bodette troupe sat nearby. And that was it; that was their family. Months ago, when Zeke visited Charlotte in New Mexico, she'd made her granddaughter's excuses. "Aubrey's just started a job at a newspaper in New England. She and Owen are trying to start a life. It's taken her so long to get to this point, Zeke. You and Nora understand. She sends her best wishes . . ."

He'd been disappointed but accepting. Zeke would do anything for Aubrey, including stay out of her life, if that's what was best. It was especially true now.

"Is it time? I think it's time," Nora said.

In the history of brides, she was probably the first one to show up early to her own wedding. But the gush of happiness wasn't lost on Zeke. He'd just have to protect Nora while negotiating around circumstance. In the back of the church, Zeke scrunched his toes inside the tight rented patent leather shoes. He looked at his sister and tried to match her radiant smile.

"You saw him, right? I mean, Ian's here." Nora giggled, taking a bouquet of pink cabbage roses from Dee. "Of course he's here! Last night, Ian said heaven and earth would have to come apart to keep him away—and even then." She blinked, damp-eyed, at her brother, who found himself pissed off by the lump in his throat. Nora leaned forward, peeking through the crack in the vestibule doors. Organ music faded, and a soprano voice flooded the sanctuary with an effusive rendition of "Ave Maria."

"What?" Nora said, focusing on her brother. "Happy. You told me you'd be nothing but happy today."

"I am." Zeke glanced about, struck once more by the irony of the location.

"Then why are you looking toward that dais like your stare could set it on fire?"

"Just getting my head around it. All that money, the world as your altar. You could have been married on either coast, their Vegas resort, or an orchard in Maine. I don't get here."

"Zeke, that's not happy." Her wide smile collapsed. "That's arguing. Not now, not today."

Dee glanced between the siblings and busied herself with tiny netted bags of birdseed.

"Sorry. I just—"

"What you're thinking of . . ."

Zeke looked at Nora, imagining if she could read his mind.

"Don't. Just don't. Mummy and Daddy, they were married in this church. We were both baptized here." She thrust the bouquet forward in a poignant gesture. "I bit Father Hannigan's hand myself, right at the altar during my First Communion. It's like they're here, even if they aren't. Don't you feel it?"

Zeke looked down at the shiny shoes that did not belong to him. Then he looked at Nora, who did. Among his less vengeful vows was the one he'd taken in front of fresh graves, the first time he'd taken off from a foster home. He swore to Kieran and Ailish that Nora's first thought each day would not be their dead parents. That her last moments each night wouldn't be wet with tears. "You're right," he said. "Nothing but unicorns and four-leaf clovers the rest of the day. I swear."

Nora tipped her chin toward the vestibule doors as they opened. "I don't need unicorns or Irish luck. I've got Ian—and you." She pecked him on the cheek. "One last hair check." The gown swished as she twisted toward Dee.

Zeke faced forward and slipped his hand into his pocket. His fingers brushed against a piece of notepaper from Hingham Hardware, Mankato, Minnesota. Scribbled on the back was next Wednesday's date and six random numbers. On his last trip to Charlotte's, it had finally occurred to Zeke that the odd numbers might be lottery wins. It was worth finding out, and he'd taken the notepaper in addition to the winning ghost gifts he'd come to count on.

Over time, as he'd clawed his way into Jude Serino's inner circle, those ghost gifts had supplemented Zeke's income. Serino Enterprises pay had been meager but necessary for his survival, if not his cause. As he and Nora waited for the "Wedding March" cue, Zeke considered the turn of events. He'd never anticipated irony of this magnitude—a rocket propulsion thrust, not into Jude's inner circle, but directly into his family.

Music played, and Zeke touched the notepaper once more. He moved forward while reaffirming his vows—the ones about Nora's happiness and the ones about revenge. He avoided Jesus's glance and attempted to focus on the moment. Ian waited at the altar, anxious but looking like a guy who wanted to get married. Ian's innocence radiated, and Zeke had his suspicions as to why the brothers had so openly welcomed their fair-haired half-sibling into the fold. Ian had arrived from England with no skeletons in his closet and a shiny degree from the London School of Economics. Surely his background and blank slate would be of use to Serino Enterprises.

As Zeke and Nora reached the altar, the Serino's family history and the Dunne's looped over and over through his head. It was history bound by many threads; Nora and Ian's marriage would be one more. Zeke held himself responsible for that. If it weren't for his determined infiltration into Jude Serino's life, Nora would not have come within a thousand miles of Ian Montague. Solemnly, he placed his sister's pale but steady hand in Ian's, kissing her on the cheek and whispering, "You'll be happy, Nora. I swear."

Then he turned away and took his seat. The specifics of the ceremony grew fuzzy, and Zeke attempted to order his thoughts by counting the things he knew to be true: One, ghost gifts were real. Two, Ian Montague had barely known his father. He wasn't a true Serino. Three, Jude was now at the helm of the family. The eldest son. The only downside: Giorgio Serino was already dead. Pneumonia, apparently—not terribly painful or vengeful. Lastly, a similar fate would not hold true for Jude. This was something he knew, a prognostication of his own, because Zeke Dublin had every intention of killing him.

CHAPTER SEVEN

Surrey, Massachusetts
Present Day

Aubrey sat inside Euro, a trendy downtown bistro. It opened the year before, filled with large doses of atmosphere and intimate dining nooks. Places like Euro had helped the town recover from tabloid notoriety. Surrey was no longer known as the place that was home to a murdered girl and the duplicitous men involved in her sad life. A new town council had done a fine job of reclaiming Surrey's status as a pleasant place to live, even bumping up amenities with a science museum and refurbished town common. Today, a text message had brought Aubrey to the bistro. Typical Zeke shorthand, noting a time and place—carnies and drifters weren't much for details.

As she waited in a dim booth, Aubrey's usual defenses felt off. In their place was an altered state of awareness. If she were to encounter a presence, what sort of message would it bring? After the Prudential Tower debacle, who knew? She sniffed the air and calmed. The aroma of coffee was the only obvious thing, internally or externally.

In anticipation of Zeke, Aubrey had ordered a carafe of coffee; he'd always been a java junkie. Euro was the perfect setting, known for its morning blends and nightly espresso shots. She sipped her tea, startling when a waitress appeared out of nowhere, asking if she wanted more. The booth was secluded, particularly with a midmorning lag of customers.

"Sorry. Didn't mean to give you a jolt. But the manager, Dashiell"—the girl pointed toward a half-hidden corner—"he doesn't like to see customers with empty plates or cups."

Aubrey leaned, looking in the direction the girl indicated. "Uh, sure. I'll have more tea. My friend must be running late. It's nice that *Dashiell* is so concerned about his customers."

"Not likely." The waitress snorted a laugh. "It's more about pushing the fresh-baked goods on a slow morning." She looked in the direction of her boss. "That's when Dashiell's not smoking his little French cigarettes out back or stealing from our tip jar."

The bistro owner stepped into view. He read as European, particularly for Surrey—a sleek suit that you couldn't buy in town and an aura that didn't blend with picket fences. He sniffed in her direction, his pointy nose and chin turning away. An ethereal female voice made a beeline for Aubrey, heady perfume overtaking the smell of coffee. "Tell you what," Aubrey said as the server supplied more hot water and another tea bag. "Send over a blueberry muffin, and tell Dashiell that *Vivian* says he can quit wondering. She knew about them all."

"Vivian?" The girl stopped pouring. "Dashiell's wife? She's been dead two years."

"Yes. I know."

A queer smile spread across the server's face. "Then you know the stories too. Dashiell married her for his green card, then he used Vivian's life insurance to open this place." She set the carafe of hot water on the table. "What do you mean 'she knew about them all'?"

"Every woman Dashiell cheated on her with. Vivian says . . ." Aubrey tipped her head, listening to an onslaught of expletives. "Oh my . . . she, um, Vivian says they'll discuss it when she sees him—which will be on . . ." Foretelling information bled into Aubrey's brain and she shut up; her trite amusement at a specter appearing turned on both her and Dashiell.

The waitress backed up a few steps before darting toward her boss. Uneasiness gripped Aubrey, and for a moment she wanted out of her own skin. She shook off the fortuitous entity and focused on her steeping tea. Seconds later, a blueberry muffin was delivered via Dashiell's yellow-stained fingers, the plate rattling as it made unsteady contact with the table. "Your, um . . . your muffin." His words were thickly accented.

"Uh, thanks." Aubrey didn't look up, and the pungent odor of gasoline stripped the air of perfume. "Do you happen to have a boat?"

"*Oui.* I do. How is it you know this? And how do you know about Vivian—or any of my business for that matter? Did Trina send you, perhaps Joanna? Women scorned," he huffed. "I thought it was a silly American idiom. Is this some kind of hidden camera joke?"

"No . . ." She glanced up, and Dashiell looked anxiously around his restaurant. "But you might want to be careful of that boat, booze . . ." Aubrey pointed. "And those tiny French cigarettes near the gas line."

His gaze moved to Aubrey, but the ghostly connection ended abruptly with Vivian vanishing. A plus-size woman came around the corner. Dashiell looked in her direction. "Ah, excellent. A taker for the double chocolate muffins; two, no doubt." Aubrey's mouth gaped. She was about to call Dashiell out on his fat-shaming remark, maybe spelling out his fate. She didn't; her attention was diverted. Behind the woman was Zeke, his width eclipsed by her frame but not his height. Dashiell pivoted. With his chin high, he nodded at the two patrons, brushing past both. Zeke glanced at the persnickety owner but quickly headed for Aubrey.

From the private alcove, she rose to greet him. He smelled like Zeke—a whirl of yesteryear, laced with the memories of carnival days, sugary cotton candy, sweltering July afternoons, the scent of endless open air. She wanted to ask where he'd found cologne infused with their youth.

"Aubrey, sorry I'm late, sweetheart." He kissed her on the cheek, his mouth warm, the reminiscent feel of his arms folding around her.

Aubrey closed her eyes and sank into the lure of comfort. "Sweetheart" hit her ears like the cologne did: with pleasant, welcoming memories. He grazed his fingers against her cheek, a punctuation mark on the hug. A wave of familiarity pulsed through her. It was positive and safe and good. "After the tower explosion, I wondered if you decided to pack up and go."

"I don't scare that easy, and I'm just glad you're okay. Crazy, wasn't it? I tried to find you, but the crowds were so . . ."

"Packed like a carnival?"

He laughed. "More cops than I care to recall. Police . . . people everywhere . . . I wandered for hours looking for you."

"I, um . . ." Aubrey started to explain, but with so much catching up to do, she decided against the particulars. "I looked for you too. Same result. With all the chaos, eventually I just went home."

Physically, he hadn't changed a smidge since she'd last seen him at a carnival troupe reunion. But Zeke tended to be like that, an endless hourglass of life. No deep lines on his face—only the expected scar above his eye. Not a strand of gray on his head. Or maybe Aubrey only noticed since she'd taken to coloring her own hair not long ago. Today he sported a few days of scruff. Aubrey stared. It was funny curious. He appeared to be a carbon copy of the man she'd fallen in love with in her youth. She shivered, goose bumps rising. "The money-grubbing proprietor ought to turn up the air conditioning. With so few customers, it's like a refrigerator in here."

"Yeah. Maybe it is cold. Nothing a good campfire couldn't fix."

Aside from the reunion, they'd had little contact over the years. It was Charley who kept in closer touch with him. The two were old-fashioned pen pals, exchanging handwritten letters. From them, her grandmother kept Aubrey updated on Zeke's adventures and Nora's family. "Tell me," she said. "How is . . . *life?*"

"Good question."

"We haven't talked face-to-face in what, five years?" She found it hard to fathom—Zeke had once defined so much of her life.

"I've had my share of changes lately." He hesitated. "Work . . . other things."

"That's right. Last time you were in town, you made quite an impression. Levi and I could hardly believe you work for Serino Enterprises. Small world." Aubrey ran her fingertips over her still-chilly arms. The small-world discovery had surprised her then, not having thought about her encounter with Eli Serino in years. He was the nephew of Zeke's boss and the boy who'd committed suicide in the house on Acorn Circle, an angry spirit who'd scared the bejesus out of her. "Remember, I told you I had a, uh . . . *run-in* with the Serino's dead son. Is that what you still do, work for the Serino family?"

"The brother, Jude. Actually, we parted ways." He was quiet for a moment. "I finally worked up my nerve, hit a final straw, and cut ties—permanently."

"Oh, I'm sorry to hear that. You seemed to like your job." Zeke glanced at the carafe of coffee. Aubrey leaned in the direction the server had gone. "The waitress certainly disappeared. Did you want something to eat?" Aubrey poured coffee in his cup, nudging a stack of sugar packets toward him. "Maybe the muffin?" Without a thought, she split the fat pastry in two. The communal gesture made her think of all the things she and Zeke had shared, the ways they'd shared them.

"I'm afraid I didn't bring my appetite, sweetheart." He leaned his arms on the table. "I just wanted to take a good long look at you." He grinned, a sight that still made Aubrey breathe deep. "You're pretty as ever."

Aubrey picked at the muffin, gazing into the teacup. "Definitely not aging as well as you."

"I wouldn't say that."

And now it sounded like she was fishing for a compliment. "So you've left your job with Serino Enterprises. What will you do now?"

"I don't need much moneywise. Lately it doesn't even feel like I need that. Kind of liberating. I'll be okay for a while. I'm not sure what comes next." His stare lingered. "Maybe I'll shop around. See if there are any carnivals for sale. Does Craigslist have a category for that?"

Aubrey laughed, but she didn't want to pry at what sounded like a downturn in Zeke's luck. At the Heinz-Bodette reunion, he'd hired a limousine to transport their group—Aubrey, Nora, Charley, and Yvette. "Change can be a good thing." But as Aubrey looked at him, the dashing, tux-wearing Zeke from that night seemed to have vanished. In his place was long-ago Zeke: A worn flannel shirt—the kind she used to swipe from him at the end of every season, an annual Zeke keepsake. A dark T-shirt with a frayed edge peeked out from his collar. Jeans. Not exactly executive attire.

"I could always pop in on Nora." Zeke's usual confident look faded. "Can't quite recall the last time I saw her."

"She's still living near Las Vegas?"

"She is. Her son, Kieran—he's a teenager now. Their little girl . . . Emerald, she won't be far behind. So tell me," he said, switching gears. "I want to hear about you and—"

Aubrey cut him off. "So you're going to take some time now that you've left Serino Enterprises. Sounds reinvigorating."

"Closer to reinvention. My last job with Jude, I was working on a residential development in Maine. A different leg of Serino Enterprises—riskier." Zeke sighed, which read as uncomfortable. "Anyway . . . the last business prediction I made for Jude, it was a big investment. It didn't turn out the way he'd anticipated."

It seemed safe to assume that Zeke had been let go from his job, and Aubrey focused on nibbling on her half of the muffin. "Sounds like maybe old times are still the best times to talk about when it comes to you and me."

"Can't disagree. Carnival days were good. In the moment, maybe we didn't know how good."

"Years ago, you couldn't have convinced me of that. But definitely simple . . . sweet, compared to now."

"Aubrey?"

Hearing her name forced eye contact.

"What's wrong with now?"

And for as well as Aubrey could read Zeke's mind, clearly he could read hers. "Life . . . Levi, things are just . . . complicated right now." She busied her mouth by sipping tea. Discussing her relationship with Levi was a line in the sand. Yet Zeke was still her oldest confidant. And honestly? She could use one. "Actually . . . we're, um . . . we're not living together."

"Really?" Zeke nodded slowly. "Charley didn't say anything in her letters. I'm sorry. He, uh . . . Levi seemed like *the guy*."

"The guy?"

"Yeah. The one who gets the girl. The one I'm supposed to hate."

It all flowed back into her brain, the delicate, heartfelt memory and Zeke's vow—to loathe the man who won the woman.

"Is it temporary, or are you two heading to something more permanent?"

"Like a divorce?"

"I don't mean to be blunt, but since you mention it . . ."

"A divorce would be highly unlikely." She paused. "Especially since Levi and I aren't married."

He stared as if "married" required a definition. "Really?" Zeke reached for the coffee cup but appeared too stunned to pick it up. "You never . . ."

"Tied the knot?" Aubrey untucked and retucked a piece of hair behind her ear. "Nope."

"Really?" he said again.

Aubrey rolled her eyes. "Okay, could you find another interjection? And you don't have to look so surprised."

"I'm not." Zeke frowned, running a hand through his dark hair. "Okay. I am. I'm totally surprised. Last time I saw you . . . you never indicated *not* being married." He blinked. "And the way Charlotte talked about you and Levi in her letters . . . I assumed. I mean, there was a suddenness to it all, a letter . . . what? About a dozen years ago . . . ?"

"Thirteen next summer," she said, factoring in her pregnancy and Pete's age.

"Even so, when Charlotte told me she was going to be a great-grandmother. Heck. I thought she just spared me the wedding-day details."

Aubrey stared into her cup. If tea leaves had been floating, she wondered how they might have read. "To be honest"—she looked up—"I don't have one clear reason why Levi and I never married. I don't know why I didn't tell you last time I saw you." She shrugged. "Levi fits well into a lot of things . . . a suit, fatherhood—which he surprised himself with—his job. Marriage is more of a mold." She thought for a moment. "I'm not sure it comes in Levi sizing."

"Fair enough. But I know you, Aubrey. That kind of commitment was always high on your list. If I recall, lack of commitment is what did in husband number one."

"Thanks for the reminder."

"There's nothing wrong with wanting those things. It was the ticket for Nora and bumbling Ian—two kids and a collie."

"Tell me more about them. I need more than a mention." She smiled. "I miss Nora."

"Change of subject. Got it."

"Not a change of subject. I'm just always glad to hear about her, that she's happy. Your sister was never you, Zeke—fate was a little harder on her." Years ago, in quieter, more personal moments, Zeke had confided the details of what had happened to Nora, how he blamed himself almost as much as he'd blamed the boy who'd raped her.

"True." He smiled, though it looked like sadness, and Aubrey felt time turn back. "So if that wasn't a cue to change the subject, tell me why you and Levi never got hitched."

"I'm not going to get away with 'it's complicated.'"

"You can if that's the bottom line."

"It's a two-part bottom line." Aubrey drew a contemplative breath. "I'm sure Charley told you about the whole Missy Flannigan story. I know you read the book; you sent me a copy to sign."

"One of many proud Aubrey Ellis moments."

Aubrey's face warmed. "Anyway . . . by the time all that came to pass, after Levi nearly died from a gunshot wound and Pete was born—both things were so unexpected and life altering . . . because Levi and I shared so many profound experiences . . ." Aubrey paused; the finer details were difficult to articulate. "A piece of paper didn't seem to matter so much."

"If you say so. Your tea's getting cold." Zeke cleared his throat and pointed. "Anyway . . . I've seen Levi . . ." Aubrey knotted her brow. "On TV."

"Right." Sometimes Levi's public personality slipped her mind. "*Ink on Air.* The newsmagazine format has done well for him."

"That's good, I guess. But I am sorry you two aren't faring better. Like I said, he definitely struck me as 'the guy.'"

"Me too."

"And Pete?" She was grateful as the topic finally advanced. "You haven't said a word about him. At the last reunion, you brought an entire photo album."

"I did not," she defended. "Just what I deemed reasonable for an iPhone."

"How is he, your son?"

"Actually . . ." Her muscles tightened, tiptoe to jaw. "He's living with Levi." Aubrey pasted a steady gaze on Zeke. "And if you say 'really' again . . ." She picked up the muffin half. "You'll wear this."

Zeke held up a hand, and Aubrey eased into the curve of the booth, trying to corner emotion.

"And you're good with that?"

"We agreed it's best for now . . . for Pete." Aubrey bit down on her lip, certain how Levi would feel about her discussing their son with Zeke. But the need for someone to listen was too great, the plausible options too small. "Zeke, I, um . . . I did want to talk to you about Pete . . . confide something. Would you believe he has a gift something like mine?"

"I would have been more surprised if you said he didn't." He folded his arms and leaned into the table. "Is it just like yours?"

"We don't know. Maybe." She shook her head. "At first we thought it was more like Charley's gift. That he might dream of the living connected to the dead. Many of Pete's encounters occur at night, in his sleep. But they spill over; they're more intense than Charley's dreams. And now . . ."

"Now what?"

"I don't know how to label it."

"Still can't google an explanation, huh?"

"One thing we have determined, whatever is happening to Pete, it's not as much a dream as it is an experience. Are the dead speaking to him? I'm not sure. Is my son terrified by it? Definitely." She blinked back tears, wanting Zeke to reach across the table, squeeze her hand. He didn't. "Pete's visions don't seem to be about messages, not like mine." Aubrey thought for a moment. "They're more about events that are occurring . . . in his head . . . in his dreams . . ."

"Like what?"

"I almost want to say 'like in reality.' But I know how abstract that sounds."

"Not if you're up to speed on the Ellis family gift. I take it Pete . . . and maybe Levi, are having issues with the concept." He waited a moment. "Or is that the whole problem—they can't handle it, period?"

"The last part. I never realized the blessing and benefit of my childhood. Not until Pete. I didn't just survive my childhood because of the carnival. I flourished in it. I never sat in a classroom or went to sleepovers. I never encountered peer pressure or had to negotiate my gift in the confines of what society deems 'normal.'" Aubrey air quoted the word as she said it. "That's left me at a deficit with Pete. I don't have any applicable advice for those situations."

"And Levi, he's not about to run away and join a carnival for Pete's sake."

"No. Definitely not. Pete's gift—whatever it is, it intensifies by the year. This past one has been particularly rough. When he wakes up . . . it's like he's stepped from a war zone or some other catastrophic event. Sometimes . . ." She stared at Zeke. It was comforting to see thoughtfulness, not shock or disbelief. It spurred her on. "Sometimes there are even marks, bruises on him. And as Pete's gift evolves, Levi is determined to use common sense, intelligence, and his own life experiences to guide him." She huffed again, considering their last loud argument on the subject.

"That's a reasonable theory," Zeke said. "Until you try to fit Pete's gift inside the parameters of rational life experiences."

"Right?" Finally, an agreeable ear; she didn't realize how desperate she'd been for one. "The situation has pushed Levi and me to the breaking point. It's pushed my relationship with Pete to the same place. He's angry with me, Zeke. My son blames me for saddling him with something less than a normal life. And he's not wrong." Her voice pinched. In a thinking habit, Aubrey ran her fingers over the traffic jam of earrings that lined her ear. "As a family . . . as a couple, we drift further apart every day."

"Maybe you need to give it more time." And Zeke did reach out, his fingers squeezing hers, both their hands icy cold. "Aubrey, think how long it took for you to grasp your gift, learn what it was all about. Charley too. Imagine how many years she dreamed of living people before connecting them to your ghostly encounters."

"That's true."

"Of course, there is one other consideration . . ." He withdrew his hand. "What about your father? Your son's namesake. Do you think their gifts connect?"

"No. I don't." She shook her head hard. "And thank God for that. But it's interesting you should bring up my father's gift." Aubrey dried a stray tear. "I wanted to talk to you about him too."

"Did you?" Zeke eased back. "Why's that? I never met him."

"Maybe not, but you never missed a trick, Zeke. I want to know if you knew anything about him that I didn't." He was quiet, too quiet; Aubrey tilted her head at him. "You do know something. Did you know he had a box of ghost gifts—like mine, but not like mine?"

He continued a silent stall, and Aubrey swore she felt the chill in the room grow colder. "Yes."

"Yes?"

"Not one of my prouder secrets, but yes. I know about the letter box."

"How? Why didn't you ever tell me?" Her voice rose, and she glanced around the deserted space. In a hushed voice, she asked, "Do you know what's in it, the box? Do you know about the predictions?"

"Aubrey, slow down."

"No, I won't slow down. I want to know exactly what you know. *Everything.*"

"All right. I can't see any reason to keep quiet now." His full lips defaulted to a tight line. "Years ago, when you were a teenager—I was maybe twenty—I overheard a conversation. Your grandmother and Carmine. I was grabbin' a cold drink outside the Winnie. They were talking about a leather box, pieces of paper, future predictions. They were talking about your father." He shrugged. "Hell, anywhere . . . anybody else, and you'd think it was nothing but carnie talk—the setup for a new act."

"But not with the Heinz-Bodette troupe. Not with me."

"More like not with the Ellis family on the whole. I listened when I should have minded my own business. I heard them discuss your father's penciled-in predictions." Aubrey's jaw slacked at the bullet of information. "I heard Charlotte and Carmine say that many of those predictions had come to pass."

"And you never thought to tell me?"

"No. I thought way more about *not* telling you. Didn't seem like the kind of thing I should be running my mouth on—especially since I was eavesdropping on the boss's conversation. Like you wouldn't have gone straight to Charlotte and asked?"

"Zeke, the other day . . ." Aubrey offered a diffident tip of her head. "The explosion at the Prudential Tower, I had a forewarning about it. While I was waiting for you, a specter showed up. Historically, he was, uh . . . well, the point is he told me about the explosion *before* it happened."

"Before? Like a prognostication? Like your father?"

"So it would seem."

"And that's never happened before?"

"No. Nothing remotely close to this. I offer closure, messages from loved ones." Aubrey held out her arm, pushing up her sweater sleeve. "On rare occasions, there have been encounters with the darker side of death." She pondered what suddenly felt like a lesser evil. "I don't fore-tell the future, Zeke. Not until yesterday . . . and now this morning."

"This morning?"

"Right before you arrived. It happened again. Smaller scale, just as foreboding. A brief encounter with the proprietor's dead wife." She pointed in the direction of the main dining room, where the staff had gone since Zeke arrived. "I thought she just wanted to scare the crap out of him. But then . . ." Aubrey leaned, resting her head on her fingertips, her temple pounding. "She told me when her living husband, Dashiell Durand, would die—the date . . . and how."

"You're kidding."

"I wish I were."

"That's amazing. And scarily similar to your father's predictions."

Aubrey pressed her fingertips harder into her forehead and squeezed her eyes closed.

"Those predictions. They're what drove your father mad, aren't they?"

She nodded, tears seeping out from beneath her lids. Aubrey felt a tug on her hand. She kept her eyes closed as Zeke's voice sank into her soul.

"Listen to me, Aubrey. I know I've been gone a long time. I know I'm not part of your life anymore. That it seems like I've turned up out of the blue. But I need you to know something. Just like always, sweet-heart . . . I'm only here because I love you."

CHAPTER
EIGHT

Surrey, Massachusetts
Five Years Earlier

Aubrey came around the corner wearing a form-fitting dress. In the arched alcove of the dining room, she struck a pose. An array of papers were fanned out in front of Levi, who was seated at the table. He didn't look up. Since she'd left the room over an hour ago, he'd gone from contemplative to brooding. In seven years of cohabitation, this kind of moodiness had never been a good sign. "Still no decision?" she asked.

"Nope." With his fist kneading his temple, he shook his head. Aubrey weighed further advice. To anyone else, the contract under his nose would be a dream job on paper. But Levi was never a fan of fanciful ideas, and his next thought reflected as much. "Aubrey, I know newspapers. I know how to go after a story, be the editor in chief of the *Surrey City Press*. I've even risen to the challenge of running newsroom personnel."

"No question about it. Not to mention a minor miracle."

He didn't respond to the sarcasm and continued to stare at the contract. "What I don't know is how to do any part of that job in front of a camera. Better still, why I would want to?" He sighed and adjusted his glasses. Glancing up, Levi did a double take. "Wow . . . exclamation point—make that two."

"You'd never put one exclamation point on a sentence. Two, and you'd reassign yourself to writing obituaries." Yet the persuasiveness of her little red dress was gratifying. With a beaded clutch in hand, Aubrey took a full turn in the living room. "So you like it?"

Levi leaned back in the chair. "'Like' would be a disturbingly weak adjective."

"Good." Aubrey brushed a hand over the front of the fiery dress with its Bardot-style band top, complemented by a keyhole front. The frock was an edgy choice, and she'd debated for the better part of an hour in the boutique's fitting room. "It's not every day the Heinz-Bodette troupe has a reunion—why not, right?"

"Makes me think I ought to work harder at date night around here. Instead of a movie next Friday, I should take you to Paris." Aubrey smiled and Levi stood, checking his watch. "But being as it is Friday, and you have some time before your entourage arrives . . . maybe I could examine up close for a zipper?" Levi approached and looped his arms around her waist. "I'd love to know how you get into—or better yet, out of—that dress."

"Are you kidding?" Since she hadn't applied lipstick yet, Aubrey kissed him. "Not a chance. You should have come upstairs while I was in the tub. An hour ago, I would have been a sure thing."

"Damn. The costly price of brooding." He stepped back, engaging in a roving glance. "And we're definitely going to Paris next Friday."

Of course, before next Friday would come Monday, the day Levi would owe MediaMatters an answer about their *Ink on Air* proposal. Years ago, the print media entity had saved itself from extinction by successfully expanding into on-air markets. *Ink on Air* was their latest television venture; all they needed was the talent. Levi was CEO Carl

Toppan's immediate choice. Clearly, from the state of reshuffled paperwork, Levi wasn't as convinced.

At the dining room table, Aubrey started to sit, suddenly acutely
aware of the dress's constricting nature. Sucking in her breath and easing
onto a chair, she said, "Whatever note of clarification you need, I have
no doubt you'll find it."

He nodded, returning to the paperwork.

Levi had gone as far as to record an on-air test segment, if only to
appease his boss. The concept was to revitalize time-honored journalism
by spotlighting (literally) the last of Levi's breed—no-nonsense news-
persons with the highest journalistic integrity. It was the on-air part
Levi couldn't get his head around. He'd gone into the test segment with
little expectation and even less trepidation. Lackluster interest had backfired, and his calm, commanding nature drove on-air rapport. Aubrey
overheard a post-test conversation between Levi and a jubilant Carl:
"Incredible, Levi! Just what we're looking for—brilliant journalistic
skills, rock-steady persona. Jesus himself would swear you're a Hunter
Thompson, Edward R. Murrow, and Gregory Peck combo incarnate.
Audiences will love you!"

After he hung up the phone, Aubrey had shrugged and said, "I
don't know about Jesus, but if it helps, I'm getting a good Thompson-
Murrow vibe of approval." He made a face and worked his way to where
they were right now: Levi brooding over opportunity.

He picked up the contract page detailing specifics like salary. "I don't
need this," he said. "Okay, I'm not that obtuse. Anybody could use this." He
dropped the page onto the table. "But I like my job. I love our life." Aubrey
hummed in agreement. She was all for whatever choice made him happy.

Pete wandered in from the kitchen, which only seemed to validate
Levi's argument. In his hand was a frozen fruit bar. Their son's above-
average height was currently dwarfed by the authentic World War II
airman bomber jacket he wore. "Mom say you could have that?" Levi
asked.

"Uh-huh." The boy leaned into his father, the leather jacket creaking as Levi's hand clutched around his shoulder. He grazed his fingers through Pete's coffee-colored hair. "Pa, I set up a new militia front line in the basement." He had a slight lisp to his speech, which Aubrey found endearing. So much so that she was taken aback when his first-grade teacher called to suggest speech therapy. "It's a right-flank attack. Want to come see? The marines will be there soon, help the French and Brits out. A blue battle for sure."

"I suppose it's better than bloody red." Levi spoke softly over his son's head, glancing at Aubrey.

"It's okay," Pete said. "The Seventy-Third Machine Gun Company will push 'em back. Daly's got 'em riled, he asked those sons of bitches if they wanted to live forever."

"What in the world . . ." Aubrey blinked at her son's lispy decree. "Pete—"

Levi held up a hand. "Pete, I'll have to talk to Granddad again about appropriate military talk."

He looked up at his father. "Granddad wasn't there. He wasn't even born. Not in the blue wood."

In recent months, Pete's out-of-place phrases had become increasingly common, more worrisome. For now, Levi patted his son's shoulder. "Well, wherever you heard it, we don't use language like that, okay?" Pete's expression slipped to defeated, like maybe he'd lost the forward push. "I'll come downstairs in a few minutes. Just let me see your mother off." Levi reached to the lazy Susan and grabbed a napkin, handing it to Pete. "But take that popsicle into the kitchen first and finish it over the sink." Pete followed the order, Levi's voice trailing behind him. "And wash your hands. Nobody likes sticky militia."

"Remind me to write that militia remark down," Aubrey said. As Pete's dreams grew more active, repeating words and phrases, she'd taken to recording them in a notebook. For a moment, she fixated on the kitchen doorway. She sighed, letting her son's military talk and how it connected to his gift go, at least for now. She turned back to the other issues at hand. Picking up the thumb drive that contained Levi's on-air test, she felt Levi's eyes follow her movement, the tight red wrap of the dress.

"I, um . . . I'm a little surprised by the outfit."

"Why's that?" With her fingers and polished nails—another uncharacteristic detail—she tapped the thumb drive on the tabletop.

"For one, the color."

She shrugged. "It will be a room full of people I've known all my life. Color isn't a factor this evening; I'm comfortable with all their ghosts." They traded a look and conversation unique to their lives. "I thought you liked it."

"I do. I would—if I were coming along. If you really wanted me to go, you should have said so."

"I would have loved for you to go, meet everyone, or the parts of the troupe you never have. Joe will be there with his new wife, and Benny G. I told you about him, a mind-reading magician who gives people like me a bad name. And Zeke . . . I mentioned he was coming. He didn't make the last reunion."

"Right," Levi said. "Zeke."

"Dublin," Aubrey supplied.

"Sounds like a carnie . . . excuse me, stage name if I ever heard one."

"It, um . . . it is."

"You're kidding." He blinked at her.

"Actually, no." Among the things she did know about Zeke's past was a clear recollection of spirited Irish brogues, the mother and father who watched over their children. Several more intimate details Zeke had shared years later. "His last name has more to do with heritage. That, and Zeke insisted a different last name was one way to keep the child welfare system from finding them."

"I supposed running away to join the carnival would be another."

"Why thank you so much for not saying 'circus.'" Aubrey smirked at him.

"Welcome. So what was it?"

"What was what?"

"Zeke's last name before it was Dublin."

"Why would it matter? Charley paid him and Nora off the books; it's not like she collected social security numbers."

Levi continued to stare.

"Dunne," she finally said. "Like I said, Irish heritage. Zeke and Nora, they didn't have an easy go of it."

Levi held up a hand. "You can spare me the details. I believe you."

"Good," she said, leaning across the tabletop, kissing him. Aubrey was just as happy not to delve into the things she did know about Zeke.

"So whatever Zeke's mysterious background, he's the Heinz-Bodette's grifter who made the rest of you look like homebodies."

"He's not a grifter. But yes. And it was Zeke and Nora together."

"Yeah, but you only had a steamy love affair with one of them."

She hummed under her breath. "I'm not sure Nora would describe it as steamy. More like a first love; much more innocent."

"Cute, Aubrey. And even better, you'll be spending this evening, wearing that dress, with old Zeke."

"And so what? Like I was *your* first date?" She folded her long arms. Considering the dress, her arms felt like the most malleable part of her body. "I recall a drunken New Year's Eve confession you once shared. Let's see, it was a summer semester at the University of Chicago, a journalism professor with a sexy French accent."

"She's from France. The accent's kind of hard to avoid."

"*Oui, monsieur.* Hard to avoid, as was the rest of the *affair*, I'm guessing." She winked at him. "I believe her educational focus was supposed to be working the delicacies of foreign sources."

"Which she did, expertly."

"Ha! And that's not all *Professeur Renard* worked—teaching her young protégé how to whisper dirty little things in ten different dialects."

Color rose at the base of Levi's throat. "Which is why I no longer drink champagne."

"And perhaps the reason you still get a Christmas card from her every year."

He refocused on his *Ink on Air* contract as Aubrey went on. "At least Zeke wasn't my polished-yet-amenable-to-sleeping-with-a-student professor. Besides, he was definitely more the rough-and-tumble type." She admired Levi's looks—more dashing than daring. "My tastes have changed. Besides, Zeke and I were best friends longer than we were anything else. That's the part I'll be reunioning with tonight."

"I wasn't worried." Levi's gaze flicked between the paperwork and Aubrey. "Even so, I could grab a quick shower, throw on a suit. A few hours away from this stuff might be what I need. Clear my head."

"Fine with me, if it wasn't for one thing."

"What's that?"

"Everyone who would babysit for Pete is going to the reunion. Your father's in London. Remember, that's why you decided to stay home."

"Right." He ran his hand over the unlikely stubble on his jaw. "There's that."

Wide awake, Pete appeared like most seven-year-olds, maybe one with a particularly active imagination and unusual vocabulary. It was the sleeping hours that kept standard babysitters at bay.

"Besides, you'll have a better time not worrying if I'm bored." Levi shuffled several stacks into one. "And let's make it a deadline. By the time you get home, I'll have reached a decision."

"Sounds like a plan."

He refanned the neat stack he'd just made. For a long time—since the Missy Flannigan story and a near-fatal gunshot wound—Levi had been satisfied running the *Surrey City Press*. On occasion, he'd dive into a series on the environment, the economy, and even politics.

But restlessness had evolved, and Aubrey knew he was no longer content. Regardless of the television format or his willingness to admit it, MediaMatters' proposal had reenergized Levi—a point he'd refused to acknowledge so far.

Aubrey was about to offer one more word of input when the doorbell rang. They both rose from the table, Levi peeking out the dining room window. "A limo?"

"A what?" She peered at the same view. "Wow. News to me, but not a total surprise." She stared at the high-end mode of transportation. "You never know exactly how Zeke Dublin will turn up."

Opening the front door in his gray sweatpants and worn T-shirt, Levi fought a footman vibe. The thought intensified as a dark-haired man wearing a tux glided through the doorway. Levi had never followed the scent of a man's cologne before, but it was impossible to avoid as the visitor paid him no attention, rushing toward Aubrey. Levi blinked as she squealed Zeke's name, her tux-wearing first love swinging her in the full circle that ended many 1940s films.

"Look at you, sweetheart! You are more gorgeous than I remember." The motion stopped; Levi's focus didn't. "And I remember quite a bit." On that remark, Levi shut the door loudly and moved toward the couple in his living room.

Aubrey took a step back, though her hand was still clasped in Zeke's. "It's good to see you too. Charley keeps me updated. She loves getting postmarked letters from you. Kind of a lost art."

"Least I can do for one of the women I credit with saving my life . . . and Nora's."

"You're being dramatic." She glanced in Levi's direction. "He's being dramatic."

"I don't think so," Zeke said. In turn, he never took his eyes off Aubrey. "Without you or Charlotte, who knows what would have become of Nora and me."

"Guess we know what became of her." Levi hooked his arm around Aubrey's shoulder. He looked directly at Zeke: sharply dressed, movie-star-grade scruff, lean, and with a height that rivaled Levi's. Rough-and-tumble was not making his short list of Zeke observations.

"Zeke, this is Levi." Aubrey tapped the beaded clutch against his chest.

"Right." He grinned, and Levi thought the expression might be visible from the next county. "So you're the guy I'm supposed to hate."

"Pardon?" Levi said.

"Ah, it's nothing." Zeke raised his arm, lightly touching Aubrey's cheek. The motion was fleeting, barely noticeable. Yet Levi noticed—completely. Zeke tucked his hands in his pockets, the sleight of hand vanishing. "Years ago, I told Aubrey someday the right guy would come along, win the girl. I said I'd hate whoever the son of a bitch was." Zeke's reminiscent tone faded, and he cleared his throat. "Then I was being dramatic, of course." He extended a hand. "Zeke Dublin."

Tentatively, Levi shook it.

"Nice to meet you. Charlotte's mentioned you over the years."

Aubrey leaned, looking out the screen door. "Zeke, what's with the limo?"

"Oh, that." He flashed the smile again. "It's not every day the Heinz-Bodette troupe has a reunion. Being as I missed the last one, I thought I'd escort us to this one in style. Your grandmother, Yvette, and Nora are already tucked inside. Nora can't wait to see you. Thought it'd be easier to come in, collect you myself."

"And you didn't bring a corsage?" Levi said.

Zeke didn't reply to Levi's sarcasm, but he did give him a long once-over. "Damn. I like him, Aubrey. Everything Charlotte said—direct, honest oozes off him, so does smart."

Levi could not say the feeling was mutual.

"Definitely an improvement over husband number one."

And Levi's estimation dipped another notch. On the other hand, he noticed that Aubrey did not correct Zeke, telling him the two of them were not married. While Levi never considered their relationship anything less than lifelong, marriage wasn't a subject that got much airtime anymore. At least not until Zeke Dublin had shoved it in his face by showing up.

"Pete!" Aubrey said, clearly deviating. "You need to meet my . . . *our* son."

"I'll call him." Levi backed up a few feet before pivoting toward the kitchen and basement stairs. A few moments later, he returned with an annoyed-looking Pete, several plastic army men gripped in one fist.

"Pete, this is Zeke," Aubrey said. "He's an old friend, from Nannie's and my carnival days." Zeke held out a hand, and Levi's fingers crunched harder into his son's leather-clad shoulder. "And what do we say?"

"Nice to meet you."

"Looks like I interrupted a battle. Sorry." Zeke squatted, tapping a finger on the plastic soldiers. "But I've been looking forward to meeting you. Your mom and I . . ." He rose and tousled Pete's hair. "You sure are the spittin' image of your dad, 'cept for the eyes. Got your mom's eyes. Is he, Aubrey? Much like you?"

"Well, he—"

"Pete, head back downstairs," Levi said. "I'll be there in just a minute."

"But you told me that, like, a million years ago. The blue-wood battle is almost over. We're no *Teufelshunde!*"

"What?" Levi said absently.

"Devil dogs," Pete said. "That's what the Germans call us."

"Okay, fine. I'll be there before the French surrender." Levi's arm wrapped reflexively around Pete's chest, patting it.

"Germans, Pa. We'll run those Germans right out of the forest." Clutching his plastic army men, Pete ducked out from under his father's hold and was gone.

Levi turned back to the adult conversation. "So what is it you do, Zeke?" He glanced toward the curbside transportation. "Other than pick up old girlfriends in limousines."

"I work for a large conglomerate—hodgepodge of holdings, newer residential projects, multiple resort ventures. In fact, we just finished up a new casino project in Atlantic City—the Galaxy Resort."

"The Serino Enterprises project?"

It was Zeke's turn to offer a curious look. "Yeah. How'd you know that?"

"We covered the casino opening at the *Surrey City Press*. I'm the editor in chief there."

"Right. Charlotte mentioned that." He shook a finger at Levi. "Maybe it was at breakfast this morning." Zeke looked at Aubrey. "Did she tell you I'm staying with her and Yvette?"

"She said she insisted on it."

"Anyway," Zeke said, "an Atlantic City casino doesn't seem like news for around here. What's the Serino connection?"

At the mention of the Serino name, Levi felt Aubrey stiffen. It'd been some time since their disturbing encounter with one ghostly member of the Serino clan had come up. Levi moved on with the less personal, news-oriented Serino link. "Local connection. One of the Serino brothers lives in the area. In fact, he used to live in Surrey. Bruno Serino."

"Of course, that's not really why we know them," Aubrey said softly.

Zeke focused on Aubrey, and Levi stared at him, aware that Zeke's knowledge of Aubrey was thoroughly intimate. "And why do you know them, sweetheart?"

And Zeke's last word felt *too* intimate to Levi, who narrowed his eyes at Aubrey's date.

"I, um . . . I had a little run-in with their dead son, Eli. It was ages ago."

The house on Acorn Circle and its ghost—their ill-fated visit had been Aubrey's attempt to introduce Levi to her unusual skill set, a disconcerting experience, to say the least.

"It's ancient history," Aubrey insisted. "When Charley said you were working for a company with Vegas ties, based in California, I didn't even think about Serino Enterprises. Small world, that's all."

"It's a big company." Zeke's focus stayed tight on Aubrey.

"Still an interesting coincidence," Levi added.

"Actually . . ." He finally offered Levi his attention. "In recent years, I've worked for Bruno's brother, Jude, exclusively. I don't have many dealings with Bruno—though I know he's driven. Both brothers are competitive in different ways. And Nora. She's, um . . . she's married to their half-brother, Ian."

Aubrey furrowed her brow. "Oh, I didn't realize that."

"No reason you should," Zeke said. "I'm not surprised Bruno owned a property around here. In fact, it might have been where they first broke ground on their residential projects."

"I think I recall that." Levi thought for a moment, reaching for his Serino facts. "But like you said, they're big into all sorts of ventures. Wide holdings—residential to commercial."

"Right. It might have been an easier gig, working for Bruno. He's just a nose-to-the-grindstone kind of man. But a while back, I caught Jude's riskier eye with a few windfall predictions."

Levi gestured toward the street. "Then I guess tonight's mode of transportation is indicative of risks that paid off."

"I spent a lot of years living hand to mouth. It was hard on me, harder on my sister. Maybe I went a little overboard with Charlotte and the rest of the troupe." Zeke nudged a shoulder toward the car. "I wanted Aubrey to know that I amounted to something. You get that, right?" he said to Levi. "A man wanting to make his mark beyond what's expected or average?"

Before Levi could reply, Aubrey grasped his wrist, turning the leather-banded watch toward her. "Gosh, traffic into Boston will be murder if we wait much longer. Why don't we get going? Just let me put some lipstick on." She flashed a smile at both men, retreating to the back hall, which accommodated a powder room addition.

Levi pointed. "Did you want to wait on the front porch for . . . Aubrey?" For the first time in seven years, Levi found himself lacking the words "my wife."

"I can wait alone. Seemed like your son was looking for you."

"Patience is a good quality. Let him work on it for a few more minutes. I'd be interested to hear more about you."

◆ ◆ ◆

It was after one in the morning when Levi heard the front door open. The hall light turned on and a low glow filtered into the bedroom. The soft luster illuminated Pete, who slept crooked in his father's arms. The third step creaked, and the tenth, before Aubrey's shadow fell over them. Her painted fingernails moved over her son's face, brushing a tear Levi had missed. "How bad?" she asked.

"Medium. I couldn't make sense out of any of it. Only whoever, whatever was in his dream, his room . . . his mind," Levi said, "they were definitely from another era."

When Aubrey and Levi weren't discussing television jobs or entertaining her past, Pete's scribe-like gift dominated most conversations.

"I swear he said 'mustard gas' at one point, and muttered phrases—*in a French accent*." Aubrey put her fingers to her lips, and he spoke more quietly. "Aubrey, they're things no seven-year-old should know. Fortunately, he calmed down and fell asleep as soon as I brought him in here, so that was a plus."

"I'll put him back."

"No. Just leave him here."

She nodded and backed away. Aubrey shimmied out of the dress and Levi was surprised to see it involved no zipper, the clingy fabric peeling from her body like the petal on an exotic flower. Her slender figure hadn't changed over time, and it still fascinated him that he'd been so physically attracted to the wavy raven hair, her elegant tall frame. Blondes and petite had always been his go-to image. Aside from the physical, Aubrey had been so different from any woman who'd come before her. Even more interesting was how Aubrey turned out to be everything Levi had ever needed or wanted. How fate, not his dogged determination, put her in his life. Levi eased his arm out from beneath Pete, propping himself on his elbow. "You know," he said, "I think I will move Pete back. He's in that snorey, super deep sleep."

Aubrey didn't object as he slipped from the bed and returned their son to his room, only a few feet away.

He waited at Pete's bedside for a few moments, satisfied when the boy only rolled to his side, clutching an overly loved stuffed monkey named Moe and popping his thumb into his mouth. It was the comfort habit of a baby that Levi wouldn't dare attempt to correct. When he came back to bed, Aubrey was already in it. He slid under the covers, intrigued by her choice of nightgown—nothing. "How was your date?" he asked, kissing her shoulder.

"My date?" She rolled in his direction, and Levi kissed her, tasting a trace of lipstick and champagne. "My date was fine."

Levi loomed over her, Aubrey sinking into the mattress. "So you agree that your past showed up here with an agenda?"

"I agree that my past showed up wanting to show off his present. Zeke's probably on Charley's front porch right now, sneaking a cigarette. I'm right here."

"Fascinating," he said, touching her face, but distracted by the tidbit. "I wouldn't think a smoker would have ever appealed to you."

"One of many things that made Zeke *not* the right guy. He tried. Quit smoking more than once for me, but somehow his love of Camels always won out."

"See that? With me, you only had to overcome a few hundred layers of stubbornness."

In the moonlight, he could see her roll her eyes. "Levi, don't make me compare. I might have preferred the challenges of a chain smoker. As noted, I'm right here. What do you want to focus on, Zeke's bad habits or me?" Aubrey's fingers hooked around the edge of his boxers.

"Definitely you. But as far as your evening goes, I reserve the right to revisit tomorrow."

"And I'm not completely sorry you noticed my evening away from you. It may have saved you from that date-night trip to Paris."

Levi skimmed off the boxers, dismissing nearly all other thoughts. "Just one more thing," he said, his hands moving in a practiced downward direction.

"What's that?" It came out in a lusty breath, as if Aubrey were disinterested in anything he wanted to verbalize.

Poised over her, Levi moved forward, and she locked an elegant long leg around him. "Just so you know, I think maybe it is time to up my career game. My goals. I decided to take the TV job."

CHAPTER NINE

Boston, Massachusetts
Present Day

On Piper Sullivan's desk was a picture of a blonde-haired girl who looked so much like her mother no one ever asked, "Is this your daughter?" It was the way Piper answered the follow-on questions that awed Aubrey. The photo invited the inevitable: *"How old is she now?" "What does she do?" "Is she like you—a bloodhound of an investigator?"* Piper had routine answers: "Sadie would have been twenty-one this year." "She was eight in that picture—my daughter was crazy for American Girl dolls and glittery rub-on tattoos." "Two weeks after that photo was taken, she was murdered, so I don't know who she would have turned out to be."

That was the pattern when new people entered Piper's office—cursory conversation followed by humbling silence. The day Aubrey entered Piper's office for the first time, things went differently. For one, Aubrey knew she was looking at a photo of a dead girl. She knew Sadie's name and that her murder had been solved. Her killer was a neighborhood teenager, a troubled boy with a twisted mind and heart. Sadie's death eventually spirited Piper to this area of law enforcement, overseeing cases involving missing children in New England. She'd needed to get out of the South, where due process had brought Sadie's killer to justice, though it had never brought closure to Piper.

Not until Aubrey arrived.

Piper had been a skeptical but intrigued reader of Aubrey's book. She'd wanted to talk, ruminate over a couple of cold cases on her desk. Aubrey didn't take offense when Piper said she'd wasted days on crazier leads. Sadie's presence had been immediate and overwhelming; Aubrey delivered a long-awaited message of closure, not necessarily to Deputy Chief Sullivan, but to a dead girl's stunned mother.

It was as far as the two women had gotten that day. The connection to Sadie plunged the hermetic investigator into emotion buried deeper than her daughter's coffin. A week later, Aubrey came back. She wanted to help, but she was also leery. Aubrey didn't want this to become her life's work. It was too much. When you lived with the dead, you had to choose, where you could, what you let into your life. In turn, Piper selected cases with care, only calling on Aubrey when certain elements surfaced—icy-cold leads and vague disappearances being common threads in the dark current of missing children.

From their distinct vantage points, the women hit a stride with difficult and hard-to-hear information. In more instances than not, Aubrey supplied critical information, the abduction and recovery of Lily North being their most recent triumph. The more devastating cases were harder to process, though Piper assured Aubrey, for the families involved, it was better than never learning what had become of their children. Unfortunately, it was a fact Piper knew all too well.

Aubrey believed that working with Piper was her current calling. The *job* was more intense than her previous spiritual employment—ferrying messages between the dead who resided in properties that were for sale and their loved ones. Maybe it was also part of the reason she'd written *The Unremarkable Life of Missy Flannigan.* It could be that this was what Missy meant by *"You could do more . . ."* Without the book, she would have never met Piper. It all made sense. The arrangement and general pattern of their work had been productive for a number of years, with Aubrey going home to a near-perfect life, always tucking Pete in a little tighter after a day with Piper. She had Levi—a breathing rock of stability, someone who encouraged but was always cautious about new challenges.

Psychic challenges and everyday life balanced, or at least they did until things went haywire and Pete's gift turned into something more than disconcerting dreams. Now, with the apparent change in her own gift, the curious discovery of her father's ghost gifts, not to mention an estranged Levi, Aubrey sighed, wondering how disheartening a prognostication of her own future would be.

Waiting for Piper, sitting in the chair across from her desk, Aubrey struggled for a grip on the things she could control. In the moment, it didn't seem like much. She bit down on her lip, sinking back into the chair. Her work with Piper: that was something about which she could say yes or no. Maybe the time had come to move on, resign from the ominous world of missing children, thereby removing one disturbing element from her life. It could be the reason Aubrey had woken with an urge to call Piper and ask for today's meeting.

"Recovered from the other day yet?" The office filled with Piper's drawl, in turn chasing the immediate ghosts from Aubrey's head. She took the seat behind her desk. "I was thinking, you ought to write another book: *My Life as a Terrorist—One Psychic's Day in FBI Hell.*"

"I'll get right on that," Aubrey said dryly. "Actually, I was thinking." She sat up straight. "The reason I called, after the tower incident and my prior warning . . . after what I learned about my father, where Levi and I are, together and with Pete . . ." She wallowed in an ambivalent pause. No. This was the right call. "Maybe I should take a break from this."

Piper's energy was almost a visible thing; it stopped dead. She cranked her body into slow motion, drawing her chair closer to the desk, then pointing a finger at Aubrey. "I get that. It was a rough day. Nobody likes being held in a cement-block basement room, having their civil rights trampled on, or being accused of representing the New England chapter of ISIS, but—"

"Piper, I was clear when I agreed to this. It wouldn't be forever, and I would get out when I felt like I'd done all I could for you. I think I'm there."

"Is this Levi's two cents talking?"

"Levi doesn't have anything to do with it. I just think as few distractions as possible are the best right now, especially when it comes to Pete."

"Makes sense." She nodded, blonde curls bobbing. "'Course, I didn't realize your son had moved back in with you, away from his daddy."

She hesitated. "He hasn't."

"Oh, then I guess your theory's changed from what you told me months ago—that it's better to keep busy than keep wringing your hands over Pete. I mean, the boy's safe. He's with his dad, who, if I'm not mistaken, you still think is a pretty good man example."

Aubrey made a face.

"Even I'll admit Levi's no chest-beating gorilla. Not like that Fed contact of his, Dan Watney, super-agent deluxe." She put such a sharp twang on *luxe*, the sound ricocheted off the walls. "If you ask me, there's something to be concerned about."

"I realize Dan's methods are a little . . . *cowboy* compared to yours. That said, I don't think Levi's at an age where he'll be influenced by peer pressure."

"I meant your son. Watney might have him stacking empty shot glasses before his thirteenth birthday."

"Ha! Levi would never . . . besides, they don't even socialize; not as far as I know." Aubrey scrunched her brow. Of course, it had been months. Who knew how Levi's life had changed. Her imagination defaulted to a messy, dorm-like condo, late-night poker games, and double bourbons all around. Aubrey rolled her eyes—like Levi would tolerate an open bag of chips in the common room, never mind dirty laundry on the floor. She shook her head. "The point is there are more unknown variables than ever in my life. It's too much." Aubrey wrapped her fingers around the beaded necklace she wore, tugging hard, then smoothed the front of her pale blue dress. "My work here is one thing I can control."

"So what's your plan? To sit at home and wait for Levi and Pete to come around, maybe spend your time worrying when and where your daddy's gift might pop up again? You'd feel safer holed up in your house, is that it?"

Aubrey nodded fervently, and the two women stared at one another.

"Okay." Piper splayed her hands wide. "If that's your decision, I respect it. I told you the day you rocked my world, this gig is your call. You may never have walked in my shoes, but I've certainly never treaded in yours."

"Well, all right then." Aubrey shifted in her seat, not exactly sure how they'd reached the mutual conclusion. "We agree. My life is far too complicated right now, and I should—"

"But before you go . . . I've been meaning to give you this." Piper spun her chair around. From the pages of a Bible, tucked amid procedural manuals and case histories, she plucked a cream-colored envelope. "Darn thing kept slippin' my mind. You know me. Not much for sentiment, no time to read anything but the files on my desk."

"What is it?"

"Addressed to you."

"It's open." Aubrey took the envelope, and Piper shrugged, busying herself with a folder. Aubrey huffed, wrestling the note from inside. As she read, her eyes misted and her throat tightened. The note was from Lily North's parents, a page of heartfelt praise and deep gratitude. A little girl had been found alive, terrified but essentially unharmed. Her life might be forever altered, but thanks to Aubrey, she'd have one. She stuffed the notepaper, now with one teardrop spot, back into the envelope. "That was a really cheap trick, Piper."

"And some of us didn't get the kid back, Aubrey." She flipped the folder closed, her expression solemn. "You possess an ability that makes mine pedestrian. I'll use dirty tricks and carnie sleight of hand to keep you on this job. What happened the other day and your personal life,

103

while currently out of sync, doesn't match what these parents are experiencing—their child is missing, maybe dead, maybe worse." She poked at some papers. "If I can prevent one parent from enduring my living hell . . ." Piper's voice pinched. "I'll do it."

Aubrey sank back into the chair and peered across the desk. "So what am I doing here?"

"Beats me," she said. "After your tower debacle, I assumed your focus would be off, or not of particular use to me. Go home; lock yourself in for a day, if it helps. Take a long bath. Maybe put some energy into sorting out your daddy's gift. Lord knows I'd be curious."

"I should. Take a close look at what's in that letter box. I guess I just don't want to do it alone."

"Invite a friend to tag along," Piper said.

Aubrey rolled that short list through her head.

"'Course, if it were me, I'd want the most methodical mind in on that case."

"Levi?"

"I said he was a stubborn ass, honey. I didn't say he wasn't whip smart and then some." Piper pulled a dark blue folder from a stack of white ones—new cases versus old, so Aubrey had learned. Her gaze jerked from the blue folder to Piper. "Go," Piper said. "If you don't want to deal with the letter box right now, do something else. Get yourself a mani-pedi. Better still, didn't you mention an old carnie buddy being in town?"

"Uh, yeah. Zeke Dublin." It seemed like weeks ago. "We had coffee yesterday . . . at Euro."

"Cozy." She frowned, looking between the folder and Aubrey. "Do I also recall you saying he's more of an ex-boyfriend?"

"Yes, but that was ages ago. Zeke, he's . . ." She thought for a moment. "Just someone from my past whose timing is pretty good in the present. Right now, I could use that friend you mentioned."

"Hmm . . . good for you. A friend. Copy that."

"I didn't mean it like that. Not that you and I aren't . . . it's just I've known Zeke forever. We go so far back."

Piper laughed. "You can't insult me by wantin' to sit at someone else's lunch table. I get us, darlin'. No worries."

Aubrey shook off the misstep and reached for her satchel.

"But here's my two cents, even if you didn't ask. Given your present, you might be a little vulnerable. Could be coffee was just an icebreaker. Is this Zeke hanging around town for a while?"

"He didn't really say. And you're wrong. Zeke and I, there's nothing . . ." Aubrey rewound their coffee "date" and Zeke's *"I love you . . ."* parting words. The way he'd reached for her hand and touched her face. The lure of yesteryear had pulsed off him—a place that was safe and steady and whole. She squeezed shut her eyes; the aura of Zeke was almost tangible. "I wouldn't let anything like that happen between us."

"Funny, that's what my ex-husband said right before he put on his best dress shirt—long sleeved—and went to a high school reunion to 'catch up.'"

"Huh. I don't think you ever told me that story. How did it turn out?"

"Good. For him. 'Catching up' with his high school sweetheart . . ." Piper finger quoted the air. "She's the reason he's been my ex-husband since Sadie was four."

"I'll bear that in mind." Aubrey cleared her throat. "But Zeke's good people. He'd never . . . it was a lifetime ago and . . ." She wanted to say it was kid stuff but found herself replying, "He wasn't the guy. Zeke knows that."

"If you say so." Piper glanced between the dark blue folder and Aubrey. "Now shoo; I've got work to do."

Aubrey started to rise but was drawn, once again, to the folder. "New case?"

"Sort of. Not New England. But, you know, sometimes they ask."

Aubrey nodded. It wasn't unusual for individual states to seek out Piper's input.

"Tucson-area Feds just turned it over to me for a look-see. They couldn't get anywhere with it."

Aubrey sat again, her sight line moving between the new folder and an older one marked "Trevor Beane." It was a Pennsylvania cold case, a missing sixteen-year-old boy whose file landed on Piper's desk months ago. Aubrey got involved back then, but there hadn't been a vibe of insider information, nothing penetrating from Trevor Beane's case file or personal belongings. Aubrey always perceived zero insight as a plus—she didn't sense death.

Trevor had vanished after ice hockey practice, not far from his home in Glenmore, Pennsylvania. Because of his age, law enforcement had leaned toward a runaway scenario. Piper felt Trevor didn't fit the profile— good student, popular, happy family life, no peculiar interests or friends, a computer hard drive that showed nothing more alarming than a few sites featuring nude women. "*Not* finding naked women . . . possibly men, would have been stranger," Piper had insisted. At the time, Aubrey made a mental note about paying closer attention to Pete's web-surfing habits.

In the parking lot of the ice arena, police had found Trevor's goalie mask, one skate, and some tape. Green tape. The kind you'd wrap around a hockey stick. But did the items indicate a struggle or just stuff left behind by someone making a mad dash out of town? There'd been no conclusion or progress. Aubrey had physically handled Trevor's personal items, the ones found at the scene and those gathered to create a DNA profile. To her, it'd all been as cold as the blade on Trevor Beane's ice skate. But now, staring at the closed folder, Aubrey was oddly swamped by recall, the specifics of a case for which she'd been no help. Also, on the back of her palate was the sudden sharp taste of a sour green apple, then a rush of sugar.

Piper was talking; Aubrey cleared her throat and looked up. "I'm sorry. What did you say?"

She spun the blue folder in Aubrey's direction. "Girlfriend, I think you really should just go home. But suit yourself, I have no qualms taking advantage. I said this is fourteen-year-old Liam Sheffield. He lives in the suburbs of Tucson, or he did until ten days ago."

Piper opened the folder, and Aubrey absorbed the image of a brown-haired boy, his nose taking up a chunk of his face. Unassuming brown eyes. Definitely in the throes of puberty, with a ruddy complexion and gangly appearance. "Anything outstanding about his disappearance?"

"I've only glanced at it. I was about to get into it when you called. Arizona state police sent Liam's personal items. That's them." Piper motioned to a box on a side chair and skimmed the notes made by Tucson authorities. "Supposedly, Liam was on his way home from a friend's house, right around dusk. His bicycle was found near a vacant lot in a residential area, a gym bag with it." She flipped the page. "Nothing worth noting—usual stuff: shorts, Axe deodorant, chewing gum, two dollars in change, a half-eaten lunch . . . boy junk. Guess they'll throw anything in a bag, huh?"

"They will." She knew Pete would. "Piper, could I see the list?"

The deputy chief turned the paper and held it up.

"No. *See the list . . .*"

She obliged, holding out the report. The paper was warm to her touch. Aubrey felt a connection between the two boys and reached for Trevor Beane's file, which was also now warm.

Piper walked around to Aubrey's side of the desk. Pictures of both boys were attached to the paperwork. "Interesting. Put young Liam here on a Proactiv plan for a few weeks, and I'd say these two could pass for brothers."

"Exactly what I was thinking," Aubrey murmured.

"And what else are you thinking?"

She shot a sideways glance in Piper's direction. "Do you still have the personal items recovered from Trevor's disappearance?"

"Yes. In here." From a locked cabinet, Piper produced a numbered cardboard box. "With nothing new, I was going to send it back to the PA staties. Do we have something new, Aubrey?"

She didn't answer, taking the lid off the box and examining the contents she'd readily recalled. "Hockey," she said, the word floating into her ear.

"What about it?"

"I'm not sure." She shuffled, irritated; the urge to squirm felt like ants on her legs. "I don't know the first thing about hockey." But as Aubrey said the words, her head swam with suspected hockey jargon: *slap shot, body-checking, drop pass, hat trick.* "Can we take a look at Liam's personal items?"

Piper cleared a space on her desk and plopped down an identical box. The lid opened, and a rush of cold air came at Aubrey, like the box led to the Arctic. She took a step back. "That's really weird."

"For you or for the rest of us?" Piper said.

"Uh, me. When you opened the box, I felt a rush of cold air, and not the kind that accompanies the dead. More like a physical cold, like a place." Aubrey moved her gaze around the office. There was a flickering ethereal presence, then nothing. She looked back at the box. Taking up most of space inside was Liam's gym bag. "Did Liam Sheffield play ice hockey too?"

"I don't think so." Piper picked up the boy's profile, flipping through. "His parents list video games and swimming. I doubt there are many ice rinks in Tucson." Piper flipped the page. "Oh, wait. It does mention street hockey. According to his parents, Liam had recently taken an interest in street hockey. But so what?" She rested her hand on her hip, glancing between the folders and Aubrey. "Aside from a brotherly resemblance and some basics—male, white, middle-class, teenagers, equally baffling disappearances—there are no decisive facts. They disappeared two thousand miles and months apart. Sadly, I could come up with a dozen other cases bearing the same similarities."

But Aubrey wasn't listening; she was unzipping the gym bag. The pungent odor of sweaty boy rushed forward, enough that Piper wriggled her nose, and Aubrey had to turn her head away for a moment. She dug into the bag, and not of her own volition, her hand burrowing into Liam Sheffield's belongings. The motion became frantic, forceful.

It was as if someone were physically pushing her. Oddly, the taste of sour apple invaded again, then vanished. If not for the relative safety of Piper's office, Aubrey wasn't too sure she'd be going along with it. "Here. This." She withdrew an inventoried plastic bag. Aubrey dropped the bag onto the desk. Inside it was a roll of green tape.

Piper rummaged through Trevor's inventoried possessions. Seconds later, she came up with a similar roll of green tape, which Aubrey recalled seeing months ago. "Kind of interesting. But hardly like finding identical voodoo dolls, pins stuck through the same body parts."

"The places your mind will go . . ."

"All I'm saying is it falls more to coincidental than suggestive. Tape does not register as even a vague indicator of their disappearances correlating."

But Aubrey couldn't let it go, taking the plastic bag from Piper and picking up the one she'd dropped on the desk. They bordered on hot, and Aubrey was surprised not to find the plastic melting. She drew a breath. Instead of heat, icy cold filled her lungs. "I still say the tape connects them."

"Hon, you're going to have to give me a little more to go on. I'm not even seeing a path to start down on, not based on rolls of green tape you can buy at any sporting goods store." She took the bagged tape from Aubrey. "I think you're understandably overwhelmed. You should go home and forget about two random boxes that happen to contain rolls of green tape. It's not exactly a smoking gun."

Aubrey's head shot up, hearing a voice that wasn't Piper's. "You're right. The tape's not worth noting." She turned toward the dedicated agent. "Not unless you just heard a third boy telling you to pay attention to it. Not unless he's hissing it in your head, insisting that these two boys and their disappearances are connected. That and this ghost—it tastes like the most god-awful sour green apple flavor."

Piper stared back, drawing her own breath and conclusion. "Well, damn, would you look at that."

"What?"

"Smoke from a gun."

CHAPTER
TEN

With a bestseller behind her and *Ink on Air* in its fifth season, money was not one of the problems Aubrey and Levi faced in their present-day lives. They could have easily moved to a fancier neighborhood but had felt settled in the house on Homestead Road. Together, they'd remodeled the kitchen and added a spacious master suite. When things were good between them, Aubrey and Levi had done the obvious, like buy new cars, invest in Pete's education, and generously support several favorite charities. They occasionally toyed with the idea of buying a summer place on the Cape. Even then, they had enough to buy Charley a seaside home in a North Shore retirement community. They were all decisions the two of them had made together.

As Aubrey pulled into Charley's driveway and Levi got out of his car, "together" was not the word popping to mind. While she'd taken Piper's advice and asked Levi for his help with the letter box, it was downright weird to arrive at the same place apart.

"I should have called you," he said, walking toward her. "We could have carpooled."

Carpooled. The word came out coolly, as if Aubrey had been an afterthought regarding school pickup. "I suppose I've gotten used to it, coming here alone."

"I've been by."

"I heard. Charley said you met the roofer here last month, made arrangements for the repair it needed. That was good of you."

"Look, just because you and I . . ." Levi stopped, adjusting his glasses. "No matter where we are, I have no intention of abandoning your grandmother."

So it's just me, then . . . good to know . . .

"Why, um . . ." Aubrey pointed to the front door. "Why don't we just go inside? See what this letter box is all about."

On the way in, they talked briefly about Pete, Levi saying that he needed to be home by four thirty. That was when basketball practice ended. Over her shoulder, Aubrey uttered a curt, "I know."

Yvette ushered them inside. She was helping Charley get to the box, which she kept in a deep walk-in closet. She left Aubrey and Levi in the living room, saying they'd be right back. Aubrey sat at one end of the sofa, Levi sitting in a chair across from her. She glanced at the empty seating for two beside her.

"I just prefer the chair," he said.

Aubrey shot him a narrow-eyed glance. "Sit anywhere you like. Seriously, Levi, I got your message the day you moved out."

"And I thought we'd calmly reasoned through that. Everybody needed space. We wanted a better environment for Pete. Not one where he felt like the catalyst for every argument."

Aubrey ran a hand through her hair, looking out a window that took in a garden view. "Rest assured, there's plenty of damn space now."

They fell silent as Yvette wheeled Charley into the room. In her lap was the letter box she'd described—a large leather thing, shallow but long. Seeing the box made Aubrey's mind reel back the memory of a high closet shelf in her parents' bedroom. "Charley, years ago, did the box arrive from Greece with my parents' other belongings?"

"Actually, your father sent it to me a few months before they passed away."

"Did he?" she said, curious. "I remember the box in Greece. I remember after they died, when a trunk and some crates arrived. We were in the rental house in New Mexico. There were books and pictures, a little of my mother's jewelry. But you're right. I don't remember the letter box, not then."

"Indeed. You wouldn't have." As Charley spoke, Yvette parked the wheelchair midway into the room.

"Did he say why he sent the letter box?" Levi asked.

"Only that he wanted it somewhere safe. It was one of the last and most lucid conversations I had with him. By then," she said to Aubrey, "your mother did most of the talking during phone calls. Peter was often heavily medicated, and when he wasn't . . ." With crooked fingers, Charley stroked the box's lid. "My son certainly wasn't himself." Silence settled over the room. "The dining room table would be better if you want to look through it. As you'll see, the box is quite full."

They all moved toward the adjacent dining area, Aubrey saying to Levi as she strode past, "By all means, you decide where you want to sit first."

They ended up side by side, just circumstance—Charley's wheelchair naturally fit best on the open side of the table—and Yvette busied herself as hostess, ferrying glasses of iced tea to the group. But as Aubrey stared at the box, trepidation rose.

"You okay?" Levi tugged at the leather tie, a thin strap wrapping around it twice.

She hesitated. "Yes. Of course." Along with the reply, she moved her hands in a flighty fashion, finally knotting them in her lap. Levi swung open the lid, and a burst of air rushed out, the dank smell of timeworn paper permeating the room. This much was pedestrian, the sights and smells anyone would sense delving into a sealed old object.

Aubrey focused on separating ordinary effects from those apparent only to her. Unknotting her fingers, she moved her hand forward, covering Levi's. "Do you hear that?"

"Hear what?"

Aubrey cocked her head and gripped her hand harder into his. "A buzzing. It's very distant. Or, I don't know, maybe it's the hum of people talking . . . yelling." With her other hand, Aubrey swiped at the bead of sweat that had gathered above her lip. A prickle moved like Morse code up her spine, and she shuffled in her seat.

"Do you want me to stop, close it?" He asked this, she realized, because her fingers were clamped around his.

Emotions converged on Aubrey, most of them emanating from the box. But it was all too surreal and vague, like some of her own ghost gifts. She let go of Levi's hand. "No. Don't close it." She focused on the mosaic displayed in front of her—scraps of paper of every pigment, shape, texture, and size. It wasn't completely new. Her gaze moved back and forth; she remembered looking inside the box, if only a handful of times. "I . . . keep going, but I don't want to touch any of it."

A practiced Levi took charge. "Fair enough. Let's see what we've got here." Levi took a moment, rubbing his hands on his pant legs. From there, he segued smoothly into reporter mode, and the hunt began. Aubrey hadn't experienced this part of Levi in some time; it was curiously comforting. He needed to make sense of the box as much as she did. On the surface, the contents challenged his orderly nature. At a glance, matchbook covers and business cards were visible, a plethora of notepaper, and even the shorn corner of a pizza box sticking out from the top layer. A few minutes into his search, Levi stopped to retrieve a fresh legal pad from his car. Some rules of order were nonnegotiable. He returned, going about the task of detailed note-taking.

He withdrew the papers one at a time—a fishbowl of prognostication. He read each one slowly, allowing everyone time to absorb the information. As he began, a white tablecloth patterned in lilies and butterflies dominated. Over the next two hours, the cheery print vanished, with Levi converting the potpourri of paper scraps into a filing system. He stopped several times and murmured, "This is just . . ."

"Amazing," Aubrey said, finishing the thought. "Just amazing. Even for somebody who is used to everyday conversations with the dead."

At one point, Levi withdrew a candy wrapper. It'd been torn open at its seams, making for one flat piece of shiny cellophane. A smile broke into his serious mood.

"What?" Aubrey said, looking at the dark pink wrapper marked "Cadbury."

"English chocolate." His tone had shifted to wistful. "On our annual pilgrimages to London with Pa, it was a game. How much candy could Brody and I get our hands on without him catching on? We'd gobble it down the second Pa's back was turned, under the covers at night. I haven't thought of it in years. And this wrapper . . ." He shook the crinkly paper. "This was a coconut Cadbury. They only produced it for a short time. Anybody who's English associates a dark purple wrapper with the chocolate, but I remember this one." He turned it over. Wistfulness vanished as he read the message on the reverse side. "Jesus . . . 'Harrods' . . . '1983' . . . 'detonation' . . ."

"A department store bombing, right?"

"Yes." Levi shook his head. "My father was called in to consult. I remember him talking about it afterward." He placed the outrageous prediction in its chronological location, which surely conflicted with the logical thoughts in Levi's head. "My God, Aubrey, this is a treasure chest of history before it ever happened."

She scanned the table, the lilies and butterflies nearly obscured.

"So tell me." Charley's query was filled with far less fascination than her guests' observations. "Aside from amazement, what is it you've determined?"

Yvette took the seat beside her wheelchair, looking on as well.

Levi lightly tapped his knuckles on the legal pad, glancing between his notes and the prediction-filled papers. "My initial thoughts, based on simple sleuthing . . . some rudimentary organization of information, if we look at the predictions on the whole—"

"Levi," Aubrey said, hearing the tip of an oration.

"Right. Sorry. First off, did you know there was a pattern?"

"A pattern?" Yvette said. "In that mess?"

"Yes." Aubrey had noted the same thing. "My father begins receiving or at least collecting the messages when he's fifteen." She pointed to the papers filed farthest left. "This would be the year. Right, Charley?"

"Yes," she said. "That's correct."

"So from here to about here." Levi reached across the table, his index finger landing on the wingtip of a monarch butterfly. "These all are past predictions, and all disastrous. Like you told us, there was the earthquake in Turkey, the girls' names from the Cape Cod murders . . ." For a moment they all looked solemnly at the heart-shaped papers Charley had described. "The department store bombing and about two dozen worldwide events in total. It's just . . . *staggering*."

"And correct me, Levi, if my assumption's been wrong all these years," Charley said, "but if not for your unique perspective, you wouldn't believe a word of it."

"That's a fair statement, for me. For any ordinary person who might look through this box."

"But we do have a different perspective." Aubrey continued to stare at the now-organized papers. "Almost as important, seeing all this clarifies the intensity of my father's burden. I can't even imagine how it felt to know all this, the encumbrance."

"Indeed again." Charley pointed a crooked finger. "And this pattern. Explain what you've learned, please."

Levi pointed to the far end. "Like Aubrey said, from the time Peter was fifteen, there are multiple predictions every year, several tragic, a few—for lack of a better word—that appear frivolous. The things you mentioned the other night, Charley—sporting events, a couple of more complex predictions that have to do with earning potential."

"Could you be more specific?" Charley said.

Levi picked up a sheet of ordinary computer paper. "This one jumped out at me."

Charley raised her chin and squinted, reading: "'Lisa project. Buy into it.' The crayon drawing of an apple. I've always wondered about that message. It seems more like . . . *gibberish* than some of the others."

"The Lisa project," Levi said, "was the codename Apple computers used during its developmental era, back in the early 1980s. It was the name of Steve Jobs's daughter, but it also stood for Local Integrated Software Architecture."

All three women stared at him, Aubrey saying dully, "And people find my base of knowledge inexplicable."

"The point is, had Peter or anyone decoded this prediction in real time and invested, they would have made a fortune." Levi held out the paper. "It's a lottery ticket."

"Okay, so we'll add that one to the positive prediction pile," Aubrey said as Levi moved the paper. "But then there's a break. Starting in the mid-1990s through present day, the good forecasts fall off. You never noticed this?"

"Not that I recall. Years ago, Carmine and I spent time focusing on the predictions, but—"

"Charley, hang on a sec," Levi said. "Besides Carmine, who knew about the predictions? I'm curious." Aubrey sat up straighter. That question hadn't occurred to her, though she knew the real answer differed from the one her grandmother would give.

"Only Yvette, Carmine. Peter's wife, of course. My late ex-husbands. Peter's father passed before any of this started to manifest itself. That's it." Charley looked over the sudden organization applied to her son's chaotic life. She looked at Levi. "Why do you ask?"

Levi pointed to the table full of predictions. "Just another piece of information that needs to be factored in."

Aubrey ran her fingers over the earring that trailed down her lobe and was quiet as the conversation continued.

"And here's another. Carmine and I did draw one inference," Charley said. "Although perhaps I was only giving myself permission to put the box away, stop looking at the messages."

"What was that?" Levi asked.

"While Peter was given future predictions, perhaps he was never meant to prevent the tragedies attached to them." She looked to her granddaughter. "It's Aubrey who took this curious gift to the next level, offering messages of closure. Asking Peter to prevent such larger calamities from happening . . . it seems a little Herculean for one man."

"Or makes him a descendant of Nostradamus," Levi said.

"Unfortunately, I can only quote our family tree to the early nineteenth century. As for my son, I'm afraid he was as much a victim as every person whose life he couldn't save. As I told you both, I did consider burning the box after Peter's death—again a few times after that. The urge to preserve it always won out."

"Huh." Levi tapped a closed fist to his mouth. Then he shook an index finger in Charley's direction. "Let's explore that for a moment— the urge *not* to destroy the box. Let's assume it still exists for a reason. The fact that Peter sent it to you for safekeeping before he died speaks to that. It's almost as if—"

"He knew the tragedy that awaited him . . . and my mother." Aubrey was quiet for a moment. "He wanted to make certain Charley had the box because he knew there were predictions yet to come."

"Maybe a specific one or two that would be relevant." He shook his head at the mystery laid out before them. "But bigger or smaller than an earthquake, more or less personal . . . who knows?"

"Levi," Yvette said, "is there an end to the predictions? We know they went beyond Peter's death, but have they stopped completely since then?"

"I was just getting to that. There are four or five I can't decode, fit into my filing system." His finger landed on two pieces of green construction paper and a blue paper star. They were unlike anything else in the box.

"Seems like those three get filed in their own category of vagueness," Yvette said.

"For now, I'd agree. The construction-paper messages, they're different. Peter's handwriting—it's erratic throughout." Levi pointed to various examples: cursive writing, all shaky but legible scrawl. "Then we get to construction-paper messages and . . ."

"They're not as complex." Aubrey eyed the closest deep green piece of paper, its edges jagged, as if it'd been torn away from a larger portion. "Maybe it's the crayon."

"But several predictions are written in crayon," Levi said, noting another detailed drawing of a bumblebee and a locker, the apple. Levi refocused on the first piece of green construction paper. Written on it was the word "Springfield," and next to it was a modest drawing of a house. "Interesting. The numbers written on the house, 2017 . . . it could be the year."

"Or an address." Levi picked up what appeared to be its mate, the other piece of green construction paper. He tipped his head at the lesser illustration. "Huh. A large bearded man wearing an old-fashioned sleeping cap. A few more stick houses surrounding him. What do you make of that?" Levi said.

"Uh, Santa Claus, maybe?" Aubrey bit down on a snicker. "A little imagination, Levi."

He shot her an annoyed glance. "Right. Yes, I suppose I can see that."

"Looks like a bunch of giant *V*s drawn behind Santa," Yvette said from her across-the-table view. Levi turned the paper around. "Oh, I see. They could be mountains in the background."

"Or tepees." Aubrey furrowed her brow at the rendering. Levi laid down the pieces of green construction paper. Boldly, she reached past them, touching the edge of the blue star. A sense of déjà vu filtered through her fingers and into her head. "These messages on the construction paper . . . they're abstract. But the blue one, it's warm."

"And is that connecting to anything else?" Levi asked.

The cutout star depicted a house with a red roof, yellow sun, and what looked like waves in the foreground. The word "SUN" was printed out with an arrow, not pointed at the circular sol, but more toward the house. At least that was Aubrey's interpretation. Before she could deduce anything more, a zing of pain shot through her temple. She let go of the star and jerked back in the chair.

"Are you all right?" Levi said.

Vagueness overrode what was beginning to feel like a cohesive memory. "Yes," she said. "I think so. That was bizarre." The pain eased, and she shook her head. "You know how you might have the urge to sneeze and then it vanishes?" They all nodded. "It was like that, something on the rise, then nothing—only sharper." She felt Levi's intent stare. "What?"

"Nothing." He hesitated. "It's just for everything I might list on a legal pad, organize on a tabletop"—he pointed at the mishmash of papers finessed into Levi logic—"it's often your cryptic insights that deliver the most critical facts."

"And it's what makes you two fools a brilliant team."

"Charley," Aubrey said softly, her glance catching on Levi's. But he looked away, busying himself with the spelled-out future in front of him.

"My apologies," her grandmother said. "I didn't realize the obvious was off-limits."

The room went quiet. When it came to partnerships, Aubrey knew how well they worked together on a story—things with lots of moving parts. After the Missy Flannigan case, after Levi recovered and Pete was born, the two of them had collaborated on a few news assignments. None had come close to the mystery involving Missy or the one in front of them now. Still, Aubrey recognized the energy. Until recently, they'd never stopped working together. They'd repurposed, applying intrinsic partnership skills to their life. Aubrey sighed, at a loss to pinpoint where the ability to solve things together had gone.

"On the other hand," she said hopefully, "without effective organization, cryptic information can remain just that."

But Levi wasn't listening to melancholy compliments. Instead, he tapped his pen rhythmically against a single stack of segregated messages. "These ghost gifts are also different from the larger mélange of predictions. They do, however, follow a pattern of their own. Each paper contains a series of numbers and dates." Levi fanned out the papers, more than a dozen. Aubrey knew the look on his face; it was the visible manifestation of the gears turning in Levi's mind.

"Five or six random numbers on every paper," he said. "Each bearing an equally random date. No digit higher than sixty-nine. What am I missing here?"

Aubrey focused too, noticing a gap in papers and dates, starting a few years before the turn of the twenty-first century.

With his right hand, Levi picked up one of the curious scribblings. It was written on notepaper from Packed Tight Moving & Storage, Arlington, Texas, and dated November 16, 1987. Then, with his left hand, he picked up another paper, transferring it to his right hand. "February 3, 1991 . . . five more random numbers." On the side of the notepaper, in pretty script, were the words *Honor's Guests, In-Home Catering, Rye, New York.*

Aubrey raised her arm, fingertips hovering over yet another. Levi bumped her hand away, picking it up. It wasn't deliberate, he was merely deep into his own thought process. With his index finger, Levi pushed one more paper a few inches along on the tabletop. This ghost gift contained five digits, dated October 15, 1993. Notepaper from

Baskum Machine & Tool, Meridian, Idaho. "These messages, the series of digits, and a date. Your father recorded each one on notepaper originating from a different state, which we can tell by the businesses."

"And this one." Aubrey reached for a lone paper. "Kind of takes it to another level."

"How so?" Charley asked. "Looks like all the other papers bearing random digits."

"Except this one is from Surrey—Hennessy's Funeral Home, on Warren Street." Aubrey placed the paper on the table, tapping her fingertip on the noted address. It was warm, not unlike the blue star.

"Better yet," Levi added, "it's a future date, not too far from now."

"So while the others are in the past, this paper boasts one more foretelling." Charley pulled in a reverent breath. "But what do they mean: notepaper from unrelated businesses, each with yesteryear dates and this one, all bearing . . . what?" she said, looking to Levi. "Five or six digits?"

Levi looked at Aubrey; his gaze was confident. "Are we on the same page?"

"A pattern within the pattern. Makes sense to me."

"I'd appreciate it if you'd share your 'makes sense' discovery with me," Charley said.

"Me too," Yvette chimed in.

"Before, the flip remark I made about the Lisa project prognostication being a lottery ticket." Levi placed all the papers back on the table. "I think that's what these are. The digits accompanied by specific dates and locations. They're lottery numbers. And the arbitrary businesses . . . not so arbitrary." He bore down harder with his index finger on Peggy's Alterations & Custom Sewing, Doylestown, Pennsylvania. "They're a time-stamped road map to . . ."

"A pot of gold," Aubrey said. "They point to the location, state, and date where my father, or anyone who deciphered the message, could purchase a winning lottery ticket."

CHAPTER
ELEVEN

Las Vegas, Nevada
Twelve Years Earlier

Taking a life wasn't beyond Zeke, especially when it was so obviously owed. A younger Jude Serino had witnessed his parents' murders; he was the son of the man who'd ended the lives of Ailish and Kieran Dunne. While these facts were clear, the eye-for-an-eye killing of Jude was understandably complicated. He wasn't the kind of man you could walk up to and shoot in the head, not like Zeke's father. The CEO of Serino Enterprises had layers of protection and plenty of eyes on him. Yet, over time, Zeke had remained vigilant in his quest. He might have executed his plan by now, if not for two things: Nora getting pregnant and the fact that Ian's degree from the London School of Economics did not come with a certificate of common sense.

Zeke had pondered this for the last hour, seated at the Montagues' kitchen table. Across from him was Nora, her frail frame looking as if she swallowed a beach ball, a salt sea of tears running down her face.

"Is it really as bad as the cruise line mess?" Zeke was trying to assess the damage, and Nora was not great with numbers. She was hysterical enough to get that much of the story wrong.

"It depends on your perspective." She sniveled, and Zeke handed her another Kleenex. "The cruise fiasco was close to a million dollars. Ian said this is only two or three hundred thousand, at least to get the books looking right."

"Two or three . . ." Zeke's jaw slacked. Even if it wasn't a million dollars, he wasn't sure Nora comprehended the amount; it didn't matter. Regardless of the sum, the Serino brothers would not be pleased.

Not long after Nora and Ian married, his half-brothers had put Ian in charge of a modest day cruise line that operated out of South Florida. In record time, he'd managed to run the cruise line aground. Literally might have been better. At least that way the Serinos could have collected the insurance. Surprisingly, Bruno Serino had been forgiving, insisting he and Jude give Ian another chance. They'd offered him a position with a small chain of restaurants that operated out of Serino resort properties—established eateries, backed by successful hotels: Aspen, Las Vegas, and Miami. *"How bad could you possibly screw it up?"* Jude had said, slapping the back of Ian's reedy frame.

Nora sniffled again, rubbing her hand over her stomach while verbalizing her brother's memory. "All that joking about the impossibility of Ian messing up again. I never imagined it could happen. And now . . . you should know, it's not just the business problems."

"Meaning what?" Zeke leaned closer to the table and his puffy sister.

"I'm leery of them. Jude especially."

"Why, did he threaten you? Did something happen?" Zeke rose from the chair, thinking today might be the day for cold-blooded murder.

Nora shook her head adamantly. "No. Nothing like that. But there's more than meets the eye. Did you know the IRS audited Jude's side of the business—twice? And as for Bruno . . ." She hiccupped again, her eyes, red-rimmed, darting away. "It's just the most dreadful story, the kind that never dies. Bruno and Suzanne's teenage son, Eli, he committed suicide while she was off skiing and Bruno worked at one of the Serino European resorts. Apparently, Suzanne was devastated—as she should have been. I heard she suffered a mental breakdown; Bruno had her locked away in a psychiatric hospital. It was that bad." Nora's hands gripped protectively around her round belly. "Then, Bruno, nearly the moment after they buried their child, he went back to his Boston office as if nothing happened. Can you conceive of anything so cold?" Nora's hazel eyes drew wide, and Zeke sank back into the chair. "As for Ian, I have no clue how he got into such a mess with the restaurants. It had to be an accident, or maybe the business was faulty to begin with." She aimed a wet blink at her brother. "Do you think they teach math differently at the London School of Economics?"

Zeke didn't reply, sure the catastrophe had less to do with Ian's arithmetic skills than his inability to grasp the wants and needs of vacationing Americans. Having been raised in England's Notting Hill area with nannies, private schools, and safari retreats to Africa, Ian's knowledge of middle-class American desires ran puddle deep.

"Zeke, I'm worried about what will become of us if the brothers fire Ian. Did you know Serino Enterprises holds the note to this house?" Nora pointed a trembling finger at a spacious kitchen, connected to a pleasant upper-middle-class home.

Zeke followed her index finger, calculating yet another complication. No, he wasn't aware that the Serino brothers held the mortgage. Nora had been so excited to move into her new home, the one that came with a garden and a foundation. *A house, Zeke! I've never lived in an actual house! There's even a tub with bubbling water! Can you believe it?* Nora's dream come true had affected him deeply, a willowy echo of all the things that Aubrey had once desired. Even if he hadn't seen her in years, every part of him wanted happily-ever-after for both women.

Nora went on with her concerns, smothering Zeke's comparison. "Jude's such a powerful man." She blotted her runny nose. "I prefer not to learn how ruthless."

Sadly, Zeke could answer Nora's concern. He wanted to tell her "The hell with the Serinos. Forget Ian." The two of them could leave town—damn, the one thing they knew how to do was vanish. Zeke could protect his sister, even his niece- or nephew-to-be. But sitting at the kitchen table, a near-empty pot of coffee between them, Zeke couldn't suggest any such thing. Nora loved her husband; she'd never leave him. His sister loved the life she thought she had. He reverted to his initial thought: maybe today was the day. Snuffing out a chunk of Nora and Ian's problems and avenging his parents' deaths in one fell swoop.

He turned the prospect over in his mind. But Zeke couldn't risk that scenario this second. Not with Nora a week away from her due date, wanting no more than the everyday things anybody had a right to: a home, a family. A blatant, front-page murder—committed by her brother—was not in Nora's best interest. Maybe it wasn't in Zeke's either. What if he got caught? It was a rational concern, and part of the reason he'd been so long-suffering in his goal. When Zeke took out Jude, he planned to do it cleanly. A half-cocked plan would jeopardize his endgame. Right now, he needed to be present for Nora. In that effort, Zeke defaulted to the vow that rivaled revenge—Nora's happiness.

Maybe he could manage that much. Last winter, Zeke had made his annual pilgrimage to Charlotte. She was still living part-time in New Mexico, traveling between her Albuquerque rental and Aubrey's Massachusetts home. After midnight, when the house was dark and Charlotte asleep, Zeke made his way to a cedar storage closet where Peter Ellis's letter box lived. Like previous visits, he carefully chose his next handful of ghost gifts.

Over the years, he'd never removed a noticeable amount of predictions. Other thieves might have gotten greedy; Zeke did not. A good grifter had his lines and limits. Zeke had maintained modest wins, never wanting to draw suspicion from entities like the IRS, or worse, Peter Ellis's ghost. He'd also taken to giving away a solid share of whatever a ghost gift yielded. It seemed fair. While Robin Hood moments left Zeke with a clearer conscience, it also left him living, for the most part, off his Serino Enterprises paycheck—an unforeseen irony.

He mentally rewound hunches that had turned into advantages: the nonsensical numbers scribbled on notepaper were indeed lottery wins. His first drawing, from Mankato, Minnesota, had been small—a $10,000 ticket. A year later, the next set of numbers he'd taken proved a more profitable $25,000 win; he'd given nearly half to Chicago Children's Charities. Today, in his wallet was Zeke's only remaining ghost gift—a slip of paper from Jed's Log Homes in Aberdeen, South Dakota. It noted tomorrow's date, and on it, Peter Ellis had recorded the numbers 23, 9, 41, 29, 59, 31.

"Nora, listen to me." She tried to halt her jerky breaths. "Focus." She blinked at him, and Zeke spoke in the reassuring tone that had held together his sister's whole broken life. "Tell Ian not to do anything stupid and to give me twenty-four hours. He can do that, right?"

She appeared to think for a moment, then nodded. He came around to her side of the table and crouched, gripping Nora's swollen but small hand in his.

"I can't promise for sure, but I do have one Hail Mary pass. I'm willing to throw it for you."

Not long after, Zeke left for the plains state, unsure if the lottery win would be pocket change or the kind of money that would get Nora and Ian out of a serious jam. No predictions had been life-altering wins. Hell, it was a fucking ghost gift stolen off a dead guy. There was no guarantee Zeke would recoup the plane fare.

Arriving in Aberdeen, Zeke made his way to Jed's Log Homes. Next to the lumber-inspired business was a Fresh Start convenience store. It'd been part of the notepaper prophecy and pattern: every business address was within eyeshot of a liquor store, gas station, or convenience store—the places lottery tickets were sold. Zeke picked his numbers and bought a Hostess fruit pie, bag of Doritos, and a six-pack of Coors

Light. Then he hunkered down in a Days Inn motel and waited for the local eleven o'clock news to end.

At 11:35, that year's buxom soybean queen pulled white plastic balls that popped like corn while Zeke's leg did a junkie's jiggle. His heart rattled as she read thirteen as the final number drawn. Then the soybean queen giggled, saying, "Whoops! I mean thirty-one!" With astonished relief, Zeke yelled, "Oh, thank God!" and threw himself flat onto the bed, reaching for the phone. The win had wholly exceeded his expectations.

Not long after, Zeke stood in a hospital room, where he presented a stunned Ian and Nora with the ultimate baby gift—a winning lottery ticket for $200,000. In his sister's arms was his nephew, Kieran, born that morning.

For the first time since rifling through Peter Ellis's ghost gifts, Zeke felt no guilt. He even reasoned out his thievery: Nora's troubles were the reason he'd discovered the ghost gifts in the first place. Maybe Peter Ellis had even seen to it from afar. Zeke also vowed that was it. He wouldn't push his luck, swearing on a dead man's soul that his dubious association with ghost gifts had come to an end.

♦ ♦ ♦

All was well for the next month; Ian righted the restaurant books, and Zeke considered his options. They ran the gamut, from slow-cooking revenge to how he might live a life not subsidized by ghost gifts. He was mid soul-searching, getting to know his new nephew, when one of Kieran's other uncles called. Jude Serino insisted that Zeke pay a visit to his Rancho Mirage home in California. Zeke hung up the phone with a bellyful of foreboding. He wondered if it was similar to how Peter Ellis felt after noting an avalanche to come.

Since being hired by Serino Enterprises, Zeke had never been to Jude's private estate, tucked into an elite edge of California resort land. The idea of being invited to his target's home had felt surreal. Now that he was there, Zeke's reaction hadn't changed. The grandeur of Jude's everyday life was truly disturbing. So much so that upon arriving, Zeke had to say, "Uh, what? I didn't hear you," to Jude as a burly manservant ushered him into an office the size of Nora and Ian's first floor.

"I said, glad you could make the trip." Jude sat behind a mahogany desk, his dark hair freshly coiffed. Behind him was a panoramic scene: pristine grounds, movie-star-grade pool, all bordered by a mountain view that looked as if it'd been placed there for Jude's enjoyment.

Zeke's resentment ran as wide as the San Jacinto range, with memories as far-reaching. *All this, and where are my parents?* Instinct dominated. Diving over the desk and choking Jude to death suddenly seemed urgent and appropriate. Zeke glanced over his shoulder at the dual gorillas standing guard. He wouldn't make it past knocking the smug look off Jude's face. He twisted back toward Jude, who was telling him to take a seat. But on the turn, Zeke's eye caught on several easels, each showing off a map.

"Ah, our newest Serino project. I'd be glad to show it to you."

"Opening casinos in all those states?" Zeke squinted at the maps. "Gambling's not legal in Pennsylvania, not unless you found a local Indian tribe to front you."

Jude laughed. "No. Nothing of the kind. Casinos are actually the smallest part of our holdings. But I understand your assumption. Working in Bruno's part of the business, those are the assets with which you're most familiar. Overall, we own a diverse portfolio that we like to keep fluid." He smiled. "Also keeps the IRS guessing." He walked toward the easels. "These are projected sites for upscale residential communities. We've entered a new century, Zeke, and the market is ripe for this kind of growth. Bruno and I have decided to take the plunge. Where to build," he said, "is an ongoing discussion. My brother is partial to the East Coast, naturally. He's already built himself a spec home in Massachusetts." Jude pointed at maps that also displayed Maine and Pennsylvania.

"And you?" Zeke asked.

Jude stepped closer to the map. "I'm drawn to warmer climates. I have my eye on land in Florida." He tapped his finger on Arizona. "Even more interesting, there's some abandoned property here, a place called Santa Claus, Arizona. I could buy it for pennies on the dollar. Interesting how brothers can differ—at least when it comes to weather." He guffawed. "We've actually discussed making it a competition, see which of us can build a more profitable neighborhood."

He pointed to a tufted leather chair. "Care for a drink, maybe a cigar?" Zeke sat, and Jude opened a box on his desk; inside were his trademark Arturo Fuente cigars. Zeke was familiar with them, having seen the remnants after board and dinner meetings. With their distinctive red-and-gold bands, the eighty-five-dollar-apiece beauties, imported from the Dominican Republic, were hard to miss.

"Uh, no thanks. Neither." Zeke patted his empty shirt pocket, the place a once-standard pack of Camels lived. "I quit a long time ago. Slipped back into the habit, quit again last year. Like to keep it that way."

"Better for your health, I'm sure." Jude snapped closed the cigar case. "Interesting path we've traveled here."

"How so?" Zeke asked, though Jude's observation did mirror the thought in his head.

"Before your sister married Ian, you did what for Bruno exactly?"

"Well, there's about a dozen bosses between me and your brother, but I was a floater between your Aspen resort and Vegas casino. I worked my way up to assistant management for two properties, go where I'm needed."

"And now?"

"Same thing. I wasn't expecting a promotion because my sister married your half-brother, if that's what you're getting at."

"I wasn't suggesting anything of the kind." Jude held up a hand. "To be honest—"

"Honest?" Zeke's tone strained.

"Yes. Honest." Jude tipped his head diffidently. "What I'd like to know is the details of how you managed to fish young Ian out of his latest financial debacle."

Jude turned a silver pen over and over on his desktop, a tiny motion that struck Zeke as precision filled. The sight drifted into a hypnotic fantasy: Zeke ramming the pen through Jude's neck, seeing what sort of blood and darkness oozed out. He blinked and reverted to the conversation.

"Ian," Jude was saying. "He has a few brag-worthy traits—if you're his mother. Among them is the inability to maintain a lie. Bruno and I, we knew about the restaurant books. It didn't take more than a brusque conversation for Ian to admit that you bailed him out. Moreover, he said you did it with a lucky lottery win." He stared at Zeke for a moment. "Ian was fascinated. So am I."

"Just fortunate timing."

"And an explanation I wouldn't believe if I read it in a blockbuster novel."

Zeke stared back and grappled for the grifter persona he'd relied on since he was fourteen. "Too bad you can't disprove it."

"And perhaps I wouldn't try, except for one thing. When Ian gets nervous, he babbles." Jude rolled his dark eyes. "When he sank the cruise line, your sister's husband couldn't supply us with enough details. Not that it changed anything. But this time, it's *you* Ian went on about."

"Me?"

"Yes. Apparently, it's Dublin family lore. When it comes to money and gambling, the luck of the Irish follows you like a leprechaun's shadow."

Zeke fidgeted, recrossing his legs.

"So we're clear, I don't believe in luck. Not the kind that made your nominal, if not numerous, bets on Miami's Flagler Dog Track a sure thing. I also don't believe luck had you placing wagers on next year's Super Bowl champs, preseason through the playoffs. Never a miss. Not once. We have them all on camera, documented." He pointed the pen at Zeke, who suddenly wished he hadn't been so lazy. Lazy enough to place bets at the Serino casino instead of venturing to the competition across the street. "I also understand, according to Ian, this lottery win wasn't your first."

"So I've had more than my share of money luck. I could tell you a story or two about things—times and places—where I wasn't so lucky."

Jude motioned to the bar, and one of the men near the door supplied a drink to Zeke. "Please go on," Jude said. "I'd like to learn more about you. Perhaps my brother hasn't taken full advantage of your . . . *skills*."

Jude's thoughts on luck were needles to Zeke's skin. Revealing his greatest hardship—his murdered parents—rode the tip of his tongue. The cool grifter in him rattled, and he dove without forethought into a subject that was a close second to that stinging memory. "Luck didn't win me the girl. All the money in the world won't change that fact."

Jude bobbed his head, sleek jet-black waves of hair riding along. "Was she one of our Vegas girls? Maybe I can talk to her."

"No. Nothing that simple. Nothing you could touch—ever. Years ago." Zeke wasn't sure why he expounded on Aubrey; maybe he only wanted Jude to see that he was a flesh and blood man. "Nora and I spent a chunk of our *unique* youth traveling with a carnival. Heinz-Bodette troupe, maybe you heard of them?"

"Carnivals. Wouldn't be an interest of mine or Bruno's."

"I guess not. Anyway, the owner's granddaughter and I . . . well, it worked out until it didn't. Aubrey's better off. She married some computer genius. She, um . . . she wasn't the type that was going to end up with a carnie hand."

"What does background matter when you have such an ability to provide? Or, if we use your explanation, lead a life jam-packed with such implausible luck."

"Beyond some money, I'm not so fortunate."

The two men eyeballed one another, and for a hair-trigger second, Zeke was tempted. He wanted to blurt out how misfortune didn't begin to describe his parents' deaths; how he held Jude responsible. Instead,

Zeke drew the glass to his lips, and Scotch older than the memory slid down his throat. He calmed and kept his focus on the endgame.

Jude was quiet, sipping his drink. "You must be a hell of a card player."

"Pardon?"

"Unlucky in love, lucky at cards . . ." He brushed a hand over the leg of his slacks. "I can relate to that."

"To my life? I highly doubt it."

"I spent a decade abroad—University of Zurich. I met a woman there . . . Tilda. She was my . . . what did you call her, *Aubrey?*"

The glass squealed in Zeke's hand; he wanted to rip Jude's tongue from his throat for saying her name.

Oblivious, Jude continued on. "It was my intention to never leave her or Europe."

"Interesting," Zeke said, relishing the fleeting chance to dig into Jude's wound. "Doesn't seem like something you'd admit to, a woman throwing you over. Is that your sad story? Did Tilda leave you?"

"In a way." Jude took a larger sip of his drink. "She died. Cancer." Jude's dark eyes stared past Zeke, aiming emotion at the far wall of his office. He tilted his head, his brow furrowing as if absorbing a sharp pain. Then he looked back to Zeke. "Tilda had an Ingrid Bergman accent and she was twice as beautiful. Kenzo Flower. It was the perfume she wore. Tilda smelled like a powder compact, filled with the mysteries of the Far East." Then, like the snap of a compact, nostalgia vanished. "When the treatments ran out, when she died, I couldn't find a reason to remain abroad. Eventually, I returned to the States. Of course, it's all many years ago."

Zeke didn't offer sympathies. Tilda might earn the tally mark of unhappy history. None of it was an excuse for a blood-soaked day in Chicago that changed his and Nora's lives forever.

"Seems we've both lived through unfortunate circumstances," Jude said. "I suspect, given Aubrey and Tilda's presence, we might have turned out to be other men."

Zeke snorted under his breath. He did not imagine Jude Serino making a statement with which he would agree. "Was there a point to your invitation? I take it you didn't summon me here to discuss old girlfriends—dead or alive."

"You're right. Let me get to my point. The reason I asked you here is because I want you to come work directly for me. Your *system*. I want in on it."

"System?"

"Yes. I believe I've made clear my disbelief in the 'luck of the Irish.' Ian, your sister, they're a shot glass short on common sense. Yet between them is a well of naïveté."

Zeke couldn't argue.

"You and I . . . we're different. Wiser souls."

"If a grifter's soul makes me wiser . . ."

"However you explain it." Jude sniffed, as if "grifter" might come with an odor that had so far escaped him. "According to Ian, from what I've ascertained, your wagers are never wrong. Wisely, you've managed to fly your *system* under the radar, keep the IRS at bay. Impressive."

Zeke didn't respond.

"That said, I'd like to change your position with Serino Enterprises. Move you from the humdrum, clock-punching world my brother runs to mine. Between my more intriguing ventures and what seems to be your unique abilities . . ." He waved a hand across the desktop separating the two of them.

Zeke snickered. "You mean supply whatever information you think I have for your own use."

"I'm a businessman. I look for opportunities. I like the one you represent."

And for as much as he wanted access to Jude's inner circle—the kind even related by marriage couldn't get him—Zeke wouldn't use Aubrey's father. He rose from the chair. "Go to hell. Even if I did have a system, I don't owe you a single fucking thing."

"No. But Ian does."

Zeke, who'd turned to leave, pivoted. "He owed you 200K; he repaid it."

"Yes. For the restaurants." He recrossed his legs, adjusting his tie. "Did you really think Bruno and I would simply absorb the cruise line mess? We were generous in our positioning of Ian. We're not a charity. Ian's known for nearly two years now that the debt is his."

"What sort of debt?"

"The kind that runs seven digits deep. Your brother-in-law assured us he'd repay it on a schedule." Jude opened a folder. "Care to take a look at how much he's repaid so far?"

Zeke stared at a stream of red numbers that appeared endless.

"Amazingly, that's not the worst of it. Turns out, poor liar is a brag-worthy trait when it comes to Ian. Bad gambler is the one I called you here to discuss. Ian's been to every casino in Vegas, attempting to put his own gaming systems to work, all with good intention, I'm sure."

"He tried to win back what he owes you."

"You know what they say about desperate men. Unfortunately, what he owes us has turned into what he owes *them*." Jude slid a paper from beneath the pile. "Casino debt, bookie debt. It's quite staggering, and it's due—now."

Caught between the exit and Jude, Zeke felt the room close in around him.

"And while I'm sure your compassion for Ian is finite, I suspect you'd go a great distance to protect your sister from any unpleasantness."

"She doesn't know."

"Would you like to keep it that way? From what Ian's confided, her mettle, ability to cope, is somewhat questionable."

"And where does the blame—" He stopped.

"I imagine you'd very much like to protect her future, and her son's. You can keep Ian's burden from becoming hers, keep the roof Nora loves over her head, and her husband in one piece."

"And if I had a system, why wouldn't I use it to get Nora and Ian out of a bind myself? What do I need you for?"

"Quite simply? Time and money. You don't have the capital to draw from. Do you think I'd call you in here without knowing your exact net worth?" He rose from his chair and strode toward Zeke. "Nowhere near the value that will help out Ian. Even if you started placing larger bets tomorrow, you couldn't make up the deficit—not that fast. Not without drawing suspicion from every casino in town. Of course, maybe you could put your lottery skills to work—I'd be curious to see what that might yield."

So would Zeke. The largest win in a dozen years had been the one he'd just handed Nora and Ian. Ten thousand, or even twenty-five, it wouldn't put a dent in what Ian owed. "I get it. In exchange for making good on Ian's debt, you'd want in on my system—assuming I have one."

"See that. I knew one of you Dublins was a clever thinker."

Zeke teetered on a precipice. He was trapped between the man whose father murdered his parents and the monstrous debt it looked like he'd soon owe in Ian's name.

"Other than repayment, what's in it for you? Like you don't have enough Monopoly money, courtesy of Serino Enterprises."

Jude turned away and paused at the wet bar, pouring himself a drink. Standing at the window, glass in hand, he pointed at the expansive view. "I'm not a mountain climber, Zeke. That's not my adrenaline rush." He turned back. "I don't skydive or do drugs beyond an occasional social drink. I've no desire to invent a better light bulb. I don't consider women conquests." He sipped his drink. "The only one I ever wanted is dead."

Zeke nodded, aware of Jude's marriage résumé—two, both short and disposable.

"But I do have a penchant for inexplicable chance." He shrugged. "I enjoy the rush of winning. I love the idea of controlling fortune beyond common means, for me . . . perhaps my many acquaintances. What you've done with your ability . . . your system, it's rather . . . *one-note*. I want to expand upon it."

"And if I don't agree?"

Jude furrowed his wide brow. "Then I suspect Nora's future isn't looking quite so bright, her fragile happiness in jeopardy. Better still, understand that her fate lies solely in your hands. What are you going to do about it?"

Zeke stepped forward; he could feel Jude's assistants behind him. He picked his drink up from the desk. Striding to the same view Jude enjoyed, Zeke swallowed a burning gulp. "I'd want conditions."

Jude offered a sideways glance and refocused on the scenery. "Name them."

"If I come over to your side of the business, I want a substantial position, an opportunity above the fray and of value. One with more than a nominal income. Got it?"

Jude's brow remained wrinkled. He too sipped his drink. "Agreed. If that's what you want, I have no issue gainfully employing you. Choose your own lane within our various businesses." Zeke glanced over his shoulder, looking at maps that showed the way to the next big Serino project. Upscale residential living; at least it would keep him out of Vegas.

"And you'll put Nora's house in their name—no note."

Jude hesitated. "I will as soon as you earn its value in profit. Not before." He finished his drink. "You can tack it on to Ian's debt." He smiled directly. "We'll even make it first on the payoff list, just as some added incentive."

Zeke nodded at the steamy mountain view, which was starting to resemble a heaping pile of dog shit. "Fine."

"Very good. I think we're done here, then." Jude looked toward the exit.

Zeke turned for the double doors, setting his glass on the bar as he went. "By the way, you should know, I think your Tilda was very lucky." Jude offered a quizzical look. "Lucky to have died when she did." His expression sobered. "I'll call you when I have something."

Zeke left, hoping common luck followed, finding him an open seat on a flight to Charley and Peter Ellis's letter box. As odds went, and gambling often played out, Zeke suspected things had finally caught up with him: the consequences of profiting from ghost gifts that were never his.

CHAPTER
TWELVE

Surrey, Massachusetts
Present Day

Sitting on the far end of the porch swing, Aubrey had hoped for a breeze. It seemed to have arrived with Zeke, who sat opposite her, asking, "And a look through your father's ghost gifts, it didn't set off any alarm bells?" He rocked the creaky blue swing, and the wind picked up, blowing back Aubrey's hair. "I'd be curious to know what you learned."

"There was a definite vibe when I first saw them." She thought for a moment, absorbing the cooler air. In fact, everything felt a little better since Zeke had showed up. "For the most part, I didn't touch the predictions. Levi wouldn't let me."

"Ah, the hero plays the part, even if he's currently living offstage."

Seated closer to the house than her, Zeke reached back, and Aubrey heard his knuckles knock against the clapboard siding. She made a face in reply. "It's more complicated than that, but Levi gets my gift. Don't sell it short. It's a huge part of what connects us . . . or did."

"Sorry. I didn't mean to dis the life partner. But know I'm always going to take your side, no matter what. You know that, right?"

"Even if I rob a bank?"

"I'll help count the money." Zeke's grin took a solemn turn. "Anything, Aubrey. Anything you need. I'm here."

"Good to know. When it comes to Levi, I just wish there weren't any sides to take."

"It'll work out. Exactly the way it should." Zeke reached over, his fingertips grazing the knee of Aubrey's skirt. "Tell me more about how Levi divvied up the ghost gifts. You said he came up with a filing system?"

"Ah, well, to completely understand that, you'd have to really know Levi. He's a master at forming cohesive information out of chaos, finding common threads, solving a mystery." She paused, crinkling her brow. "Okay, so his organizational skills could pass an OCD litmus test. But it's a useful thing in a situation like this."

"And did his tactics solve every mystery surrounding the ghost gifts?"

"Not yet. Although we did identify various patterns."

"Like what?"

Aubrey hoisted her hand upward, thudding it onto her lap. "A lot of tragic events. But also predictions that indicate windfalls."

"Windfalls?" The swing swung harder. "What, um . . . what sort of windfalls? Tell me."

"This is going to sound wilder than the ghost gifts, but among the many prophecies were a lesser number of gaming predictions—a mini Vegas, only no chance involved."

Zeke stared quizzically.

"You know, like who won the World Series in 1986, major prize fights, things like that."

"Go on."

"Well, it gets even more curious. This sounds impossible, but we think certain predictions are lottery wins."

"Lottery wins? You're kidding."

"I mean, they're not marked 'Hey, Peter, shuffle off to Buffalo and play these numbers on this date.' It's more cryptic. But Levi managed to sort out most of it."

"In one sitting? Impressive. Must be that dazzling brain Charlotte wrote me about years ago, the one that caught your eye."

Aubrey whacked a toss pillow at him. It missed, hitting the swing. "Do you want to hear about my father's ghost gifts or not?"

Zeke feigned a defensive position. "Sorry. Go ahead. I'm dying to hear how your dad predicted Secretariat's 1973 Kentucky Derby win."

Aubrey cocked her head at him. That exact prediction was among the earliest. It was written on a vintage Heinz-Bodette flyer. Hard to miss. "Did I mention anything about Secretariat?"

Silence swung with them for a moment. Zeke stared, then he laughed. "Come on, Aubrey. Even an average trivia buff could come up with that moment in sports. It's like saying 'Do you believe in miracles?'"

She wagged a finger at him. "US Olympic hockey team, 1980."

"See. And I know how closely you follow hockey."

She couldn't disagree. "As for the assumed lottery wins, we'll see if the theory pans out. There's only one prediction like that left."

"Is there? One prediction?"

"And would you believe it's from right here, in Surrey?"

"Right here. Wow again."

Aubrey nodded and drew her knees to her chest, the long skirt falling around her. "Overall, it was fascinating, like watching Levi organize a timeline of my father's life." Aubrey hugged her knees tighter and turned her head toward the neighboring fence line. "Huh. The Langfords must be having a barbecue. I swear I smell hot dogs." She scrunched her brow. "And hear party music. It almost sounds like a carnival." She turned back to Zeke. "There's something else about the ghost gifts: the winning predictions break from the pattern. There are gaps, years where positive predictions are missing."

"Maybe there just weren't any predictions like that during those years. Not to disagree with Levi, but I'm not sure how you could commit to 'a pattern,'" Zeke said, air quoting the words.

"Point taken. But I know Levi, and he knows when he's onto something." Aubrey let go of her knees and lowered her leg to the porch, pushing off with her toe. The air penetrated, and she swung a sweater that had been lying between them over her shoulders. "He's working on verifying the lottery theory. That will take some digging. But in a few weeks, none of it will matter anymore."

"Why's that?"

"Because aside from the one lottery-like prediction, the only ghost gifts left appear to be gibberish, nonsensical words, peculiar drawings on construction paper. I can't imagine how they'd add up to anything. So I suspect soon, all Peter Ellis's ghost gifts will be history."

Zeke reached for a pack of cigarettes tucked in his shirt pocket. A sharp glance from Aubrey halted the action. "Even if your father's predictions do end, that's a lot of secrets for one old letter box."

Aubrey tipped her head. "Did I say they were in a letter box?"

"Uh, yeah. I think you mentioned that the other day, when we met for coffee."

"That you didn't drink!" She leaned forward, her fingertips grazing Zeke's leg. "After you left, the waitress wanted to know if there was something wrong with it."

"Are you sure we just didn't order a second pot? I was wired like a junkie for the rest of the day." Zeke laughed. "I went back into the city and wandered around for hours. But you're sure about the lottery predictions. They come to an end?"

"Yes. Whatever way Levi's theory proves out, he can absolutely read a calendar." She pushed off once more with her toe. "It will take some time; Levi's busy on a story connected to his day job."

"The hectic life of a television reporter. Did he snag an interview with a Kardashian?"

"Now you would have definitely insulted him." Aubrey leaned into the cushioned swing and breathed deep; the scent of safety wafted off Zeke. "Actually, Levi's working on something with a contact, Dan Watney. He's, um . . . Dan's kind of a wild gun, government law enforcement. After Levi and I left the paper, we both fell into work that involves government connections. Dan and Levi team up from time to time. This go-round involves a John Doe discovered in a Maine swamp. Definitely a homicide."

"A homicide in Maine?"

"It was a nasty scene, from what Levi said." Aubrey frowned. "Dan doesn't have much to go on with the body—no ID, execution-style murder. It's a puzzle."

"And so he put a call in to his best puzzle solver."

"Something like that." Aubrey shared the rest of what she knew, which was little more than what Ned Allegro had reported in *Surrey City Press* coverage. "Male. White . . . midforties or so . . . that's all I know."

"No other insider details, like who the dead guy is, or who did the crime? Levi or his FBI contact, they're not close to solving the case?"

"Why are you so curious? Are you writing a book?"

Zeke laughed, and the tense look riding his face eased. "No. Of course not. Just sounds more interesting than a Kardashian interview, getting an inside scoop on a homicide investigation."

"For everyone but the victim."

They were quiet for a moment, and Zeke changed the subject. "His job, it must be different from your work with Piper."

"Did I tell you about that, my work with her?" Aubrey touched her fingertips to her forehead.

"Last time we talked."

"Sorry—my mind's been in such a whirlwind. With Piper's work, my abilities have proved useful. And it's gratifying, being able to assist with cases involving missing children. She had a new one recently, and I did make a connection with it and an older one."

"In the realm of psychic information or standard?"

"A little of both, which is the way Piper and I work. Two missing boys, two thousand miles apart. I got a vibe off the belongings of the first boy . . . a Trevor Beane. He went missing about six months ago. I really felt bad coming up cold when Piper first brought the case to my attention." She leaned back in the swing. "But this time, when I opened a box containing Trevor's personal items, I sensed cold air. Definitely *indoor* cold air, like a freezer." Aubrey closed her eyes. "Or maybe like a hockey rink." She concentrated on inbound information, like someone or thing were whispering softly in her ear. "The second boy, Liam Sheffield, he's from Tucson. The authorities found his bike, a gym bag." She focused on Zeke. "Stuff from the gym bag, it was jarred loose during a struggle. The tape . . . it wasn't in the bag; it didn't belong to Liam."

"Is that something Piper told you?"

Aubrey looked from the porch floor to Zeke. "No. More like a puzzle piece that was just handed to me. The tape didn't come from Liam's bag. It belonged to whoever took him." Her gaze drifted back to the porch, and Aubrey tucked a piece of hair behind her ear. "That's definitely a piece of information Piper should have."

"You're not a bad puzzle solver yourself. Maybe Levi could use you."

On his words, Aubrey's phone, which had been sitting between them, dinged. She glanced at it and joked with Zeke. "Wow. Your own psychic prediction . . ." She picked it up, reading Levi's text. A wide smile drew across her face. "Levi's on his way over . . . and he's bringing Pete with him!" She put the phone down. "This will be great! You can see Pete again. You'll be amazed how much he's grown since you met him. What was that, five years ago? He was just a little boy. Now he's practically a teenager." Aubrey stopped talking, realizing her eyes were damp. "Actually, I may be amazed by how much he's grown. I haven't seen him in a month. Maybe this is a good sign. Maybe Pete wants to come home!" She reached over, touching Zeke's hand. "Wouldn't that be the best news ever!"

"Guess the only thing that could beat it would be if Levi brought his suitcase too."

Excitement dampened. "I won't hold out for a miracle. Hey, would you excuse me for a few minutes? I feel like kind of a sticky mess. Until you got here, the air was absolutely stagnant."

"Sure. Go. I think you're gorgeous, but far be it from me to stop you from primping."

Aubrey rose from the swing and strode across the porch in her bare feet. As she reached the front door, she turned back to Zeke. "I'm really glad you came by today."

"Me too."

CHAPTER
THIRTEEN

Aubrey came back through the living room, and familiar voices rose from the porch. She smiled silly at rumblings about the Red Sox's chances of making the playoffs. Hurrying to the door, she pushed open the screen. Motherly instinct charged forward, but the cautious parts of Aubrey hit the brakes. "Pete. You're here."

"Hey, Mom." He stood in front of Levi, his preteen frame coming chest-high to his father. Aubrey breathed a sigh of relief. Aside from being in the 95th percentile for height, which she knew, Pete didn't appear different than a month ago. When considering things like posture, height, stubbornness, and occasional brooding, Pete could have stepped from Levi's reflection. When their son was younger, the physical resemblance had given her hope. Perhaps Pete's gifts would mirror his father's, not hers. The theory had not panned out. Silence lingered now, and Levi made contact, poking his index finger into Pete's back. The boy shuffled forward, and Aubrey couldn't help herself, gathering her son into a massive hug.

"I, um . . . I've missed you."

He didn't say anything. Pete didn't whisper longingly in her ear, *"I miss you too . . ."* But she wasn't mistaken; his grip tightened, even if it didn't last. Aubrey buried her nose in his dark head of hair, which she swore still smelled of baby shampoo. She squeezed her eyes shut, and a million memories collided—rocking a fussy Pete at three months old, reading to him as he sat cross-legged in her lap, pounding at a brightly covered book, asking, *"One more, Mama."* Her mind flashed forwarded to a vacation in Yellowstone National Park, an awed five-year-old Pete watching from the window of their cabin as a family of bears wandered by. Images of the first day of school dominated, as did the dusky evenings the three of them sat on the porch, eating ice cream, watching day fade into night. All of that was before nighttime overtook Pete's life, his dreams turning so vivid they were like touching a hot stove.

Aubrey held tighter to her son; his first disturbing encounter was also a potent memory. Pete had stood at her bedside, relaying vivid details about a battlefield. It was knowledge no small boy—not even one as smart as Pete—should possess. After a few years of that, the entities became intruders. They no longer appeared solely in Pete's dreams, but showed up as visitants, dragging their son, willing or not, into another world. At least, to this point, that was Aubrey's best interpretation. The experiences had driven him to the door, and he largely blamed his mother for a burden he did not want. A burden that no one, including Pete, could define.

He backed up into his father and flashed a terse smile at her.

"I'm so happy you're here," Aubrey said, clasping her empty hands together. She was determined to keep an even keel. A *perfectly normal mom,* the kind who had it totally together. That was the only thing she wanted Pete to see. "What, um . . . what brings you both by?"

"Pete had half a day at school. We had lunch, talked some. We thought it would be good if he came to see you. We discussed how living at the condo is a break, not a solution."

Solution for what, Levi? Our son . . . the three of us . . . you and me? Could you shed a little more light on that? But because pressing Levi would only unleash emotion she was burying like a body, Aubrey nodded and smiled at the narrow clarification.

"It was Pa's idea. Since I don't drive, and we were closer to here than home, here we—"

"Hey." Levi gave him another poke. "Did our discussion go in one ear and out the other?"

"Sorry. I'm sorry, Mom." Yet Pete took a step away from both of them. "How, um . . . how's work?"

She started a reply and stopped. Any mention of her work with Piper would only highlight their curious skill sets. "Fine. Nothing unusual to report." She pointed toward the house. "I think your models have missed you."

"I'll go see them while I'm here."

"The only reason I go down to the basement is to do laundry, and there's not so much of that with only . . ." Aubrey cleared her throat. "I'm just happy you're here, Pete, even if it's for a visit."

His curt smile repeated, answering for him.

"Oh, I have a friend I want you to—" Aubrey turned toward the swing, which was empty and moved ever so slightly. "Where in the world did he . . . ?" She moved past Levi and Pete, peering into the street. Wrapping her hand around the porch post, Aubrey tapped her finger against it. Twenty yards away, a sedan that looked like a rental made a right onto Halifax, exiting the tree-lined curve of Homestead Road. "Nice, Zeke," she whispered. "I would have thought you gave up vanishing acts with the carnival."

"Aubrey, who are you looking for?"

"Zeke." She turned back to Levi and Pete. "He stopped by." She pointed in the direction the car had gone. "He just left. I wanted to reintroduce Pete. Do you remember him? Zeke and I used to . . . well, he dates back to my carnie days with Nannie."

"Nope. Not a clue," Pete said. "But since I'm here, I wanted my longboard. It's out in the garage. Can I go get it?"

"The idea was to visit with your mother."

"Just let him go." She looked dejectedly at Levi. "It's fine. Maybe he can tell me about school, talk after he gets his skateboard."

"Or I can just longboard back to the condo."

"Or you can just leave the longboard right in the garage—period," Levi said.

Aubrey was quick to offer a keep-the-peace suggestion. "How about you put it in the car? Fair enough?"

Pete narrowed his eyes at both his parents and darted off the porch, disappearing around the side of the house.

She traded parental glances with Levi. "I guess in selecting his runaway destination, Pete forgot he was choosing the disciplinarian parent."

"No worries. He's frequently reminded." Levi's gaze settled on the porch's potted plants. "Although I make every effort to see that he's *not* living with my father."

"I know that." Crooked in Levi's arm was the letter box and an accordion folder—a Levi trademark. So taken aback by their visit, Aubrey hadn't noticed those things either.

With his free hand, Levi pointed to the garage. "But he had that warning coming."

"I don't disagree. I'm just not in a position to be as hard-assed as you at the moment. Or do I need to remind you who he's going *home* with?"

"No. I guess you don't. So you saw Zeke again?" Levi looked past her head, toward the swing. "That's what? Two . . . three visits since he's in town?"

"Just two. Remember, we missed our first connection in Boston."

"Right."

"He came by to talk. Gets lonely around here with both of you gone."

"Did all the neighbors move?" Levi jerked his head toward Diane Higley, who was pushing a mower across her lawn, and Paula Dunlap, who appeared to turn on cue, waving from her mailbox. Levi smiled stiffly, offering a brief wave back.

"It's not like I could do more than chat about the weekly Stop & Shop specials, or even gossip about the PTA meeting. Their kids all go to public school."

Levi nodded at this much.

"But I can have a slightly more meaningful discussion with Zeke."

"Convenient."

"What's that supposed to mean?"

"Nothing."

Tension rose with the breeze, and Aubrey changed the subject. "Why do you have the letter box with you?"

"I wanted to take another look, point out a few things. Can we go inside?"

"Of course." Aubrey wanted to say, *"It is your house."* She didn't. It might lead to a risky reminder that Levi no longer saw it that way. He headed in; before following, Aubrey looked at the swing. Maybe Zeke was wise to make a preemptive exit. Five years ago, Levi hadn't been keen on that visit either. Frustrated, she sighed. Based on what was in front of her, the only comfort available seemed to be her past. Was that any more her fault than Levi's? She made a lackluster attempt to smooth things over and called after Levi, "You know Zeke's just an old friend."

Inside the living room, he placed the letter box and folder on the coffee table. He studied her for a moment. "Not always the way you would have described him."

"Like a hundred years ago." She flailed out her arms, slapping them to her sides. "So what? Do you want to go another round about your University of Chicago journalism professor?"

"That was sex, Aubrey."

"Why, thank you for the vivid clarification. Your point?"

"It ends my definition of the *relationship* I shared with her. A woman I haven't communicated with since then."

"Except for your annual Christmas card exchange."

"Except for that," he said dryly. "But can you really say old Zeke fits in the same box?"

"I don't know, Levi. Compartmentalizing life is your ritual, not mine. On the other hand, I'm not the one who packed a bag and left. Keep that in mind."

"That was about Pete, and you know it." Levi stiffened his chin. "It's also not what I came here to discuss."

"Fine." She took a turn around the living room. "We'll consider all talk of Zeke Dublin officially closed. I probably won't even see him again."

"For some reason, I suspect other—" He huffed and stared at the hardwood floor. "Forget it." He made calmer eye contact. "I came to talk about the research I've done. It proves out your father's predictions."

"Go on." Admittedly, Aubrey was intrigued. "What did you learn?"

"I've verified the majority of his predictions, including the old lottery wins, which took some digging." He opened the accordion folder, unpacking his notes and computer-printed news stories. "Using a sampling of old numbers, I contacted the lottery commission in several states. Most weren't willing to go fishing for such old information, but eventually . . ."

"Let me guess. Your quest presented a 'being social in the right situation' moment, and you charmed them into talking."

"It did." He looked over the rims of his glasses. "And I was." He flipped a few pages into a legal pad, pointing to neatly recorded rows of numbers. "The point is the sequenced numbers were lottery predictions, all of them winners."

A hum of nonsurprise seeped from Aubrey.

"Not huge wins, but impressive nonetheless. Overall . . ." Levi shook his head at the box. "The facts and corresponding results are astonishing."

"And something for which you'd have a dozen logical explanations, if not for your unusual insights on what's possible."

"Believe me, the urge to disprove the predictions wasn't totally absent. Yet . . ." He pointed to the box. "Here we are." They both sat with a thud on the funky orange 1950s sofa. "So that leaves us with the last lottery prediction, which doesn't occur for a while."

"And so we just hang around, wait? Proving what?"

"That's an interesting question, and part of my conjecture."

Aubrey furrowed her brow as Levi opened the box. The buzz of energy she anticipated was present but distant. Levi withdrew the paper stamped *Hennessy's Funeral Home, Surrey, Massachusetts*, bearing six digits and a date. "We could watch the drawing, or we could play."

"Do we need the money?" Aubrey glanced around the paid-for craftsman and thought of their bank account, which wasn't lacking. If only their relationship was in half as good a condition as their finances. "We're not exactly big spenders, Levi."

"If it's a win, we could donate it."

Aubrey tipped her head at his suggestion. A charitable donation sounded fine, but it didn't feel like the reason for the last lottery prediction or the sudden spotlight on her father's ghost gifts. "I suppose—"

"Aubrey."

She stopped talking.

"There's something else. This is conjecture, but hear me out. With the gap in good predictions, I believe someone pilfered through the letter box over time, took your father's ghost gifts."

"And?" she said warily, positive Levi's conjecture wasn't complete.

"The last lottery prediction is right here in Surrey." He paused. "So is your old boyfriend." Levi was quiet, his mental nudge poking hard at her. "Aubrey?"

If it was possible to be silent on top of silent, that's what she was doing. Unfortunately, it backfired, and silence translated into a loud confession.

"He knows about them, doesn't he? Zeke Dublin knows these predictions exist."

"Yes. Zeke knew about the predictions." She twisted toward Levi. "He mentioned it when we had coffee the other day. He was aware of my father's ghost gifts. But that's it," she said hurriedly.

"Knows." Levi narrowed his eyes. "He *knows* they exist, Aubrey." His face fell solemn, the same look as the day he announced that moving out might be best. "You're not this naïve. Tell me it hasn't occurred to you that Zeke is responsible for the missing predictions. Maybe more relevant, his prior knowledge is the reason for his sudden visit to Surrey. You don't think he's here to make another withdrawal?"

Aubrey ran a hand through her hair, running defenses through her head. "If that was true, why wouldn't Zeke have taken the lottery prediction last time he visited Charley?"

"If you're an accountant, and you're skimming off the books, you don't steal all the money at once. Not if you're smart. You only take what you need—especially if you have access."

"Okay, but Zeke hasn't even been to see Charley on this trip. Not yet. She told me that herself." Levi started to speak, and she held up a hand. "He also just sat on our porch swing, appearing very surprised about the more specific details of my father's ghost gifts."

"Zeke *appeared* surprised?" Levi said. "How far would that be from acting surprised?"

Aubrey opened her mouth but didn't offer anything more. Instead, she folded her arms and leaned hard into the sofa. She didn't want to believe it was a remote possibility. It didn't matter; Levi was right there with an accusation.

"Could it be that Zeke was quick enough to get up to speed on everything that's happening with you and realize your father's ghost gifts are suddenly a hot topic of conversation? Maybe he's gauging the situation before making his move."

"Levi, that's absurd. You're making leapfrog assumptions. I know Zeke, and he would never betray—" The kitchen door burst open, thudding hard into the wall. A month's absence didn't cause a moment's hesitation. Aubrey and Levi both said, "Shut the door, Pete!"

Loud conversation and a gush of bathroom humor hijacked the house. Like any ordinary day, Pete and Dylan Higley made a rowdy entrance. The boys didn't attend the same school, but they'd grown up across the street from each other. They'd been skateboarding buddies until Pete moved out. Dylan—a curly-haired kid with fat dimples and bright eyes—burped loud enough to rattle bric-a-brac. Pete sucked in a huge gulp of air. Looking at his parents and with his cheeks puffed wide, he expelled the air in one silent breath. Aubrey wanted to shout, *"Go for it! Yes! Do something disgustingly normal in your own house!"* Levi's disapproving look said Pete made the right call.

"Hey, Pa, can we skateboard over at Greenly Field? Dylan said they put in a new ramp." His father didn't reply. "My spare helmet and knee pads are still in the garage."

Levi glanced at Aubrey.

"It's fine. Let him go." She thought maybe a taste of what he'd missed—even if it wasn't her—might remind Pete of the good things he'd run away from.

"Okay." Levi looked at the ghost gifts scattered on the coffee table. "I was kind of in the middle of something with your mother. Can you wait twenty minutes? I'll drive you over."

"Oh, it's cool, Mr. St John. You don't have to take us. I skateboard over to the park now. It's only three blocks."

"Yes, but you have to cross Piedmont. That's a busy road."

"It's not a big deal. We'll be fine. There's a traffic light. Besides, you know my mom." Dylan rolled his eyes. "She's got more rules than you."

Aubrey stifled a laugh.

"That militant?" Levi said.

The boy produced a cell phone. "GPS with boundaries, plus I have to check in every hour. I swear, I've done it, like, a gazillion times."

"Well, if it's a gazillion times, then I guess it's probably . . . *fine?*" Levi looked at Aubrey. While Levi was the strict disciplinarian, Aubrey tended to make the everyday calls.

"Hard to argue a gazillion safe trips." But as Aubrey spoke, her nose filled with the scents of rose water and dresser drawer sachets. She tasted sugar cookies. She looked at Dylan, acutely drawn to his bright eyes. They weren't just in front of her, but clear in a photograph in her mind. "You have your grandmother's eyes, don't you?"

The boy gave her a squirrelly look. "Uh . . . I don't know."

"She passed away not long ago, didn't she?"

Dylan's puckish grin faded. "Uh-huh. But, like, last Christmas or something. I remember 'cause my mom didn't want to put a tree up." Dylan bumped Pete's arm. "Let's, um . . . let's go."

"Hold on a second, guys," Aubrey said.

The boys turned back, Pete looking warily at his mother. "Mom . . ."

Over the years, on occasion, the dead connected to Pete's friends had made themselves known. Naturally, Aubrey never deemed it an appropriate conversation with a child. She'd shut down any burgeoning entities, shooed them all away. But Pete knew enough to detect his mother's connection to a spirit. And right now, Dylan Higley's grandmother was beating a war drum in her ear. "She was your mother's mother, right?"

"Mom," Pete said again, even his boyish timbre so like Levi's.

Dylan blinked at her, considering lineage the way a twelve-year-old might. "Yeah. That's right. She was fun. Never forgot my birthday." He smiled. "She used to make these heart-shaped cookies on Valentine's Day, put my name on them. Was cool when I was, like, six."

Aubrey took a step closer, and Pete's eyes went wider. "She . . . your grandmother passed away very suddenly. Your mother was so devastated."

Dylan's expression morphed from squirrelly to screwy. "She had a heart attack, I think. My mom went to see her like she always did. She found her on the bathroom floor." It came out deadpan, the asked and answered question no adult should demand of a child.

Yet she couldn't make it stop.

"Aubrey?" Levi said. "What are you doing?"

She shook her head, her thoughts detached from her controlled stream of consciousness. The urge to speak about Dylan's grandmother connected like an overriding circuit.

"Uh, listen . . ." Levi looked at his watch. "I have a work call at four, so if you guys want to get any skate time in, you'd better be heading to—"

"No!" she shouted. Levi and Dylan looked startled; Pete appeared mortified. "They can't. I mean . . ." She focused on the hardwood flooring as yet another prognostication filtered into her head. It wasn't a simple connection, a grandmother reaching out to her grandson. It was a clear warning. *"Don't let my grandson go . . . an accident on Piedmont. It will happen . . . if he's there, he'll be here before his mother can say good-bye again . . ."* Then it vanished, just like Paul Revere, just like Dashiell Durand's wife.

Aubrey was perched on her knees, looking over the back of the sofa; she dug her fingers hard into the cushion. Her mouth went dry, the smell of sachets fading. "You can go, Pete," she said tensely. "But only if your father drives you."

All three nodded vaguely, the boys slowly backing away.

"And as long as he picks you up!" she added. "Promise me!"

Aubrey's demand came with so much authority no one argued. Levi glanced at her and pulled a set of car keys from his pocket. "I'll be back in about ten minutes. Sounds like we have more than a box of ghost gifts to discuss."

As he stepped toward the back door, behind the sofa, Aubrey grabbed his arm. "Go down Chestnut Street, the back way. Don't cross Piedmont for any reason, okay?"

Levi nodded at a route that would take twice as long. "In that case, I'll be back in twenty."

CHAPTER
FOURTEEN

As the car drove away, Aubrey decided she'd had enough. Whatever this new facet of her gift was, she refused to spend years adjusting to it. She'd earned a normal life, and Aubrey was determined to be the entity in charge. She turned back to the sofa, and her line of vision caught on the letter box—a tangible marker of her father's tormented life. "I'll just have to be cleverer than any future predictions." She gulped and shrugged. "How difficult could that be?"

In the quiet of her house, Aubrey sat. She flipped open the box's lid and gazed into a past of future predictions. "Okay, fair warning, *box*. I'm expert at navigating ghost gifts, the spectrum of good and evil you represent." She glanced around the silent room, which showed nothing more apparent than a coat of dust. Scents weren't aligning either, only the faint aroma of a bayberry candle mingled with yesterday's take-out, Thai dumplings. Regardless, she continued. "So we're clear, I don't spook easily. Know that." Aubrey snatched up the lone lottery prediction. Her resolve strengthened when the paper felt warm but delivered nothing more obvious or ominous.

In fact, the sensation reminded her of her old real estate listing sheets. The same feeling had emanated off them. It translated more like a compass direction, rather than solid information connecting to any entity—the latter always occurred after she arrived at a property. *Interesting,* she thought; real estate listing sheets and the assumed lottery predictions: both involved addresses. Of course, the paper from the box didn't belong to her, and the address, Hennessy's Funeral Home, reflected a less-than-appealing destination. "Irrelevant," she said to herself. "I'll take that as no more meaningful than notepaper from Medfield Lumber or Tony's Pizzeria." In truth, if making a top-ten list of least-favorite psychic locations, funeral homes and morgues made the top five. Aubrey looked up; the sound of distant sirens bled through. She reached for her cell and texted Levi; voice messaging would deliver it as he drove. *How's your ride going?*

The siren noise intensified and so did Aubrey's heartbeat. After a few seconds of silence, his app generated a reply: *Fine. Back Soon.* She glanced once more at the open living room window and distant sound of trouble. "What was I supposed to do? Race like a lunatic over to Piedmont and direct traffic?" She widened her eyes at the word "lunatic," the ease with which the label would apply to any such behavior.

Feeling bolder, maybe thoroughly pissed off, Aubrey pulled the letter box closer. The mosaic appearance was gone. Levi had transformed the contents into a tidier system, filing predictions by subject and date. It was like graffiti had marked the contents: *Levi was here.* "Thirty years of Pandora's box, tamed in a few days by Levi St John."

She perused the stacks of paper-clipped past predictions, the graver events Levi had verified. It was amazing, the range and accuracy. In some instances, the messages read like misfit puzzle pieces. Other tragedies were more recognizable, easier to piecemeal. Things like a deadly 1980 head-on train collision in Curinga, Italy—twenty-nine fatalities. Another forewarning told of April rivers of blood in Africa—a macabre prognostication that Levi had linked to the Rwandan genocide. Looking through the accordion folder, Aubrey found corresponding news stories validating each prediction.

Whether tragic or bountiful, Levi had finessed almost all her father's prognostications into order. Silently, she acknowledged how he'd done the same thing with her life. It was the comforting, if not calming, effect of Levi. Whether it was this box, Aubrey's frustration over a case on Piper's desk, or their son—for the past dozen years of her life, Levi had been present.

Until now.

Aubrey was drawn back to the myriad of ghost gifts and thoughts of her father. A different singular thread stuck out. It was something not even Levi could assign to a list or flesh out in his head: the burden of knowing the future. Aubrey now had a clear picture of her father's haunted guilt; the weight of realizing how prediction A connected to tragedy B, but only after CNN had reported it. Her fingers fluttered over Levi's companion news reports. People were dead, families devastated, and in front of her were bits of paper that foretold it all. Her hand hovered near another example: a prediction that bore a clear forewarning about a cruise ship sinking in the Mediterranean Sea. It was around the time her parents had relocated to Greece. Aubrey imagined her father's angst. He would have been within half a day's trip of the predicted tragedy. She rummaged through the accordion folder until she found a *New York Times* article on the all-too-real Greek tragedy—a bomb had been the early determination.

Had her father attempted to intervene, one of two things would have occurred: Peter Ellis would have been labeled mad for suggesting the future, or held responsible for having known about it. None of it was too far from what had happened to Aubrey at the Prudential Tower. "Talk about a lose-lose situation." She held on to the cruise line prediction, scribbled on the torn edge of a menu written in Greek. A solid number of prophecies had occurred after his death, and Aubrey felt reverence for the posthumous predictions. "No more responsibility, no liability." For the first time since she was five, Aubrey had an inkling of understanding: Peter Ellis would have perceived death as more peaceful than the burden of living.

The kitchen door opened and, of course, shut; Levi came back into the room. Distant sirens still pealed through the space, and Aubrey stood, both of them looking toward the living room windows. "I took a turn down Blakemore," he said. "The intersection at Piedmont was blocked off. Looked like a nasty accident." He pushed up his glasses and stared blankly. It'd been some time since Aubrey's gift had put such a mystified expression on his face. "Am I correct in assuming that Dylan's grandmother warned you?"

Confirmation seemed pointless. "Could you see if anyone else was seriously hurt?"

"The vehicles looked totaled, but no. It appeared to be cuts and scrapes, even from a distance. Answer me, Aubrey, about Dylan's grandmother."

"Yes. She warned me. Begged me, actually, not to let him skateboard to the park. That if he did, Dylan would . . ."

"He would what?"

"Die."

Levi ran a hand through his dark hair, a hint of gray encroaching at his temple. Aubrey sometimes wondered about the lines on his face, if she'd put them there. "So you didn't just decide to act out on a friendly visit from a specter, this was a prognostication like your father's."

"I couldn't help myself. Although this prediction did appear to be on a smaller scale—not some national disaster."

"Or it could be the entities in charge want to give you a few practice rounds first, work you up to the big-ticket stuff."

"I did manage to keep Dylan, maybe even Pete, from harm," she snapped. "It wasn't a negative thing."

"And so now what?" Levi frowned, his head moving in anything but an agreeable motion. "We start living our lives in fear of the future? That's great, Aubrey . . . just great. When you call to tell me not to get on that plane or insist Pete shouldn't go on a field trip . . . well, I suppose we could build a bunker in the basement." He threw his car keys onto a side table, metal careening into the ceramic dish where he used to keep them.

While it cracked in two, Aubrey didn't react, not outwardly. "It's not like I chose this, Levi. What do you want me to do—get a lobotomy, maybe some shock therapy, see if we can waterboard it out of me?"

He scraped a hand around the back of his neck. Confounded was not a look Levi wore well. "No," he said more calmly. "Of course not. Of course I'm glad you were able to circumvent any tragedy today." He thrust his hands to his waist, his dark irises looking solemnly into hers. "I only thought when it came to *your gift*, at least we had that much figured out. I wasn't anticipating a plot twist."

"Enter the 'life is full of surprises' cliché." They were the same words she'd offered years ago, when informing a still-recovering Levi that she was pregnant. After a near-fatal gunshot wound at the hands of Missy Flannigan's killer, she wasn't sure how he'd take the news. His initial surprise had worked its way around to guardedly anticipatory. "I get it, Levi. It's a lot to negotiate on top of everything with Pete." Aubrey dropped onto the sofa.

But as he so often had—and despite problems in play—Levi continued to support her. He sat beside Aubrey, his hand squeezing hers. "Hey, you and Pete are a package deal—no matter what. Yes. This is an unforeseen complication. But we'll figure it out."

With her left hand clasped in his right one, Aubrey couldn't help but wonder if a ceremony at city hall, a piece of paper between them, would make a difference. She sighed. What did it matter now?

"For what it's worth," Aubrey said, "I told that box I'm not having any of it. I won't let this . . . *aberration* of my abilities affect me like it did my father."

"Then that box had better heed its own forewarning. Listen." Levi waited until she made eye contact. "With things how they are right now . . ."

Aubrey looked away; he didn't need to finish the "between you and me" part.

"With everything that's going on with Pete, I admit I don't have an instant solution. But I've witnessed your command, Aubrey. If necessary, all ghost gifts will come to fear you. You are a tower of strength."

She wanted to tell him the tower interior was not a stand-alone structure, that contrary to his statement, Levi was a load-bearing wall. She thought better of it. At the moment, adding pressure to the delicate scale on which their relationship balanced was not a great idea.

Aubrey looked at the culprit box, examining the last random papers, several predictions neither Levi nor Aubrey could decipher. "Did you have any more thoughts on these?"

"A few. It's one reason I asked Charley if I could keep the box for a while."

"Makes sense." Aubrey tipped her head at the unidentified scraps of paper but didn't pick them up. She was wary of them. *This is bullshit . . .* Ramping up her in-charge attitude, Aubrey plucked one slip of paper from the pile. There was definitely heat, more so than lottery expectations and real estate listing sheets.

"That one crayon drawing," Levi said, "it's so detailed, but I can't figure it out. I do see the drawn predictions as more like a puzzle."

They both stared at the paper, which was about the size of an index card. On it was a clear sketch of a locker, the kind you'd find in a bus station. Next to it was an even tinier but precise drawing of a bumblebee.

"Funny," Levi said. "It reminds me of that old game show, *Concentration.*"

Aubrey offered a vague look.

"Right. No TV." While Levi's childhood had been strictly monitored, Aubrey's didn't even include cable. "The contestants," he explained, "revealed puzzle pieces that used pictures to represent words. If you put it together first, solved the puzzle, you might win a washer-dryer, maybe a trip to Cancun."

"And let me guess, you solved every one before the contestants."

"Not so amazing. I doubt their contestant pool was selected from Mensa."

An urge to laugh was derailed as searing heat ripped through Aubrey's fingers, and she dropped the paper. "Damn it!" She shook her hand. "That *ghost gift*," she said with gritted teeth, "just went from tepid to burning bathwater." She continued to stare at the drawing. Below the locker and bee was a curious scribbling of numbers: "55 06 56 003 21 31," different from lottery numbers. "Oh my God . . . Levi." She touched his arm. "I know what these numbers mean."

He spun the paper toward himself, taking a closer look.

"They're coordinates." On her words, Aubrey's nose filled with the smell of jet fuel, and her ears rang with indiscernible noise, then a loud pop. "There wasn't enough time for anyone to scream."

It seemed to flip a switch in Levi's head, and he pounded his index finger into the drawings. "Lockerbie," they said simultaneously. Levi pulled out his phone, navigating to Google Maps and punching in the coordinates. He showed the result to Aubrey. Lockerbie, Scotland, the site of one of the most horrific bombings in airline history.

"Can you imagine if my father had figured it out ahead of time?"

"Maybe worse, put it together the day after." He drew a breath. "Incredible."

"Which part?"

"It makes me think about *my* father," Levi said. "Broderick St John was—still is—a tough man who faced many a battle on a field. But at least he had a choice; at least he had some idea of what was to come. Even someone as tenacious as him . . . I can't fathom how anybody would handle this. It's mind-boggling . . . cruel."

Aubrey rose from the sofa and walked to the fireplace mantel. She reached up, her fingertips fluttering over Peter Ellis's face. Rarely had he smiled in photographs. His blue-gray eyes appeared hollow and lost. And now, it was as if she could see the terror. "What is it they say . . . something about walking in someone else's shoes." She looked at Levi. "What if I'm suddenly plunged into the same fate, Levi? What am I going to do?"

"We'll figure it out." In a heartbeat, he was beside her. "Like you said, this gift won't own you. You have to hang on to that." Her chin quivered, fingertips pressing to her mouth. She didn't want a future filled with incoming disaster; she wanted her life back—the one that included Levi, her son, and everything she'd earned. Everything that made their home normal, such as it was.

Aubrey was unsure if Levi tugged her to him or she reached for the safety of his hold. It didn't matter; she just held on.

"Maybe there's a reason your father's gift turned up at this point in your life," Levi said. "For me, the timing is like a clue—your father's predictions coming to an end just as yours kick in."

Into his shoulder, she absently murmured, "That's kind of what Zeke said."

He let go, backing up. "Zeke said?"

Aubrey swiped a single tear. "Uh, yeah. In our brief conversation about the predictions . . . we were at Euro, and Zeke suggested the same thing."

"I see." He returned to the sofa.

"Do you, Levi? He's just someone close to me who was trying to shed light on a subject I can't share with many people. Don't read into it."

His glance moved between her and the bits of paper in front of him. She could see him weighing his words, seeking something that wouldn't set off another argument. "Fine," he said tightly. "We'll label it *gratitude*, input from a third party, someone who gets you."

Aubrey forced the conversation elsewhere. "As for shocking predictions, let's just hope the remainder of my father's ghost gifts are benign."

"Based on recent events, what are the odds of that?" He shot a sideways glance in her direction. "Sorry." Levi filed the Lockerbie disaster with other tragedies from the 1980s. He reshuffled the last of the unidentified ghost gifts, as if the motion might jar a thought. With the Lockerbie prediction resolved, and aside from the possible lottery prediction, three ghost gifts remained: each written on construction paper; two green scraps, one blue star.

One green construction paper read "Springfield," and like several of Peter Ellis's predictions, it was written in crayon. The other green paper depicted the Santa Claus sketch and more stick houses. On this fresh look, Aubrey felt more certain that the pointy brown ridge represented a backdrop of mountains. The final prediction was cut from sky-blue paper, star-shaped. It showed off another house, this one with a red roof. Dark blue waves took up the foreground, and a giant yellow-rayed sun overwhelmed the entire scene. It was completely primitive, somewhat nonsensical. Spelled out in yellow printing was the word "SUN."

"Well, duh," she said. "Now if he foretold us that the sun, along with the sky, were to fall, then at least we could all run around like Henny Penny." Aubrey muttered this as she stared, but instead of trepidation, she had the urge to pick up the construction paper star. "Huh. This ghost gift is familiar warm."

"Familiar warm," he said. "What does that mean?"

"Best I can explain, in addition to general warmth connected to a spiritual presence, there's also an intense sense of déjà vu attached to it."

"But no more than that?" Levi asked. "You can't place the déjà vu?"

"Not really." She switched the paper from one hand to the other, as if this might make a difference. Aubrey concentrated on the construction-paper drawings. "Levi, do these ghost gifts stick out because they're different than the others? On the whole, construction paper is no stranger than the torn corner of a pizza box or yellow pages torn from a phone book."

"True. But I'm wondering if it's the simplicity of these drawings making them stand out, more so than what they're written on."

"I was thinking the same thing."

Levi reached for the Lockerbie drawing again. It was a good sketch, with fine, discernable detail. "If nothing else, why is your father's drawing here so detailed . . ." He placed it next to the construction-paper ghost gifts. "And not nearly as much on these?"

She tipped her head, glancing between the drawings. "Well, for one, my father was heavily medicated as the years went on. It could have affected his ability to transcribe . . . capture whatever message he was receiving."

"Point taken," Levi said.

Aubrey refocused on the green pieces of paper. Another wave of déjà vu—like that oncoming sneeze—rose and faded. Boldly, she picked them up.

"Aubrey?" Levi said cautiously.

"They're warm, but I'm not feeling as drawn to the green papers as the blue. The blue star, there's just something . . ." She reached for the word that kept rolling through her head. "*Personal* about the star. The green papers, it's more like they contain information I'm not getting." She clamped her hand over her mouth, stifling a gag. "And oh my God, they stink!"

"Stink?" he said, looking queerly at her. "Stink like what?"

"Pete's gym bag." The reply was reflexive. "Not Pete's, exactly. Any teenage boy's gym bag. No," she said, a tiny trail of information seeping into her head. "Make that two teenage boys." The taste of sour apple rolled over her palate again, followed by sugary sweetness. Combined with the gym-bag stench, a hint of nausea rose, and Aubrey cleared her throat. "The green paper, it's just like . . ."

"Like what?"

"The green tape."

"Green what?"

She focused on the Santa-like drawing, but Aubrey found herself more drawn to the background mountains. "Levi, how many states border the Grand Canyon?" It was like asking him the weather outside the window.

"Three. Utah, Nevada, and mostly Arizona."

"Arizona."

"A little more information, please?"

"I don't know if it's information or speculation, but when I saw Piper last week, we talked about two cases on her desk. Two teenage boys; one boy was from Arizona. She didn't think the cases were related."

"I'm guessing you disagreed."

"Nothing concrete, I just sensed a connection. The first boy was from Pennsylvania. But the other, he was from Tucson." She ran her fingertips over the triangular mountains.

"Okay, but what does it have to do with elementary art and your father's predictions?" Levi pointed to the letter box and all its contents.

Aubrey wanted to pounce on a conclusion but found she had nothing other than psychic conjecture. She sat back, slamming herself and a toss pillow into the sofa. "I don't know. It's all so vague . . . discombobulated . . . *old*." She looked at him, feeling oddly frustrated. But the thought faded as the sensation of being physically pulled forward dominated, an entity urging her to look at the green construction paper. A shadowy image, a specter, filtered into her head and the room. It was eerie and uncomfortable and she'd seen it before—*somewhere*.

A practiced skill set allowed her to shut it down. But before she could, the specter shoved rolls of green tape into her sight line. Aubrey heard the words, *"It doesn't belong to them. Look harder. Ask the ace reporter what he knows about green tape . . ."* Then the voice vanished, the pulling sensation and vision ceasing on the entity's exit.

"Okay, so that was truly weird." Aubrey sat pole straight.

"Weirder than normal or . . . ?"

"There was a specter present for a moment." Aubrey's gaze darted around her living room. "It didn't belong here, like a stranger walking through your front door—I felt it, he knew it."

"He?" Levi said.

"What?"

"You just said 'he knew it.'"

"Definitely a male energy—and not a particularly pleasant one. It wanted me to look at the green construction paper. It said . . ." She shook her head. "It doesn't make sense. It sounded like total rubbish."

"What sounded like total rubbish?"

"Okay, let me, um . . . let me throw this out there. The boys I was just telling you about, they vanished months and two thousand miles apart."

"So not exactly a 'what do these two things have in common' scenario."

"No. Not with a couple of thousand kids reported missing every day. And maybe it's not an inference even a trained eye would make."

"But to your eye . . ."

"The older case, a boy named Trevor Beane—he's a sixteen-year-old hockey player from the Philadelphia area. The second boy, Liam Sheffield, was two years younger."

"He's your Tucson kid."

"Right. He also played street hockey, a newer interest, according to his file. Like Trevor, Liam all but vanished into thin air. There hasn't been the tiniest lead in either case."

"And, um . . ." Levi hesitated, knowing the first thing Aubrey was often called in to rule out.

"No. I don't see them as dead. In fact, not only do I sense these boys are alive, I think their disappearances are connected."

"And Piper doesn't agree?"

"Piper's on the fence—where she should be at this point. That's her job. But now . . ." Aubrey picked up the pieces of green paper. "Levi," she said, fishing a bit. "Among Trevor's personal belongings was green hockey tape—exactly the color of this paper. Color that would stand out to me. Similar tape was found with items from Liam's gym bag. The Tucson authorities assumed the tape belonged to Liam. I don't think that's the case."

"I don't follow. Why would green tape be of any significance?"

"Because the entity that was just here, I'm pretty certain he was also in Piper's office the other day. He keeps showing me the tape. He just reinforced the idea that the tape found at both scenes didn't belong to Trevor or Liam. And he said one more thing."

"What was that?"

"To ask you what you know about green tape." Aubrey expected the vague look on Levi's face would grow more unclear, that he would shake his head and say he didn't have a clue what she or any entity was talking about.

Instead, his jaw slacked and his breath visibly caught. "Holy shit."

"Holy shit what?"

"Your ghost is right."

"He is?"

"The Maine homicide, the one Dan Watney called me in on . . ."

Aubrey craned her neck forward, listening harder.

"Our dead John Doe, there were a couple of things I didn't mention about him. One was a custom letter *E* tattoo. We still don't know what it means or if it connects to anything case relevant. The other has to do with the victim's wrists—or what was left of them. They were bound with green tape. At the time, on the scene, I said it looked like electrical tape, not the usual duct tape you'd find in situations like that. But now that we're both seeing green . . ."

Aubrey shrank back, astonished. She hadn't imagined even a dotted-line link to the dead body Levi had recently encountered. "Is it possible? Could Piper's missing boys and Dan Watney's John Doe be connected?"

"Speaking at a purely pedestrian level, I'd say the odds of a connection between Piper's and Dan's cases are more plausible than a box of predictions about the future."

"Good point." Aubrey's gaze drilled into her father's ghost gifts.

Levi turned his attention to the mismatched, curious collection laid out before them. "So put it together. What do we have here? Two missing boys, one unidentified dead body—white male in his forties or so—and your father's letter box. I don't know about you, but the next question seems obvious to me."

"That being?"

"Are the last of Peter Ellis's ghost gifts a road map to solving all of it?"

CHAPTER
FIFTEEN

"Aubrey, I'm not saying you don't have a connection here. I know better than to dismiss you." In a terse, side-to-side motion, Piper swayed in her chair—one of few outward habits that expressed irritation. "I'm just reiterating my focus, which is two missing boys. How that connects with decoder-ring Watney's dead John Doe, I can't fathom."

"I only thought a conversation between the four of us—you, me, Levi, and Dan—wouldn't be the worst idea." Aubrey eased back in the chair, feeling more like she'd suggested a foursome dinner date than a meeting. "Look, I know government agencies aren't keen on sharing information, but if Dan's case and these cases connect . . ."

"Based on green tape and some miscellaneous ghost gifts from your father?" Piper huffed, looking past Aubrey's head and into the swarm of field agents in the outer office. "I'm sorry, sweetie. That's not enough for me."

"And a strong indication from a specter, based on my perspective, that's not enough either?"

"Maybe what I'm hearing is translating more like wishful thinking—at least in this case." Piper tapped her dark-purple-painted fingernails on a maze of folders. "Look, this goes outside the box that contains you and me." She jutted her hand between them. "So take it for what it's worth. Currently, you and Levi aren't in a good place. Am I right?"

Aubrey nodded small. "If you want to understate it."

"Okay. And it would be wonderful if something besides disagreements over Pete took center stage, even for a little while."

Aubrey shrugged, feeling ghostly transparent.

"So how great would it be if three totally unrelated cases suddenly and mysteriously connected, courtesy of your father. I get it—it's hopeful. It puts you and Levi back on the same team. So I can see—"

"I'm not doing that, Piper. I get it. These boys' lives are at stake. A murdered man deserves justice. At the very least, an identity, notification of the next of kin. But it's also unfair to think I'd manipulate psychic evidence for my own benefit."

Piper held up her hands in a placating motion. "I don't believe you'd consciously do that. I only thought it might be worth pointing out."

"Okay; fair enough. I admit, I don't know what will happen between Levi and me. When it comes to him and predictability, you can count on a made bed that would pass a military quarter snap, work habits as meticulous as a Swiss watch. After that . . ." Aubrey sighed. "For one, what you're suggesting, even if that's what I'm doing with these cases, it won't *fix* us."

"And two?" Piper wriggled her brow. "Where there's a one, there's always a two, honey."

"I'm starting to lean more toward *not* fixable."

Piper was silent, shuffling a few folders. "Then let's just move forward with what we might be able to resolve. I'm hesitant about what a sit-down with that rogue ex-commando will accomplish, but if you feel strongly about it, fine."

"I guess we'll see. Besides, it was Levi's idea to put our heads together. Dissuading him when he thinks he's onto something is never a good idea."

Piper offered a look. "Kind of like taking the bone away from the dog?"

Aubrey nodded, and both women looked at the wall clock. "Of course, had I known you'd asked Trevor Beane's mother to come in, I would have told Levi and Dan to arrive later."

"I have my instincts too, Aubrey. And the break in the Lily North case didn't happen until we interviewed then-suspect Errol Pope with you in the room. I thought a one-on-one with Trevor's mom might prompt a lead. Your kind."

"Fine with me, but you explained my role, right? The mom was still willing to meet with me after . . ."

Piper's expression suddenly reeked of avoidance.

Aubrey started over. "When it comes to family members, people who are not suspects, you explain *me*, give them an option. That's our agreement, Piper."

Any chair swiveling ceased, and the deputy chief focused on her desktop. "I'm aware of our agreement." She finally looked at Aubrey, smiling her crooked smile. "Sue me. I didn't have time when it came to Mrs. Beane."

"Piper!"

"Look," she said, sighing. "It's a given that all parents of missing children are terrified. Some come more unstrung than others. A few might even lash out, considering the circumstances." She tapped her fingers on the desktop. "As for Mrs. Beane, I suspect, on average days, she's the one holding high court at the church social."

"Great." Aubrey slumped back in the chair, hardly in the mood for incredulity.

A young woman knocked on Piper's open door. "Mrs. Beane is here." Behind her was a white-haired woman whose colorless bob read more like a life statement than being age related.

"Mrs. Beane . . . thank you for making the trip from Philly. Please, come in." Piper was out of her seat, guiding the woman to the chair next to Aubrey's.

The moment she sat, the space began to buzz with spectral energy.

"Fabulous," Aubrey muttered.

"You say something, Aubrey?"

"Uh, no. Not really." Her gaze flicked around the room, and Aubrey had to give in to the notion that Piper's idea was on point. Along with the woman came an obvious presence. It wasn't her son; it wasn't Trevor Beane. But it did swoop fast, stealthy and with a wide wingspan—like a bat. Frankly, it made Aubrey want to duck. Her glance tracked to the corners of Piper's office. She'd seen this presence before.

"Aubrey?"

She looked between Piper and the woman, who held out her hand. "Sorry."

"I said this is Trevor's mother." Piper smiled tightly.

"Connie Beane." As the woman repeated her name, Aubrey shook her hand. "Piper said you work here as well. Are you assigned to my son's case? Do you have something new?"

Other than the bizarre presence that followed you in here and a "paper-thin" connection? Not so much . . . "Not exactly new information." Aubrey glanced at Piper. "I work in more of a freelance capacity with Piper's team. I wanted to ask you a few questions."

The woman's expression drifted to annoyed. "I've answered every question they've asked a dozen times over—the local police, the Philadelphia task force on missing children. The CMEC. Never mind hours of interviews overseen by the deputy chief here. It's all in my son's file."

"Mrs. Beane, Aubrey profiles cases a little differently. She's actually had some amazing results. If you could just bear with us and—"

Aubrey had the sudden sensation of walls closing in—claustrophobic, almost a choking sensation to her neck. She thrust a hand to her throat and stood, sitting again in an antsy whirl of motion. Both women stared. The impressions faded, though Aubrey was now sure of one thing. The entity in Piper's office was the same male presence that had turned up in her living room. The apparition who didn't belong, who insisted she look closely at the ghost gifts made from green construction paper.

The ghost's words filtered in, just as they had in her living room. *"Ask her about Derek . . . go on . . . do it!"* Aubrey leaned back in the chair, not appreciating the tone. Command was everything when it came to strong-willed spirits, and Aubrey was about to demonstrate who was in charge. But before she could, a finger poke was applied to her back, and she lurched forward. "Hey, what gives!"

The two women offered queer stares.

"Uh, back spasms . . . they tend to pop up out of nowhere." She cleared her throat and smiled at the white-haired woman. "Mrs. Beane, can you tell me about Derek?"

Connie Beane looked between Piper and Aubrey. "Seriously?" she said to Piper. "You bring me all the way to Boston to talk to a woman who hasn't even done her cursory homework on my son's case."

"I'm sure Aubrey meant to be more specific, Mrs. Beane," Piper said. "I'm certain she's well aware that Derek is Trevor's older brother." She shot Aubrey a "get it together" look.

On the mention of Derek Beane's name, images flashed through Aubrey's mind, among them was a sheet of ice. Like her last visit to Piper's office, a myriad of hockey terms filled Aubrey's head: *blue liner . . . sin bin . . . wrist shot . . . suicide pass . . .* She took a guess. "He played hockey too . . . right?"

"Plays . . ." The woman batted her eyes. "Derek plays for the Anaheim Ducks. All Trevor wanted was to follow in his brother's footsteps. Derek's even put up a $50,000 reward for his brother's return. Again . . . all in the interviews I've given. I don't understand. Every agency has asked nearly as many questions about Derek as they have Trevor—if he had any enemies, the people he knows, or if he bets on hockey games, gambles. For goodness' sake, I even told them that he

spent his high school years training here in the Boston area. What does any of it have to do with Trevor's disappearance?"

And another sharp poke was delivered to Aubrey's back. She jutted forward, this time having to grab on to the edge of Piper's desk. "Knock it off," she hissed.

"Excuse me?"

Piper shot her a warning look.

"Uh, Mrs. Beane. Sometimes an investigation works better for me if I get information directly from the source, as opposed to reading it from a report."

"Why?"

"Why?" Aubrey repeated.

"Yes. What difference could it possibly make?"

Her mouth gaped. If Aubrey offered a psychic reveal, not only would Connie Beane be heading out the door, she'd be on her way to suing Piper's task force for negligence. "It just does. It's how I roll." She smiled at the woman's cold stare. "Like Piper said, if you could just bear with me. About your older son . . . *Derek*," she said with more command. "You noted that he trained here in Boston. Where? When was that?"

"Keep going, lady . . . finally. You're on the right track . . . I knew it years ago, when we first met."

First met? Aubrey glanced around, but nothing beyond a few words revealed itself. There were no telltale hints, no scent of aftershave or cigarettes or even the backwash of booze on her palate. It seemed like cigarettes and booze might go with this particular spirit. She tasted nothing but could hear something crack or pop. *Gum?* The damn ghost was chewing gum. In addition to the little she could surmise, Aubrey also didn't feel like the entity connected to anyone in the room, not directly.

Mrs. Beane offered a languishing sigh. "Derek trained outside Boston more than a dozen years ago. Ninth grade through his senior year. It was a big decision, but there's a skate club in Sudbury. They've produced a number of professional hockey players, Olympic-grade athletes. Derek had that kind of talent—unlike some boys whose parents bought their way into the program."

"In Sudbury?"

The woman nodded.

"I'm from Surrey," Aubrey said. "Interesting. That's not too far from where I live."

"Fascinating, Miss Ellis. Does it get me any closer to getting my other son back?"

"What do you mean by parents who 'bought their way into the program'?"

The sigh repeated. "You know—people with money and influence. People whose sons didn't have talent like Derek's. Money won't buy everything, but it can secure your child a spot in a program like the one at Velocity Skate Club. Is that the information you were after?" Connie Beane's lip twitched, and her body language oozed anger. She exhaled, staring at her clasped hands. "I apologize. I don't mean to come off as so acerbic. I'm sure you understand how stressful this is. If my boys were here, they would have stopped me sentences ago. They're both wonderful people, good boys." She withdrew a package of Kleenex from her purse and dabbed at her eyes. "Champions in so many ways aside from sports."

"In what way, Mrs. Beane?"

She rolled her teary eyeballs. "I was being figurative, Miss Ellis. I just meant—"

The feel of a finger dug into Aubrey's back. "No. Be literal. Very literal. How were your boys *champions* aside from sports?"

"Please, Mrs. Beane," Piper prompted.

"Well, for one, Trevor worked with kids with Down syndrome, taught them how to skate, play hockey. Despite his dedication to such a rough sport, Trevor was . . . *is*," she corrected, "a very sweet, passive boy. He'd be any mother's dream." She paused to blot her nose. "As for Derek, nowadays he's involved in all sorts of charitable causes through the Ducks. Of course, years ago, he was as likely as Trevor to champion the underdog. I remember one boy in particular . . ."

The pressure eased in Aubrey's spine, but it was as if the spirit were breathing in her ear . . . down her back. The male entity that had followed Connie Beane loomed large, dominating Piper's office.

"This one boy, he wasn't very talented and not well liked by the others. Oww!" Connie Beane's hand flew to the top of her snow-white head. "I'd swear someone just pulled my hair."

Piper widened her eyes at Aubrey, who inched the dialogue along. "Please, Mrs. Beane, go on."

She glanced around and refocused on Aubrey. "This boy's parents literally bought him a spot on the team by making a huge donation. I believe it paid for a new rink. But really, it only added to his troubles. The other boys saw right through it, teased him mercilessly. Derek befriended him—or at least he tried. The boy was quite troubled."

The entity moved again, buzzing steadily in Aubrey's ear—not words. It was noise, a stream of angry emotion escaping through whatever connected this world to the next—or maybe the one in which he was stuck. Aubrey's pulse quickened, and she sensed an all-over prickling of sweat, a small wave of nausea. Really, she just wanted to leave.

"Aubrey, are you all right?" Piper asked.

She closed her eyes and then looked at Connie Beane, focusing on the son who had gone missing. But her mind was being nudged, like a hockey puck in the mud, to another place—she saw a large house and marble-clad entry. A pinging noise she couldn't place echoed. She smelled frozen cold. She'd been in this house before.

The voice, more distant, spoke again. *And just to make it interesting . . . that Arizona kid . . . I know about him too . . ."*

Aubrey stifled a gasp. She wanted to demand the rogue specter quit with the cat-and-mouse game. But it all vanished—the images, the sounds, the smell of frozen air, the voice, and the popping gum. It all cracked like thin ice. Aubrey kept her composure and turned back to Trevor's mother. "What, um . . . the boy Derek befriended; do you happen to remember his name?"

The woman exhaled, a sound of frustration. "It was so many years ago; it wasn't as if Derek became best friends with the boy. I just recall the stories, how the boy's parents constantly left town, left him home alone. I believe he got into a good bit of trouble just trying to get their attention. It was Eric, maybe. No . . ." Then she looked directly at Aubrey, Connie Beane's fingertips fluttering over her mouth. "Oh, good Lord, I don't know how I could have forgotten this part—the boy, he's dead. And his name was Eli, Eli Serino."

CHAPTER
SIXTEEN

Arriving at Piper's office, Levi and Dan passed a red-faced woman with snow-white hair. Levi had the strong impression that the conversation she'd just left wasn't an easy one. Aubrey sat quietly in a chair. Levi recognized her state of mind—tense, queasy . . . *spooked*. "Aubrey, are you all right?"

She nodded but didn't look up.

Piper stood near the edge of her desk. "I'm not entirely sure what just happened here, but I don't think it was good. At least not for Aubrey." She looked from Levi to her. "Sweetie, I have to ask . . . is . . . did someone or thing indicate that we're not searching for a live Trevor Beane?"

Aubrey continued to sit with her elbow on Piper's desk and her head pressed to her fingertips. They dug in harder. "No. Nothing like that." She spoke through gritted teeth, eyes closed. Her behavior was evident to Levi—spirit-induced nausea. "I'm fairly certain Trevor's alive."

"Thank God for that much." She tipped her head at Aubrey, then turned to Levi and Dan. "That was Connie Beane you passed. Mother of the missing teen from the Philadelphia area. I thought a meeting between her and Aubrey might spark some sort of connection." She crouched, facing Aubrey at eye level. "Can I get you a sip of water . . . something stronger? I have three kinds of bourbon in my desk."

"Huh." The audible grunt came from Dan; Levi and Piper looked at him as he shrugged. "I only have two."

Piper turned back to Aubrey. "I'm not sure what or who was here, but I hoped we'd secure ourselves a few more Trevor Beane clues."

"Aubrey." Levi said more forcefully.

"I'm all right." But it came out weak. She glanced at him; quick eye contact read as tense. The intimate, unspoken exchange wasn't the kind of look she would offer to Piper.

Aubrey wore a deep-rose-colored shirt—new, Levi thought. But more importantly, the bright fabric read like an open invite to any circling entities. "Who was here besides Trevor Beane's mother? Tell me."

Aubrey took a huge breath and sat up straight, flesh tones returning to what Levi might have described as a ghostly tinge. Her jaw slacked as she made steadier eye contact. "Would, um . . . would you believe our old ghost from the house on Acorn Circle, Eli Serino?"

The next hour was filled with a ghost story, a riveted Dan and Piper listening to the tale of Eli Serino and how he served as Levi's introduction to what the afterlife held. How early one morning, years ago, a visit to a reproduction colonial on Acorn Circle changed the way he viewed the world. Levi did the majority of the telling, explaining that the whole sordid story dated back to Aubrey's home portrait days, when they both worked for the *Surrey City Press*. "Aubrey was desperate for a way of convincing me of her gift. She got more than she'd bargained for."

"What I got was an irate specter, desperate to move his energy and looking for a way out."

"The specter wanted to use Aubrey as his conduit. The whole scene, the discussion afterward, it was quite a morning."

"And even after our visit to the house, my explanation, you *still* didn't believe me."

Piper and Dan shared a look, which was an odd thing to Levi. In his experience, they didn't like to share breathing space.

"Okay," Dan said. "So I gotta know. What, exactly, happened in that house?"

"The wrath of Eli Serino's ghost." Levi said this as casually as saying, *"Pass the salt."*

Piper appeared gripped by the details; Dan looked markedly more skeptical. He didn't necessarily buy into the idea—more like a noncommittal hum of acknowledgment. Levi got it; it was a politer response than he had offered years ago.

Aubrey looked from her pockmarked arm to Dan. "I don't know how much Levi has told you, but not every spiritual connection is about information or messages of closure. On rare occasions, the entities I encounter would prefer to do more harm than good. Eli was a ghost with an ax to grind."

"But as I recall," Levi said, "as terrifying as he was, he was also stuck in that house."

"And what did I warn you about specters and where they reside?"

"You said eventually Eli would find his way out."

"Apparently he has."

"So go back to my initial question," Levi said. "Are you all right, and what the hell was he doing here?"

"I am—just a tad queasy." But she sat up taller, looking more like herself. "Eli still harbors a lot of angry energy. But without his family home to back him, it wasn't nearly as threatening as our meeting on Acorn Circle. It turns out that Eli was a long-ago friend of Trevor Beane's brother, Derek."

"Derek Beane, who plays for the Anaheim Ducks?" Dan said.

"Oh, here we go—testosterone cues recognition." Piper rolled her eyes and folded her arms.

"I think it's worth noting," Dan said. "The brother's a sports celebrity. Might not mean anything to you." His gaze swooped over Piper.

"But that kind of status can lead to all sorts of possibilities when it comes to a missing younger brother."

"Why thank you, Agent Obvious. It never occurred to my feminine sensibilities to consider a possible link."

The red of Dan's hair mirrored his face.

"Not a single thing out of order. Derek has nothing to do with his brother's disappearance. But if you'd like to check my work . . ." Piper drew her hand across a file-filled desktop.

"Uh, we're good," Dan said.

"Back to the point," Aubrey said. "Derek surely connects, just not in a traditional manner. Eli's presence seemed to be about making damn sure the conversation between Trevor's mother and me got around to him. But unless Eli's abducting teenage boys from beyond the grave, I have no idea how he relates to the Beane case—or Liam Sheffield's disappearance."

"Did that come up?" Levi asked.

"Not in our *live* conversation, but Eli indicated that he was aware of Liam's disappearance too."

"Really?" Piper said. "So somehow this old ghost connects to the disappearance of two boys, two thousand miles apart."

"I believe it does. Eli wasn't more forthcoming than that. He, um . . . he kind of left the room once Connie Beane acknowledged him, brought him into the conversation. It was more like a clue than anything fundamental."

"So wait. Back up a few steps," Piper said. "His death. What happened to Eli Serino? Was he abducted? Maybe that's how it all ties together."

"Uh, no. Nothing that would fall onto your desk, Piper. You remember that Mrs. Beane said he was a troubled boy, that Derek tried to befriend him."

Piper nodded.

"I'm afraid Eli's troubles exceeded the healing power of friendship. He killed himself. Hung himself from the foyer staircase. Suicide, as Levi can attest, can result in all sorts of otherworldly ramifications—some bad, others quite heroic."

Levi eased back in the chair as very real images of Brody St John filled his head. In that case, his own brother's suicide had ultimately saved eleven-year-old Levi's life. The reverent memory of Brody was strong, and for a moment Levi reflected on his own loss. "According to Aubrey, and based on my own experiences, the spirit of a person who takes their own life does appear to revisit with a greater presence, larger agenda."

"So like they're stuck in purgatory, waiting for an opportunity?" Dan said.

Levi and Aubrey exchanged a glance, Dan having concluded precisely the same thing Levi did when first introduced to the concept.

"I wouldn't call it that," Aubrey said. "*They* don't call it that. But there's definite accountability for those who try to leave this world by their own hand."

"Try to leave?" Piper said.

"An irony of the act, I believe." Aubrey clasped her hands in a prayerful gesture. "If you need to simplify it as good or bad—those who take their own life are subject to different circumstances. To their surprise, I don't believe death gets those souls what they truly desired."

"Which is?" Dan said tentatively.

"Resolution to whatever drove them to such desperation in the first place."

Levi listened quietly; Dan's look of disbelief was enough to keep him busy. Aubrey smiled at his befuddled expression.

"Listen, I don't have answers that you can verify with a Google search or take to your lab for analysis. I only can tell you . . ." She paused, running her finger across the scar on her chin. "Ending one's own life doesn't resolve pain or rectify demons. The reasons why a spirit remains so earthbound after a self-inflicted death . . . I'd say the explanations vary as much as the individuals who take their own lives."

"And this Eli kid," Dan said. "That's why it played out badly when you visited the house where he died years ago?"

"Not as bad as some of my encounters," Aubrey said. "But yes, Levi and I had plenty of signs, if not proof, of a tormented soul."

"Eli Serino was a ghost with a lot of anger," Levi interjected, offering his own take on that day. "That's not a conclusion I would have imagined offering back then, before that event. And it brings us to now. Other than an old connection to one missing boy's brother, what does Eli Serino have to do with the disappearance of these two boys?"

"Wait," Dan said. "Eli Serino—any relation to Serino Enterprises?"

"Yes," Levi said. "Bruno, he's one of the sons. Do you know the family?"

"A shorter list would be who doesn't know that family."

"Hmm . . ." A throaty noise of agreement pulsed from Piper. "Even I'm aware of who they are. So based on everything we know, what ties this together?" She looked at Dan. "What's bringing your John Doe case to my neck-deep ocean of missing children?"

"Maybe what Dan has in that folder." Levi pointed. "It's speculative, but something Aubrey and I came up with."

Dan placed a folder on top of Piper's desk, opening it. They all winced, basic human recoil as a photo of bone and flesh, swamp-eroded green tape crisscrossing the wrists of the remains, filled their collective points of view. Piper picked up the photo, examining it more closely. She moved to a locked cabinet and retrieved two boxes, withdrawing large, marked envelopes from each. She handed one to Levi. From the envelope she held, Piper withdrew a roll of green tape. "This was found at the scene of Trevor's disappearance."

The outside of Levi's envelope was marked "Liam Sheffield," and Levi removed a roll of identical tape.

"So the same green tape as our John Doe," Dan concluded.

"My guess is some lab-coat analysis will back that up. And so fill us in on the latest, Agent Dan," Piper said. "What have you learned about your victim?"

"Not much more than we did on scene. The natural elements did a number on any physical evidence." He drew a small notepad from his shirt pocket. "Male, some dental forensic evidence. But nothing telling unless we find the dentist. Coroner concluded his age to be between forty-five and fifty-five. Fingerprints were a total no go. The biggest plus was a faint tattoo. Decomposition wasn't at an even rate."

"Meaning?" Aubrey said.

"Uh, due to the elements and the victim's clothing—which fared better than him—certain areas of skin were intact, others . . ." He pointed to the photos of skeletal remains.

"Sufficient explanation," Aubrey said.

"Check out the other info." Dan pointed, and from beneath the pile, Piper came up with a drawing sealed in a plastic bag. "Our gal . . . sorry." Dan tipped his head at Piper. "Our lady forensic artist reproduced the tat, coming up with this rendering."

They all studied the symbol; Levi had been right in his initial assumption. It was a fancy capital *E*. "Definitely looks like custom body art."

"I've got a team scouring tattoo parlors throughout New England," Dan said. "Maybe one will come up with a hit. But I'd say that's a one-of-a-kind symbol."

"And you can add this to the little we do know." From the inside pocket of Levi's jacket, he produced a small plastic bag. "The day we found the body, I found this on the side of the road. Cigar band, I believe."

"Withholding evidence?" Dan said.

"Not really. It got sidetracked that day with Aubrey . . . Pete. I honestly forgot all about it until this morning. I checked the pocket of my shirt before dropping it at the cleaners and bagged the cigar band."

"Interesting." Dan took a closer look. "Arturo Fuente. Pricey cigar."

"And you think it ties to your dead body?" Aubrey asked.

They all stared at the loosely linked pieces of evidence, adding the cigar band to the inventory. "Possibly." Levi narrowed his eyes at the newer puzzle piece. "That body was found in an extremely isolated area—the middle of a swamp." He shrugged. "The distant aesthetics were noteworthy. The unique ocean view, private cove with nooks and crannies—million-dollar houses. But other than that, my vantage point, the rural road leading in, would only lend itself to bird-watchers and bikers. I don't know how many people pass by smoking expensive cigars."

"Somebody could have easily tossed it out a car window," Piper said.

"Mmm . . . I disagree," Dan said.

"Of course you do." Piper countered.

"I'm just saying. That particular cigar isn't like the Dutch Masters you might keep, along with your bourbon, in your desk drawer. You don't buy them in your local liquor store. You even have to prepare it, cut the tip, toast the foot. A smoke like this is an art—meant to be enjoyed. You don't light one up while driving."

"Interesting," Piper said. "That's the first time I've ever heard a cancer-causing agent referred to as *art*."

"Hey, don't knock it until you've tried one."

Levi was barely listening, another point occurring to him. "Don't forget the houses in that cove. The upscale development is within a few miles."

"And there you go," Piper said. "Now you've got neighbors who might smoke expensive cigars. Perhaps one lit up in his house and decided to finish it while taking a drive in his Mercedes convertible. Either way, I believe that dilutes any connection to your body."

"While it pains me *not* to disagree," Dan said. "I can't. And that's too bad—not only because I so enjoy sparring with the deputy chief here, but I did like the idea of that cigar band connecting to our guy." Four collective nods bobbed. "So what now?"

"I suppose we all go pursuing our individual leads, see if they circle back around to one another," Piper said.

Aubrey touched the tape, which radiated heat. She touched the grisly photo, which did the same. She looked at Piper. "That's all fine, but for two people who have nothing in common, you and Dan are dismissing the biggest clue."

Piper cocked her head at Aubrey. "That being?"

"Eli Serino," Levi said.

Aubrey smiled brusquely at Levi and their government cohorts. "Séance, anyone?"

CHAPTER
SEVENTEEN

Dan headed out first, fielding phone messages, his giant strides putting him a good distance ahead. That was fine with Levi, who stopped Aubrey midway through the parking lot. "There is another angle here. Something I didn't want to bring up in front of Piper or Dan. Something you refuse to consider."

"What's that?"

"Zeke Dublin."

"Levi, Zeke has nothing to do with any of this—a John Doe or those missing boys."

"How can you say that? He works for Serino Enterprises. He just *happens* to be in town. At the very least, it's remarkable timing."

"Remarkable how?" She folded her arms. "Thousands of people work for Serino Enterprises. Are they all under suspicion? And suspicion of what, exactly? To think Zeke knows anything about the disappearance of two teenage boys . . . it's ridiculous."

"I wasn't necessarily thinking of Piper's cases. Hell, based on what just happened back there, I'd be more inclined to suspect a dead Eli Serino."

"I believe you can count out a dead Eli as much as a live Zeke. Spiritual entities, no matter how unpleasant, aren't capable of kidnapping." Yet

Aubrey's glare, which continued to skewer him, told Levi she was far from finished. "And neither is Zeke. It's absurd. File it under 'unrelated circumstance.'"

"I agree that Zeke, in all likelihood, is not tied to the disappearance of those boys. But as for our John Doe . . ."

She huffed in reply.

"Don't let sentiment cloud your judgment, Aubrey. We do have a dead body found not that far from here. I know a little about Jude Serino; compared to his brother, his business practices aren't what I'd call squeaky clean."

"So what's your plan? Throw everything remotely connected to Jude Serino on the wall, see what sticks, including Zeke."

"Stranger things have been determined with less. How about we add some green tape to the clues, see how that sticks together?"

"Clever, Levi." She narrowed her eyes. "Too bad you're out of the headline business: *The Green Tape Caper*."

"Fine," he said. "I've no problem approaching this from the status of hard facts."

"Here we go," she muttered.

"First, Zeke Dublin shows up in Surrey with impeccable timing, just as a dead Eli Serino elbows his way into the conversation. Point two: While it's a bizarre clue, there's no dismissing green tape located at the vanishing point of both boys. From there, it grows even murkier when the same tape turns up binding the bones of a dead body in Maine. I can't connect any of it just yet, but I also find it fascinating that"—Levi arched his arm past Aubrey—"all this occurs as your gift starts to mirror your father's. A man who had secrets and ghost gifts, things no one knew about but your grandmother, her dead husbands, Yvette, Carmine . . . and Zeke Dublin."

"Zeke did not come here to steal more ghost gifts."

"How can you be so sure of that?"

"Because he told me why he's here."

Levi's gaze turned laser like. "And that would be?"

"He cares about me, Levi. Zeke just wants to be present . . . listen to me, help me through a tough time. Sorry if that doesn't cause a spike in your sinister meter."

He shook his head and stared at the pavement, mustering every ounce of reason. Finally, he looked up. "Come on, Aubrey. You're not this naïve."

"It's not naïveté. It's me knowing Zeke as well as I know you."

He cleared his throat. "Thanks for the clarification."

"Stay on point, and don't overread Zeke being here. No matter the facts, I wouldn't dump you into a scenario involving missing boys or unidentified dead bodies. That's guilt by association."

He hesitated. Anything more would be asking for a major fight in a public parking lot. Instinct wouldn't let go. Levi lowered his voice. "I'm just asking, what is Zeke's connection to the Serino family—*specifically*? You tell me his work for them is mainstream and beyond reproach. You claim he's no more than a charming ex-boyfriend, something that dazzled like the Ferris wheel lights from your carnival past. That he's here in the name of friendship. But his knowledge of those ghost gifts, these curious extenuating circumstances . . . it all suggests I question that."

"You're projecting because you don't like Zeke."

Levi glanced back toward Dan, who was clearly trying not to hear what sounded like a nasty husband-and-wife quarrel. Despite the absence of a legal union, Levi supposed it was exactly that. "You're being ridiculous."

"Am I?" Aubrey firmed up her point and position. "This rant, your suspicions. It's all because you don't like that I had coffee with Zeke last week or a relationship with him years ago. You're annoyed because he turned up present day on your porch swing. So really, which one of us is making assumptions based on emotion?"

Forget communicating with the dead. Aubrey's real talent had always been getting under his skin. Not today; not over this. "That's a great question. Maybe you should spend some time thinking about it. It's your conjecture that Zeke took off from my porch swing because that's . . . *how he rolls*," Levi said, brushing his arm through the air. "I say it's more of a thief-in-the-night maneuver. Zeke vanishes before he has to answer a question from anyone but you—his biggest fan."

"Doesn't change the fact that you've disliked Zeke from the moment you met him five years ago."

A flat-out charge of jealousy shut him up. Levi loathed the idea that such a thing could influence his perspective. He shook his head—not at Aubrey, but at himself. He wasn't doing that. "I think you're the one who needs to remove emotion from your opinion. True. I may not like Zeke, but I'm not the one whose calling card is stamped "grifter, first class." Look at how he's lived his life. What does it tell you?"

"It tells me you don't know the first thing about Zeke. Not the things that matter." Near-visible steam hissed from her; Levi was just better at hiding his. "And to be honest, I'm disappointed that you—the five-star fact finder—would leap to conclusions based on what you *think* you know."

He blinked at her accusation.

Aubrey took a tight turn in the dusty parking lot, her fuming gaze moving over him. "Just FYI, Levi, channeling your narrow-minded father is not your best look."

"So enlighten me. If my Zeke facts are limited, it's because that's the way you wanted it. Other than his vague carnie existence and labeling him the first big love of your life, it's all you've given me to go on, *sweetheart*. Sorry if you don't like the picture that paints in my head—particularly, as you note, when it turns up on my porch swing years later."

The energy around Aubrey quieted. Her tightly folded arms eased. "You're not wrong."

"Is that anything like saying I'm right?"

"Just shut up if you want to hear this."

Levi stood down, trying to relax his posture and unfolding his arms.

"I never told you about Zeke's past because . . . well, it happened long before I knew him. It's not something he likes to talk about, or even talked to me about that often. Out of respect, I never brought it up to you. Fair enough?"

"Go on."

"The reason Zeke and Nora eventually joined up with the Heinz-Bodette troupe is because they were runaways from the Illinois foster care system."

"I believe I recall a mention of foster care from a conversation we had about Zeke years ago."

"Right. Well . . ." Aubrey pursed her lips, a breath rising and falling from her chest. "The two of them had been through several homes together. On their last placement, they were separated. The home Nora lived in, there was an older boy. She was raped . . . repeatedly."

For the first time, when it came to Zeke Dublin, Levi felt a step behind.

"While that's shocking to hear, it only competes for the worst part of the Dublins' story. The reason Zeke and Nora ended up in foster care is because their parents died."

And like a fine sliver of light, Levi could see Aubrey's acute attraction to the carnie grifter. "So they were gone—like yours."

She nodded.

"Was it an accident?"

"The police concluded it was murder-suicide."

"Also a similar theory to what may have driven your parents off that mountain road in Greece."

"Possibly. But Zeke has a different theory."

"That being?"

"He believes they were murdered." Aubrey shook her head. "Something to do with retribution. I don't have any concrete details. Although I do know it was gruesome and violent. His mother was riddled with bullets. His father died from a single gunshot to the head.

That's where Zeke always clammed up, maybe the reason he appears a little vague on the whole. Dead parents are a difficult thing for any child to navigate—something I know a little about. It's something Zeke and I had in common. I'm sorry if you can't get your head around that bond. Whatever happened to his parents, what were the odds I'd run into somebody with a relatable story?"

"Not huge."

"And now you know what I do about Zeke. He lives with a lot of ghosts, Levi, some I can't even fathom. But I do know that as a teenager, Zeke got his sister out of a bad situation. He made sure nobody ever hurt her again. That single act earns points in my book—somebody who'd go to such lengths to protect you. It's the kind of respect speculation and wild theories won't shake."

He opened his mouth to speak, but she held up her hand.

"I'm sorry if Zeke's life comes with details you didn't anticipate. That he was more than some wild kid who ran away to *join the circus*. But I also don't think Zeke has to prove anything to you."

"All right," Levi said, processing an unexpected punch of compassion. "That does cast him in a different light. I give a teenage boy credit for having the presence of mind to come to his sister's aid, provide for her as best he could. Anyone would agree it's commendable."

Aubrey tipped her head at him. "Why do I hear a 'but' in there?"

"There isn't."

She tipped her head the opposite way.

"Fine. There's a 'but.' Go beyond that dark period. In addition to heroic, you just defined a person who is smart, clever, and resourceful. All positives."

"So?"

"Have you ever stopped to consider the negatives? Haven't you ever thought about those horrible things that happened to Zeke, and how they might have shaped the adult he became?"

"In what way, exactly?"

"Say everything you told me is fact, including a double homicide. I have no way of knowing if it's true, but Zeke believes it is, and that's all that matters. What becomes of a boy whose sister was raped at the hands of a system that was supposed to protect them? Or it could be the boy skips right over the system and ends up blaming himself for what happened to her. And if that's not enough, where does a person's head end up if they believe their parents were brutally murdered?"

Aubrey's eyes searched his.

"You're missing a few chapters in Zeke's story, Aubrey. He grew up a grifter with a series of heartless experiences connected to his background. You can't discount that."

"It doesn't tie him to Piper's or Dan's cases, not beyond circumstantial."

"It doesn't tie him to your father's ghost gifts either—not directly. But I'd say all things considered, it's enough to prompt a dialogue. You feel you're so right about him. Let me have a conversation with Zeke, and let him prove me wrong."

CHAPTER
EIGHTEEN

Las Vegas, Nevada
Six Months Earlier

"Zeke! I'm glad Max located you. Please come in!" Jude was on the phone but motioned anxiously to him. It was as if the room were his domain and their conversation would be casual. "Good to see you. Such a bustle of people for a family party. I thought it'd be easier to speak in here."

Zeke took in Nora and Ian's study, amazed that one small room could hold his hatred for Jude Serino and their unfathomable fates. Today's unexpected venue was compliments of Nora and Ian—not deliberate but effective. Much to their delight, seven years ago, the Montagues had extended the Serino and Dublin connection when Nora gave birth to a daughter.

Ceremony had brought them together today. Earlier, Zeke sat at the First Communion of Emerald Montague, amazed that God didn't deviate from the forgiving of sin to strike dead a visiting uncle or two. Not when, inside the sanctuary, so many choices made for easy targets.

Jude placed his hand over the phone, saying, "Hold on. I'll be right with you."

Wait for Jude? He didn't think so. "I can talk to you lat—" Zeke turned, finding Max stationed at the door.

"No . . . no. Please sit." Jude waved his arm toward a chair as if it were a friendly gesture. "I won't be more than five minutes. We'll talk before they serve cake—marvelous-looking creation, buttercream frosting, I think." He appeared to glow over the promise of family celebration, as if their niece's religious milestone wasn't anything but an excuse. Jude returned to his phone conversation, his tone reverting to business. "Exactly, Rudy. Building costs are skyrocketing—outrageous compared to when we started these communities a dozen years ago. I want a real-time update on the Maine development. The Five Points at Blue Cove cost overrun is inexcusable. Then go back to our Arizona property—costs are piling up there as well. I didn't purchase a fucking desert for pennies to end up in a hole! Extravagant swimming pools, I get. But a fucking ice rink? Who the fuck ordered a custom indoor ice rink!"

Zeke's mind defaulted to his old job. He looked out at Nora and Ian's Vegas backyard. An indoor ice rink didn't sound like the worst idea. Not in Arizona or Vegas; at least today was atypical, with a breeze and the thermometer holding in the low eighties. The Montague backyard included a swing set, built-in pool, and, presently, many guests. Standing near the study window, Nora hugged Emerald's shoulder, stroking her red hair, so like Ailish Dunne's. In a muffled motherly tone, Nora could be heard warning Kieran to be careful on the diving board.

Resigned to his immediate fate, Zeke dropped into a leather wingback chair, adjusting his tie and everything else that was a discomfort. Jude's ongoing phone call was a tactical delay, providing a window for Zeke to reflect. For years, he'd been schooled in this behavior and every other unsavory quality attached to Jude. What began as an exchange of information to repay Ian's debt and guarantee Nora's happiness had eventually gone as crooked as a country path.

Initially, Zeke supplied enough ghost gift victories to not only clear the deed to Nora and Ian's house, but repay his brother-in-law's gambling debts. In turn, Jude had kept his word, and Nora never learned of Ian's true financial crisis. What Zeke didn't do was break the vow he'd made to himself—not to profit anymore from Peter Ellis's ghost gifts. He viewed this as the hard-fought pledge of a compulsive gambler determined not to roll another die.

The delivery of ghost gifts became unavoidable background noise. Instead, Zeke focused on carving out an honest position within Serino Enterprises. He'd proved his worth as a land location manager. There were endless things about Jude Serino that Zeke loathed, ironies that he was forced to live with. Conversely, Zeke couldn't say he disliked the opportunities the situation had afforded. He'd earned a solid salary by employing a grifter's soul, traveling like a gypsy from one project to the next. It had suited him; it was a lot for guy who'd never excelled at anything but survival.

The Tucson development, upscale Spanish-style homes, had flourished like a cactus in the sunbaked ground of Santa Claus, Arizona. Buyers with money and a taste for arid living were drawn to the climate, privacy, and the affable repurposing of worthless desert. Over time, Jude and Bruno expanded upon their housing communities with development deals in Pennsylvania, Massachusetts, Maine, and Florida. It'd been interesting to watch: Jude working every angle to accumulate power and wealth, while Bruno was determined to do the same by way of eighty-hour work weeks and business dealings beyond reproach.

Most recently, on Zeke's land proposal idea, Jude had made an unusual slingshot move up the East Coast. Construction on pristine Maine acreage was under way. Like past land ventures, Jude had started out on the high road by dedicating land to a nature preserve. Once the locals were on board, he began to weave in moneymaking interests, like a proposed golf course. It'd been slated to abut protected swampland. At least that's where Zeke had left Five Points at Blue Cove when he left Jude's employ.

Waiting in the Montagues' study now, Zeke felt his animosity renew. For the sake of the day, he tried to deflate it by sucking in air and mentally popping tiny bubbles of hate. Maybe all Jude wanted was input. He appeared frustrated enough with Rudy, who'd taken over much of Zeke's responsibilities. But realizing how tightly his fingers were gripped into the chair's leather arms, it was clear that Zeke's body knew better than his brain.

While employed by Jude and bound to servitude because of Ian's debt, Zeke had considered other ways out, but Nora was never in a place where he could risk it. His sister had had two miscarriages before Emerald and suffered a scary bout of postpartum depression afterward. In more recent years, Nora had developed asthma and anxiety issues, something for which Zeke absorbed a chunk of the blame.

He might have physically saved Nora from a heinous situation by stealing her from foster care, but she'd never gotten the proper psychological help. It simply never occurred to a fourteen-year-old boy. Nora's only healing resource—whether it was their parents' deaths or the traumatic assaults she'd endured—had been time. It wasn't enough. And because of this, Zeke and Jude saw the same thing: a fragile woman who craved a stable life.

Finally, an uptick of hope had bloomed. Ian seemed to be holding his own as the manager of a single car-rental franchise the Serino brothers had bought for him. Nora thought it was generous, especially after the pool-cleaning service Ian had drained of any profit and a Vegas Strip tour service he'd imploded two years before that.

Six months ago, Zeke saw his chance and he took it; he owed Jude nothing but a bullet to his head. He demanded out from his boss's heroin-like addiction to winning prognostications. To his surprise, the CEO of Serino Enterprises agreed and let Zeke go from his obligation—and his job.

Initially, Zeke reined in the shock. The good news was his hard-earned freedom; he could find other employment. So far, those efforts hadn't unearthed much. Currently, Zeke was behind on the rent and not sure where, after today's First Communion spread, his next meal might come from. Yet only a small part of him regretted not using the ghost gifts for his own gain, or at least a rainy day fund.

Admittedly, his current situation added to Zeke's desire to see Jude dead. It ranked high on his list of motivating factors, though not near as much as avenging his parents' deaths. Giorgio Serino's son might not have pulled the trigger, but it was complicity; Jude had stood by and watched murder happen.

Aside from the disruption of today's "family" activity, Zeke was almost there. He'd even purchased a .22-caliber revolver. According to talk at the Nevada shooting range where Zeke had practiced, it was the perfect weapon for up-close murder. The .22-caliber revolver was quieter compared to other guns; it left little evidence. A bullet discharged to the head tended to remain in the skull, spinning around and causing catastrophic damage, an almost-no-margin-for-error painful death. Aiding his murderous scheme, Zeke knew enough about Jude's comings and goings to formulate a promising plan of action.

Zeke recrossed his legs and focused on Jude's dark head of hair, the brain beneath it. Of course, Nora's study wasn't the location Zeke had envisioned for long-awaited retribution. That and he hadn't thought to bring the .22 to a First Communion. He didn't imagine Ian's half-brother would show up. In his experience, Jude paid almost no attention to the Montague children.

Shifting in the leather chair, Zeke dumbed the moment down to a curious hitch. What else could it be? And what could Jude possibly want? This was no more than the universe tapping Zeke on the shoulder, saying, *"Murder. Tough move, even for someone like you . . ."* Zeke nodded firmly at Jude, who was still deep in conversation. *"Doesn't matter. It'll be worth it. And whoever I'll owe, they can have this grifter's soul . . ."*

It prompted Zeke into spur-of-the-moment action—he didn't have to listen to a damn thing Jude had to say. He rose sharply from the chair. Jude ended his conversation, and Zeke pounced on another one. "Don't even bother. I told you we were through; I meant it. You won't get another thing out of me that makes your pulse beat any faster." Jude stared, clearly not used to such a dominant Zeke. What the hell? What did it matter if Ian had steered the car-rental franchise into red ink or the goon behind Zeke beat him to a pulp for noncompliance? Not in the Montagues' study, but at an appropriate time, of course. Jude could no longer fire him; he had nothing to hold over Zeke's head. Nora might be the only thing left to sway him, but what could Zeke honestly do? Aside from any fresh threats, the letter box containing Peter Ellis's future ghost gifts had nearly run dry. "I don't have one fucking win to offer, not even a craps game on the old Vegas Strip."

Jude stood and removed his suit jacket, hanging it over the back of the chair. "The atmosphere is always so damn oppressive in this state." He sat again, offering no outward reaction. "I see where we are. We've reached our biannual negotiation."

"We're not negotiating anything."

Jude tapped his fingers on the desktop, swinging the chair slightly to take in the party view. Father O'Laughlin patted Emerald on the head; Kieran dried off near the edge of the pool. "How about this?" Jude swiveled back around. "I understand your state of employment continues to be . . . *fluid*. By now you've learned that decent work for a grifter, even one with a surprisingly good résumé, is difficult. My guess is you might be open to opportunities. I have one. I'm even willing to up the ante. It comes with a title: vice president of land development— residential and commercial projects. Has a nice ring, wouldn't you say?"

"You're not getting this. I'm done." Zeke rose from the chair.

"Hear me out for old times' sake." Jude pointed to the door, and Max shored up his shoulders, which ran nearly the width of the exit. Zeke begrudgingly sat again. "It's an interesting endeavor. Serino Enterprises has a small but special casino project going. We're calling it 'the Eli.' It's part investment, part family honor. You have strong feelings about family, right, Zeke?"

"Mine. Yes. But—"

"Bruno's wife, Suzanne, she spearheaded the idea." Jude breathed deeply, as if the memory troubled him. "It's yet another attempt to pay homage to their dead son. Terribly . . . terribly sad story, have you ever heard it?"

"Bits and pieces. And I'm sorry for their loss, but it's not going to—"

"Years ago, the boy hung himself in the foyer of their Massachusetts home." Zeke blinked at the blunt fact. "Could you imagine having to endure anything so awful?"

"As a matter of fact, I—"

Jude kept on talking. "While Eli's death was more than a decade ago, I suppose it's the kind of thing from which a parent never really recovers. I felt it important to show solidarity. My support means a great deal to Bruno." He smiled at Zeke. "And keeps him guessing as to how deep my loyalty runs." He sighed. "Sadly, Suzanne's been in and out of mental health institutions since the boy's suicide. She's had the most difficult time keeping a grip on reality. Bruno's tried—he's gone as far as to purchase her a home in every community Serino Enterprises owns. Regretfully, a change of scenery hasn't done much to dilute her demons."

"Maybe she's earned them."

"A possibility, I'm sure." Jude looked down at his tie, straightening it. "To be perfectly frank, Suzanne's mental health is my lesser concern. A larger one is the price of indulgence, what Bruno's appeasement has cost Serino Enterprises." He brushed at the silky neckwear and refocused on Zeke. "To assuage Bruno and ease our development costs—God knows what he'll build next to keep Suzanne's feet planted in reality—I agreed to support the Eli project. Bruno and I have even made a 'blood bond' over it, so to speak."

"A what?" Zeke shook his head at the dizzying streak of information.

"Not so much blood—that would be a bit *Game of Thrones*-ish, but a bond, nonetheless." Jude unbuttoned his crisp shirtsleeve and hitched it up. On the inner part of his forearm was a tattoo, an emblem that appeared to be a dark brown swirling capital *E*. "If nothing else, it makes for a fine logo, interesting family pledge of body art. We've never had a crest. This seemed appropriate. The tattoo unifies the Eli project; in fact, we'd like everyone involved to get one. And just to deepen that well of loyalty to my brother, I'm paying a $5,000 bonus for takers. The Local 409 Cement and Plasterers Union signed right up."

"Uh-huh. If that's your next play, Jude. But I don't see what any of it has to do with me."

Jude bent his head, resting it on his fist. He made some notes on a piece of paper as he spoke. "While I initially hired you as part of our terms for repayment of Ian's debt, I must admit your negotiating skills have impressed me." He looked up. "You did a good job for us, Zeke. You added value to my side of the business."

Guilt and irony dug further into Zeke. Apparently, the only way he could achieve anything in life was by way of the family that had killed his. "Look, I—"

The study door burst open and Kieran plowed through.

"Hey, kid!" Max said. "You can't just—" He took a menacing step toward the boy.

Jude held up a hand. "Max. Don't be absurd. This is Kieran's home. I should think he can burst in wherever he likes." Clutched in the boy's hand was a remote-control helicopter. It went with the train set Uncle Jude arrived with that day. "Kieran, did you have a good swim? Come around here and see me." With the gift in hand, the boy obeyed, Zeke fighting the urge to scoop him up as he darted past. Damp bathing suit and all, Jude pulled the boy to him.

"You said we could fly it! Can we, Uncle Jude?"

"Of course we can. I just need to finish up a chat with Uncle Zeke—you know he works for me."

"Used to," Zeke said.

Either way, the boy shrugged, spinning the copter blades with his finger.

"Back to our initial conversation and my point. After a stretch of unemployment and some reality, would a prominent position and title sway you?"

"You're not getting this, Jude. I can't give you any more winning predictions because I don't have any. It's over. They're gone."

"Gone?" Jude rolled his dark eyes. "Really? Then at least do me the courtesy of explaining why a sure thing has suddenly gone south. Whatever your formula or system . . . I'm to believe it's magically come to an end?"

"It's not a system. It's not a formula or insider information."

"Then what is it?" Jude huffed, tolerating what surely he deemed a stall tactic.

Zeke began a reply, opened his mouth, and closed it. "What the fuck," he muttered.

"Uncle Zeke!" Kieran's fair eyes peeled wide.

"Sorry, Kieran. Unfortunately, cursing is at the low end of the things I'm going to owe for." Zeke hesitated, and let the truth fly. "It's a box, Jude. An old letter box full of paper scraps. Anyone who didn't know better wouldn't look twice at it, would label it junk and throw it out. But the crazy truth is that it's filled with foretelling promises. Predictions, none of which ever belonged to me. The winnings you've benefited from . . . and other more ominous foretellings."

"Ominous foretellings?" he said, as if listening to a fable.

"Most prognostications are about accidents and crimes, catastrophes and horrible events. Others weren't. Years ago, when Nora and I were homeless teenagers, I took one of the positive predictions. I shouldn't have. If I hadn't, I wouldn't be sitting here now while you try and bribe me, after blackmailing me for years." Zeke's gaze drifted to their nephew. "Or are we back to that? No matter what gifts you arrived with, I can see it. Are Kieran . . . Emerald, next in your game of threats?"

Jude was quiet, his wide brow tightening. Then he laughed, hugging their nephew harder. It was a great, Santa-like belly laugh, laced with a touch of insanity, and it had Kieran laughing too. Jude pointed a finger at Zeke. "You almost had me. I mean, it's as good an explanation as any for such innate knowledge."

A humorless Zeke stared back. The boy squirted from his uncle's grasp, fiddling with the helicopter at the edge of the desk.

"Fine. All right. I'll play." Jude folded his arms and settled in for a story. "If that's the case, tell me more. Who did the predictions belong to, and how did this . . . *soothsayer* arrive at both such ominous and profitable conclusions?"

Zeke's expression went blank; he guffawed. "Sure. If you really want to know, they're ghost gifts."

"*Ghost . . . ?*"

"Gifts," he said. "An unexplainable psychic phenomenon, passed from the spirit world to a man in this one. Why or how, I couldn't begin to explain. They belonged to Peter Ellis. He's dead now—a long time. So good luck tracking him down, squeezing him for any more prognostications."

Jude shook his head. "What a ghoulishly delicious tale, but I don't follow the specifics."

Zeke thought for a moment. What further harm could come from the truth? "Peter Ellis had a psychic gift. I never met the man—I know his mother and his daughter."

"Aubrey Ellis."

Hearing Jude speak Aubrey's name, Zeke startled. On second thought, maybe honesty wasn't the best route.

"I never forget a name, Zeke. Especially if it belongs to the woman a man in my employ happens to be in love with." Jude grinned at the fact Zeke did not want him to touch. "We spoke about her years ago, when you first came to work for me. Don't you remember? We were exchanging love stories about loss. I told you of my Tilda."

He did his best to recover, to protect Aubrey. "Aubrey has nothing to do with her father's gift—not that it matters, because like I said, he's dead, and the winning names and numbers are gone."

Jude studied Zeke with a long, leering gaze. "How incredibly convenient."

"It's not convenient. It's the truth."

"It's the most farcical explanation I've ever heard." Jude huffed at him. "From liberals to grifters, people will say anything to keep capitalists from benefiting."

"Uncle Jude, can we go now?" Kieran said, the child having exhausted his patience.

"We'll go when we're through here!"

The boy gulped, inching closer to Zeke.

"Kieran, go see if your mom knows where the batteries are. I think that helicopter's going to need a handful." Zeke gave him a nudge toward the door, which Max opened, and the boy sprinted through.

"I don't want to hear any more absurdity about *ghost gifts*, Zeke, or boxes brimming with foretellings of the future. I came here today bearing more than an olive branch. I brought you a fucking tree." He blinked hard, his expression grim. "Be smart and plant it. I've never asked for a specific prediction, but I need one now. I need the winner of the Lopez-Wilder fight. In return, I'm offering you an executive-level position. It's beyond fair. Why the fuck are you being so stubborn?" On his arm, a vein wound through the decorative *E* tattoo; it pulsed, casting an eerie effect on the body art.

"Why do you need it?" Zeke countered. "Why is it so important? So you can unfairly win a prize fight that in the Serino world amounts to chump change? For a cheap thrill and an excuse to smoke one of your fucking eighty-dollar cigars—buffer the memory of the dead love of your life? I don't get it. Smoke the fucking cigar anyway. And like I said before, your Tilda's better off without you."

From the look on Jude's face, Zeke guessed the last remark went too far. But what the fuck, he'd already said it.

"You're incredibly naïve, Zeke. Do you really think this is about an expensive cigar, or even a distraction from my memories of Tilda?" A laptop sat on the desk. Zeke hadn't realized it belonged to Jude. He opened it and spun it toward Zeke. On the screen was a spreadsheet. It was similar to ones that tracked Serino real estate profits and losses. The amounts escalated, well into hundreds of thousands of dollars, dozens of entries. Zeke furrowed his brow. But this wasn't Serino Enterprises accounting. Zeke had heard these names over the years, people attached to Jude's conversations. Most had reputations more unsavory than Jude's. Then it crystallized, the ways in which Jude had expanded upon and profited from Peter Ellis's ghost gifts.

"Understand, Zeke—these aren't just my wins. You're a fool if you think I'm the only one who's benefited. My ability to be the crown prince of gaming—whether it's lottery wins or a myriad of sporting events—has turned many heads. Over time, people who wield a great deal of power, in return for a sure thing, have provided me with substantial leverage in business dealings, as well as a percentage of their earnings." He picked up the helicopter, which Kieran had left on the desk. "Take a look." He motioned to the screen. "It's kept me a step ahead of Bruno, and it's far more than *chump change*."

In reply, Zeke banged an index finger against the screen. "That's your doing, Jude. Your mess." Zeke leaned back in his chair. "I told you, I can't help you."

"I wish your regrets were that easy. A simple request, followed by an artless decline. But the fact is I have no intention of disappointing my investors. I can't, Zeke. Not because you've grown some balls, found a backbone."

"I can't give you what I don't have."

Jude nodded fervently. "Hardball it is."

Zeke glanced over his shoulder at Max. He tightened his jaw, wondering how badly it would hurt when it came unhinged. But Jude wasn't giving his gorilla a command; he was shoving papers in front of Zeke.

"What?" He half looked at the thick packet of pages. "Has Ian imploded another Serino business, or have you just gone full tilt and rigged his complete financial ruin?"

"No, I feel we've run the course with Ian, don't you? Besides, I don't have any janitorial positions to offer him. That said, you're remarkably close." Jude's dark gaze met Zeke's. "I haven't rigged Ian's financial ruin. I've rigged yours."

For the next half hour, he listened to Jude's well-drawn plot, which by comparison did make Zeke's murderous revenge look like a stick-figure sketch. With salivating energy, Jude explained that along with his own wins and the wins of his investors, he'd been doubling down on his bets and winning for Zeke as well. "Honestly, it just didn't strike me as fair," Jude lamented, "that myself and others should be the only ones profiting from your brilliant predictions. But as you'll see, according to these statements from the IRS, the government has caught up with your unreported earnings."

"My unreported earnings?"

"Why yes." He pointed to a paper that referenced Zeke's Serino Enterprises W-2 and a shitload of wins Zeke linked to bets he did not place or profit from. "Naturally, as your former employer, the IRS began their inquiry with me and my knowledge."

Zeke gulped at the setup—more like the tip-off Jude had supplied to them.

Jude paused his plot to extract a signature cigar from his suit jacket and went about the process of cutting the tip. "So here's the deal, Zeke." Jude never took his eyes off the pricey smoke. "Your decision today will greatly influence what I decide to tell the *bookkeepers* at the IRS. This is your call." He examined the cigar and the precise cut he made. "Those papers could be nothing more than a simple mix-up—I have contacts at the IRS. There are as many employees willing to . . . *look the other way* as there are bloodhounds for the cause." He glanced at Zeke and back at his cigar. "However, with no assistance from me . . ." Jude produced a lighter, toasting the foot. The air filled with the acrid scent of rolled tobacco. "I suspect it's the bloodhounds that will have your name. Even worse, they might have my cooperation regarding your ill-gotten gains." He pointed the cigar at the paperwork. "Among the details, you'll find a large-print notation citing the potential forty-year prison sentence regarding tax evasion of this magnitude."

Slow realization sank in. By way of Peter Ellis's stolen ghost gifts, Zeke had become Jude Serino's mark. He thudded into the leather chair, wishing he'd brought his gun to the First Communion. In this moment, he would have guiltlessly splattered Jude's blood and brains all over the Montagues' homey backyard view.

"Naturally," Jude said, interrupting Zeke's mental collision with reality. "I appreciate how upsetting a situation like this is. I wouldn't want your cooperation without reward, so here's what I'm willing to do. I'll keep that leafy tree I offered extended. You're welcome to return to my end of Serino Enterprises. All I ask is you bring your assets and that we don't have this conversation again. In return, I'll almost guarantee—"

"Almost?" Zeke said.

With a practiced turn, Jude rolled the cigar between his lips, letting the flame lap at the end. He removed the cigar, staring at Zeke. "Surely you can agree. What good would an instant correction to your life do me? I believe that's the basis of a persuasive argument." Jude glanced around the desktop. "Damn. I don't believe the Montagues own any ashtrays." He dumped the pens from the pencil holder of the leather desk set, repurposing it. "The Lopez-Wilder fight is months away. Whatever your method, that's plenty of time for you to come up with the winner. Pedestrian predictions are heavy." He puffed on the cigar, the red tip burning steadily in Zeke's face. "The right bet, the right winner, and I'm claiming a heavy purse, along with my many investors." Zeke opened his mouth and closed it. "Do the smart thing, Zeke. Come up with that winning name."

The leather squeaked as Zeke pressed into the chair, cigar smells weaving tightly through the study and his lungs. His stomach lurched on the potent scent and promised future. Zeke stared at the hot red glow; it looked like hell. Without a ghost gift to be had, Zeke could see Jude's point. A cigar was the least of what was about to get burned.

CHAPTER
NINETEEN

Surrey, Massachusetts
Present Day

Aubrey wasn't exactly sure how they ended up in her bedroom. When Zeke arrived, the impromptu visit began on the porch swing, but cloud cover and a chilly wind had driven them indoors. She'd gotten further behind on chores: general decluttering, unloading the dishwasher, watering plants. Necessity drove the tasks as a soothing back-and-forth exchange accompanied Aubrey, fluffing sofa pillows and sweeping dust bunnies out from beneath the dining room table.

Much of the sedate chatter focused on Zeke and Aubrey's past, the old days. It was a time when problems came and went with the towns they traveled to, and life on the whole seemed to stand still. The memories were secure, and this made Aubrey feel better. Since Levi left and then Pete, the anchor of happy, everyday talk was gone, and Aubrey felt as if her life had been set adrift. Sometimes the ache was outright unbearable. So it seemed good, even right, having someone familiar and handy to spend time with. What was so wrong with that?

It's what Aubrey asked herself as chores wound down to a large basket of laundry that belonged in the bedroom and after her mention of an eye-catching addition to the house. "I think Levi nearly drove the architect mad, but it really did turn out beautiful. There's a preserve behind the house, and the view is really something."

A few minutes later, the observation became an invitation. Zeke sat on a cushion-topped storage box, absorbing the scene Aubrey described. The day had begun as early autumn impersonating summer. As the afternoon wore on and Zeke sat, clouds thickened even more. Aubrey thought it was the kind of weather where God couldn't make up His mind, sending shimmering rays of sun peeking through thick puffs of blackness. It was eerie and beautiful.

Aubrey stood on the far side of the bed, methodically folding clothes. The room turned quiet, and a lump settled in her throat as she realized that everything in the basket belonged to her. It'd been a mix until then—a golf shirt of Levi's that she'd washed again and again, trying to dislodge a grimy stain. She'd refused to let it go. Maybe it wasn't so much the stain, but to set aside the last piece of Levi's laundry felt like she was giving up on them. It'd been easier to hang on to the essence, if not smell, of Pete. Until a week or two ago, she'd still been retrieving the odd sock from under his bed, a T-shirt thrown in the bottom of his closet. But now they were just her things—alone things.

"Aubrey."

She looked up. Zeke seemed to sparkle with hope, or more likely, the strange light coming through the bedroom window.

"It will fix itself. Give it more time."

"But that's not like saying Levi will come back, even if Pete does."

"I'm not saying he will or won't. I don't know him well, at all really. But you do." He rose from the window seat. The peekaboo sunlight must have been warm, and Zeke rolled up the sleeves of his long-sleeved green flannel. He was such a contrast to the angst in Aubrey's life, the calm of a millpond separating from a rough ocean. His longish hair, the stubble of a beard, and a sinewy frame, none of it had changed from the images that lived vividly in her mind. Yet it was Zeke's voice that brought the most comfort—not necessarily his words, but the sound. The way its timbre settled into her bones, more real than the life currently surrounding her.

Years ago, she'd so admired Zeke's fierce loyalty to Nora—something Aubrey thought she'd found with Levi. And while it was unintentional, Aubrey drifted toward the memory of a love affair, the one she'd shared with Zeke. But now time had softened the rough edges. Staring at him— his dark eyes, the scar above—Aubrey let go of turmoil and gave in to warmer recollections. Zeke smiled, and the lump in her throat melted. She looked back at the layers of laundry, grateful it was folded and sorted and taking up much of the bed.

"You have to believe that," he said.

"Believe what?" she said, blinking at him. "Sorry, I lost my train of thought."

"Believe that things with Levi will work out for the best." He laughed. "Remember, I'm supposed to hate him. How pro-Levi do you want me to be? Knowing him like you do, that should tell you every-thing, even how this will end. Listen to it."

The remark teetered between ominous and encouraging. "You'd think I'd know his mind, especially with so much time and a son between us." Tightness swelled, then it ached. "Levi never was and still isn't what anyone would call *easy*. That imperfection, it's what drew me to him the most. It's his greatest asset and his biggest fault. As long as you're not the thing he's resisting, it's mesmerizing."

"Ah, I take it I fall to the resistant side of Levi's brain."

"You do." The remark highlighted their current location. Aubrey ignored it but was cued to the point Levi had made about Zeke. Maybe now was a good time to bring up his sudden appearance in Surrey. "Zeke, I wanted to ask you something. Well, to be perfectly frank, it's Levi's question more than mine."

He frowned a bit. "Go on."

"It's about your work with the Serino family. I told you once I had an encounter with Eli Serino—a rather angry spirit."

"Vaguely. Coincidence, I think that's what we concluded."

"It seems the coincidence has grown more curious. Recently, since you came to town, I had another run-in with Eli Serino. Two, in fact. Remember, I told you about the missing boys—a teenager from outside Philly, another from Tucson."

"Right. You're helping out your friend. Piper, was it?"

"I'm not sure you'd define her as a friend—"

"Not like you and me, anyway." He arced his hand through the air between them. "Not that kind of bond."

"No. Not like us." Aubrey smiled at him. "The point is Eli somehow connects to these missing boys. How, I haven't figured out."

"Not sure I can help with that. Angry spirits aren't my thing. I told you. I just want to help you."

"I didn't think you could help directly with Eli. But Nora is married to a Serino half-brother. You did work for them."

"That's right, I worked for Jude."

"And you indicated that your departure wasn't exactly . . . amicable. Could, um . . . could you tell me more about that?"

"Like a lot of long-term business relationships, it went south. It wasn't a pleasant ending."

She thrust her hand back in the laundry basket, plucking out a towel, folding and then refolding it.

"Aubrey, is there something specific you want to ask? Up until now, your fine motor skills seemed to be working okay."

He moved closer, his steps airy, almost a glide. Looking him in the eye suddenly didn't seem like an option. Her gaze moved downward, past the buttons on his green shirt and onto the rolled-up sleeve. A gasp fluttered from her throat and she squashed it sharply. A tattoo peeked out on Zeke's forearm. Aubrey reached; there was no resistance as she turned his arm upward.

"Where did you get this tattoo? It's very . . . *unique.*" It was also a dead-on match to the artist's rendering of the tattoo from Dan Watney's dead body.

"The Serinos, they branded me."

Aubrey looked up as a grin spread across Zeke's face. "Is that a joke?"

"No. It was a job requirement. Last commercial project I worked with them."

"What does it mean, the tattoo?"

"It's symbolic. Sorry—I didn't see any reason to mention it. But you're right. It is connected to Eli Serino. The Eli, it's what they named a casino built in his memory. Something about honoring the dead boy and meant to appease Suzanne Serino."

"Eli's mother."

"That's how Jude explained it to me. Apparently, she's not been right in the head since the kid killed himself. As for the tat, that was about . . ." He squinted, glancing toward the bedroom ceiling. "Oh, I guess about six months ago. Jude gave a 5K bonus to anybody on the payroll who agreed to get a tattoo."

"And that's why you got one?"

"No. Nothing so simple. The promise of $5,000 wouldn't have persuaded me to change a light bulb for Jude, never mind brand myself. I got the tattoo because I was his right-hand man, because that's what you did if you worked for Jude. Like I said, I was in deep, and the relationship didn't end well—particularly for him." Zeke glanced at the tattoo. "An unwanted souvenir of my association. That's all."

Aubrey's breath tremored on the way in. "And this tattoo, this souvenir. Did Jude have one too?"

"Yes. Of course. Lots of people connected to the project have one. He set the example." It was quiet for a moment. "Aubrey?"

She blinked into his eyes. It was an absurd thought. It was years of living with Levi. But she knew Zeke; Levi didn't. When she didn't reply, he inched closer. Something was off in Zeke's presence; something wasn't reading right. Zeke's fingertips came forward, touching her cheek.

"Remember. I'm just here to help you. You know how I feel about you. That's never changed."

Suspicion wavered. In the tight proximity of the large bedroom, a tingle wove down Aubrey's spine. There wasn't any trepidation—just the reassuring scent of Zeke, the fact that he was there for her, the encouraging timbre of his voice.

It was the sudden drill of Pete's voice that startled Aubrey, the sound of the screen door creaking and slamming. "Mom! Mom, are you here?" Feet pounded up the stairs, and Aubrey's heart raced. "Mom, you won't believe what happened—Mom . . ."

"Pete," she said breathlessly. His bedroom was first in the hall. She heard him go in, still calling her. She glanced at Zeke, who didn't make a sound. Two things ran through her mind: Was asking him to shimmy down the trellis rude? And thank God it was only Pete's hurried boyish steps, only his voice she heard. "You should probably go." Slight panic rode her tone.

He only shrugged softly. "He's a lot like you, Aubrey. I think he'll be fine."

Zeke's cryptic reply hit her ears as Pete bounded into the bedroom. "Mom, where the heck is my—" He gripped his fingers around the door molding, applying brakes that shot him back toward the hall with the force of a bungee cord. Pete blinked like the scene wouldn't come into focus—his mother standing with a man, who wasn't his father, poised at the edge of the bed. "What the . . . ?"

Aubrey moved fast, putting herself closer to her son, farther away from Zeke. "Pete, you remember Zeke—or at least me mentioning that he was in town. He, um . . . he stopped by, and I had a lot of things to do." She pointed to the laundry and tried to keep it casual, as if Pete had found them in the basement as opposed to a bedroom. "We got to talking. That's all. I finished everything I had to do downstairs. I was showing Zeke the view, putting wash away." She stood directly in front of Pete, her height still challenging his, though probably not for much longer. Regardless, her son peered past her shoulder. His expression shifted, a look Aubrey associated with Pete's dreams—bizarre confusion and outright terror.

His mouth gaped. "Mom . . . he's, um . . . what's he doing here?"

"Hello, Pete," Zeke said.

The boy's mouth clamped shut. He squeezed his eyes shut tight and opened them, color rising in his cheeks. She needed to fix this, and fast. "I'm the one who should be surprised. A good surprise, of course. What are you doing here?" Tucked under his arm was a basketball.

He didn't answer, Zeke's voice rising from behind them. "I think it might be better if I left. I don't want to get in between any mother-and-son reunion. I know the way out."

Aubrey turned and mouthed "thank you" to Zeke. He strode across the carpeted floor and she stepped aside. In turn, Pete planted himself flat against the hall wall, his eyes wide as two moons as Zeke passed by.

Pete didn't move, fixated on the staircase; a creaking sound rose as Zeke passed the midway point—a step Levi had been meaning to fix. Aubrey struggled, trying to find her mental footing. *Okay, maybe that was a little weird . . . but it's not like anything inappropriate was happening . . .* She wondered if Levi had gone as far as to mention Zeke to Pete, and not in a positive context. Then she got her own back up against the wall. *If you and your father hadn't left . . . if our life wasn't completely upside down, Zeke wouldn't be in a conversation, never mind my bedroom . . .*

"Pete." Aubrey led with her most motherly tone. "Are you going to tell me what you're doing here and why you're so excited? I heard it in your voice the second you came through the front door."

"I'll bet you did." He peeled his gaze from the staircase. "Basketball. I made first string. Only seventh grader to do that."

"That's fantastic!" She couldn't help it, throwing her arms around her son. His reaction was clear.

"Don't do that. Don't touch me!" He repelled, dropping the basketball. It hit the floor with a thud and rolled until it bounced down the stairs, crashing hard into what Aubrey guessed was the potted peperomia at the bottom.

It wasn't the action; it was Pete's anger-laced tone. Nervously, she folded and unfolded her empty arms. Was it guilt about what Pete had walked in on, or what he might have walked in on given another five minutes? "I'm sorry," she said hurriedly. "I'm excited for you. That's all. I know how much you love to play. It's a big deal for a seventh grader to make first string."

"Yeah. Must be awesome when something normal swoops in to save the day, or just maybe your conversations."

"I don't know what you mean."

"That guy. He doesn't belong here. You brought him here, into our house."

For a moment, Aubrey wasn't sure if she was talking to Levi or their son; his tone was so similar to his father's. "It was nothing, Pete. Zeke and I, we're old friends."

"The creepiest kind."

Aubrey found her face hot and her emotions defensive. "I get that finding Zeke standing in the bedroom was . . . *awkward*, but nothing was happening." She pointed to the bed. "I was folding wash. He was looking at the view. We were talking. That's all."

"That's not all," he shouted. "You're just too fucked up to see it! Totally fucked up!" He shook his head hard, his face crimson with rage. "God, I so wish you weren't my mother!"

"What the—" Levi's voice boomed from the bottom of the stairs. He pounded up them, clearly taking two at a time. Seconds later, the three of them stood in the bedroom, eyeballing one another. "What the hell is going on? Why is there a smashed plant at the bottom of the stairs? And why," he said, shooting an angry glare at Pete, "are you talking to your mother like that?"

Aubrey assumed coming clean was her best bet. "Zeke was here."

"In the house?" Levi said.

"In the bedroom," she replied, keeping her gaze steady on Levi's.

"Like it matters what room," Pete muttered.

"He was where?"

"It was nothing," Aubrey said. "We talked downstairs for a while. I mentioned the bedroom addition while I was doing chores. I showed it to Zeke. That's all." She pointed to the light-filled space, her aim landing on the laundry-filled, neatly made bed. "Pete came in and . . ." She sucked in a breath and fought wet lashes, blindsided by tension on the verge of bursting. "It was nothing, Levi."

The look he offered said it was something more than nothing. In reply, Aubrey wriggled her brow, seeing a fresh scratch on Levi's cheek. "I'm surprised you didn't pass him on your way in. He just left."

Pete snickered, and Levi's attention whipped toward him. "Something funny I'm missing, son?"

Pete knew better than to challenge sentences that ended with an uptick to "son."

"We'll get back to your visitor, Aubrey." He turned to Pete. "Use language like that again within earshot of me, or more importantly, in reference to your mother, and you'll be off that first-string basketball team as quick as you were on it. Is anything about that unclear?"

Pete narrowed his eyes at both his parents. Then a twelve-year-old Pete looked a little older, a lot angrier. "Sure. Control me by threatening to take normal away. That's great, Pa." He started for the stairs, clearly aiming to be out of Levi's reach. "Maybe I'm wrong. Maybe it's the both of you who are completely fucked up." At the bottom of the stairs, he yelled, "I'll be at Dylan's when you're done fighting."

The observation, Pete's unlikely expletive, left them both dumbfounded. Levi spent a moment examining his shoes, then pushed his glasses tighter to his face. "And I think we're back to the reason moving out seemed like a good idea."

Aubrey offered a feeble nod, taking in the large square footage of the bedroom. She preferred to remember the reasons they'd built the space, how many good years there'd been compared to moments like this.

"It was nothing, Levi," she repeated. "Zeke stopped by . . . we were talking. That's it. I admit Pete startled me. But it's not like he walked in on anything remotely inappropriate."

"Call me old-fashioned, but I'd say your ex-lover visiting your current bedroom on any level is inappropriate."

Aubrey folded her arms. "Right." She looked him right in the eye. "And what label would you like to put on yourself?"

Stymied was an unusual look for Levi, and his dark gaze jerked away from her. "If Pete's reaction was over the top, I can't say I'm surprised. The first-string basketball news was an unexpected high in what's been a rough few days for him."

"Why? What happened?"

"Three nights of excessively disturbing dreams. The first one was about what he'd been experiencing here for the past year—talking in his sleep, then a lot of yelling. He repeated a woman's name during the dream. It was mixed-up sentences about people and places. Yet it was like he was there, like Pete knows the people in the dream."

"Levi, how many times do I have to say it—"

"I know. You don't think they're 'dreams,' per se," he said, air quoting the word. "Sorry, Aubrey. But 'dream' is the best description my common mind can process."

"Which is why he should be with me, or better yet, both of us."

"Do you want to hear this or just finish the fight our son just called us on?"

"And you need to understand that Pete not being here makes it twice as frustrating for me."

"Maybe so, but at least your life came with the starter kit."

She narrowed her eyes at him.

"Whoever Pete's been dreaming about . . . or the place he's a part of," Levi said, giving her the benefit of the doubt. "He's definitely afraid. And all three nights, he repeated the same name."

"What name?"

"*Esme*. Weird, right? Over the years, we've heard him say countless random names—different languages, even different dialects."

"True. Everything from a thick French accent to what sounded like Native American names. But I don't recall . . . wait." Aubrey darted to the window seat. From a built-in drawer, she retrieved four journals, each filled with words and phrases captured from Pete's dreams. "I made a list of names in one of these."

In an instant, Levi was by her side, scouring through too. They read like a history lesson, like Pete's sleeping brain was a map of the world and his dreams a dart aimed at random events.

"Here." She trailed her index finger down the page, Levi tight by her side. Aubrey turned to the next page and then the next. "Not a single name repeats."

"Not until three nights ago."

"Were you able to define a time period? What was he saying about this *Esme*?"

Levi shook his head. "It sounded like a war zone. He talked about planes, so, twentieth-century history rather than earlier. But my real concern was more about his level of distress. It was unprecedented."

"What sort of things did he say?"

"It all happened so fast. I was trying to wake him up, and he was just fighting me—physically at several points." He brushed a hand over the scratch on his face.

"Pete did that?"

"And a nice bruise on my shoulder." He rubbed his hand over the sports-jacket-covered shoulder. "He's getting stronger, Aubrey. And the dreams . . . *episodes*, they're growing more intense. Whoever, however this Esme connects, there's something terrifying in her presence."

"So what's happening to Pete, if it's growing more intense . . . vivid, it's another good reason why it would be better if there were two of us to deal with him."

"Possibly," he conceded. "But after the past few nights, there's no way I'd leave you alone with him."

Aubrey went back to scanning journal pages, unsure if Levi meant he'd be inclined to come home with Pete. Or perhaps he'd simply hire live-in help to assist.

"I understand this is all beyond Pete's control," Levi said. "And I don't relish saying this about my own son, but disturbing episodes are rapidly turning violent." He lowered his tall frame onto the window seat. "I'm scared for him, Aubrey. I don't know if what's happening at night will start spilling over into his conscious hours. If it does, what do we do then?"

Aubrey's gaze didn't travel to Levi but moved to the chest of drawers. On top of it was her father's box of ghost gifts. "If that were to happen in a rational, standard-behavior kind of world, I don't want to imagine how society would label him." She forced a gulp down her throat.

"I like to think that here I can protect him—at least as long as I'm his father and there's some breath in me. But I've been thinking, more and more, about a possibility where I won't have any control."

"Like what exactly?"

"What if you're right?" Levi said it fast, as if tearing off a Band-Aid, conceding to possibility. "What if these . . . *visions* aren't fantastical dreams? Fighting that premise . . . it's part of what made me move out, the idea that the people or places Pete is drawn to is something . . ." He sucked in a breath. "I can't believe I'm saying this. But what if it's *real?* I know how much it hurt you and us, when Pete chose to come live with me. But now . . ."

"Now what? Levi, what is it you're considering when it comes to Pete's dreams?"

"What if Pete wakes up one day, and you and I . . . no matter where we live . . . what if here and now is no longer our son's reality?"

CHAPTER
TWENTY

Concern for their son was enough to keep Aubrey and Levi together, at least for the evening. That and Pete had called, asking if he could go to the movies with Dylan. More than ever, Levi was agreeable to normalcy. Then Pete had said, "Dylan wanted me to sleep over, but . . . you know." As Pete's words hit Levi's ears, any hard-ass reaction to his son's earlier outburst waned. Among other things, it was a piece of childhood tradition that Pete had missed out on.

A few years ago, when Pete had declined one overnight invite too many, Dylan accused him of being a bed wetter. Aubrey had called Diane Higley, Dylan's mother, and smoothed things over, politely asking that Dylan not make accusations he knew nothing about. "Sleepovers just aren't something Pete prefers to do. Can we leave it at that?"

Diane, being a bit of a helicopter parent, profusely apologized for her son. She went on to offer the name of a good psychologist, maybe a psychiatrist. Perhaps Pete was dealing with emotional issues beyond Aubrey and Levi's grasp. Listening to Aubrey convey the conversation, Levi had rolled his eyes, saying, "You think?" He left the room, muttering, "Sure. A psychiatrist. That's what we need—the medical world's take on diagnosing the incomprehensible."

Thoughts like that seemed to be weighing on Aubrey's mind as she appeared in the living room, holding her father's box of ghost gifts. She didn't open it but went into the dining room alcove, where she placed the box on the table. "Do you want to order a pizza or something?" she asked. "Pete won't be back until after nine."

Levi didn't reply.

She pointed toward the door. "Or maybe you just want to leave and come back later."

"Pizza's fine." Levi took a seat on the sofa. "I have some work to do." He'd retrieved a leather valise from the car and proceeded to unpack folders. Among them was the information Dan had supplied about the Maine John Doe. Aubrey's involvement in Piper's case had prompted Levi to start a second file. It contained the information about the two missing boys. While the only tangible connection was some peculiar green tape—hardly a flashing neon clue—he didn't dismiss Aubrey's ethereal hunch.

After ordering the pizza, she paced the living room and fiddled with her phone. Usually, Aubrey's phone sat with its charger. When she looked out the window for the third or fourth time, Levi put down the legal pad. He'd been resisting her mood; he didn't want to tempt another argument. He couldn't help making an observation. "Expecting someone?" This time he pointed to the door. "Maybe you were hoping I'd take you up on option two and leave."

"Levi—"

He held up a hand. "I withdraw the question." He picked up a pen and looked down at his work. Then he tossed it on the table. "Aubrey."

She turned toward him.

"You get that *not* moving back home isn't my long-term goal. I mean, I shouldn't have to spell it out." He huffed and attempted to go back to his paperwork. But Levi couldn't see the pages in front of him— the dense remark was occluding his vision. For as close as they were, it'd never been easy for Levi to verbalize emotion. It was something he continued to work on—but surely more so with Pete than Aubrey in the past year. "Sorry," he said. "That was abrupt."

She shot him an angry glance.

"Stupid."

"Better," she said over her shoulder.

"We've hit a rough patch, Aubrey. We haven't skidded out of control."

She put her phone down and wrapped her arms around herself. "Right. A rough patch."

But he couldn't gauge whether it was placation or agreement.

"But since you're clearly wondering, I don't keep inviting Zeke here. He just sort of keeps showing up."

"Unusual for a guy whose MO was always about vanishing."

"Mmm . . . maybe on the surface. Maybe to other people. But that's not how I saw Zeke."

"And how did you see him?"

She turned, the last few sentences having been directed out the window. "As safe. We had things in common, granted, a lot of it tragic. Yet there was a bond . . . trust. Zeke was the person I counted on when my ever-evolving adolescence felt unsteady. He's someone from the past that eases the present. Is that so difficult to grasp?"

As Aubrey's sentiment unfolded, Levi knew he'd fallen decidedly short on emotional awareness. Admittedly, there were times when exhibiting emotion felt more like he was moving an internal mountain. But there were solid examples of growth, like when Pete was born, and the joy he readily recalled from vacations and holidays, simple Sunday barbecues. Time spent with his son and Aubrey—his family. She'd done this for him, cleared a path to a whole new life. So why couldn't Levi close the gap? Why couldn't he give her the space and understanding she needed about a man from her past? "Aubrey—"

She cut him off. "Levi, there is something . . . *more*," she said. "Something I need to tell you about Zeke."

His stomach knotted at her tone, a reaction rarer than the emotions he could not navigate. "Okay," he said tentatively. "But let me ask you a question first. Should I be grateful I'm already sitting?"

♦ ♦ ♦

The arrival of the pizza interrupted Aubrey and what, to her, was starting to feel like a confession. While Zeke's visit was innocent, the discovery of the *E* tattoo was not. In fact, it felt as if she were suppressing evidence. She stalled, doling out paper plates, pizza, and napkins. Levi didn't bite into his, pushing the plate aside. Aubrey had no appetite either, placing her slice next to his and sitting on the sofa.

"Aubrey, look, we know putting my feelings front and center is not my strong suit. But I can't believe Zeke, no matter what he was in your past, can just dive in here and—"

"Would you just let me get this out? My first instinct was not to tell you. But . . ." She wavered for a moment. "While I share a longtime kinship with Zeke, my loyalty is to you. Know that."

It seemed like Levi exhaled the breath she'd inhaled.

"Even if we're just talking about something work related."

"Work related?"

"Yes." Aubrey opened the folder marked "Physical Evidence."

"This sketch. The tattoo. I know what it is, what it ties to."

Levi squeezed his eyes shut. "Sorry. I didn't realize we'd moved on from you and . . ." He picked up the slice of pizza. "Really? I can't wait to hear this. So it'd be a fair guess to say the ink has something to do with Zeke?"

"That's a matter of opinion. He has this tattoo, Levi. I saw it on his arm today."

Pizza on the move toward his mouth froze. "That tattoo? On *his* arm?"

She nodded.

"Did you ask him about it? Did you tell him our John Doe has the same tattoo?"

"No, not that part. But I did ask Zeke to explain it."

"Actually," he said, reevaluating, "that was smart thinking. Probably best not to share too much information right now." He moved his eyes over her. "I don't want you alone with him again, not for any reason—old times' sake or . . . emotional support."

"I knew that's right where you'd go. It's also why I hesitated to tell you. Just listen. The tattoo represents the Eli casino. It's a new Serino property in Vegas." Levi's laptop sat on the coffee table, and Aubrey googled the name. "That's what I was doing with my phone before, looking it up. See." Along with a variety of glitzy images came the forty-story-high crafted *E* emblem, the hallmark of the property.

"I'll be damned." Levi put aside the pizza slice and took the laptop from her. "That's one mystery solved."

"Yes. And you can thank Zeke for the explanation. It gets more interesting—and complicated. He said a lot of workers associated with the project got the tattoo. Apparently, Jude Serino used it as a lure to spark comradery. The whole project was built to appease Suzanne Serino, in memory of her son. According to Zeke, she's never been able to deal with his death. Jude paid anyone who worked on the project a $5,000 bonus if they got the Eli tattoo."

"And Zeke signed up?"

"Zeke didn't do it for the bonus. He just did it . . . because it was expected of him, because he was Jude's right-hand man."

"And I'd say that further defines Zeke's deep ties to the Serino family—more than just his sister being married to a half-brother. More importantly, it should lead us to an identity, give us a road map. Surely with a five-grand payoff, there's a list of people who got the tattoo. Maybe Zeke even has a record of tattoo takers. I take back my earlier protest. Give him a call." Levi cocked his chin toward her phone. "Let's sit him down and ask him. I can even call Dan and—"

"Slow down, Levi. I can't do that."

"Why?"

"Zeke had a falling out with Jude. He doesn't work for him anymore."

"It doesn't mean he won't have a list on a computer, some kind of record." Levi reached for his phone. "What's his number? I'll call Zeke myself."

"No. I don't want to drag him into this. I don't want a confrontation between the two of you. If you want the list, ask Jude Serino." A stare wavered between them. "Besides, knowing what you think of Zeke, I'm guessing you'd be more inclined to believe verifiable information, from the source."

He appeared to weigh his options. "All right. I'm agreeable to that." Levi clicked on the website's corporate contact link. "Let's see how difficult it is to track down Zeke's old boss."

Aubrey sank back in the sofa and watched as Levi slipped seamlessly into reporter mode. As the call connected, he was clever and loquacious, quickly navigating to Jude Serino's administrative assistant.

He replied with "I see," and "uh-huh," starting and stopping several times. From what Aubrey could overhear, the female voice surpassed Levi's loquaciousness. "That's right, Levi St John from *Ink on Air*. The television newsmagazine." An audible buzz of excitement rose from the other end of the call. "You don't say? Well, I'm glad you're a fan . . . Holly, was it?" He nodded, smiling at Aubrey. "Yes. You do sound exactly like a former Miss Oklahoma . . ." He rolled his eyes. "Like I said, we're considering your boss for a piece on . . ." Levi ran his hand through the open air in front of him, a stalling gesture. "American-bred business dynasties, large and small," he quickly said. "We're inquiring with the Walton and Cargill families too. We wanted a cross section, and we thought the Serino family might be interested." He listened for another moment. "Naturally, I understand that you can't discuss Mr. Serino's schedule in depth, but—"

Aubrey bit into her pizza, impressed by Levi's progress.

"He's away that long?" He furrowed his brow, listening. "And that's not unusual? Right. I understand. A man in Mr. Serino's position would certainly require downtime. If you could just . . ." Frustration edged into his expression. "Like you said . . . you'll add my message to all the others. Got it . . . yep. Great talking to you too, Holly. And absolutely, I'll keep that in mind." He ended the call, dropping his cell on the coffee table.

"You'll keep what in mind?"

"After her stint as the reigning Miss Oklahoma—before her job as Jude Serino's administrative assistant—Holly was the weather girl in Tulsa. She'd love to get back into TV."

"Oh. I see. And what about her boss?"

"Jude Serino takes a six-week, zero-communication sabbatical every year. He left about a month ago. Apparently, both brothers do the same. She said she'd be happy to forward my request along with the daily data dump she sends him."

"So a dead end for now."

"Yes and no."

"Clarification, please?"

"Sometimes the best leads are born out of inconsequential references. While explaining that she couldn't share privileged information, like Jude's sabbatical destination, Holly did mention her last verbal communication with him."

"And that was?"

"From here. She spoke with Jude when he was at Logan's international terminal. So we know it was right before a flight to an undisclosed location abroad. Apparently, the East Coast was a pit stop. He wanted to check on progress on a residential community Serino Enterprises owns."

"And that's curious why?"

"It's in Maine, Aubrey. A place called Five Points at Blue Cove." He withdrew a paper map from a folder marked "DB Location Info."

He moved the pizza and opened the folder on the coffee table. Aubrey assumed the red-circled piece of swampland bull's-eyed the location of the body. Levi clicked on a pen and circled an area not far from it, prime real estate that boarded the ocean. "And about here is the half-built project. A few high-end properties surround the cove. I got a glimpse of them while I was standing over Dan's dead body."

Aubrey sat up taller. "That is, um, curious. And it does appear to broaden the Serino connection."

"Yes, it does. And I haven't gotten to the most curious part yet—something you're not going to like very much."

"What's that?"

"Jude's assistant, our former beauty queen, said that when her boss left his Rancho Mirage home on a flight to here, he had his right-hand man with him—Zeke Dublin."

CHAPTER
TWENTY-ONE

Palms Spring, California
Two Months Earlier

"Mr. Serino will be in shortly. Have a seat." Max rammed a hand into Zeke's shoulder. He winced and spilled into Jude's Palm Springs office. His previously dislocated shoulder remained painful to the touch. Zeke muttered an expletive at Max, who left. He shuffled forward. At the office bar was a decanter of Scotch, and Zeke helped himself to a drink—a double, neat. Then he spied a bottle of vintage Macallan. With the full glass in hand, he took two achy steps toward a mini potted palm and watered it. He served himself an even larger portion from a bottle that cost about three hundred bucks. If his gaze hadn't caught in the mirror, Zeke might have felt a dollop of satisfaction.

A beating like he'd never endured was still evident: puffy, bloodshot eyes, bruises that had turned like an angry sky, going from black to purple to faint patches of yellow. And forget his nose. Once a feature that complemented salient bone structure, it now sat slightly left of center. "Jesus . . ." Zeke downed a pain-killing gulp. It burned in his throat, but not nearly as much as the cuts and bruises that went with his busted face and cracked ribs. The image that stared back, it was Jude's payback for Zeke's losing prediction in the Lopez-Wilder championship fight. "I knew I should have called fucking tails."

Without a ghost gift to deliver, it was how Zeke had settled on a future outcome. After supplying Jude with a name, he considered boarding a flight, choosing a destination as far from his boss as possible. Two things had stopped him: concern for Nora and the clear suspicion that he was being watched. That part was confirmed when Jude's handy helpers showed up before losing ticket stubs could be torn in two. Zeke had been sitting in a bar on the outskirts of Biddeford, Maine, where the Serinos' latest development project was under way. A tall beer sat in front of him as he swallowed down the ESPN London feed of the fight. The bad choice and subsequent beating remained vivid as Jude entered the office.

"Zeke, have a seat." He pointed to a chair.

From the mirror's reflection, he watched Jude stride across the room. Before turning for a chair, Zeke made steadier eye contact with himself. *We are done, you son of a bitch. You are going down . . . harder than Wilder, count on it . . .* It should have never come to this. Zeke should have taken Jude out a decade ago, and this was karma's payback—for being a coward, for always finding a reason to hesitate. He should have never strayed from the objective: avenging his parents' deaths.

If he could have snuck his gun inside Jude's house, here and now would have been a fine location for murder. Zeke no longer cared if killing Jude meant spending the rest of his life in prison. The little life he had, Jude had made a living hell. Slowly, Zeke eased into a chair. "Forgive me," he said cynically. "My range of motion is still recovering."

Jude waited until Zeke situated himself. "Honestly? A part of me feels the need to apologize for your, uh . . . unfortunate state."

Zeke widened his eyes until the tender muscles surrounding them strained. "Not really what I thought you'd lead with, considering your response to the fight and the two muscle-bound minions who escorted me here."

"And in what other way could I have ensured your arrival?" From behind his desk, Jude leaned back, his face oddly contemplative.

"I don't know, Jude. *Not* beating the shit out of me might have made this a friendlier invitation. I told you months ago—"

Jude held up a hand. "That your resource for the predictions was gone." He drew a measured breath. "But you have to understand, Zeke. You endured the wrath of one man's loss. In turn, I was subject to the reaction of my many associates, who, cumulatively, were deprived of millions, not to mention their initial bets." He glided a look over Zeke. "These weren't blue-collar workers who placed twenty-dollar wagers in a break-room pool. To be quite frank, I'm somewhat surprised I didn't end up like you."

"Wouldn't have hurt my feelings."

"Fortunately, at this level of gaming, we respond like gentlemen. While my peers will require restitution, taking it out of my hide would not be the message they'd send. That's reserved for . . ."

"Schmucks like me."

Jude lightly shrugged his shoulders.

"So I'm here because you want . . . ?" Zeke brushed a hand through the air. "I told you months ago, back in Vegas at Nora and Ian's, I'm tapped out. You think it's total bullshit, a grifter's scam."

"I did back then."

"And my story hasn't changed. Or maybe today is the real payback. Should I expect a government raid at any moment for back taxes owed? I don't know how many ways I can say it. Nothing will change the fact that there are no more—"

"Ghost gifts," Jude supplied.

Zeke was taken aback. "What did you say?"

Jude retrieved a folder from a desk drawer. "After your misinformation on the Lopez-Wilder fight, after I calmed a bit, I did some research." He reached past the cherry-crafted cigar box and picked up a pair of glasses. "Eyestrain," he said. "Worse by the day. This year, my entire being may drown in my upcoming sabbatical." He continued on as if the two had met for a friendly midmorning coffee. "Serengeti this year, big game hunting. I'm quite excited."

"Uh-huh," Zeke murmured as Jude slipped reading glasses to the tip of his nose.

"As I said, the Lopez-Wilder snafu forced me to reconsider the absurd—surely you realized an inaccurate prediction would only lead to . . ." He peered over the rim of his glasses. "Your current state. While you are a grifter, Zeke, and we established your proclivity for cheating ages ago, I had to ask myself why you would have deliberately misled me. I could only come up with one answer."

"And that is?"

"You had to be telling the truth." Jude opened the folder.

The moment his eyes registered its contents, Zeke's heart began to race. Even from his upside down view of the pages, he saw what Jude had researched.

"Fascinating story. Although it was her significant other that led me to the jackpot." Beneath the papers were photos. One was a head shot of Levi St John. "I've caught his *Ink on Air* program. Mr. St John is adept at his trade. But her," Jude said, tapping a manicured finger on a candid picture of Aubrey. "She's the one with a singular gift." He spun in his chair, reaching for a book on his credenza. "Incredible read." He spoke while fingering the pages of *The Unremarkable Life of Missy Flannigan*. "Miss Ellis, the author, the woman you've been in love with since joining up with her carnival past, she's the one with a remarkable life, isn't she, Zeke?"

"You leave Aubrey the fuck out of this. She can't help you. She has nothing to do with—"

"Zeke, let's not waste time. She has everything to do with it. And from what I've unearthed, despite her low-key, below-the-radar life, when added to what you professed about her father . . . well, I can only imagine how much they have in common." He removed the glasses, making clear eye contact. "If it weren't for years of unfathomable predictions, I might have labeled her story pure fiction. But when you put it all together . . ."

"Aubrey's gift, it's not like her father's. Yes. She can communicate with the dead, but she can't predict the future. Her gift doesn't work like that."

"Or maybe it's where you obtained some of your best predictions." Jude wasn't listening, surely thinking he'd found the Holy Grail of future wins. "I understand she also has a son. The information on him is unclear. But wouldn't it be interesting to learn if the boy shares in his mother's . . . and his grandfather's unique traits?"

Ignoring the ache of sore ribs, Zeke sucked in a breath. "It's not going to happen, Jude. You won't get anywhere near Aubrey or her family."

"And why's that? You're going to stop me? Or perhaps you'll try and head me off at the pass, forewarn her yourself. Nonsense." He glanced at a second folder. "My IRS plan, while on hold, is easily set in motion. A lot of good you'd do your Aubrey from jail. No, Zeke, that's not what your future holds. Moreover, I don't need any crystal ball to tell me as much."

Zeke was a word away from going across the top of Jude's desk. He calmed. The only way out of this was to be smarter than Jude—something Zeke had a history of falling short on. He willed himself back into the chair. "You're right," he said, his tone cooperative. "I can't deny Aubrey's gift. I also haven't had much contact in recent years, no matter what you might think. Like your Tilda being gone, it's just too painful. I lost the girl . . . the incredible woman she became. I suppose a piece of that mind-set was shame. I should have never touched Peter Ellis's ghost gifts to begin with. If Aubrey found out . . ."

"Why should she?" He rocked in his chair, pressing his fingertips together. Zeke recognized the gesture—Jude was engaged in the art of snake-oil crafting. "I'd say this presents no more of a problem than you working your way back into Aubrey's life. Clearly, you'll have to get over the 'difficult to be around her' part. Aside from recommending a good therapist, I can't help you with that."

"Wouldn't matter, I have no desire to *get over* Aubrey. Not unlike your Tilda, it's something I've learned to live with."

"True. There's that—the solace of separation by death, as opposed to simply not being worthy." He pointed to the photo of Levi. "I suspect he'd agree with me on that."

"From what I know about Levi, if he were here, the thought would have never made it out of your head, never mind your mouth."

"Then lucky for me it's you, not him, I'm left to deal with. So let's share some details, an angle that puts you not only back in Aubrey's life, but in her good graces as well."

"If forced to help you . . ."

"And you are."

"I want something in return."

"Make this work, and I'll see to it the IRS matter is completely and permanently erased."

"No, it's not that—and, hell, I see that as the upper hand. I might not be able to help Aubrey from a jail cell, but it wouldn't do you much good either."

Jude wagged a finger at him. "See, you are educable." He sighed. "Is it something for Nora? Sorry, but I won't put that money-bumbling husband of hers back at the helm of any Serino business greater than an ice cream stand."

"No, Nora's content. I'd like to think even you wouldn't threaten the delicate happiness of her life, the lives of her children."

"It wouldn't be my first choice . . ." He swept a hand past Zeke. "So then, what? What is it you want, Zeke?"

"I want the truth." He sat straighter, a position that sent a zing of pain through his shoulder.

"The truth about what?"

"My parents—Kieran and Ailish Dunne," he said. "Their deaths."

Jude showed no outward reaction as Zeke spoke his parents' names. His nemesis merely stared, his eyes lifeless, shark-like. "What makes you think I know anything about the demise of—"

Zeke held up a hand. "After all this time, the years of blackmail, I'm asking for the truth—grifter to gentleman."

"The truth about your parents' deaths."

"Yes. I want you to tell me it wasn't a murder-suicide. That my father didn't kill my mother in cold blood. I want you to admit that your father was responsible."

"My father?" With a sliver of a smile, Jude tilted his head at him.

"End it, Jude. I've known the truth since the rumors that ran through my old neighborhood, since the day I first came to work for Serino Enterprises."

"You surprise me, Zeke. I didn't think you had it in you. It takes a lot of nerve to make that kind of direct accusation."

"Not nearly as much as it does to gun down two people. Leave two innocent kids to fend for themselves. Do you have the same set of balls your old man did, enough to tell me the truth?" He gripped the leather chair, his fingertips digging into the arms. "Do it, and I'll give you what you want." Zeke played it tightly; Jude needed to believe what he was hearing—surrender. "Tell me, and I'll give you Aubrey Ellis."

Jude cleared his throat and leaned into the desk. "Fine. Just to prove that much to you . . . yes. My father wanted yours dead. Your mother's even bloodier death was meant to send a message: crossing my father could only result in one thing." There was a visual standoff. Jude conceded the contest by selecting a cigar from the humidor.

"You son of a bitch. You miserable, fucking, cock-sucking piece of—" Zeke managed to heave himself from the chair as forcefully as his beaten body would allow. But the yelling was enough to bring Max thundering into the room. Jude never even flinched as Max easily subdued a weakened Zeke. He rammed him back into the chair like a puppet.

Zeke struggled for a breath that didn't incite searing pain. Jude waited, tapping the cigar on the desk. "You can go, Max. I'm sure Zeke realizes the foolishness of any physical recourse." He swayed gently in his chair, his gaze contemplative. "Since we're starting a new chapter here, one that apparently is predicated on honesty, let me enlighten you to a few more truths. I've been well aware of our connected pasts since your meager beginnings at Serino Enterprises." The swaying ceased, and Jude ran the cigar beneath his nose like it was a drug. "Do you truly believe it was cupid's fate Nora and Ian crossed paths? Although, I admit, I was stunned when it turned out the two dolts proved to be a match made in heaven."

Zeke blinked at him, comprehending the depth of Jude's strategy. How it was even more calculating than Zeke's. "You're out of your fucking mind."

"Don't be ridiculous. I'm a shrewd businessman who's been doing precisely the same thing as you."

"And that is?"

"Keeping my enemies close."

Zeke forced a dry swallow through his throat, absorbing his miscalculation, praying he didn't make another one.

"Back to the point. You wanted the truth. Fine. Be a man. There you have it."

Zeke focused on his folded hands. He only wanted to hear a little more. Between a confession of the crime Jude's father committed and Jude's new target—Aubrey—Zeke no longer wavered at the precipice of revenge. He was there. "It's, um . . . it's good to know, better than the alternative in a lot of ways."

"It was a different time, Zeke. Comeuppance was doled out in a way that not only compensated for the misstep but sent a reminder to the many onlookers. Your father had been providing information to the authorities. It was a leak that cost my father money and assets. If not strongly curtailed, it was information that might have brought down Serino Enterprises, put my father in jail. How would that have looked?"

He shifted his sore shoulders. "Like maybe justice was served."

"Well, regardless, we have little hope of changing any of it now, don't we? My father was obligated to not only repay your father's disloyalty but to send a message. I believe that came to pass. Is that what you wanted to hear?"

"Part of it." Zeke reached for his glass, the tea-colored liquid sloshing as he downed a mouthful. "That day, in my parents' apartment building. You were there, weren't you? Afterward, part of what I overheard was that the hit was a demonstration, a grooming lesson for Giorgio's son. You stood there and watched, didn't you? You did nothing while your father killed mine, while he murdered my mother."

Jude laid the cigar on the desk and folded his hands, his expression introspective, solemn. "Because I promised you the truth. Because gentleman to grifter, I want to keep my word . . . so you'll grasp how serious I am about your need to facilitate Aubrey Ellis's cooperation, I wasn't *present* that day, Zeke." He picked up the cigar and cutter, sharply clipping the tip. "I pulled the trigger."

CHAPTER
TWENTY-TWO

Surrey, Massachusetts
Present Day

It was like the box had eyes. The next morning, Aubrey moved around her living room, in and out of her kitchen, all too aware of the letter box that sat on her dining room table. She finally took a seat, poking a butter knife at it. "What?" she said to whomever might be listening. The rising hum she'd heard when Levi first opened the box penetrated. "Could I please eat my breakfast in peace?" She spread strawberry jam across a piece of whole wheat toast. Aubrey flicked her gaze between the jam jar and box until she missed with the knife, and a gooey glob landed in her lap. "Great. Thanks so much." Aubrey scraped red jam off the casual white linen nightshirt she'd worn to bed. "Like that'll ever come out."

She proceeded to dunk a tea bag, nearly drowning the thing, when a tapping sound rose. Having bit into the toast, she stopped chewing. She forced the toast down, all the while squashing a visual: a gathering of spirits en masse. She blinked at the letter box and sat taller, stiffer. Her heart thumped an extra few beats, then slowed as the tapping turned to knocking. *The door.* Brushing crumbs from her hands, she sighed and rose, wondering if it might be Zeke. One thing she did want was more information about Zeke's relationship with Jude. On the other hand, if it was him, she needed to be more direct while not inviting Zeke beyond her living room.

Peering through the slightly raised window, she didn't see Zeke or his rental car but spied Levi's Volvo. Loudly, she said, "It's your house. You don't have to knock." The knob turned as he inserted a key. A moment later, Levi stood in the living room, looking much like he had for years: dressed in khakis, although it was a Saturday, his only real weekend giveaway a casual cloth jacket. Still, less a suit, it was the Levi that belonged to her, in this house, at home. Aubrey wasn't sure if it was memories or longing that heightened the sense of loss. "Pete?" Concern eclipsed her own desires.

"He's fine. He had early Saturday basketball practice. He's skateboarding afterward."

"Good . . . that's good." She leaned back in the chair, though the tense feeling didn't ease. She looked at the letter box, then at Levi. "So you're here because . . . ?"

"Because we're not done talking about last night. Pete got back earlier than expected, and—"

"Yes. I'm well aware of the part where he didn't want to come inside, calling you from the driveway."

"So you know, I tried talking to him about it on the way back to the condo."

At least he didn't say "home." "Do you want to sit? I can make some coffee." Coffee was on the list of things Aubrey missed. While she didn't drink coffee, she loved the aroma, the cup after cup Levi might have on a Saturday morning.

"Thanks, I already had plenty." He took his usual seat at the end of the table. The action was comforting but short-lived, his expression somber.

"Levi, what's going on? You're starting to freak me out more than that box." She pushed it a few inches away. "Tell me. Did Pete have a particularly bad night?"

"No. He was quiet. My phone rang late, so I was up. I checked on him a few times. Pete was only mumbling in his sleep, which given some of his nights . . ."

"Is fairly unremarkable. And you're sure he didn't say anything on the way home?"

"Not much. Definitely wasn't in a sharing mood. But I do know finding Zeke Dublin here got under his skin."

"Just *his* skin. Good to know."

Before Levi could clarify—or not, Aubrey's phone dinged. She looked to the vintage 1950s blond sideboard where they charged modern-day electronics. Levi leaned over and retrieved the phone, handing it to her.

"A text from Piper. Huh. Looks like you can file this under 'interesting.'" Her glance moved between Levi and the phone. "The deputy chief's lab personnel, with some help from 3M, determined the green hockey tape came from the same manufacturer. And while they couldn't prove it came off the same roll, analysis concluded that the tape found with Trevor's belongings, on his hockey stick, and the roll found with Liam's effects were manufactured around the same time."

"I'd say that makes it all something beyond coincidental."

"It'll be interesting when Dan gets his final lab analysis back on the tape connected to your victim."

"I suspect it will. Aubrey," he said.

She quit poking at her phone and made eye contact.

"It's why I'm here. Our victim. I came by because regardless of any green tape, enough things are falling beyond the lines of coincidence. Particularly after what we learned last night."

"Ah," she said, putting her phone down. "We're back to Zeke. And what did we learn? Other than the origin of a tattoo and that it could belong to any white male."

"For one, we learned Zeke was with Jude Serino before he took off on his yearly sabbatical—a trip where no one has heard from him for weeks."

"And you have no reason to believe that's suspicious. His assistant told you it's typical behavior, not atypical. Did she seem concerned about him?"

"She seemed pleased that online shopping was her only purpose at the moment. She wasn't looking for a concern. But thanks to Jude's weather girl Friday, we also know, before leaving on his trip, Jude stopped here to check on the Serino's Maine development. Weeks later, and Zeke is right here too. Surely you can't dismiss all that?"

"I'm not dismissing it." Aubrey concentrated on her toast, reapplying jam. "I'm just trying to separate facts from overzealous investigative reporting. Information gathered by someone with a bias."

"I'm professional enough to recognize a dividing line. But forget my take entirely. Last night, the late call that woke me up, it was from Dan. I'd left a message earlier, asked him to call no matter what time."

"And what? When the bars closed at two, he—" She cleared her throat. "Sorry, that was a Piper-inspired remark. What did you and Dan discuss?"

"Aside from fleshing out Zeke's association with Jude Serino, Dan had some new information. That's where I had the coffee this morning. We met up to trade details."

"How simpatico. Identical hair triggers when it comes to anything that remotely resembles a lead—especially if it's aimed at someone you don't particularly care for."

"And you can't say the same for Dan. He has no prior opinion about Zeke."

"Except your current influence."

"You know me better than that. Facts influence me, Aubrey. Not my personal opinion of Zeke Dublin. Not when it comes to something this serious."

She shoved the butter knife onto her plate. "Mind of steel. Got it."

"The point is, I told Dan what we learned about the tattoo, how it ties to the Serino family. You can't possibly believe that wasn't worth sharing?"

"As long as you also told him how *E* tattoo takers were paid a $5,000 bonus for getting one. With all sorts of blue-collar workers involved, hundreds of men could have that tattoo."

"But only one ended up dead in a swamp with a bullet through his head. And I might be inclined to agree with you, less the new information Dan brought with him."

"Which would be?" She folded her arms, staring at him.

"Yesterday, Dan's forensic team revisited the crime scene. The marshy surroundings have made a thorough investigation nearly impossible. Considering the lack of red-flag evidence, which now includes a common-hit .22-caliber bullet, Dan thought another walk through at low tide was reasonable."

"They found the gun?" Aubrey's body braced.

"No. No gun." From his jacket pocket, Levi produced a photo. "This is a picture of what they found tangled in a heron's nest."

The photograph depicted a cigarette butt with a Camel filter end. Nervous laughter sputtered from Aubrey. "What are you telling me, Levi? That instead of a smoking gun, you've just got a smoker?"

"Not any smoker, and you know it."

She narrowed her eyes at what would be Levi's stellar recall.

"I remember the story. The one you told me when Zeke was here five years ago. You said back in the day, he was always trying to quit smoking for you. You even went as far as to note his brand of choice— *Camels*." He paused while she too rolled the late-night exchange through her head; she'd just arrived home from the Heinz-Bodette reunion. "Am I wrong? Put it together. Nobody's heard from Jude Serino since he went on his trip."

"And according to Jude's assistant, he's on a preplanned sabbatical—"

"There's more." Levi retrieved his phone and clicked on the screen until an image appeared. "It's from a piece *Dolce* magazine did a few years ago. That's Jude Serino, and in his hand is an Arturo Fuente cigar."

"The cigar band you found near the road."

"Maybe it puts the victim . . ." He hesitated. "And Zeke at the scene."

Aubrey glanced between the picture on his phone and the photograph. "I don't have Piper's or Dan's credentials, Levi. But I know enough about evidence and probable cause. I agree, it's a coincidence that should be questioned. But any decent lawyer will also tell you it's no more than circumstantial. Not unless you have something more damning . . . a fingerprint, DNA?" While Levi's case was gaining momentum, Aubrey wasn't about to abandon Zeke. Not when she might be the only person left to defend him. "You don't even know who your victim is. Go back to Jude Serino. Does he have a wife, a family member raising a concern?"

"He's divorced. Jude Serino doesn't have any children. Bruno Serino hasn't returned my calls. Even so, add it up. It's not rocket science. We have motive, opportunity—a prime location that guaranteed rapid decomposition. Hell, we even know Zeke made the trip east with Jude. What more do you want, a confession from Zeke?"

"As opposed to conjecture? Yes. I might find it more convincing than roadside litter, or a cigarette butt that a bird or the tide could have carried for miles."

"And I suspect it's what a good defense attorney will say too." Levi stuffed the photograph into his jacket pocket and clicked off his phone. "Regardless of your reservations, it's enough for Dan. He's started a formal inquiry. His team is in the process of collecting Serino DNA. According to Dan, Bruno Serino is currently abroad—China, then Europe, so it's a little slow going. While we wait, I'm here to make an informal inquiry. You tell me Zeke doesn't work for Jude anymore.

You never conveyed any details, if it was an amicable parting or something—"

"Something like what?" she said snappishly.

"Something like the specifics surrounding Zeke's split with Serino Enterprises. Surely he's discussed it with you."

Aubrey remained silent. Internally, she was wavering on Zeke's involvement. Externally, she wasn't ready to hand Levi information that would sound like a motive—namely Zeke admitting to parting ways with Jude on less-than-good terms. Her chest tightened, but then so did Aubrey's resolve. Her bond with Zeke was stronger than circumstantial evidence.

"I'm just asking," Levi pressed, corralling her attention. "His sudden nonemployee status is a relevant question." He paused, a note of graciousness. Otherwise, she might find herself the subject of a Levi St John interview. "Aubrey, we can ask him—or somebody like Dan will."

She started to reply, then stopped. Instead, she picked up her cup and swallowed down cold tea. While Aubrey fought fissures of doubt, she didn't want Levi to see any of it. "You're going to feel ridiculous, Levi, when it turns out your John Doe is from the Local 409 Iron Workers Union—or wherever. A person Zeke Dublin's never even met. That your victim had a gambling debt or drug habit, someone who owed money to the wrong people." She flailed her arm upward. "Or it could be he's just a poor schmuck who looked the wrong way at some street punk's girlfriend and ended up dead in a Maine swamp."

"I hope so, Aubrey . . . I really hope so."

"Sure you do." Her cup made clinking contact with its saucer, her face warming at the prospect of being wrong.

Levi focused on his folded hands. She knew the habit: controlling emotion before replying. "So while you and I are in this *really good place*," he said dully, "let me tell you the rest. While Dan works the Serino end of this case, I've taken it upon myself to investigate Zeke's past."

"You what?"

"I'm checking off the things somebody like Dan will if given enough cause. If it comes to that, nobody on Dan's team will be looking to exonerate Zeke."

"And you are?" she said, incredulous. "What did you do, Levi?"

"I called an old . . . friend."

"Facts. I want specific facts."

"You said Zeke was from Chicago, right? You know that much about him, before he and his sister joined up with the Heinz-Bodette troupe."

Aubrey nodded.

"You also told me his parents' deaths were . . . *questionable*."

She reluctantly repeated the gesture.

"A few days ago, I called Geneève Renard."

She laughed. "Should I be surprised you did that, or just that an opportunity to do so took this long?"

He ignored the dig. "Geneève is still on staff at the University of Chicago. Since I'm at a distance, and not in a position to fly off to the Midwest, she was agreeable to do some digging for me."

"What is this, Levi?" This time Aubrey's hand smacked hard against the table. "Twisted payback for Zeke showing up? Drop a dime to an ex-lover, ask her to check out mine?"

"No. It honestly struck me as a perfectly logical move. Geneève knows Chicago inside and out. She has a lot of connections; she knows how to discreetly and thoroughly pursue a background investigation."

"And she was ecstatic to hear from you, more than happy to help you out."

"She didn't turn me down." He tilted his head at her. "Are you more bothered that I called her or that I asked her to look into Zeke's past?"

"Neither!" She seethed. "Sorry to disappoint you, Levi, but a phone call to an old flame isn't going to get a rise out of me."

"Maybe what she found out will."

"What's that?" she said, forcing a tone of total disinterest.

"Newspaper stories that reported the murder-suicide of Zeke's parents."

"And?"

"And Genève's a stellar investigative reporter."

"So multitalented?"

"In a few phone calls, she managed to get beneath the surface of the story. The trail is old, and the sources weren't great, but a rumor still runs through Zeke's old neighborhood. Your footnote about their deaths being retribution was correct. Apparently, there's suspicion that his parents' deaths weren't murder-suicide but retaliation linked to organized crime."

Aubrey straightened her spine. "I see where you're going with this. You think your ex-professor slash summer lover stumbled on a five-star motive." She closed her mouth and stared him down. "Stop looking for a *Zeke* headline."

"I'm not doing that."

"Aren't you? Has your holiday-card-giving ex come up with anything besides ancient rumors? Until she does, we're done with this conversation!" Aubrey jerked up from the table, slamming her chair into it. The sudden force was enough to send the box of ghost gifts flying forward.

Or was it?

"What the hell?" An always self-possessed Levi leaped up as if he'd seen a ghost.

From the alcove of the dining room, they stared at the aftermath. The leather tie had been loosely fastened. The force of the fall—or throw—caused the lid to open, ghost gifts fluttering like dust bunnies across the hardwood floors.

"Okay," Aubrey said. "I lost it there for a second. But I didn't slam the chair that hard. Did I?"

"Not unless you've been injecting steroids I don't know about."

Aubrey was about to say something else, but the buzzing sound from the box intruded, and she slammed her hands to her ears. "Oww . . . holy . . ." It was ferociously loud.

"Aubrey?" A second later, Levi was by her side, herding her toward the front door. "Outside, now!"

Bent at the waist, Aubrey shook her head and forced herself erect. She pushed away from Levi. "No," she said to him, shouting, "Knock it off!" in the general direction of the room. The high-pitched buzz ceased on her words. She looked at Levi and stiffened her frame, though her fingers clamped into his forearms. "I put that damn box on notice days ago. It's not in charge." Her gaze darted around the room. "Not in my house. Do you hear me? You're not doing this in my house!"

"You want to fill me in on what's happening here?"

She continued to glance about, like a swarm of angry insects was buzzing through. "I'm not sure—someone or thing connected to that box. It was like a burst of rage, pent-up frustration. Our escalating argument was not going in the direction it wants."

"So that was the box's attempt at counseling?"

"Don't mock, Levi." She furrowed her brow. "It took serious energy to move the box like that. I'm sure me slamming the chair into the table helped channel the anger. But you saw it; it was hardly enough force to do that." She pointed at the fallen letter box and scattered ghost gifts. Just as she did, a hefty breeze rose from the barely open window. It muscled its way through the room, robust enough to lift two papers, separating them from the rest.

Levi looked toward the window and now-still curtain. "Okay, so I won't even attempt to assign logic to that." Together, they approached the papers.

"And these." Aubrey picked up the two pieces of green construction paper. "It's not just the box. The entity that's here now, I assume it wants us to focus on these." Not only were the papers warm, but they vibrated under Aubrey's touch.

Together, Aubrey and Levi said, "Eli Serino."

"And it's not just Eli," Aubrey said. "These two ghost gifts, we know they're different from almost everything else—a drawing of Santa Claus, some simple mountains, and the word 'Springfield.'"

"Wait. Let's invite some logic into this. What are the common denominators here? What are we overlooking? Green construction paper . . . both pieces torn from the whole sheet. Like you said, different from most everything else in that box."

"Yet . . ." Aubrey tipped her head at the box. "Somewhat similar to the blue construction paper, the star." They both turned, looking at Peter Ellis's box of ghost gifts. The star remained inside, undisturbed. She stared, a wave of yesteryear encroaching on the foreground waves, stick-drawn house, and bright sun with the word spelled out. "Right now, the blue star just feels . . . *nostalgic*." Aubrey looked at Levi, the word slipping from her stream of consciousness. "But I'm not getting anything more than that off it."

"Okay, so let's stay with the green construction paper for now. Springfield," he said. "Springfield, Mass—sounds like a town to me."

"Could be. But google it. Do you know how many states have a city or town named Springfield? It's hardly a map."

"Okay, so it's an idea."

"I suppose, but what do green construction paper . . . the possible town of Springfield, somewhere, USA, and these arbitrary drawings lead us to? Moreover, other than a vague connection to Trevor Beane's brother, what does any of it have to do with Eli Serino?" The bizarre taste of sour green apple and sugary sweetness rose from Aubrey's palate. "Yuck. What is it with him and that taste?"

"What taste?"

"A sweet-and-sour apple flavor. I've been associating it with Eli Serino for a while now. I think it's gum."

As the dead boy's name hit the air, a pinging noise sounded. It came wrapped in a web of déjà vu and rose, distinct and rhythmic. Levi was silent, his gaze pinned to Aubrey. The taste grew strong, and so did a memory. "Levi, you told Piper and Dan the story about us visiting Eli's house years ago. Do you recall the specific details—other than him scaring the bejesus out of me?"

"Uh-huh," he answered but didn't move a muscle. "You mean things like the smashed glass of a French door and a bloody rash around your throat? Pretty tough to forget."

"And you also know my beliefs about spirits and suicide—people who succeed in the act, ironically, their connection to here remains strong. Their inability to move on is tied to unfinished business."

"Like Brody." It came out reverently, Levi referencing his brother. As he spoke, his gaze finally detached from Aubrey, darting around the room.

"Exactly. Brody couldn't move on until he'd made peace with you. A difficult task, but one we accomplished." Their gazes met again. "But Eli Serino—he was so troubled, angry, in life and in death. He's been hovering. We know that." The pinging sound amplified, like a homing signal telling Aubrey she was on the right path. "I think part of what Eli's been trying to convey is that his ability to communicate is restricted, maybe by setting."

"What brings you to that conclusion?"

She pointed to the box. "He just did. Insofar as Eli's been present, the best way I can describe his manifestation is 'shadowy.' At first I thought he was being stubborn, a troublemaker. But now I don't believe his behavior is intentional; I think it's stunted."

"Makes sense. Your strongest connections are facilitated by setting, a physical element, or loved ones. But even so—"

"It's more than that." Aubrey felt positive she was onto something, the pinging rattling like steam through metal pipes. "Eli could have spelled out his message on any number of occasions. Right here or in Piper's office last week."

"Don't discount the other option, Aubrey. 'Friendly ghost' didn't describe him all those years ago. It could be a sadistic spirit luring you toward more harm than good."

Absently, Aubrey drew her fingertips over the half-moon scar on her chin. "I don't think so, Levi. Not this time."

"So what's your bottom line? What are you saying when it comes to Eli Serino's ghost?"

She stared at him. "We need to go back to the house on Acorn Circle—for Eli, and for whatever it is he so desperately wants to communicate about those missing boys."

"And what, specifically, makes you say that?" His gaze had stopped moving too, reconnecting with Aubrey's.

"When we were at the house on Acorn Circle, do you remember the pinging sound? It was so distinct, connected to Eli from the moment we went inside."

He offered no reply.

"What if I told you I heard it right now—since about the time the letter box took flight? Would that be enough to convince you?"

"Not really." His dark stare moved from hers to the far corners of their living room. "It probably has more to do with the fact that I hear it too."

CHAPTER
TWENTY-THREE

Whether the body in Maine turned out to be an unrelated John Doe or Jude Serino, Aubrey and Levi agreed to table that much while seeking out Eli Serino. "Hopefully, home-field advantage will give Eli the platform he needs." Aubrey said this as she settled into the passenger seat of Levi's car. Instead of a listing sheet, she held on to the two pieces of green construction paper.

Interestingly, accessing the house on Acorn Circle proved to be a low hurdle. It had been years since they'd visited the property, the odds greatly in favor of an occupied house. But a search of public records had left Aubrey and Levi intrigued. The house had been bought and sold eight times in the past dozen years.

"Must be some kind of all-time high," Levi had said as Aubrey switched from scrolling through town records to her old haunting grounds: Multiple Listing Service. She found the house, which was, once again, listed with Happy Home Realty—the real estate firm best known for hard-to-move properties. But Aubrey didn't recognize a single realtor, including Dawn Carmichael, who currently represented the listing. Levi and Aubrey decided the easiest way in would be to pose as interested buyers. When Dawn recognized Levi's name—*Ink on Air's* most popular news contributor—she was quick to forgo realtor basics, like financially qualifying potential buyers. They grabbed at the perk, and Dawn agreed to meet them at the house on Acorn Circle.

The car slowed as Levi navigated the long, winding driveway. "What, um . . . what's your plan when she wants to accompany us on the tour?" he asked.

"I was thinking about that. One possibility, you act standoffish." She flashed a smile at him. "Shouldn't be a stretch."

Levi smirked in reply.

"We could tell her I'm the one who's dying to see the house. You keep her talking outside while I take the tour." The car stopped twenty yards short of the house.

"You're not serious? Aubrey, if you think I'm letting you go into that house alone . . ." He shook his head. "Then clearly *you* forget the details of our last visit."

Aubrey stared at the once-pristine property. Years of come-and-go owners had taken their toll; the reproduction colonial hadn't fared well. Overgrown shrubbery swallowed the front, a tired façade, and paint-chipped shutters. The once-stately property bore all the markings of a movie-lot haunted house. Regardless, she addressed Levi's remark as if they were approaching a house with a welcome mat that said "ordinary."

"I'm not that person anymore, Levi. You should know that. As for future predictions, am I concerned I may have to navigate new and not particularly inviting aspects of this gift? Yes."

"Okay, then—"

"But the gift, I know; it hasn't owned me in years. I'm not afraid of Eli Serino." She ran her fingers over a pockmarked arm. "I'm not foolish either. I'm not sure you'd get me to take a return trip to a motel room on the Delmarva Peninsula." It was the place Aubrey had experienced her evilest encounter with the spiritual world, resulting in bite marks on her arm, the scar on her chin. "But this," she said, pointing to the house, "I can handle. Eli was a bully, not a true threat."

"I'm not trying to scare you, but maybe he's upped his game."

Even in their current turmoil, Levi's protective instincts were touching. "Let's just see how it goes." She pointed to a young woman who stood in front of a luxury sedan, her realtor smile beaming from afar. Levi sighed and drove forward.

Introductions proved insightful. While Dawn recognized Levi, she clearly didn't have a clue about Aubrey. After a blip of conversation, Aubrey suggested they go inside. At that point, it was Miss Carmichael who seemed standoffish. "Uh, of course . . . the house tour." She twisted her hands in a wringing knot. "It's why we're here, right?"

"You know . . ." Levi wrapped an arm around Aubrey's shoulder, hugging tight. She glanced queerly at him. Even in peak relationship mode, Levi wasn't much for public gestures of affection. "Can I be candid with you, Dawn?"

"Oh, absolutely! All my clients can count on complete discretion."

"Good to know. The truth is Aubrey's had her eye on this house for ages. Every time it's up for sale, she's says, 'Levi, now's our chance! I just know this is the house for us!'"

"Really?" the young realtor said. "Well, it does have some . . . *uncommon* features."

"And she feels it's serendipity that so many owners have come and gone over the years."

"Wow. I suppose serendipity would be one way to spin it."

"Anyway . . . being as we're not exactly complete strangers. I mean, you did say you watch *Ink on Air* religiously."

"That's true." She smiled brightly. "Your reporting is just . . . well, wow!"

Levi cleared his throat, Aubrey cued to his response over the underwhelming adjective.

"And, my gosh, your on-camera appeal is just . . ."

"Wow again?" Aubrey offered.

"How'd you know what I was going to say?" The girl giggled, and Aubrey giggled back, patting Levi's chest. "I'll even tell you a little secret, Dawn." She dropped her voice to a pseudo-whisper. "Don't tell Levi this, but the camera's love for his face, it's most of the reason MediaMatters hired him."

"*Ohhh* . . . wow . . . wow . . . wow," she said in a breathy gasp. "And here I thought his stories were pretty good too."

"Okay, that's enough—" But Levi shut up as Aubrey discreetly elbowed him.

"Show business!" Aubrey said. "You've no idea how many hours Levi spends answering fan mail, signing eight-by-ten glossies. Anything to keep up his image."

The realtor continued to nod, her gaze going starry. Aubrey patted him again, a prompt to speak.

"Uh, that's right," he said. "So all things considered, would you mind terribly if Aubrey and I toured the property alone—privately?"

"You mean I wouldn't have to go in?"

"It's not a problem for us," Aubrey said. "I'm sure you're busy. Maybe you have some phone calls to make?"

She giggled again. "Gosh, I can only think of about a dozen realtors who'd love to know I was showing this property to Levi St . . ." The realtor stifled her remark. "I mean, I do have some appointments to confirm. If you really don't mind."

"Not at all," Levi said. "I appreciate your understanding. Clearly, you know how to work with your clients."

A few moments later, Levi and Aubrey made their way up the front walk to the pillars and rotunda entry.

"I see being social in the right situation is still one of your strong suits."

"Don't complain. We're in." Levi punched Dawn's realtor code into the lockbox. "Just be glad I didn't have to agree to after-the-tour drinks."

Aubrey laughed.

"What could possibly be funny?"

She pursed her lips. "Sorry. It's still a cheap thrill when your reporter prowess is eclipsed by your sex appeal."

"Keep it up, Aubrey."

Humor vanished as the lockbox popped open, and Levi inserted the key in the double front doors. They opened in a gliding motion, as if butlers drew them steadily from either side. Aubrey inhaled deeply, her lungs filling, her mind whirling. While the memory of their last visit was clear, being there came with a tad more caution. In front of them was the expansive, marble-clad foyer, the turned staircase from which the original pinging noise resonated.

"Are you sure you want to do this?"

She half shrugged and nodded. "Guess I'm not the only one who's come a long way in the past dozen years."

"How so?"

"Last time, I had to drag you in here, totally pissed off, under protest and complete disbelief."

"So we agree you and I have both benefited from a learning curve. Do you suppose Eli has?"

"Only one way to find out." But Aubrey didn't move forward. Old instinct edged in, her mouth went dry, and her feet stayed planted at the entry. Levi's hand closed around hers and she shut her eyes. His ability to bridge the ethereal and earthbound remained a strong guiding force. They moved forward together.

Last time, aside from Eli, the house was empty. This time it showed the wear and tear of many owners. The upscale layout remained, though it felt abandoned—dirty floors and banged-up walls, naked curtain rods and empty boxes strewn about—the result of an intense lack of attention or just the fast exit of terrified homeowners? Instead of an angry spirit, Aubrey had the profound sense that the emptiness before her was exactly how Eli Serino had perceived his life—hollow and abandoned. As the thought settled in her head, so did the presence of a specter.

Aubrey looked toward the balcony rail from which Eli had hung himself, bracing for the gory visual. Thankfully, it wasn't there. He'd harbored enough energy to show himself last time, and Aubrey had never gotten the image out of her head—a gruesome glimpse of Eli's earthbound corpse. His ghost had stood by the grand staircase, near the spot in the airy foyer where his body had twisted for nearly a week.

Eli's ghostly account of what had happened was unforgettable: the suicide had been an accident—a cry for help gone wrong. Anticipating his parents' arrival home from Europe, and prepared for a good show, Eli had slipped on the balcony edge. The seventeen-year-old boy ended up executing the act, as opposed to merely scaring the shit out of his parents. Aubrey imagined how it must have haunted the Serinos— Suzanne and Bruno. Had the couple returned on schedule, they might have found their son in time.

Instead, the house phone had rung as Eli twisted. He heard his mother's voice laced with cursory interest as her son gasped, his legs kicking vainly. Eli's mistake. He'd been unaware, until her call, that his parents had extended their European trip. The boy listened as he slipped from life to death, Suzanne conveying the message between her pro skier lesson and hot rock massage.

Aubrey shuddered at the horrific event. Back then, Eli's spirit hadn't been able to escape the house. She suspected the number of owners and waning aura of the Serino family had weakened his tie to the property. She assumed that eventually his earthbound soul had broken free, at least from the house on Acorn Circle. She glanced around the foyer; even so, this was still home to Eli.

"Anything?" Levi's hand was still tight around Aubrey's.

"Uh, yes, actually. Eli is definitely here." The pinging rose on cue, and she smiled. "Look on the bright side; he could have heaved a cur- tain rod at us. Compared to Piper's office or our house, his energy is significantly stronger here."

"And should we take the pinging as a 'he's come in peace' sign?"

"Maybe," she said warily, the hint of sour apple tickling the back of her throat.

"So what now, we take the tour, or—"

"Mmm . . . I'm pretty certain this foyer is Eli's hot spot."

"Can't say I'm sorry to hear that."

Aubrey let go of Levi's hand, but he remained shadow-like, less than a body width away. From her shoulder bag, Aubrey withdrew the two pieces of green construction paper. "Okay, Eli. You've got our attention. How about a little cooperation? What's this all about? I'm listening."

The air was filled with nothing but dust. While the sugary sour apple was slight, Aubrey didn't hear a voice, not even a whisper. At the very least, Eli didn't appear to be on the attack—his sole goal during her last visit. There was an absence of stronger markers—scents and sounds. The lack of finer details, it was part of Eli's message. He did not have a life, but merely existed inside this house.

As she looked toward the living room, framed by massive columns, a wave of sympathy washed over Aubrey—something she'd had a hard time feeling for Eli Serino. The moment true empathy emerged, the wall sconces lit. She and Levi moved toward them.

"At least he's starting with the basics."

"Shh . . . ," Aubrey warned. "Don't spook him."

"You're kidding, right?"

With the green papers in one hand, she tugged on Levi with her other. The turning on or off of lights Levi had witnessed numerous times over the years. Aubrey dumbed it down to Specter Presence 101. Electrical current was the most basic form of communication. But in the dimly lit room, where crooked blinds were drawn, Aubrey perceived it as more of a direction from Eli.

"And so now what?" Levi let go of her hand, taking a turn around the large empty room.

"I'm not sure. He definitely wants us . . . *me* in this space." She took a few steps toward French doors at the opposite end of the square footage. They led to a brighter sunroom. To her right was a swinging door, a small glass window providing a peek into a gourmet-grade kitchen. They'd never made it that far last time they'd toured the property. Whatever specifics Eli wanted to convey, they weren't registering.

"Uh, Aubrey."

She turned. Levi stood about fifteen feet away, having cozied up to the fireplace, the sconces denoting the high and massive mantel where a mirror hung. "I think I found what he wants to point out."

Aubrey hurried to where Levi stood and peered up at the mirror. Written in a heavy layer of dust was the word "Mother."

"Oh my . . ." It was always a stunning sight, any specter's ability to expand outlets of communication. Adding to Eli's presence was the construction paper, which grew hot in her hand.

The two of them stepped back and stared up at the spelled-out word. The mirror was high; reaching it would require a step stool, even for Levi. He shook his head at it.

"The most acute sense of logic wouldn't blame that on vandals or happenstance. It's at least six and a half feet off the floor." He shrugged. "But so what? We know Eli Serino had a bad relationship with his parents. How does finger pointing at his mother mean more than what drove him to suicide?"

"I'm not sure, I—"

As Aubrey spoke, the mirror gave way and fell, crashing to the hardwood floors. On impact, they scooted back, a sea of glass shards at their feet.

"Damn," Levi said, looking at the mess. "How the hell are we supposed to explain that to Dawn?" Sarcasm was doused as the pinging noise rose, so loud and steady, Levi and Aubrey only exchanged a glance of confirmation. "Uh, listen," he said to the room at large. "Sorry about the joke. Just keep calm, Eli. We're not following quite yet, but we'll get there." He pointed to Aubrey. "Okay, she'll get there."

"No! Christ, he's stubborn. It will take the two of you . . . what you need isn't in here . . . finish what you started last time. Go!"

Aubrey jerked up her head, her gaze detaching from the slivers of glass. "Uh, sorry, Levi, but Eli just said your presence is requested too."

"So now he's willing to chat?"

"Seems so." She smiled at Levi, whose sense of humor had dissolved.

"Great. And did he happen to mention a bread-crumb trail we should be following?"

"Nothing so specific. Eli just indicated that we need to 'finish what we started last time.' What do you suppose that means?"

"Last time, we came for the house tour. We never got further than the library and foyer." Levi shrugged. "Maybe Eli's old bedroom?"

He turned for the stairs and crossed through the foyer. At the same time, Aubrey felt a firm tug on her hair.

"Oww!" She grasped the back of her head, and Levi spun back toward her. "I'm guessing upstairs is not the right direction." Rubbing her head, Aubrey hurried back into the foyer. Instinctively, she wrapped her hand around her pockmarked arm. Uninvited touch was a line in the sand; she preferred specters did not cross it. "Last time, the realtor who showed us this house talked a lot about amenities. Where's the listing sheet Dawn gave you?"

Levi pulled the folded square from his pocket.

"There," she said, pointing to a list of items that included a maid's quarters and wine cellar. There was also an asterisk and the words "bonus space."

"Interesting. All those things are on the lower level. But I don't see how you access . . ." Levi took a turn around the foyer and peered down the hall that led to the library. "Maybe the staircase is in the back of the house."

"Tell the ace reporter to think outside the fucking box . . . when they built the damn thing, they thought of everything but me . . ."

Aubrey frowned, nodding.

"What?" Levi said.

"Seems Eli's not impressed with your imagination." Aubrey stepped into the middle of the foyer, her gaze scanning the extensive woodwork, ornate wainscoting, the wall supporting the wide, built-in curve of the staircase. In Levi's defense, she did have to call upon old real estate lessons, the hundreds of houses she'd toured as the *Surrey City Press* home portrait reporter. "Look . . . here." Built into the curve of the staircase was a door, designed to be a seamless part of the molding. "Huh," she said, examining the frame. "No knob."

"But a keyhole," Levi said, spying the small lock. Upon closer examination, they could see it, the frame of a door camouflaged by woodwork. "If I go out and ask Dawn for a key . . ."

"Either she won't have a clue where it is or she'll want to come inside." Aubrey concluded this as Levi pressed forcefully on the door, which didn't budge.

Yet the steady ping persisted, indicating they were on the right track.

"Let me give it a try."

Levi pasted a squirrelly look on Aubrey; the door was quite massive compared to her.

"A little cooperation if you'd like my assistance, Eli." There was nothing to grab on to, the entry one unified piece of architecture. The door remained stationary, and then slowly it began to pivot on a hidden hinge.

Levi stepped back. "I'll be damned." He glanced at Aubrey. "That would have been genius in our master suite addition, separating the bathroom from the dressing area."

She rolled her eyes, huffing at him.

"Right. Not germane to the task at hand. Even so . . ." He paused to run his hand over the clever artisanship.

Aubrey located a light switch, which illuminated a tight metal turned staircase; it mimicked the one that led to the grand house's second story. She stepped forward, and Levi's hand gripped her arm. She turned. His expression was warier than the possibilities of a simple ghost hunt. "Right," she said. "The last time you and I ventured into an unknown basement . . ."

"At the Byrd house." Levi stared into the dark chasm before them.

"That didn't end so well, did it?" Aubrey knew their thoughts were the same, though surely Levi's was more pointed. Desperate, caught, and somewhat crazed, Violet Byrd, Missy Flannigan's killer, had shot him at point-blank range.

Levi swallowed hard. "Sorry. The similarities caught me off guard."

"Six days in ICU, eighty-five percent blood loss." Her gaze moved to his shirt-covered midriff. "Scars you can definitely talk about. It'd give me pause too. But I doubt Eli came equipped with a firearm."

"You're right." He sucked in a deep breath. "I'm being ridiculous." Levi stepped in front of Aubrey, his shoes heavy on the narrow, winding metal.

Following, Aubrey murmured, "Of course, I have no idea what other scare tactics Eli might have at his disposal."

CHAPTER
TWENTY-FOUR

A fast tour of the lower level showed off amenities they'd missed a dozen years before. Empty maid's quarters and two full baths, an in-home theater stripped of everything but electrical wires, a rec room of some sort, a wine cellar, and a spacious laundry room. This was the last room Aubrey and Levi saw, having passed, without incident, through all the other square footage. Even the pinging had grown vague. She took in the expanse of endless cabinetry, fancier than what you'd find in most kitchens.

"Maybe you should have had our architect tour this space." Aubrey took a turn around the room. "I doubt anybody would mind doing laundry in here."

"I'd think the point of *here* is that you can afford for someone else to do your laundry. I doubt Eli's mother—*or father*," Levi corrected before Aubrey could label the remark sexist, "ventured this way too often." He leaned against the folding table that housed a built-in ironing board. "I don't know about you, but seems like our trail has gone—"

"Cold," she said, sensing a drop in temperature. "Do you feel that?"

Levi shook his head, though his relaxed stance suddenly stood pole straight.

"I mean cold as in atmospheric, not ethereal." In Aubrey's mind, there was a distinct difference. "We missed something . . . something detached from everything else down here." Like the tug to her hair, she felt a sharp poke in her back. "Don't touch me!" Aubrey's teeth gritted, annoyed by Eli's continued physical contact. Yet he managed to make his point, directing them to a door at the far end of the laundry room. "The bonus space noted on the listing sheet. We didn't see anything like that."

"There?" Levi pointed to double doors that blended with the cabinetry.

"It'd be my guess." Aubrey was on Levi's heels as he approached the entry. It opened to a deep well of blackness, the light from the laundry room barely filtering in.

"Hang on." Levi fumbled to his left, inside the door, following the trail of electrical fixtures on the laundry room side. "Why is it they never flip a switch when it's basic necessity?"

"Because energy expended in that way is about communication, not your convenience."

"It was rhetor—" Levi stopped dead as he found the switch, a sea of lights illuminating an arena-like space. "Holy . . ."

"Shit," Aubrey said. "What is this?" In front of them was a circular cement floor, railing around the edge. They moved forward, onto a large pad of cement. Levi's fingers gripped around hers.

"Your hand is like ice." He looked around, then down at their feet. "And I'm pretty sure this whole place was once covered in exactly that—ice. An indoor ice rink, that's the bonus space?"

"Looks like it."

"And our chipper realtor didn't mention that because . . ."

Aubrey smiled, recalling the lessons learned from savvy real estate agents. "Because an indoor ice rink is not a perk. Unless your buyer is an NHL player, this is nothing but maintenance and an eyesore."

"So just accentuate the positives."

"I think it's page one in the realtor handbook." Aubrey was drawn away from what motivated realtors to what was motivating Eli Serino. "But an ice rink. How is that part of Eli's message?" She shivered; the space felt like a freezer. As she spoke, Levi inched back, staring at her. "What?"

"I can see your breath, like it's twenty degrees in here."

Aubrey only had to expel one to see it too. When Levi spoke, the same psychic-induced phenomenon was absent. "I'm guessing you're not feeling anything but room temperature?"

He shook his head and removed his jacket; Aubrey gratefully tugged it on.

"I suppose an ice rink makes sense. Connie Beane said Eli's parents bought him a spot at Velocity Skate Club in Sudbury. I assume Suzanne and Bruno's parenting style included indulging Eli in whatever."

"But an entire indoor ice rink?" Levi said. "That's nuts."

"Well, if you're of average means, and you're using possessions to appease, you buy the kid skates."

"And if you're filthy rich, you build him an ice rink." Levi let go of Aubrey's hand and took a larger turn around the space that had to cost hundreds of thousands of dollars. "But how does any of this tie back to Trevor Beane or Liam Sheffield? You're going to call Piper, and say what? 'My eccentric ghost has led me to a giant puzzle piece. Unfortunately, I don't have a clue how it fits'?" On Levi's words, the sound of something falling—or being thrown—echoed through.

"I think you're lucky that wasn't aimed at your head." Aubrey pointed toward what looked like a large cedar door, set rinkside. "That way. Levi, when are you going to learn, acerbic doesn't fly with them."

"I disagree." They traded a glance. "Sometimes I think it's why I was recruited for the job."

Aubrey rolled her eyes, and the two of them crossed through the center of the defunct rink. She pulled Levi's jacket tighter and squinted as they approached the door. "Huh. It looks like . . ."

"A sauna?" Levi clamped a hand around the wooden handle and yanked. The door opened and a light lit automagically. "I think that one is mere mortal wiring." He looked up at the fixture.

"But, oh my God," she said, pointing, "that isn't." In the middle of the planked floor was a black ice skate, the sharp blade thrust with knifelike force into the floorboards. Surrounding it all was a sauna that had been repurposed into a storage room. Makeshift shelving was filled with a locker room's worth of hockey equipment—a plethora of gear: skates, padding, goalie masks, enough hockey sticks for an entire team. And tape: shelves and shelves of green tape. Aside from the X-marks-the-spot skate impaled in the floor, Aubrey was keenly aware of temperature. It was odd to be freezing in a sauna. "Help me out, Eli. I'm still not getting it." Aubrey's teeth chattered, the cold penetrating like she was on an Arctic quest. "How does here get us to those missing boys?"

Levi crouched and pried the skate from its violent pose. "I think we should go." He stood, skate in hand. "The shattered mirror, this skate. Maybe Eli's not chasing you directly. But this is enough for me. It could be this has nothing to do with Trevor or Liam, and Eli's still a ghost with an ax to grind." As he grasped Aubrey's hand, she pulled away. "Be reasonable. Your lips are turning blue! This isn't safe."

"Since when does reason figure into any of this? But that is Eli's message. And the tape, rolls and rolls of it." She pointed to the shelf. "And this!" She took a step forward and plucked a roll of Hubba Bubba Sour Green Apple gum from a display box, the kind you'd find in a convenience store. "Tell me all this is not a direct link, Levi, and something Eli wants us to find. Help me solve this . . ." She put back the gum and drew knotted hands to her mouth, blowing into them. "And we'll get out of here."

He huffed, dropping the skate onto a shelf and taking her hands in his, rubbing. "So this is what, other than a cryptic trail?"

Out of sheer survival instinct, Aubrey drew closer to Levi. He let go of her hands, putting his arms around all of her and rubbing furiously.

"My guess is that Eli's definitely in the market for closure. Last time, I was a conduit for his escape from this house. He's done that. He's got no other reason to pursue a connection with me."

"How can you be so sure?"

She inched back. "Sincerity has a way of making itself known, even with the prickliest of people. You just have to be open to it. Am I right?"

Levi reverted to holding her hands, red and icy cold. He rubbed harder. "Our team effort has always been stronger than our individual ones. No argument there."

"That's good to—" A voice cut into Aubrey's head, dousing the most intimate moment she and Levi had shared in months.

How sweet. If possible, I'd barf. Actually, it'll be good news for the two of you. You're gonna need those dynamic-duo antics. But right now, if you want your road map to those missing kids, pay attention. It's not that complicated . . . consider the construction . . . *all* construction . . .*"

Aubrey let go of Levi's hands. "'Consider the *construction* . . .'? That's what Eli just said."

"Consider the construction." Levi absorbed the immediate sight lines, top to bottom. He even dropped onto his knees, running his fingertips along the edges of the floorboards.

"What are you looking for?"

Satisfied or just frustrated, he stood. "I don't know. 'Consider the construction . . .' It's like the case you solved for Piper. Lily North. Her captor held her hostage in a barn cellar, the trapdoor. It made me think of that old Edsel, how you drew it."

"And how do think that relates to this?" Aubrey's brow furrowed at Levi's dead-stop pause.

"Edith Pope, the kidnapper's mother. The reason you finally got the information that led Piper to Lily North was because of Errol Pope's dead mother. She's the one who conveyed Lily's whereabouts."

"Led me to . . . or compelled me to draw that car, underlining it like a madwoman until I put it together, until they found Lily."

"So if a son's mother was so willing to rat him out in the afterlife to save a little girl . . ."

"Maybe a mother's son is doing the same thing now."

"A mother who, according to Zeke, couldn't deal with the loss of Eli."

Aubrey and Levi traded a telling glance. "My God, Levi, if they built an entire casino to appease Eli's mother . . ."

"Imagine how far Suzanne Serino, a woman with money and means, might go to appease herself."

Aubrey's bag slid from her shoulder, and Levi retrieved Peter Ellis's ghost gifts.

"Okay, but what do a childlike sketch of Santa Claus, some mountains, and the commonly named town of Springfield have to do with this defunct ice rink and two missing boys?"

Aubrey took one piece of paper from Levi, its warmth hyper-obvious in the cold that surrounded her. "Oh, Levi . . ." She held up the paper. *"Construction."*

"Construction, as in paper, but also like a property—housing developments!" He handed Aubrey the other paper and pulled his phone from his pocket. The reporter went to work, pursuing a fluid Google search. "Here. Look." He turned the phone toward her. The screen showed off the image of an upscale desert housing location, hardly the stuff of jolly old elves and Christmas holidays. "Santa Claus, Arizona."

"And that's what, besides an oxymoron?" But as Aubrey spoke and Levi followed the trail, the cold she felt began to dissipate. Her breath was still visible, but the air temperature rose, her ears going from numb to burning. She pulled out her own phone and googled the same location. "According to this, Santa Claus, Arizona, is the textbook description—no pun intended—of a ghost town."

Levi looked at a different screen, one that showed off a luxury gated entrance. "Wikipedia needs to catch up. The Serinos bought the surrounding acreage. I came across it doing general research on Jude Serino. They revitalized a chunk of Santa Claus and turned it into a slice of desert paradise . . . golf course, self-contained community amenities, and luxury properties. Getaways and vacation homes for the ultra-rich."

Aubrey peered from her phone to his, which displayed a startlingly different point of view. "Levi, this house, the one we're standing in. It's also part of the Serino developments, right?"

"Right. I think Acorn Circle was their first foray into residential housing."

"Where was the second?"

Levi pursued another Google search. "Holy shit. I almost can't believe it took Eli Serino's ghost to put this together. Would you believe Springfield, Pennsylvania?"

"You don't think . . ."

He exited the repurposed sauna, his gaze gliding over the dilapidated ice rink. "I'd say once you've built one indoor custom ice rink, it's probably not that hard to duplicate. I'd be very curious to know if this setup exists anywhere in Santa Claus, Arizona, or Springfield, Pennsylvania."

The temperature continued to rise, as did the pinging noise—almost a bell of acknowledgment. They had the right answer. Aubrey walked back through the rink, feeling the heavy cloak of a sad life begin to lift. Midway, she shuffled a few steps in front of Levi and turned back, looking at him. "Thanks for staying. And thanks to Eli, I think we may have our road map to those boys."

CHAPTER
TWENTY-FIVE

Hyannis, Massachusetts

Aubrey, Levi, and Piper stood in the living room of a grand seaside home, walls of glass showing off multimillion-dollar views of Lewis Bay. It was a rental property but upscale enough to suit the high-end tastes of Bruno and Suzanne Serino. "Just, um . . . still just the three of us?" Levi asked. Aubrey nodded.

Eli Serino's presence had faded in the house on Acorn Circle and it had not returned. Not even after they'd arrived at Piper's office, conveying the unusual details of their morning adventure. Naturally, Piper did not argue Aubrey's conjecture about an irate ghost indicating the whereabouts of two missing boys. Nor did she question the part where Peter Ellis's ghost gifts played a role in the mystery—old predictions providing timely clues. What took time was linking ethereal clues to earthbound ones involving Suzanne Serino. But Piper had succeeded in persuading a federal judge to issue a search warrant for several Serino properties, including their temporary Cape Cod residence.

Admittedly, Aubrey was as curious as Levi to see how it would all play out. She didn't trust Eli, concerned that his silence simply meant he was lying in wait. Perhaps his Acorn Circle cooperation was Eli misdirecting energy. It could be she was no more than Eli's pawn at this point, an efficient route to revenge. Looking at the glass surround of the room, Aubrey recalled a shattered French door from years ago, the mirror Eli smashed only yesterday, a skate plunged like a knife into floorboards. Clearly, he had a quick temper, ample energy, and a penchant for sharp objects. She remained leery of what a conversation with Eli's parents might produce. As they waited, she inhaled deeply, not comforted by the scents of breezy salt air and thorough housekeeping.

Twenty minutes passed, and Aubrey assumed the delay might have something to do with the household staff that had answered the door. The woman's first language was Portuguese, making it difficult for Piper to convey her purpose—that she wanted to speak with Suzanne Serino.

Finally, a well-dressed, flaxen-haired woman entered the great room. She appeared regal and poised, her presence striking Aubrey as staged in both wardrobe and demeanor. The woman stretched out a slender arm, decorated in several diamond bracelets; at the end of it, an elegantly boned hand curled into a shaky fist. It dropped as if the intended handshake now eluded her. "My apologies," she said. "Marina's English isn't very American. We haven't had guests since moving in—I do so enjoy fall in New England. I, um . . . I needed to dress."

"That's all right," Piper said. "We didn't mind waiting . . . Mrs. Serino?"

The woman ran her fingers nervously over her long throat. She was tall, taller than Aubrey, an unusual thing in her experience. She smiled at Piper, an equally anxious gesture.

"That and I don't know whether to be fearful or hopeful that Marina misunderstood. She said you're with the government, a task force involved with missing children."

"That's right. I'm Deputy Chief Piper Sullivan. I work in conjunction with the Center for Missing and Exploited Children. This is Aubrey Ellis, Levi St John. They're, um . . . they're assisting me on cases involving two missing boys."

"So you have come about my son!" Suzanne's attitude veered, going from uneasy to expectant, and Piper glanced at Aubrey and Levi. Suzanne came farther into the room, her fingers flitting over her mouth. "Tell me, please, is it good news?"

"About your son?" Piper said carefully.

"Yes. Of course about my son. It's been ages since we've heard anything positive. Anything at all, really." Her chin quivered, jarring her smile. "But I haven't given up on Eli. He was always so determined. He can be quite tenacious."

"No argument from me," Aubrey murmured.

"Mrs. Serino," Piper said loudly. "You said you haven't 'given up'? What does that mean?"

"It means that once we're all reunited, Eli will get a second chance. We'll *all* get a second chance. I've been dedicated to practicing." She glanced over her shoulder, then pressed a finger to her lips. "That part's a surprise. Bruno prefers not to discuss our life after Eli returns. But I know he'll be pleased too. How could he not?"

"Pleased about . . . ?" Piper asked.

"Pleased that I'll be prepared when Eli returns home. Not everyone gets a second chance with their child. Do you know what I mean, Deputy Chief?"

The remark seemed to fluster Piper, the clip of conversation not only confusing but suddenly personal. Aubrey interjected. "Mrs. Serino . . ." She took a step toward the woman, Levi following. "How is it you've been practicing on being a better mother to Eli?"

Her expression muddled, like it was an absurd question. "I've read all the books on parenting—old ones and the newest titles. *Uncommon Sense for Parents with Teenagers, When Good Kids Do Bad Things, Raising Your Wayward Teen* . . ."

Levi leaned in, whispering, "Maybe she means *Resurrecting Your Wayward Teen*." Aubrey elbowed him.

Suzanne continued to prattle on. "Why, I've all but memorized them cover to cover. I see now where Bruno . . . but especially me, where I went so wrong the first time."

"Really?" Aubrey said. "Parenting. That's a topic with endless resources."

"To a point." Suzanne Serino smiled, then didn't. "After I felt ready, I moved on from the books. Of course, I'm still doing everything Dr. Klaussner recommends, but sometimes you just have to . . . fly on your own." Her subtle smile returned. "I've learned so much."

"Have you?" Aubrey said.

Suzanne inched closer, outwardly pleased to have an interested bystander. "Yes. I've been working on being precisely the kind of mother Eli deserved years ago. My son will be so proud of me."

"Mrs. Serino, I'm sorry," Piper said, drawing closer. "But I'm confused. These missing boys may relate to your son, but as for Eli, he's been—"

"Waiting for just this moment." Aubrey snatched the flow of dialogue, shooting Piper a shushing glance. "Could you tell us a little more? How is it you hope to . . ." A man appeared in the great room entry.

"Hope." The word echoed, commanding Suzanne's attention. She turned. "Hope is what my wife hangs on to." He strode forward and placed his hand on her shoulder. "Marina said you had visitors, darling. Seems we'll have to review the house rules with her again." He offered a stiff nod to the group. "Language barrier and new help; it's difficult." Suzanne stared at him, her face a combination of vagueness and need. "I'm Bruno Serino. Something I can help you with?"

Piper went another round, stating who they were and that they wanted to speak with Suzanne regarding the whereabouts of two missing boys. Bruno never left the plane of smooth talking, calmly asking, "Wait one moment," and calling for Marina. They stood in silence until the woman who answered the door turned up in the great room.

"Marina, would you take Mrs. Serino back to the solarium? Later, you and I will discuss the rules about visitors." Marina glanced back worriedly while taking Suzanne by the arm.

"But Bruno," she said, not quite willing to be led away. "Our guests. They say they have news about Eli."

He approached his wife, gently taking her hand in his. "And I'm going to find out anything they have to tell us. But remember, stress isn't good for you. Dr. Klaussner would be disappointed to learn you deviated from the program." Anxiousness faded to dutifulness, and Suzanne exited.

Piper didn't demand the subject of her inquiry stay put, and Aubrey assumed it meant she had a plan B. Impatience was a default setting when Piper felt close to solving a case—the driving hope of getting a child back alive—and the deputy chief got right to her point. "Mr. Serino, I'm going to go out on a limb here and suggest Mrs. Serino is not . . ." Having steamrolled into the thought, Piper aimed for a gentler landing. *"Well,"* she said softly.

"I take it you spoke with Suzanne long enough to realize her reality and actual reality aren't quite parallel."

It was Levi who stepped into the conversation. "Your wife believes your son to be missing, as opposed to deceased. She indicated—"

Bruno held up a hand. "Suzanne's emotional state has deteriorated over the years. In fact, I returned early from a business trip abroad because Marina became concerned about Suzanne. I don't know if you're aware of how our son passed—"

"Very," Levi said. "I covered the story years ago for the *Hartford Standard Speaker*." He hesitated. "I, um . . . I'm sorry for your loss."

Bruno narrowed his eyes. "Then I suppose you all know the grisly details, including how the press crucified Suzanne and myself for Eli's suicide."

It would not be in Levi's wheelhouse to pull punches. "I'm aware that your jet-setting lifestyle was called into question."

"Jet-setting . . . perhaps for my wife. I assure you, my focus was business. Either way, no worries, Mr. St John. While the law couldn't pursue charges, fate has seen to comeuppance. After the initial shock of losing a child, Suzanne's been subject to years of guilt. First the authorities, then the press. It grew worse when friends abandoned Suzanne at her most vulnerable. Yet without a doubt, it's self-inflicted culpability that's been most traumatic, wreaked havoc with Suzanne's mind. Her perceptions. They've spiraled steadily, deteriorated until . . . well, until it resulted in what you just witnessed."

"Would you mind clarifying?" Piper asked. "What, exactly, it is we witnessed?"

"A woman who can't distinguish reality from fantasy."

"You're going to have to elaborate, Mr. Serino," Piper said. "The lives of two boys may very well depend on it."

"I'm sorry, Deputy Chief . . . Sullivan, was it?"

She nodded.

"You mistook my housekeeper's faux pas as an invitation. I've no desire to further discuss my wife's illness or my son's death with you. I've already said more than I care to about Eli. If you don't mind . . ." He pointed toward the massive entry.

From the inside jacket of her suit, Piper produced a warrant, dropping it on the coffee table. "On the contrary, Mr. Serino. We have a court-ordered right to be here, search the place if we like. Yesterday, I amassed enough suspicion regarding your wife's behavior and unusual travel pattern in the last six months—numerous flights between Philadelphia and Laughlin International Airport, near Santa Claus, Arizona."

"I didn't realize interstate travel was illegal."

"No. But the purchase of a firearm by a known mentally ill person is."

"That's absurd. Suzanne doesn't own a firearm. You're mistaken . . . or—"

"We'll get back to it, Mr. Serino. But also know we have a receipt from an Enterprise car rental. It's billed to your wife's credit card, a franchise located one block away from a Glenmore, Pennsylvania, ice rink where a boy went missing. Trust me. It was all the judge needed to hear. Question is, would you like to hear this in your living room or the Boston agency office? I assure you, Suzanne will not appreciate the amenities. It's up to you."

After a moment, Bruno pointed to the high-end furnishings, his teeth slightly gritted. "Would you all care to sit?"

◆ ◆ ◆

Levi did the majority of the talking, Aubrey detecting a weave of sub-conscious thoughts between him and Piper. Bruno Serino was already on the defense; chances were he'd respond better to a man. Clearly, Piper didn't like it. But if it got them to those boys, she was willing to give Levi the reins. It began with a brick-by-brick inquiry, navigating deftly. Before long, in reply, Bruno Serino painted a detailed portrait of his wife's condition.

According to him, her psychosis had begun with small pockets of delusions that manifested into wider spans of neurosis. Suzanne Serino's mind-set had spread from a puddle of grief into a sea that had swallowed her.

The year after Eli's death, Bruno attempted to combat depression and guilt with trips abroad, an exotic extension of her jet-setting life. "I tried to put more substance into our itinerary, hoping Suzanne would find solace in more inspired, soul-searching destinations."

"Did you also buy her a copy of *Eat, Pray, Love* to read on the planes?" Piper said under her breath.

"Touché, Deputy Chief. Not long into our travels . . . India . . . the Far East, it became apparent our lifestyle was doing Suzanne more harm than good. Eventually, we returned to Surrey, our house."

"The one on Acorn Circle," Aubrey said.

"You know it?"

"Quite well. And how did that go?" A soft pinging rose, and she saw Levi's alerted gaze. Eli's father and Piper appeared oblivious to the sound.

Bruno Serino sat heavily, his line of vision on a well-stocked bar. "Unfortunately, the house proved more debilitating than our travels."

"How so?" Levi asked.

"I, um . . ." Bruno averted his glance to the Oriental rug beneath his feet. "This is going to sound ludicrous, but . . ." He looked up. "According to Suzanne, the house was . . . *haunted.*"

"Really?" Levi said as if he'd never encountered the word. "Can you elaborate?"

"At first it was solely Suzanne's perceptions. My work requires extensive travel. I'm very dedicated to Serino Enterprises. My wife's claims began with hysterical phone calls about lights blowing out when she'd flip a switch to more pronounced things, like books and bric-a-brac flying off shelves; the slamming of Eli's bedroom door became a nightly occurrence. Once, she sat at the dining room table and innocently picked up her wineglass. She insisted it shattered in her hand, of its own volition. I found that incident particularly disturbing."

"And why's that?" Levi asked.

"Because she ended up with eight stitches in her hand. I found it remarkable that Suzanne would self-inflict pain to such an extent. Aside from that, she spoke continuously about noises coming from the lower level—"

"Tell us more about that, Mr. Serino, the lower level." As Aubrey inquired, the pinging noise grew more acute. Still, neither Piper nor Bruno appeared aware.

"We'd built a custom indoor ice rink for Eli. The boy went through hobbies like the chewing gum we provided by the case. But this hobby seemed to stick. He was obsessed, even if he wasn't terribly good. We thought the rink would keep him occupied, out of trouble."

"More like out of your way, Dad . . ."

Aubrey cued to the voice, bracing for Eli's presence to produce more than words.

Bruno shifted in his seat. "Once Eli was *gone*, we had the floor drained, shut the rink down. I was determined to move on. Suzanne . . ." He brushed an arm through the air in front of him. "She couldn't. She called while I was on a trip to Amsterdam, insisting there was something wrong with the heat. The house, according to her, was freezing. Particularly curious, being as it was early June."

"New England weather can be wildly unpredictable," Piper said, her Southern twang seeming to agree.

"Precisely what I told her," Bruno said, nodding. "Suzanne went to the basement, intending to go to the furnace room. Instead, she ended up in the ice rink. She, um . . . she was startled to find the water system turned on, the floor refilling."

"And this couldn't be attributed to a mechanical malfunction?" Levi asked.

"Perhaps." Bruno's glance evaded his visitors. "But this disruption to my business trip . . . it was the fifth call; the fifth time Suzanne had made such a claim."

Aubrey bobbed her head in a subtle gesture; the tale did not come as a surprise.

"I blamed all the wild stories, the *crazy* incidents on Suzanne's state of mind. That's rational, right? I assumed, in Suzanne's declining mental state, that she was probably responsible . . . like the shattered wineglass. When I was home, nothing so bizarre occurred. Eventually, there was only one reasonable solution to our housing situation."

"And that was to move," Levi said.

"Yes." He closed his hands into tight fists. "My reassurances weren't helping; Suzanne was slipping further and further from reality. I was done reasoning with her, insisting she was enabling her own delusions with these *ghost stories*. At dinner one night, I made an announcement, I told her I'd put the house on the market."

"Oh, I bet that went over well." Aubrey was hardly thinking of Suzanne Serino's reaction.

"Excuse me?" Bruno said.

"Tell me something, Mr. Serino," she said. "You never believed the things Suzanne experienced in the house? You thought it was all her imagination, or more precisely, a symptom of her psychosis?"

His fisted hands slid into a twisted knot.

"It will sound ridiculous if I tell you."

"Try me," Aubrey said. "I love a good ghost story."

Bruno made eye contact with Aubrey. "It was, um . . . it was my last morning in the house; I was alone. I spent time in Eli's room. I talked to him." Bruno shrugged. "The way anyone might speak to someone who'd passed—just to the air, really. You know?"

Aubrey asked, "And what did you tell the air?"

"I said we had to go—that for Eli's mother's sanity, we needed to move. Perhaps, in hindsight, I was harsh with my words. But it's not as if . . ."

"As if what?"

"As if Eli was actually listening."

"You don't think so?" Aubrey said.

"Well, of course I didn't . . ." He seemed to retreat from his defense. "Not at that point. I was speaking symbolically—to an empty room." He hesitated. "But I did challenge Eli, ask him if his suicide wasn't enough. What more did he want? I was angry. His death, it was so . . . unnecessary. My God, you can't begin to imagine what it was like that day, to come home from an exhausting trip to find your son . . ." Bruno lurched from the chair, his fist thudding into the fireplace mantel. "The boy could have had the world."

"All I wanted was you . . ."

277

A hum rang from Aubrey's throat; it carried a sound of empathy for Eli.

"I said no son would want this for his mother—her ongoing suffering." Bruno scraped a hand over his face, blinking at the spent ashes in the hearth. "But I did tell him that he was no longer a part of our lives."

"I was never a part of your life. You ask him, lady . . . ask him what else he said . . ."

In a room of common people, common sense would say to end it there. Whatever blame belonged to Bruno Serino, his torment was palpable. But this was not a room of common people, and a fast tug to Aubrey's hair was a curt reminder. "Damn it," she hissed, grabbing her head. While Levi and Piper offered wary glances, Eli's father was too lost in his memories to notice.

"Fuck him. Distraught isn't accountability. Make my father tell you what he said!"

"Mr. Serino, is that all? Did you offer anything else, maybe parting words as you left Eli's bedroom that day?"

He looked at Aubrey as if she could see into his head. A shame-filled confession dragged from his mouth, perhaps a burden he'd been carrying like a sack of rocks. "I, um . . . I said I wished Eli had never been born." Still poised by the fireplace, he looked at a photo of Eli that seemed to look back. "Then I moved on. I threw some odds and ends, spare hockey paraphernalia . . . bubble gum Eli chewed constantly, a knit cap he wore, into a box and sealed it. Then I went to the master bath to take a shower."

"And that was it?" Aubrey tilted her head at him.

"Not exactly." Bruno pressed a closed fist to his mouth. "When, um . . . when I got out of the shower, I reached for my robe. As I put it on, I looked into the bathroom mirror. In the steam was a date—'June 29.'" His cold gaze was racked with disbelief. "June twenty-ninth was Eli's birthday." He pursed his lips. "Below the date were the words 'Sorry. Still here.'"

Piper hummed under her breath. "After that, I guess you didn't waste any time packing."

"After that, I did everything I could to preserve what was left of my wife's sanity. You can't imagine the horror . . . realization of seeing something like that. I mean, who would believe such a thing?"

Aubrey raised her brow. "Who indeed." She found him undeserving of validation; Eli's presence was not about offering closure. Her attention was drawn away from the people in the great room. Eli was the strongest entity, and Aubrey felt the anger that drove him transform into simple sadness.

"Your wife's sanity," Piper said. "It brings me to the point of our visit today. That warrant, Mr. Serino." She pointed to the document. "We have reason to believe that Suzanne is involved in the disappearance of two boys."

He shook his head. "That's absurd. My wife is under a doctor's care. She barely functions."

"Let's clarify that," Levi said. "Barely functions outside her obsession, which is to get her son back. To be prepared when he arrives. Would that be more on point?"

"What point? Suzanne can put all the energy she likes into the prospect, but unless you know of a way to raise the dead . . ."

"You might be surprised."

In reply, Bruno shot a queer look at Aubrey.

"Nevertheless, would it be fair to say Suzanne's focus has gone from mourning your son to anticipating his return?" Piper said.

Bruno looked at the warrant on the glass coffee table. "Her care is well documented, along with her progressive psychosis. A few years ago, she started working with a Dr. Klaussner. He's based in Switzerland, but he's an expert with this sort of trauma and mental breakdown. Between medication and treatment, it's our hope that Suzanne will reconnect with reality."

"What is his treatment based on?" Aubrey leaned forward, listening harder. "You couldn't find a doctor in the States to treat her?"

"We tried stateside psychiatrists. Dr. Klaussner's methods are . . . *unconventional.* It has more to do with altering the brain's wiring than it does grief counseling, which after so many years didn't seem to be helping. Dr. Klaussner believes that molding from within the fantasy is the way to break the cycle."

"Molding from within?" Piper said. "What does that mean?"

"His treatment, medications, they target deep brain therapy. It's about rewiring how Suzanne perceived life when Eli was alive. It's Dr. Klaussner's assertion that not only was Eli's manner of death haunting her, but it's the ongoing psychological trauma. It's Suzanne's perceptions about herself as a mother." He cleared his throat. "That perhaps she wasn't a very good one."

"So kind of like . . . *blame?*" Levi and his suggestion, again, met with Aubrey's elbow.

"It would be a lot for me to explain to a nonprofessional, anyone who isn't familiar with Dr. Klaussner's methods. Given permission from me, I'm sure he'd be willing to have a conversation with you. But I'm certain you're mistaken about any handgun, and I still don't understand why you're—"

"Mr. Serino," Piper said. "Take this as a nonprofessional hypothesis, but part of the doc's treatment, would that include allowing Suzanne a do-over on motherhood, whereby she possibly reinvents the past?"

"In layman's terms, that would be part of the process. A reenvisioning of life events is the preferred terminology. He feels strongly his treatment will eventually reverse her perceptions."

Aubrey heard laughter. *"Yeah, right. For that to work, I'd need different parents . . . Mom never gave a damn about anything but her next vacation, and you never gave a damn about anything but work . . ."*

"And this cutting-edge treatment, how's that been working?" Levi asked.

Bruno glanced past the inquiring group and toward the seaside view. "I'm due for a report this week. I've been busier than usual with Serino Enterprises, out of the country a great deal."

"Even so, surely you've monitored your unstable wife for safety—if not hers, other people's."

"Suzanne is not a threat to anyone. And you don't understand the demands of my position. My older brother, Jude, he's been on sabbatical. That increases my responsibilities tenfold. Jude's been out of touch for more than a month. Suzanne's condition is not new, and I have to prioritize."

"Even if that's the case, you couldn't have employed an entire entourage to oversee her care?" Levi said.

"It's unnecessary, regardless of what you may think. I prefer not to draw attention to my wife's mental state. How would that look for Serino Enterprises?" He huffed at the seaside view and looked back at Levi. "As it is, I believe I've seen signs of improvement. Suzanne's disposition has gone from permanent melancholy to, as she said . . . *hopeful.*"

"And when did you notice this change in behavior?" Piper asked.

He thought for a moment, as if trying to recall what he ate for breakfast last Saturday. "Around the time Suzanne started to divide her time between residences. She seemed to find hope while staying at a Springfield, Pennsylvania, property."

"This is a Serino residential development?" Piper's tone sharpened.

"Yes. One of several Serino Enterprises owns. It's been one of our most profitable. I feel sure it's a sign; Suzanne's truly turned a corner since taking such a keen interest in our housing developments. It's the most stable behavior I've seen from her in years."

"Mr. Serino, you're not lis—"

He cut Piper off. "No. You're not listening. In each community, there's an exquisitely decorated model home. Decorating is something Suzanne once had a passion for. Naturally, I encouraged her to get more involved. With that property, any of them, really."

"And so you supplied her with a *playhouse* in Springfield?"

"I don't see the problem. Admittedly, I found it curious she didn't have a greater desire to winter at our Florida complex. We have a gated community there as well. But Suzanne insisted on the Springfield development, especially after we discussed . . ."

"After you discussed what?" Levi asked.

"This will sound indulgent to an outsider, but Dr. Klaussner insists on supporting emotional health with tangible treatment when possible. Things that encourage Suzanne's positive parental imagery."

"Meaning what specifically—in terms of the Springfield property?" Piper said.

He hesitated. "Suzanne wanted an ice rink installed on the lower level of the house, like the one on Acorn Circle. That wouldn't be possible in Florida."

"No basements," Aubrey said.

He shook his head. "Sound mind has been in short supply regarding my wife, but money isn't. So I—"

"Indulged her," Levi said. "Just like you did your son."

Bruno narrowed his eyes. "I followed her doctor's advice."

"And after you built this mind-numbing ice rink," Piper said. "Where did you spend most of last winter?"

"As noted, I travel a great deal, Miss Sullivan."

"Deputy Chief," she corrected, the two trading irritated stares. "And your wife was left to her own devices during these periods?"

"Certainly not." He pointed in the direction Marina and Suzanne had gone. "As you saw, we have help. Granted, Suzanne goes through a good many companions. She can be difficult; she doesn't perceive herself as ill."

"Funny thing about crazy people," Piper said. "They're always the last to know."

He ignored the remark. "I was sure that eventually we'd hit on the right personality combination of caregiver . . . companion."

"So this rotation of hired help, they're not medically qualified, and they see to a variety of duties?" Levi said. "Someone who, in addition to overseeing your wife's medical state, tends to menial tasks like watering plants and changing bed linens?"

"It was an appropriate compromise. It's not as if Suzanne is a danger to anyone."

"You don't think so?" Piper scooted to the edge of her seat, her frame tensing. "Let me run a little scenario by you. After last winter and the Springfield property, I'm guessing Suzanne wanted to relocate again. This time to the Serino development in Santa Claus, Arizona."

"How do you know—"

"How *don't* you know!" Piper snapped.

"I don't understand. What are you talking about?"

Piper looked at Levi and Aubrey. "I've heard enough. Let me get Keystone and Grand Canyon State warrants moving." She stood, shaking her head at Bruno Serino. "It's amazing."

"What's amazing?"

"That you could make graver mistakes with your wife than your son." Piper left the room, making a call on her cell phone as she went.

Levi pointed to the chair. "You might want to sit again. And you'd better pray that Suzanne's eccentricities don't go beyond kidnapping."

"Kidnapping? What the hell are you talking about?"

From there Aubrey and Levi went on to explain about Trevor Beane and Liam Sheffield. When Aubrey suggested that their Santa Claus, Arizona, property also contained an ice rink, Bruno Serino sneered at the idea. Then he made a phone call to the property manager of the elite gated community. "I see," he said after listening for a few moments, then abruptly ended the call.

"And what did you learn?" Levi said.

"It, um . . . according to the property overseer, Rudy Gale, amid the standard swimming pools and tennis courts, an ice rink was installed several months ago." He dropped his phone into his lap, gripping his finger around the arm of his wingback chair. "Dear God, she's completely mad."

"And you've been completely oblivious." Levi rose from his chair.

"You don't understand. The demands of my position are arduous. The travel alone is almost constant." He was quiet for a moment, his gaze slowly moving back to Levi. "Two boys. You really believe Suzanne abducted two boys? For what? Why would she do such a thing?"

"My guess," Aubrey said, "is she's *reenvisioning* the past—especially after she was given a road map, encouragement, and permission from her doctor and husband."

Bruno's jaw slacked, but he had no rebuttal.

"Suzanne told us she's been practicing. Those were her words, Mr. Serino. Your wife's sole mission for the past year has been about preparing to be a better mother to Eli—when he comes home."

"But Eli, he's never coming home."

"I wouldn't be so sure about that either." Aubrey left the room, leaving Bruno Serino with nothing but the perplexed look on his face.

CHAPTER
TWENTY-SIX

Several hours later, Aubrey, Levi, and Piper stood in a tight circle outside the Hyannis seaside rental. A swarm of agents had descended on the interior. With her phone gripped tight to her ear, Piper nodded and replied with what sounded like positive information. "Right. Will do. As soon as we get her processed, questioned, I'll be on a flight."

"Well?" Aubrey said as she ended the call.

"That was my counterpart in DC. He coordinated team efforts that simultaneously breached the Santa Claus and Springfield properties. They found both boys—safe! Scared, sealed into ice-rink tombs, but safe."

"Oh, thank God." Aubrey closed her eyes. She could appreciate but, thankfully, could not conceive of the terror Trevor's and Liam's parents had lived with in recent months. As always, there was tremendous relief in not having failed in her efforts to locate a missing child.

"That's good news," Levi said. "How did Suzanne manage it, kidnapping the boys in the first place?"

"I only have preliminary findings," Piper said, "but according to a statement obtained from Trevor Beane, the older boy, Suzanne approached him as he came out of the ice rink where he worked. He'd closed up that night. Nobody else was around. A middle-aged woman who claimed car trouble didn't seem like a threat to him. Once he got in her car to try the engine, apparently, he felt a sharp stick to his neck."

"She drugged him," Levi said.

"Apparently, Dr. Klaussner passes out sedatives like whiskey shots," Piper replied. "Next thing the boy knew, he woke up in a dark garage, his mouth and hands bound with—"

"Green hockey tape," Aubrey said.

Piper nodded. "Here's the kicker. While delusional enough to pursue her fantasy, Suzanne had enough of a grip on reality to know she'd need assistance."

"The handgun," Levi said.

"Correct. It's how she maintained Trevor's cooperation—likely Liam's too. Then she sealed them into their ice-rink prisons."

Aubrey's fingers rose to her mouth. "Those poor boys. They could have frozen to death."

"Actually," Piper said, "they were *thoughtful* prisons. According to my DC counterpart, the rinks had adjoining interior rooms—dormlike setups, mattresses, toilets, food supplies. Junk food—"

"I suspect all Eli's favorites," Levi said, and Piper nodded.

Aubrey touched his arm. "Including sour green apple bubble gum."

Piper inched back. "DC did mention cartons of Hubba Bubba Sour Green Apple found at both locations. How did you know . . . ?"

"That gum, the flavor, it's the only taste I'd been associating with Eli."

"The things teenage boys will find appetizing. Most importantly, Aubrey, thanks to you, we can add two more kids to the win column. You should feel good about it."

"So should Eli," she said.

"To a point." Half a smile rode Levi's face. "Without a channel, a conduit, ghostly information would be nothing but static."

"It's a fifty-fifty deal," she said. "If Eli hadn't come forward . . . if not for my father's ghost gifts . . ."

Piper finished their thought. "Who knows how long Suzanne would have continued to *reenvision* motherhood."

"No argument there," Levi said. "Knowing their purpose, I imagine Suzanne's newer ice rinks were even more fortress-like than the one in Surrey. And that one had no egress, no daylight."

"I don't even want to speculate on what she might have done if she realized the hitch in her plan, that her son is never coming back," Piper said.

"Makes me kind of long for newspaper days. All of it is one hell of a headline." Levi sighed, shaking his head. "So the boys, they'll be okay?"

"From the short report I got, seems positive. I'm sure there'll be residual issues." She blinked, the lump in her throat almost visible. "Hell, they're alive. It's a better ending than a lot of parents get. I understand Connie Beane is grateful beyond measure." Piper turned and headed toward a female officer, who led a bewildered and handcuffed Suzanne Serino from the house.

"What will happen to her?" Aubrey said.

"Depends." Levi shrugged. "Charges . . . punishment, I'm sure it will hinge on a sound mental evaluation. The real shame here is that beyond blind indulgence, being obsessed with his business, Bruno Serino's committed no crime. None that would let Piper slap some handcuffs on him."

Aubrey watched the government vehicle drive away. "Not unless flagrant disregard for your personal life has become part of the penal code."

Levi looked at Aubrey. "What about Eli? I heard pinging again, while Serino was spinning his story."

"It's interesting. When we were at the Acorn Circle property, Eli's presence was intense . . . vibrant. He was here too, but his mission no longer seemed to be about retribution. He wasn't there because of his parents."

"After all those years of pent-up anger? I half . . . no. I fully expected that glass sculpture on the mantel to come flying across the room."

"In the past, definitely. But as traumatized as Eli was by his parents' neglect, the awful things his own father said to him, this wasn't about retribution. Eli's overall purpose was about finding those boys—which we did."

"And so Eli is now . . . ?"

Aubrey turned in a tight circle, as if she might find the boy standing behind her. "Oddly absent, particularly after Piper left the room to issue those warrants."

"Maybe it's what you said. None of Eli's communication was about closure."

"Possibly. Maybe it was just about doing the right thing."

"Well, it'd be a new trick for that old ghost."

Their focus diverted as Bruno Serino came outside. He seemed oblivious to Levi and Aubrey, walking past without a word.

"Mr. Serino . . . Bruno," Levi called out. Then he said more quietly to Aubrey, "We do have a Serino in our midst. I can't do Dan's job, but maybe we can get a lead out of him. Maybe he can help solve a second mystery."

"Your John Doe," Aubrey said.

Begrudgingly, Bruno stopped and pivoted. "What is it? I don't want to be too far behind Suzanne." He looked at his watch. "As it is, I suspect I'll need to cancel the day's appointments."

"I had one more question. Your brother, Jude."

"What about him?"

"During our conversation, you mentioned he was on sabbatical. When was the last time you spoke with him?"

Bruno shook his head. "Weeks . . . perhaps a month. While we both anticipate our annual break from business, it does increase the workload—the perks and responsibilities of running a family-owned enterprise." He sniffed the sea air. "My trip was to begin when Jude returns. I assume that won't be happening now."

"Yeah. Sorry about your travel plans," Levi said. "But here's what I'd like to know: Is it unusual for you to have zero communication with your brother while he's away?"

"It would be more unusual for me to converse with him during sabbatical. It's the purpose, Mr. St John—to disconnect, reenergize. As I've failed to make clear to you, Serino Enterprises can be exhausting. Is there a point to this curious shift in inquisition? Your presence has made for such a splendid day so far."

Levi hesitated. "No. Not yet. But an Agent Watney is trying to get in touch regard—"

He waved a dismissive hand at Levi. "Yes, yes . . . I received a voice mail from someone by that name. I'll get back to him eventually." He walked away before Levi could interject another word.

Aubrey took a step in Bruno's direction and Levi grabbed her arm. "Let him go. We don't have any legal standing, and Bruno's not going to cooperate with us. I don't want to interfere in Dan's investigation; he'll catch up with him."

◆ ◆ ◆

A short time later, Aubrey and Levi were on their way back to Surrey. Sitting in the passenger seat, she held the two pieces of green construction paper, now room temperature. Piper hadn't taken possession of them. The firearm, Suzanne's travel history, rental car receipt, the boys' testimony—prosecution would rely on those tangibles. Ghost gifts wouldn't be the sort of evidence to find its way into a courtroom.

"Kind of amazing, isn't it? Seeing how something my father wrote down years ago played out today."

"Kind of?" Levi said.

"What?"

"I don't know, Aubrey. Kind of makes *your* ghost gifts seem sort of pedestrian."

She smirked. "Very funny. Of course, let's not forget—"

"That you've exhibited the same penchant for future predictions. I haven't forgotten. Not for a second. We just got sidetracked."

"Sidetracked for a good reason."

"I'd say so. Listen, when we get back to Surrey, maybe I could give Pete a nudge, suggest the three of us have dinner together. How does that sound?"

"Like the best thing you could have said to me." Aubrey smiled wider and reached for the radio, turning it on. Instead of music, the only sound that rose was a familiar ping. She furrowed her brow and changed the station. Again, a soft but distinct ping vibrated through the car's stereo system. "Weird . . ." She shut it off. Levi didn't say anything, though he glanced between her and the highway. Aubrey's phone dinged, the sound muffled. "Where is my . . ."

Levi flipped open the center console. "I tucked it in there."

She rolled her eyes at perpetual tidiness and stuck her hand inside. Instead of her phone, she came up with a roll of Hubba Bubba Sour Green Apple gum. "What the . . . did you take . . . ?" Levi shook his head. Aubrey closed her eyes and laughed softly.

"A ghost gift from Eli?" he said, his eyes on the highway.

"How thoughtful." Still shaking her head and smiling, Aubrey reached back into the console and came up with her phone. Aubrey clicked on her messages. "Oh my God."

"What? Say something."

"This text. It, um . . . it says, *'My first message from here. Thanks for the assist.'* " Then her brow pulled tighter. *'Don't forget—you two work best as a team. You'll need to.'*

Levi's dark gaze made a skeptical shift between Aubrey and her phone. "You don't really think that text was from . . ."

She blinked at the phone and held up the gum. She pondered the passing scenery, her fingertips dragging through a slightly fogged side window. "Well, if they can write on a mirror . . ."

"Or project enough influence to make a person take notes . . ."

"Communication from the other side goes beyond my breadth of knowledge. Which, based on this"—Aubrey held up the phone—"does seem a little like last year's psychic technology." She turned to Levi. "Okay, regardless of Eli's choice of conduit. What does he mean?" She read the text message again. "We *work best as a team* . . . and we'll *need to*."

"Aubrey, I am flat-out done dissecting Eli Serino. We got those boys back thanks to him. Let it go at that," Levi said. "I really just want to pick Pete up and—" The thought was interrupted by Levi's phone, the dashboard display lighting up: Diane Higley. Levi hit the audio button on the steering wheel. "Sorry we're running late, Diane. We'll be back in Surrey shortly. I hope Pete's not giving you a hard time."

"Uh, Levi. It's not that. I have to tell you something."

Aubrey was suddenly hyper-tuned to the woman's voice, heavy with motherly concern. Background noises clarified, the static of a police radio and the wail of a siren.

"Levi?" Diane said. Her voice and the sounds, they lit a full-on panic inside Aubrey. "I'm sorry . . . so sorry—I thought they'd be fine."

"Piedmont Street." Aubrey clamped her hand around Levi's arm. Instead of darting to the emergency lane, Levi pulled right onto the highway median.

"What's wrong, Diane? What's going on?" he said. Aubrey's fingers were firm on Levi's wrist, and through his suit jacket, she felt his pulse pound. "Is Pete all right?"

"That's just it. I don't know." The woman's voice wavered, sobs echoing. "He and Dylan left the skate park. I told them not to; I told them they didn't have permission to go anywhere else."

"Diane," Levi demanded, "where is my son?"

"Dylan told me they were skating behind the abandoned rubber-processing plant," she said, gulping frantic breaths. "There's a bunch of ramps back there. Dylan said he got thirsty and went to the 7-Eleven a block over. When he came back, Pete was gone."

Levi dove at reason. "Maybe he got bored, went home. It's not that far, or went off to skate somewhere else."

"I don't think so, Levi. Dylan found Pete's skateboard behind the factory . . . and his cell phone. We've been to your house, the condo . . . we've been everywhere. I called the police over an hour ago."

"And you're just calling us now!" Aubrey looked in her side-view mirror and slapped her hand on the car door. "Go, Levi! Just go!"

They sped off toward Surrey, tires screeching onto the highway, solid black lines in the pavement snaking toward the unknown.

CHAPTER
TWENTY-SEVEN

Forty-Eight Hours Later

Upon their return to Surrey, a hysterical Diane Higley and Detective Espinosa had met with Levi and Aubrey. Since the Missy Flannigan story, and during his tenure as *Surrey City Press* editor in chief, Levi had kept in contact with Surrey's lead detective. Aubrey was grateful for this, as the detective was inclined to share all aspects of the investigation into Pete's disappearance. But as the first twenty-four sleepless hours came and went, Detective Espinosa had gravitated toward a scenario both Aubrey and Levi were dreading: finding themselves in the same hellish predicament as Barbara Flannigan and Connie Beane—the parents of a child gone missing.

While the Surrey Police Department did their due diligence, speculating and investigating common avenues, Pete's parents were considered ethereal possibilities. This wasn't an ordinary twelve-year-old boy who'd vanished, but one with a mysterious gift. A gift not even his parents understood. A confounded Levi and Aubrey weighed various theories, a range of risks: Pete hitting a wall of anger and taking off on his own. Option B, a more worrisome scenario—an abduction that had nothing to do with Pete's gift. A third thought finally wove its way into the conversation, something beyond Pete's anger or a criminal mind. What if Pete's disappearance was tied to his inexplicable gift?

It was a hypothesis they didn't dare share with Detective Espinosa.

Late into the second afternoon, a police car was stationed outside the house on Homestead Road. Dan Watney had been by to hear the details, offer his support. Piper remained in Washington, DC, coordinating the Suzanne Serino investigation. She'd listened intently on speakerphone, stunned that such a fate had befallen Aubrey and Levi. Naturally, both Dan and Piper pledged their considerable resources and help.

At the moment, only Detective Matthews, an underling of Detective Espinosa, remained inside the house. She'd been assigned the task and given permission to look through the personal possessions in the Ellis–St John home, including the master bedroom. Aubrey didn't like the invasion of privacy but understood the necessity. Ordinary possibilities couldn't be dismissed. After an hour of rummaging through their upstairs, the female detective returned to the living room. In her arms were Aubrey's journals—the ones where she'd recorded Pete's precarious dreams. Aubrey swallowed hard and hung on to a thread of composure. Detective Matthews wanted to know more about the peculiar handwritten notes, and Aubrey was obligated to say something. Exhausted and terrified, she was unable to grasp at a quick lie. Levi answered, the threesome standing awkwardly in the living room. "They're idea journals."

"*Idea journals?*" Detective Matthews narrowed her eyes at his explanation.

"Idea . . ." In her frightened and fatigued state, Aubrey almost mirrored the remark of disbelief.

"Uh, yes," he said. "Not so much journal writings, but story ideas. Aubrey's been putting together notes for a Harry Potter–type of series. The journals, they're like an artist's sketchbook."

"Uh-huh." The detective offered a curious look. "And you planned on naming the main character Pete, just like your son?"

"What?" Aubrey's gaze ricocheted between the windows and the detective. Levi shot her a coaxing glance. "I'm undecided." She was engaged enough to realize a deep inquiry into Pete's dreams would not be a productive path. She shrugged. "Would it be so out there to model an adventurous boy after my own son?"

The journals were tight in the detective's grip, and Aubrey fought the urge to snatch them away. "I don't know about that, but this is some seriously inventive thinking." The detective flipped one open. "You've covered history like a time machine. Do you have a degree in history, Mrs. St John?"

"Miss Ellis." Her correction was swift and sharp. Aubrey didn't want the woman anywhere near her son or his dreams. "Why don't you get the parties who are present straight before questioning my creative writing habits? And why would you ask about a history degree?"

"I just found your notes interesting . . . surreal. Why do you find my question so upsetting? I'm a bit of a history buff. Your idea journal appears to be factual . . . and yet imaginary. Biographical fiction anchored to real events."

"Again, I'm not sure as to the relevance of your question."

"I'm just here to collect puzzle pieces, Miss Ellis." She held up the journal. "This seems like one. At the very least, it shows incredible imagination laced with an air of . . . *spookiness*, the things you've written about your son."

"You mean the things Aubrey wrote about the character in her story," Levi said.

"If you say so. The writing is intense. Hence my question about having a degree in history."

"No, Detective, I don't have a degree in history. But there isn't anything in those journals a library card or Google search can't produce.

I do have a nonfiction book to my credit. My turn. How does your question help find my son?"

"I can't answer that, Miss Ellis—not yet. I'm sorry if I further upset you. I'm only exploring all realistic possibilities as to how or why Peter St John might have vanished into what appears to be thin air."

◆ ◆ ◆

Levi shut the front door and flipped the dead bolt. As far as he was concerned, there'd been enough police input for one day. Aubrey stood by the fireplace, her thumb running over the edge of a silver frame that held a picture of Pete. Levi's recollection of the photo was vivid.

His son had been four when the photo was taken, Pete seated on a spotted pony. Of all things, a carnival had come to town. Aubrey had coaxed until Levi caved. "Oh, come on. It'll be fun," she'd said to him. "I'll show you how to win at the milk bottle game. You have to know which bottles are weighted."

That day at the carnival, the games were quickly forgotten. Aubrey's fascination appeared to go far beyond the glitz of blinking lights, air scented with funnel cakes and popcorn, the whirling crank of carnival sounds. She'd been caught off guard, and her introspection was obvious to Levi. Wandering a straw-covered maze of memories, he'd followed her rapt attention, her mind clearly snagged on the past. Pete, on the other hand, had been terrified of the giant slide, even while riding in his father's lap. But the pony—Pete had loved the pony, sitting tall and fearless, like a soldier on its back.

On the ride home, Pete had fallen asleep in his car seat, his face sweaty and his head filled with dreams—Levi knew this from the way his son had thrashed restlessly, even though he'd been exhausted. At the time, an unsuspecting Levi had blamed disquiet on too much sugar. Another year or two would pass before Pete began to verbalize his dreams and lash out from a deep sleep. As for Aubrey, she'd sat so quietly beside Levi, staring out the passenger window. He'd wanted to ask what she was thinking of but didn't. For the first time in their relationship, Levi had been fearful, concerned about what her answer might be.

In their living room, Levi was confronted by the current silence, which reminded him of the carnival aftermath. But this deafening hush was removed from Levi's memories and so very different. Their life and home, it hadn't been this way, filled with raw emptiness and soundless air. Levi sat, suddenly aware that this silence was the sound Aubrey had been living with, listening to, in recent months—since he left, since Pete left. He thought about pouring himself a drink; then he thought better of it. He needed to be sharp; he needed to be present. Where the fuck had it all gone so wrong? And now this.

"We'll find him, Aubrey." He rushed into the statement with the force of a tourniquet, wanting to cut off her pain. She didn't latch on to his attempt to soothe, not even turning from the mantel.

"Detective Matthews, did you hear her tone? She thinks I have something to do with Pete's disappearance." Her voice shook. "We're not new to this, Levi. We can't count out all the horrible ordinary things that might have happened to Pete. We've seen too much. Sadly, we know too much." Misplaced laughter sputtered from Aubrey. "We both know I didn't go all Suzanne Serino on you." She faced him. "I haven't lost my mind. I don't have Pete holed up in an indoor ice rink, nor did I steal him from you because I felt you were keeping him from me. So we can erase those possibilities. But it's small comfort, isn't it? We're erasing the easy stuff." Tears ran in tiny tributaries down her face.

"Of course I don't think anything like that. Aubrey . . ."

She closed her fingers around the photo and backed away from the fireplace, from him. Learned behavior, heightened self-awareness, told him this was wrong. She should be moving toward him.

"What if it's something worse? What if it's beyond insane, and Pete's disappearance is nothing that can ever be solved like Missy Flannigan or Trevor Beane? What if it's what you said the other day? What if Pete's vanished to wherever his dreams take him—dreams that are nobody's fault but mine."

"That's not what's happening here. You—" He clenched his fists; Aubrey swiped at her tears. Levi wanted to tell her it was incomprehensible—like traveling to whatever existed beyond the farthest star. He was too cognizant of facts to do this. Levi had experienced enough of the implausible, been privy to enough ghosts. He couldn't assure Aubrey this wasn't the case. He moved closer; the photo rattled like a Halloween skeleton in her hands. He eased the frame from her grip and looked at his son, smiling atop the pony, the thick of carnival crowds surrounding him. Aubrey had preferred the black-and-white image, and it was the one she'd chosen to display on the mantel eight years ago.

Through his own glassy gaze, he looked at Aubrey—a woman who'd not been overcome but taken steady control of her life. Yet in this moment, everything trembled: her hands, her chin, and, he guessed, her heart. His own heart began to race, and he was left with two options: panic, or default to his comfort zone—steadfast logic.

He tugged on Aubrey's arms until she was in his. "Listen to me. We might not know the exact scenario, but I believe Pete is out there, within our grasp. It's not what you're thinking. He hasn't tumbled off into some parallel existence. Even for you, that's a big leap. Pete didn't go from detailed dreams to something so . . ."

"Outrageous?" She pushed away from him. "Don't look now, Levi. But it wasn't so many years ago I brokered a conversation between you and your own dead brother. At the time, it was exactly what you labeled it—an incomprehensible, impossible thought."

"That was different."

"How?"

"I might not have been on board, not right away, but you knew precisely what was happening. We're not going to lose our son to such an unknown. Something neither one of us can define. Pete isn't going to simply vanish off the face of the earth."

"Why not?"

"Because . . ." Levi's flapped his arms against his body. "Because he's got too much St John in him—we're more earthbound."

"Oh really? Want to ask your brother about that?"

"Stop it, Aubrey—just stop. Don't do this to us. Don't head down a path that—"

"A path from which we'd have no hope of recovering our son." She narrowed her teary gaze. "At least admit it's in the realm of possibility."

Levi refused. Instead, he took a lost turn around the familiar living room. Neither intelligence nor reason would allow him to argue her point. Then he sat on the sofa and placed the photo on the coffee table; Levi trailed his fingertips over Pete's face. Then he retrieved his phone, his brain frantically grasping at straws of logic.

"Who are you calling?"

"Dan Watney. When it comes to the unsolved and the missing, we do have a huge plus in Dan and Piper. Maybe one of them has come up with a lead we can follow up on. I'm sure as hell not waiting on the Surrey Police Department and Detective Matthews." He glanced between the phone and her. "We know their track record on missing children."

Aubrey moved to within his sight line; she stood with her long arms folded, her face red, and her nose runny. "You do that, Levi. And I hope Dan has avenues we haven't considered—whatever they are. At least they'll be tangible options. But just like our son's dreams, I'll be the one left here, understanding, accepting that Pete's life is full of unknowns. They're possibilities that all the Dan Watneys and Piper Sullivans of the world can't do a damn thing about."

CHAPTER
TWENTY-EIGHT

Aubrey tried to anchor herself in the surroundings. The garage of the Homestead Road house was set to the rear; behind it was the nature preserve. A massive oak tree served as the border between the field and yard. Years ago, Levi had hung a tire swing from a sturdy branch. Pete had quit coming back there and swinging from it about the same moment he had permission to leave the yard. In the approaching dusk, Aubrey had wandered out, looking for her son, searching for hope. Standing near the tree, she dug the toe of her shoe into the soft earth. Pete and her life, they both were so absent. It seemed like the past was the only thing that came with clarity right now, the only thing she could grab on to.

When Pete was born, Aubrey's longing for a normal life vanished. It was immediately transformed into the daunting task of motherhood. She'd never held a baby until they handed her one in the hospital. *"Is there a practice model?"* she'd wanted to ask. No. You just dove in with your squalling infant and significant other—a man who had only moved in with Aubrey the week before Pete was born.

It was a distant but poignant memory. At the time, it appeared perfectly logical. Levi had just recovered from the near-fatal gunshot wound; he lived and worked in Hartford. Plans came together slowly but naturally, or so she'd thought. Malcolm retired and MediaMatters offered Levi the job as the *Surrey City Press* editor in chief. Where he should reside was obvious enough; heck, they were already having a baby together.

But Pete hadn't gotten any memo about a grace period and surprised his newly cohabitating parents by arriving three weeks early. It'd been the three of them without ever having a chance to be the two of them. Aubrey and Levi had no time to agree, or not, on what shade of blue to paint the spare bedroom or to discover that neither of them could make a meal beyond toast. Still, it managed to work. Pete had solidified a bond that had a strong, if not frenzied, beginning. They were cautious parents, more inexperience than anxiety. They didn't know enough to be fearful. They might have anticipated a strong-willed son— that was a no-brainer given his father. But Aubrey had always been wary about what a son might inherit from his mother. Maybe nothing; and she never could decide if this was truly what she had hoped for. Before Pete's second birthday, she knew. It wasn't her gift, not precisely, but a curious iteration.

In the earliest years, she kept much of this to herself. Levi was tuned into the everyday moments of Pete's life, and she thought this was good. One of them was hyper-focused on the ordinary, and the other was not. Regardless, it didn't take long for Levi to catch up. Right before Pete turned three, their son woke from a wild reverie, his red face sticky with sweat and his tiny teeth chattering. As Levi held him, Aubrey stared into her son's stark, wild eyes, his whole body trembling in his father's arms. Short, sniveling breaths trembled in and out of Pete, his tiny fists clutching Levi's undershirt like this might anchor him to earth.

Aubrey had remembered reading about toddlers and their dreams; it explained that they did not yet possess the brain growth to dream like adults. Their minds weren't developed enough to induce vivid autobiographic or episodic visions. Yet looking into Pete's blue-gray eyes, maybe deep into the black center of his irises, she knew this was precisely what was happening to their son.

Once Pete quieted, over an hour later, they went back to bed. Another hour passed, and Levi's voice pierced the silence. "I've never dreamed like that. Have you?"

In a whisper, she'd answered, "No."

As he lay beside her, Aubrey could feel him think, an intrinsic stream of consciousness between Levi and her.

"There's no stopping it, is there? We'll have to manage, help him, whatever it is."

A tear had slid down her face. "Yes. It's just us and him. But it's more than I had."

In the dark, Levi had reached for her hand.

In their backyard, Aubrey pulled in a breath of night air. This would be Pete's third night gone. The tire swing caught in her peripheral vision. The heavy rubber sphere swayed in dusky stillness. She reached out and steadied it, too upset to think beyond a gust of wind she'd missed. Not when the thing she missed most could be anywhere on this earth—or not. A nearby wooden picnic table had played a part in a common family ritual, and Aubrey climbed onto the bench, her body weighted with guilt and fear. With her elbows planted on the cedar table, she folded her hands and bowed her head into her solemn knot of fingers.

When it came to Pete's fate, she didn't know whether to wish for a common crime, early teen angst, or to beg for anything but the incomprehensible. Maybe she would just pray for any answer that led to the safe return of their son. A chill spread from her spine, enveloping her whole body.

"Took me long enough to find you." The voice was scored to her soul. Aubrey looked up, nearly blinded by the eye-level sun, a knotted sphere of daylight. It seemed committed to a fiery descent, and goose bumps rose on her arms. She blinked. Zeke was there, swinging his long legs over the bench on the opposite side. "Thought for sure I'd find you in the house. What are you doing way out here?"

"I needed a little time alone. I was going to call . . . or text you. Do you know what's—"

"I know everything."

Aubrey was grateful she would not have to retell the facts, such as they were. Zeke must have had a conversation with Levi. Interesting what would bond natural enemies. "Good. It was hard enough to tell Charley. I didn't want to at first. Levi insisted."

"I think that was the right thing. She'd want to know. Everyone will want to help, sweetheart. I want to help."

She undid her knot of fingers and placed them flat on the table. "This is so surreal, especially after what happened with the rest of the Serinos, the ones you don't deal with."

"You mean Eli."

"I meant Suzanne." She furrowed her brow. "But interesting you should mention Eli. He's actually the reason—"

"I know. I heard that whole story too."

She nodded. It could be that Levi told Zeke about Eli as well—a cursory conversation, all before getting into what he really wanted: to pick Zeke's brain about Jude Serino. What was Zeke's connection, if any, to nameless remains found in a Maine swamp? Aubrey shook her head. Even the most diligent, dogged parts of Pete's father wouldn't be focused on chasing a story right now. Not even Levi could compartmentalize to that extent. At least she didn't think so.

"How did you hear about Eli, from Charley or Levi? If anything, I thought Levi would have framed it in terms of what Suzanne had—"

"I was just thinking of what you said about Eli. His manner of death, his suicide."

"What about it?"

"He helped you, Aubrey. He helped find those missing boys. I guess a soul never knows what it'll have to do to earn a ticket out of here.

Knowing you, I found that to be the more important part of the story." A Zeke grin appeared wider than the setting sun. "Do you think he did, sweetheart? Find something better than here in the end?"

Aubrey's mind wasn't on Eli Serino. She hadn't given him a thought since reading his text, right before Diane Higley called. "Could be." She hesitated, unsure how to frame her thought. "I'm not privy to details beyond what you might fit . . . in a text. Remember? I'm not that special." She blinked into Zeke's dark eyes, so drawn to the comfort of his presence. But like a taut rubber band, her thoughts snapped back to Pete. "You know, there aren't too many people I can discuss my son with. The *possibilities* when it comes to Pete's disappearance."

Zeke nodded. "His dreams."

"Yes. His dreams." She drew a thinking breath, a habit she'd picked up from Levi over the years. "His father doesn't want to hear it. It's almost like when he first learned about my gift—Levi won't accept what he can't explain."

"You're being harsh. It's a lot to get your head around."

"Wow. Are you suddenly on Team Levi?"

"'Course not. I just know what it's like to be the ordinary person in your life."

"Not how I would ever describe you or Levi."

"That's because you've never looked at it from our perspective. All the extraordinary things about you, it was enough to intimidate me, keep me running, as opposed to taking you up on your offer all those years ago. Do you remember?"

"My senior year of college, when I asked you to stay . . . or at least come live inside after I graduated."

"The night I gave you the pearl necklace."

"I still have it."

"But you never wear it."

"Doesn't change the significance of the keepsake."

"No," he said. "It doesn't. Remember that." Silence settled between them. "Not to rehash ancient history, but do you see now what a mistake that would have been? Not for me, but for you."

"You don't know that."

Zeke peered in the direction of the back door, and Aubrey glanced over her shoulder. The house had grown fainter in the waning light. "The ace reporter, *he* might not have happened."

"Again, how can you know that?"

"Because if I'd taken you up on your offer, I would have never let you go." Zeke drew his hands from his lap to the tabletop, clasping Aubrey's. Physically, he was ridiculously close compared to the house, the back door, maybe who or what was inside.

At the same time, Zeke seemed to blend into the haze of evening colors, the puddling purples and reds, a sun setting roundly behind him. Aubrey saw Zeke as close as a carnival campfire and as distant as those summers they left behind. It was all so soothing. With Levi at such an emotional distance, Aubrey wanted that almost as much as she wanted her son.

She sighed. Not even Zeke stood a chance of numbing current reality. *"If I'd taken you up on your offer, I would have never let you go."* She couldn't fake a smile at his endearing observation, and fresher tears ran down her face. She felt his hands squeeze harder around hers. "Hey, come on. You'll find him. I promise."

"So you and Levi think."

"It might be different instincts that drive us, but we're both right. Trust that." He leaned into the table, his rolled-up shirtsleeve exposing the tattoo she'd seen the other day. It brought back to center Levi's theory about recent events, and Aubrey removed her hands from Zeke's. She inched her gaze onto his shirt pocket. A pack of cigarettes peeked from the edge.

While it was a Herculean mind trick—or practiced psychic technique—Aubrey willed the conversation in a different direction.

"Zeke, I need to ask you something. Something that has nothing to do with Pete."

"Go ahead." It sounded as if he'd been waiting for her to ask.

"The John Doe found in Maine, the case Levi is working with Dan Watney. The victim, he has . . . or had, a tattoo like yours."

"Did he?" The sun and Zeke's mouth dipped downward.

"But like you said, hundreds of different men could have that tattoo, right?"

He didn't reinforce the notion.

"They, um . . . they found something else at the scene the other day. A cigarette butt caught in a heron's nest. It was a Camel filter. The same brand you smoke."

He avoided her stare. "If only I could have quit for you years ago."

"Zeke," Aubrey said carefully. "Levi's uncovered some information. He's been able to establish that Jude Serino should be well into a lengthy sabbatical."

"Jude goes annually, has since I've known him. They're the quietest weeks of my life. Of course, this year . . . I'm definitely getting an extension."

"And why, um . . . why do you say that?" Aubrey's heart pounded harder, unsure what she might do if Zeke confessed murder in the middle of her backyard.

"Because I don't work for him anymore."

"Right . . . of course." She heard the nervous flutter in her own voice. "He, um . . . Levi spoke with Jude's assistant. She said she hasn't heard from him in weeks."

Zeke shrugged. "Nothing unusual there."

"That's what his brother, Bruno, said. Jude's whereabouts didn't seem to concern him." She shifted on the hard bench, and her gaze caught on the last of a sun swallowed by dusk. "Come back to something else for me. Is it true that Jude had the same tattoo?"

"What are you asking me, Aubrey?"

"I'm asking if I should be concerned . . . if there's a reason you're not."

"I'm not sure what you mean. Are you asking if I think Jude Serino might be your John Doe, or are you asking if I had something to do with it?"

"Both," she gulped.

"I won't lie to you. I had a lot of reasons to hate Jude Serino. Some of them are connected to you. Now more than ever, I'm afraid."

"Me? What does Jude Serino have to do with me?"

"I have to tell you something."

Aubrey's knees locked hard around her side of the bench, bracing. Zeke curled his hands into two soft fists.

"The missing ghost gifts, your father's predictions. I took them— the good ones, anyway."

"You did what?" She lurched back on the bench and in her mind, repelling from Zeke.

"It started long before I ever got involved with Jude Serino. Then, unfortunately . . . I did. I worked for him for years. Of course, you know that part."

"What don't I know, Zeke?"

"He didn't employ me because I was so slick at managing off-site projects—I was capable, good at it. But Jude kept me on the job because it was a dubious trade, because I provided him with a steady supply of Peter Ellis's ghost gifts—the winning predictions."

She gripped her fingers tight around the wooden seat. It steadied her body and kept her from smacking Zeke across the face. She felt duped—by her steadfast belief in Zeke, by what suddenly seemed like Levi's realistic assumptions. "I . . . I don't understand. Why would you do that?"

"Jude's been blackmailing me for . . ." He was quiet, and in the rising moonlight, Aubrey couldn't make out his expression. For the first time in her life, Zeke appeared more like a shadowy and uncertain object.

"Years, really," he finally said. "At first it was Nora. Things connected to her life. Then he came after me. Jude would threaten and promise. From the beginning, I knew it was wrong, but I never thought it would be more than dishonest. Not until now, not with what's happened."

"What happened, Zeke? Tell me."

"You should know, I've wanted Jude Serino dead since I was a teenager. The story goes that his father, Giorgio, killed my parents. That it was retribution, meant to send a message to the masses."

Drawing her fingertips to her mouth, Aubrey took a moment to factor in the rumor Genève Renard had unearthed. "I heard . . . well, Levi . . . he asked an *old friend* from Chicago to look into the reports surrounding their deaths. She discovered the same rumors, which, I guess, are facts."

"Ugly ones. But not all the facts are right. Not even the ones tied to rumors. A couple of months ago, I found out Giorgio didn't kill my parents—Jude did. He confessed it to me; he gloated about it." He paused, focusing on his knotted fists.

"Zeke, I'm so sorry. I can't begin to imagine how that made you feel." She didn't need to further prod him and the rest of his plot spilled out.

"Long before learning that little kicker, I'd bought a gun. I had a plan." He looked from his curled fists to Aubrey. "Jude's confession, it should have been enough right there to kill him."

"But it wasn't." A flicker of hope rose. "Even after Jude told you that, you didn't follow through. You didn't do it."

"No. I didn't. Not at that point. For a lot of years, I was just too much of a fucking coward. Or I don't know, maybe I like to tell myself even grifters have some conscience. But then, even after learning that, it wasn't the outright murder Jude confessed to me. I wasn't ready to kill Jude Serino until he threatened you."

"Me? Why would he—"

"I ran out of ghost gifts, sweetheart. You saw it yourself. Except for a piece of blue construction paper, they're gone."

"And a last lottery ticket win."

"Yes. That too, for whatever it brings. The prediction your father wrote on the notepaper from the funeral home in Surrey."

"Zeke, what are you confessing to me?"

"Years ago, I accidentally told Jude Serino about you."

"About my gift?"

"No," he said calmly. "Just that you exist. That I'd been in love with you the same way Jude had been in love with a woman named Tilda. She died." Zeke snickered, a sound of self-loathing. "I was just never good enough."

Aubrey guessed he was glad for the dim light; it kept them from having to look each other in the eye.

"But Jude . . . the man does his research. He's thorough. He knew about your gift."

"He knew."

"And that's not all."

"What else?"

"Jude believed your gift works like your father's gift. That you possessed the ability to make predictions about the future." His jaw slacked, then shut. "When Jude assumed that, I told him it wasn't true. That your gift didn't work that way. But now . . ."

Aubrey inched back. "I hope you're not going to say irony's a bitch." Her hand flitted angrily between them. "I'm hardly sitting around penning predictions. So far, any ability to project future events isn't quite like my father's, not as intense or vivid. Even so—"

"Doesn't matter." Zeke raised his arm, lowering it in a defeated motion. "Jude was too deep into his own scam, the one he'd been running for years off your father's predictions. When I proved I couldn't come up with another winning bet, Jude wasn't about to give up. Not with what was hanging over his head. Not when he thought he knew how to keep the game running, the winning predictions coming."

"And?"

"And so when he threatened you, sweetheart, you have to understand—I couldn't let that happen. For years, I wanted him dead, and finally . . ."

"Finally what?"

"Finally, I—"

"Aubrey!" Levi's voice shot like a bullet through the backyard. She lurched up from the bench, stumbling to her feet. "Are you out here? Pete—Pete just called!"

She didn't look back at Zeke as she ran full charge toward the house.

CHAPTER
TWENTY-NINE

Aubrey came through the back door, demanding information on her charge into the kitchen. "What did he say? Where is he? Is he all right?"

Levi pointed. "Charley and Yvette are here." They hurried into the dining room.

"For God's sake, are you going to answer me?"

"He called." Levi held his phone in a murderous grip. "All he said was 'Pa' and . . . 'I love you.' Then the line went dead. It wasn't even two seconds. He sounded half asleep, but it was him, Aubrey. It was Pete."

"He hung up or someone took the phone from him?"

"I don't know. I've already called Dan. You don't need a time minimum or anything like that to trace a call nowadays. They should be able to pinpoint it."

She grabbed at his phone. "Did the caller ID indicate—"

"No," he said, handing it to her. "It just said 'Private Caller.'"

Aubrey ran her fingers through her hair, squeezing. "So someone took him?" She stared into Levi's face, which she guessed looked as shocked as hers. "Someone took Pete?"

"Makes basic sense. Or I'm hoping it does."

"But I did get a text from a dead Eli Serino." Her heart sank a little more. "Considering that, any message connected to a cell phone has me leery."

He reached out, squeezing her arm. "I'm going with that was your phone, not mine. Surely it makes a difference. For now, let's stay with the more grounded, logical scenario." She nodded; Levi hesitated, then didn't. "Aubrey, I need to tell you something . . . something Dan considered the moment I told him Pete went missing."

"Which was?"

"The drug cartel out of the Florida Keys. They were serious badass people. Dan may have led the raid, served justice. But I'm the one who tracked the leads, broke the story. Those drug dealers, the ones who went to jail . . . we know it wasn't all of them. Offshoot cells do exist, and this could be retaliation."

"Retaliation?"

"I didn't say anything at first because child kidnapping doesn't fit their MO." His somber face stared into hers. "I mean, what could they want? It's not like taking Pete would get their partners in crime released, or the government would be open to trading a warehouse full of cocaine and heroin for our son."

Aubrey considered the theory, expanding on what were surely Levi's thoughts. "If those people took Pete, you think it's more of an eye-for-an-eye scenario?"

"I swear, if it is . . . if this happened because of my high-profile job . . ."

She was sorry she said it aloud. "Levi. Let's not go there. Let's not play roulette with theories, not until we have hard evidence. One short phrase from Pete doesn't tell us anything—except that he's alive . . . I think."

He turned away without answering. Aubrey peeked around his frame at Charley and Yvette, who sat silently in the living room. Surely, they'd heard every word.

"Right?" Aubrey moved forward and attempted to rouse encouragement. "You two need to tell him not to go off the deep end with possibilities."

Charley said nothing. Instead, ninety years of living and the lines on her face spoke like a devastating palm reading.

"Charley?" Until that second, it hadn't occurred to Aubrey to question her grandmother's presence. "Have you and Yvette been here long?"

"No," Levi said. "They got here seconds before Pete called."

"Oh, I thought maybe you came with Zeke. He's . . ." She pointed toward the back door, but the motioned ceased, her arm dropping heavily to her side. "Charley, why are you here?" She was so quiet, her blue-gray eyes clouding with more than grandmotherly concern. "Charley?"

It was Yvette who answered. "We've, um . . . your grandmother and I have been talking all day. What we should do or if we should come. We can't begin to imagine what the two of you are going through, all the unknowns about Pete. And then we get here, and he calls." A smile pushed into Yvette's cheeks, though Aubrey thought she might as well have drawn it on. "So maybe it's nothing. Maybe you're just on your grandmother's mind, which is completely understandable given the circumstances."

Aubrey shuffled to within a half step of her grandmother and asked again, "Why are you here?"

Her misshapen arthritic hand rose, crooked fingers trembling as they pressed to her lips. "My great-grandson just called. If you'd rang me and said Pete phoned, I never would have come. I would have believed what Yvette said—you're just on my mind. It would be a reason, an explanation for why it's more likely than not that you'd . . ."

"Be in your dreams." The silence that followed said Aubrey was right.

"You were in her dream last night." Yvette's hand rested on Charley's shoulder. "But it makes perfect sense, baby. She's been so worried; we both have—"

"Except my grandmother only dreams one way, about one thing—the living connected to the dead. At least that's been the rule for as far back as my memory goes." She glared at Yvette. "Do you recall anything different? A time when Charley dreamed about someone for the hell of it? That her dreams conjured up a person out of concern because they'd been sick or upset or just on her mind?" Her voice rose with every suggestion. "Have you ever dreamed of a single person for any of those ordinary reasons, Charley?"

Yvette's grip tightened as Charley's head bowed. Aubrey's knees buckled, and Levi grabbed her by the shoulders. Really, they were bracing one other. "What did you dream about, Charley? Tell me."

"You." Her head ticked up. "Last night I dreamed of you. I've never dreamed of you, Aubrey. It's an odd thing to dream of strangers, see their faces so vivid and never, not once, dream about your own granddaughter. Not even when your parents died."

"But they've never visited me in this life, and that's not how it works. Is it?" Aubrey inched forward, her voice bearing down as if the dreams were something Charley controlled. "Is it!"

"No, my dear girl," Charley said. "That's not how it works."

Aubrey glanced over her shoulder; Levi's staid face had gone pale.

"Your grandmother, she dreamed of me years ago, right before my dead brother visited you. So if Charley dreamed of you now . . ."

"Someone close to me is bound to be dead. And my next conversation will be with their spirit."

"But Pete," Levi said, holding out his phone. "He called. We just heard his voice!"

Aubrey turned away, her pulse whacking wildly against her soul. "It's not about precise timing," she said to Levi. "It's about what will come to pass—eventually." She sank onto the sofa, though it felt more like dread pushing her down. She blinked up at him. "I did get a text from a boy who's been dead for more than a decade. Who knows where that call from Pete came from." Aubrey closed her eyes. Honestly? She wanted to close off the universe. "As far as Pete goes, I don't think earthbound scenarios carry any more weight than otherworldly ideas. Not with our son."

♦ ♦ ♦

Levi refused to give up or give in. Yes. He believed in Charley's gift. He accepted that she dreamed of the living before Aubrey connected to the dead. But he did not believe that meant his son. He would know. Fuck psychic perceptions. He would know if his own son was . . . a tremulous breath pulled into him as he sat in the leather chair. Would he? *Fuck*. He couldn't even form the word in his head and connect it to Pete. No. He'd know if his son was anything but alive, and this wasn't true. It couldn't be.

The four of them sat in silence for a time. At some point, Levi faltered to a mechanical mode and rose, fixing himself a drink. He asked if anyone else wanted one, and Yvette was the only taker. It was a useless thing to be doing, but he was at a loss to bridge two parallel trains of thought: Pete's disappearance linking to his initial instinct—a kidnapping connected to any number of dangerous stories he'd pursued with *Ink on Air*—versus something far more vague and ethereal. Earthbound bad guys connected to him: it was the guiltier but more feasible possibility.

On the other hand, if Charley's dream was accurate . . . Levi took a burning gulp of whatever he'd poured into a glass. He couldn't get his head around it, no matter how much a man made of logic swore to the existence of ghosts and a world beyond this one. He'd be damned if his next conversation with his son would be via Pete's mother.

Aubrey.

She hadn't moved from the edge of the sofa. He sat bent forward, elbows on his knees, the drink swirling in front of him as he held it. Levi supposed they were waiting for Dan's call. But even if it did register a physical address, it might not matter. Anything could have occurred after the call disconnected. Aubrey drew a prayerful, frustrated knot of fingers to her mouth. She looked at Levi, and her forehead mimicked the gesture her hands made. She glanced over her shoulder. "Wait. What happened to—"

Levi's phone rang and they hurled their collective energy in its direction. He answered. "Yeah, Dan." He listened for a few moments and said little more before abruptly ending the call. "Nothing yet," he informed them. "The brevity of Pete's call made it hard to pinpoint. The, um . . . the signal wasn't very strong, almost like it'd come from the middle of the ocean."

From her skirt pocket, Aubrey pulled out a tissue and pressed it to her nose. "Or Middle-earth."

Her lips pursed into a tight, flat line. Levi put down his drink and stepped over her long legs, bumping into the coffee table as he went. Sitting beside Aubrey, he wrapped his arm around her, and she dipped her head onto his shoulder.

"With all due respect . . ." He glanced at Charley. "Pete is not the spirit connected to her dream. Do not give up on him, Aubrey. He's *not* dead. He's not going to die."

"You don't know that." It was a scratchy, unsure whisper.

"Yeah. I do. You . . . Charley . . . your father. There's no arguing the fantastic breadth of your gifts. But I swear . . ." His own voice cracked. "I, um . . . I never told you this because . . . well, because compared to your connection to my brother, it seemed small and so what, but now . . . maybe it does matter."

"What?" Aubrey jerked her head up. "Tell me."

"It's about Brody. The night he died, the fire at my mother's house. When I got to the top of that flame-filled staircase, something inside me made a conscious choice, and I chose to save my mother. Had you put the question to me earlier that day—when I was a calm, average eleven-year-old, I would have answered bluntly . . . honestly. I would have answered 'Brody' if asked to pick. Choosing my hero over my usually drunk, often careless mother . . ." He shook his head. "Not my proudest thought, not something I like to dwell on . . . but it's true. Yet in the moment, I chose to save my mother because instinct said she was savable. Brody was not. I knew then, just like I know now—Pete's alive. I'm not arguing Charley's dream. I'm only saying that our son's ghost, it's not the spirit you're destined to meet, Aubrey."

CHAPTER
THIRTY

The four of them continued to wait; Levi alternated between pacing and sitting. At one point, he got as far as the front door. Aubrey asked where he was going. She knew her tone was as desperate as the look on his face. With his hand on the knob, Levi answered, "Door to door. I don't know. It'd be something. I can't sit here anymore."

"Levi . . ."

Logic stopped him, and restlessly, he sat again. In the meantime, Aubrey's point of view moved to her box of ghost gifts. She'd rummaged through it that morning, desperate for something to click—some yesteryear token to register a new meaning.

Its contents remained unchanged. There were ghost gifts for which she could tell an entire story—places, dates, meanings that had come with closure. Most prominent was a bag of beach sand that had led to an extraordinary connection—the spirit of Brody St John, linking Aubrey to his brother in a way that far exceeded newsroom comradery. She'd never told Levi, but eventually it occurred to Aubrey that Levi himself had been Brody's ghost gift. Reinforcing her theory, no ghost had delivered the bag of beach sand; Aubrey had gathered it herself.

Aside from this, inside her box were the odder ghost gifts, things that Aubrey could never figure out. Earlier, she'd touched each token, hoping one might lead her to Pete. Among the unexplained was a glass butterfly, smooth as velvet stone, and a vintage postcard from Bayport, New York. The card had always stood out, thought provoking and curious. The faded watercolor image showed a calm blue-green bay and long wooden pier. On the front were printed words: *Dock, Foot of Gillette Avenue. Bayport, L.I.* While the card bore a postmark, there was no written message. This had always bothered Aubrey—a postmark but no address. It enhanced the mystery, making it more personal than it appeared. The postcard had always emanated heat, but Aubrey perceived it as warmer than usual that morning. She assumed it was desperation. Staring at the box now, across the coffee table, across the room, she was disappointed that nothing connected to Pete.

Directly in front of her was her father's letter box. She and Levi had gone through it so many times, separately and together. For the most part, it seemed to have filled its prophecy and purpose—clues that had led them to Trevor Beane and Liam Sheffield.

As Levi finished a second drink, he placed his empty glass on the table and scooted the box closer. In the current chaos, Aubrey had forgotten Eli Serino's earthbound rage, tossing papers about the room, wreaking havoc on Levi's meticulous filing system. As Levi flipped the lid open, her recollection made the visual even more stunning. Instead of a thrown-together mess, the ghost gifts were neatly arranged, systematized by paper clips, and returned to Levi's logical order. "Did you do this?"

"No. I haven't touched it since we threw everything back in, since we took the green construction paper out."

"Something's missing." But she couldn't think what. Aubrey reached forward; Levi grabbed her wrist.

"Don't." His dark eyes darted back and forth, the width of the box.

"Levi? What do you see?" Charley asked.

A singular piece of paper rested on top. It was the last lottery prediction, the one written on notepaper from Hennessy's Funeral Home. "Maybe nothing."

"Gut instinct?" Aubrey said.

"I'd cop to that if it helped find Pete." As Aubrey withdrew her hand, Levi picked up the notepaper. "With everything that's going on, I'd forgotten the date."

Aubrey tilted her head at the paper. "It's today. The lottery numbers are for today." She glanced at the mantel clock. "An hour from now."

"Do you think playing them would have bearing on Pete's whereabouts?" Charley asked.

"Seems unlikely," Levi said. "Even given our extraordinary point of view. Hennessy's Funeral Home. Huh. I know I've passed by it."

"It's on the other side of town," Aubrey said. "One of those beautiful old Victorians that makes you kind of sad to realize its purpose. Aside from the building, the venue isn't exactly on my hot-spot list."

"No, I guess it wouldn't be." Levi continued to stare at the paper. "Aubrey, what's across the street from the funeral home? Warren Street. It's kind of commercial that way, isn't it?"

"For as commercial as Surrey gets." Aubrey closed her tired, burning eyes. An image flashed. A man she knew but hadn't seen since she was a child. He pointed to a sign. Goose bumps prickled, not out of cold or fear but realization. When Aubrey opened her eyes, her line of vision was consumed by Peter Ellis's photo. Air was stuck in her lungs; she was startled by the images—the one in her mind and the one on the fireplace mantel. More important was the message, and she spoke the words as they filtered into her head: "Across the street from the funeral home. There's a mini-mart, a mom-and-pop place—Idlewild's. There's a blue-and-white sign; it needs a fresh coat of paint."

"You remember seeing that?" Levi asked.

Aubrey shook her head. "No." She looked at Charley. "I think my father just showed it to me."

"Oh, my dear girl . . ." On Aubrey's words, the carnival color seemed to drain from Charley's face. "My son. You're not serious? Peter? You saw him?"

"Maybe that's why Charlotte dreamed of you, because of your father," Yvette said.

Aubrey wanted to pounce on the idea; instead she shook her head. "No. My father wasn't here. Not in the way spirits visit after Charley dreams about them. This was very distant, detached—more like a glimpse as opposed to a presence with which I could communicate."

"But still . . ." Levi's thought trailed off as Aubrey continued to shake her head.

Yet given the present circumstance, Aubrey appreciated how much the possibility meant to her grandmother, how much all of them wanted it to be true. She knew it wasn't. "But I did see my father, Charley. Even if it was for only a few seconds."

Her grandmother dabbed at her eye, Yvette patting her aged, arthritic hand.

In the same second, Levi was on his feet, moving toward the door. "Let's go."

"Where?" Charley said, sitting up taller.

"To buy a lottery ticket." Aubrey answered the question as Levi tucked the paper in his pocket. "Maybe there's a reason why my father's never been a presence, even if it was fleeting. Maybe he wanted to make damn certain I noticed when he did show up."

Aubrey and Levi pulled into the parking lot of Idlewild's. Overhanging lights lit the blue-chipped-paint sign Peter Ellis had pointed to and she'd described.

"I'll go in," Levi said.

Aubrey reached for his hand. "We'll go together."

He nodded and they exited the Volvo. Behind the counter, a young man had his nose buried in a car magazine. As Aubrey and Levi burst through the doors, he lurched to his feet. Clearly, he was wary of the late hour and a Bonnie and Clyde–like entrance. They slowed their pace, offering awkward smiles.

"Help you with something?" He remained on guard, rolling up the magazine, a weapon if need be.

"We, um . . . want to buy a lottery ticket."

The attendant motioned to a lottery-designated area. "Quick pick, or . . . ?"

"What?" Levi said.

Aubrey couldn't recall Levi ever buying a lottery ticket, and she nudged his arm. "He wants to know if you're picking the numbers yourself or you want the computer to do it."

"Uh, computer's fine." This time Aubrey tugged on his pants pocket. "No. Wait. I want to pick them."

"Whatever, man." The clerk raised his arms in stick-up fashion. "It ain't no Powerball win, but I guess two million is a decent jackpot." He turned back to his stool.

Levi withdrew the notepaper from his pocket, and moments later they placed their bet. The clerk continued with an unsure glance and completed the transaction. "You bust in here five minutes before the drawing to play one set of numbers? Lame." He shook his head, laughing.

"It was just a whim," Levi offered.

"Welp, might as well hang around. They'll pop the winning number up on that screen in about two minutes." He turned the volume up on a television that hung from a crowded piece of wall and sat again.

Aubrey and Levi staked out a rack of the day's remaining Hostess products. The thought of food made her stomach roil, and she said to Levi, "I don't see how this is going to get us any closer to Pete—whether we win or lose."

"Maybe there's more to it. If we win . . . I don't know. Maybe it leads us—"

"Zeke."

"Zeke?"

"Not necessarily Zeke, but something he told me about Jude Serino. Actually, it's something he confessed."

"What was that, and when did you talk to him?"

"In the backyard, earlier tonight. He came outside after . . ." Aubrey pressed her fingertips to her forehead, trying to steady a swirl of thoughts. "Levi, you were right. At least in part, about Zeke and my father's ghost gifts. Apparently, he's been stealing from the box for years. According to Zeke, Jude's been blackmailing him into providing him with winning predictions. A while back, he told Jude about me, my gift. He also confessed to how he'd been coming up with all the winning predictions. The whole conversation was kind of stilted . . . weird," she said, given an hour to process it. "At first, the way Zeke told the story, it was like a confession. Then it became a warning."

"What sort of warning?"

"Jude Serino believed *I* could predict wins like this." She poked at the lottery ticket Levi held. "Zeke said when he couldn't come up with any more wins, Jude threatened me. And . . . well, right before you shouted out the back door, telling me Pete had called . . . I think . . ."

"You think what?"

"I think Zeke was going to confess to killing Jude."

Levi clutched Aubrey's arm and guided her farther from the clerk, who continued to glance toward their whispery but animated conversation. "When did this happen? When did you see Zeke? I swear, if he had anything to do with Pete's disappearance—"

"Numbers are up." The clerk pointed at the screen. "Did your big hunch pay off? Store that sells the winning ticket gets about twenty grand." He held up the magazine, the cover showing off a sporty silver car. "Be a fat down payment on this baby."

Aubrey grabbed Levi's hand, and they pinned themselves to the counter's edge. He held out the ticket so all three could see the numbers. Expectation dribbled into a gush of disappointment. The clerk spoke first. "Damn. Not a single number. That sucks. Thought for sure you guys had somethin' goin' on, the way you charged in here." He laughed. "Next time, invest more than a buck. You might end up with something besides a loser lottery ticket."

Racked with frustration, Levi and Aubrey dragged themselves outside Idlewild's convenience store. Levi leaned against the car and scrubbed a hand over his face. "I totally do not get it. I couldn't really fathom a lottery-ticket connection to finding Pete, but I thought a winning ticket might be a clue. Your father's ghost gifts were all winning tickets except for this one." He ripped his arms through the cool night air and tore the ticket in half. "Why not this one?"

The lights to the convenience store shut off, and the clerk exited, locking the door. Getting into his car, a beat-up economy model, he looked in Levi and Aubrey's direction. "Man, don't sweat it. They'll play another set of numbers tomorrow. There's always hope."

Levi never looked up. Aubrey watched as the clerk's car sped off. She followed it through a light mist and the dark parking lot, all the way to the sidewalk. "What are you doing?" Levi called after her. Diagonally across the street was the glow of replica gas lampposts, aged elms dotting the perimeter of a stately Victorian. A man stood on the porch, sweeping.

"Oh my God, Levi. The lottery ticket got us to here. But I think there," she said, pointing toward the house. "Hennessy's Funeral Home. That's where we're supposed to go."

CHAPTER
THIRTY-ONE

They stepped off the curb, and Levi's hand locked around Aubrey's. Only together did she feel the tremor in hers stop. "Wait on the sidewalk," Levi said. "For a lot of reasons, I understand you not wanting to go in there."

"I don't think it's a choice." Aubrey held tighter to his hand, picking up her pace and her courage.

An older man wearing a dark suit made for an odd sight, the late hour and curious task of sweeping, though he was well lit by porch lights. Spying Levi and Aubrey, he stopped. "You folks lost?"

"Uh, no. Not exactly." Levi glanced around the wide porch. It lacked a rocker or potted plant, maybe any significant signs of life. "Could I ask, was there a viewing tonight?"

"Here? Not the kind anyone comes to. More of a humanitarian gesture. Either way, viewing would have been over hours ago. But maybe you're looking for O'Casey's Funeral Home."

"O'Casey?" Levi said.

"Yeah. They're on the other side of town. Held a big wake tonight. Evelyn Craig. Woman had a ton of family, dedicated her life to Surrey philanthropy." He pointed to the library, which sat diagonally across the street. "Left most of her money to causes, places like the library. She was a good soul, larger-than-life personality—relative of Colin O'Casey, which is why they got the call. Maybe you knew Evelyn?"

"Did we, Aubrey? Know Evelyn?"

"Uh, no. I don't think so." Their curious standoff continued; Aubrey jerked her gaze around the mist-filled setting.

"I had to hang around tonight. Like I said, my place was host to an empty viewing—loneliest kind." He arched his shoulders, broom in hand. "Had some cleanup I'd been putting off, and now seemed like a good time. People come outside, smoke . . . toss cigarette butts, gum wrappers."

"Right," Levi said. "And just to be clear, the other viewing . . ."

Levi's words faded as a dominant female voice filtered into Aubrey's head. *"You're in the right place, honey. Go in . . ."* Aubrey glanced around— no visible specter was evident. *"Tell Jimmy I'm grateful for the kind words and understanding."* Confident laughter, the kind she associated with Charley, filled the air. *"But a body can only be in so many places . . . well, until now, anyway."* Then it was gone.

Conversation continued between Levi and Jim Hennessy; Aubrey interrupted. "Mr. Hennessy, you indicated a viewing here tonight. Is that right?"

He thumbed over his shoulder. "Yeah. John Doe. Medical examiner released him two days ago. Police gathered everything they needed from the body. In cases like this, the commonwealth mandates funeral homes rotate services." He squinted toward the inky sky. "Bet it's been fifteen, maybe twenty years since I handled one. Sad. Wakes like this don't draw a crowd. Sometimes if it's a child. But that's an even rarer circumstance."

"And is it?" Levi's voice pinched.

"Tonight's viewing?" Mr. Hennessy said. Aubrey knew Levi was holding his breath as tightly as she held hers. "Gosh, no. Some fellow they found up in Maine a while back."

"In Maine?" Levi said.

"Yeah. Guess the Feds were handling it. Never identified him. Poor guy ended up at the ME office in Boston; I ended up with the body. We'll bury him tomorrow, Surrey's common area at Our Lady of the Redeemer." He made one short stroke with his broom and stopped. "Why do you ask?"

Aubrey's reply came in a question. "I know it's late, Mr. Hennessy, past hours, but would you mind if I visited with, um . . . him?" She pointed toward the Victorian's ornate carved door, heavy brass knocker. "Someone probably should."

"Don't see why not. Seems like the Christian thing to do." He motioned toward the door with the broom handle.

Levi tugged Aubrey's arm, guiding her just out of earshot from the proprietor. "What are you doing?"

"Let's just say the recently deceased Mrs. Craig is still full of goodwill. She suggested I go in. Maybe this is how we prove the body found in Maine belongs to Jude Serino. It seems logical enough—for me."

"And that puts us closer to finding Pete how?"

She opened her mouth, which dead-ended into an *O* of vagueness. "Do you have a better idea?" She tried to move toward the entrance, but Levi had her firmly by the arm.

"Think before you go in there, Aubrey. What if the message you're about to receive is that Zeke is responsible for Jude's death?"

Aubrey ran her fingers through her crow-colored hair and focused on the steady sweep of Mr. Hennessy's broom. Then she looked at Levi. "If that's what this is all about . . . then Zeke Dublin will turn out to be somebody I never knew at all." She moved forward, and Levi was right by her side. She stopped at the door. "Levi, I know you don't like the situation. Believe me, neither do I. But can you give me a little room, maybe a head start?" She saw the objection in his face. "Distracting energy will only make this more difficult."

"So you want to go in alone?"

"Yes."

"You're sure?"

"I'm not sure about anything—except that our son is missing, and my father may have handed us a clue he jotted down years ago. My gut says to go in there alone."

From his section of porch, the undertaker interrupted. "There's a waiting room outside the viewing room. You just head through there if you're going in. I'd like to get home before sunup."

"Thank you, Mr. Hennessy." Levi turned back to Aubrey, whispering in a nonnegotiable tone, "I'm agreeable to the waiting room. Take it or leave it."

Reluctantly, she nodded.

In the foyer, the beauty of the old Victorian stayed true to character, with Oriental rugs over dark hardwoods and a regal carved staircase. The lights were dim and the air filled with the innocuous scent of no-one-really-*lives*-here. Aubrey was wholly preoccupied with Pete, creating an instant guard against the dead. She sensed hundreds of specters hitting a wall of emotion. Motherly instinct wouldn't allow them to pass. She was quick to calm Levi. "About that onslaught of unknown apparitions, I'll be fine."

He offered an unsure glance.

"I'll explain later. Let's just do this."

To the left was the sitting room. A stiff-looking period reproduction sofa and several chairs cluttered the space, multiple boxes of tissues, and a podium that, she supposed, usually held a guest book.

Levi took in the same inventory. "Not my taste, but it wouldn't be so bad if it weren't for—"

"Its everyday use."

"Something like that."

Dividing the room was a sturdy set of double doors. She puffed her cheeks and blew out a breath. "I'll, um, be . . ." She pointed.

"And I'll be right here."

She moved toward the doors.

"Aubrey, wait." He didn't say anything, though Levi pulled her into the kind of hold that spoke volumes. "We're going to get through this. No matter what happens in there, I still believe Pete is okay."

"I'm hanging on to that, Levi. I'm hanging on to it." She dug her fingers into his sports jacket and squeezed her eyes shut. Like the frame of a film, another image of her father eclipsed every thought. But this wasn't a vision; it was a memory. They were in the house in Greece—Aubrey and her father. For such a tall man, Peter Ellis was awkwardly seated, knees tucked tight at a childsize table. Aubrey, maybe four or five, sat across from him. She was smiling, chattering like a monkey. The table was filled with scraps of paper and paste, children's scissors, crayons. It was a ritual, something father and daughter did together. But this time, the letter box was also there. Then the image was gone. She pushed back from Levi. "That was incredibly weird . . . and telling."

"What?"

"A totally random memory of my father and me, sitting at a little red table. His letter box was there too. I recall him sitting with me. But I don't remember the letter box ever being present." She shook her head, the imagery so detached from the moment. "I haven't thought of it in years. He'd do that, sit and draw with me sometimes." She shrugged. "I'm sure it explains how a few of his ghost gifts ended up written in crayon, on construction paper."

Levi knotted his brow. "Or maybe . . ."

"What?"

He only smiled at her. "You know, we've got enough to wade through this second. Let's circle back to that."

Aubrey glanced toward the viewing room. "I agree. Outside distractions won't help right now. Between Pete and what's on the other side of that door . . ." She held on to Levi's hand until only their fingertips touched. She glanced back. "Levi, don't, um . . . don't hesitate if . . ."

"Don't worry. I won't." Tentatively, he let go, Aubrey taking one backward glance at Levi's serious expression and his tall frame edging toward the floral-patterned sofa.

CHAPTER
THIRTY-TWO

If the light was dim in the common room, shadowy described the viewing room. A few wall sconces glowed on a low setting while two candelabra held wax candles. Their flames flickered on either side of a simple wooden casket, which was closed. She recalled Levi's grisly description of the remains. She'd seen the photos. Clearly, closed was the only choice. For a moment, Aubrey felt like her gift was more of a parlor trick as she simply waited—a sound or smell, the less-likely vision. She glanced down at her clothing—a black skirt and silvery cotton shirt, not a strong fashion statement for ghost hunting. But given the circumstances, it didn't seem like wardrobe should play a part in this encounter. Aubrey touched her fingertip to her lips, searching for the sense that was second to smell—taste. But the taste of what, assuming Jude Serino was taking up space in the casket? She wriggled her nose, imagining the bitter hint of an Arturo Fuente cigar. Nothing like that came.

Yet she felt certain there should be a validating sign. This was not the newly dead—not like Evelyn Craig, who in spite of her *recent transfer* had managed a verbal prodding. No, this person had passed some time ago. And who knew for how long the body had resided in its swampy resting place? After more moments of nothing, Aubrey's senses eased, and she sat in the end chair, first row. She saw no point in cozying up to the casket. Zeke's story wound through her head—his confession about wanting Jude dead. The telling statement sent a shiver up her back, and Aubrey ran her hand over her pockmarked forearm. She looked at her watch. Her son was missing, and this was beginning to feel like a wild-goose chase. It could be that desperation had led to misinterpretation. Maybe a physical direction wasn't the sign her father meant to deliver.

She sat a little longer. Then Aubrey decided it was enough. No spirit she wished to connect with was present; no odors or tastes invaded. Before leaving, she dug into her purse and pulled out her phone. In a grand moment of nothingness, Levi's earthbound fact-finding skills dominated. She sighed. "Okay. I'm running from the obvious." She glanced at the casket. "What am I waiting for? Jude Serino to show up and confirm that Zeke shot him with a gun he admitted to owning?"

No. It was time for Zeke to man up, fill blanks, and answer hard questions. Aubrey scrolled to the bottom of her contacts, connecting with Zeke's number. It rang; he didn't answer. *Texts.* Come to think of it, since calling from California, Zeke had communicated via text message. But before typing a new one, Aubrey scrolled through old messages—the ones starting with Zeke's Boston arrival.

I'm here. Meet me in the morning, Prudential Tower. Waterfall wall.

His next text, later that day, after the explosion: *Searched through the crowds for hours. Couldn't find you anywhere.*

Exhausted by her own harrowing ordeal, Aubrey had texted back: *Looked for you too. It was chaos. Finally took the train home. Can we catch up this week? If you're in town, maybe Euro on Thursday, say ten? Cute Surrey hub.*

Another text had followed. *If you want to see me, I'll be there. Euro.*

Aubrey straightened her posture and scrunched her brow as she scrolled past her calls. Unanswered calls. The few times she'd dialed Zeke's number, his voice mail had answered. Replies came by text message. She looked around the maudlin space. Her heart began to flutter as an evocative scent seeped into the room. It was like a rolling mist, carrying a trail of carnival smells—summer air and straw, popcorn and sticky-sweet funnel cake. The crank of carnival music filled Aubrey's head, and so did yesteryear.

With her phone in hand, she stood, taking deliberate steps toward the coffin. She glanced to her left, and the candle blew out. The mawkish shroud of death lifted, and a sense of familiarity resonated. It no longer felt like she was in a funeral home. In fact, if Aubrey closed her eyes, she'd swear she was standing on firm carnival grounds.

The vivid impressions nearly caused a panic, but Aubrey was nothing if not practiced at remaining centered. She looked at her phone again and, with trembling fingers, tapped her messages. But she wasn't looking for the ones from Zeke. She reread the text message from Eli Serino—poignant, accessible, perhaps a modern form of communication from the dead. *Hell, if they can write on a mirror . . .* On that thought, Aubrey looked, again, at the casket. "Oh my God!"

Her sight lines filled with a simple wooden coffin, and flashes of recent memories exploded in her head. Short, fearful breaths shuddered in and out as Zeke's visits mentally rewound. Euro, where he'd never touched the coffee. A place where they sat alone in the dark curve of a secluded booth. The swing on her front porch, a day when Aubrey had felt so utterly alone and lost—her once lover, her oldest friend arriving on cue. Just Aubrey, alone with Zeke.

"No . . ." Her voice was incredulous, barely managing the word. Aubrey stared at the wooden box. *Boxes.* An ornamental one shaped like a treasure chest with a coppery patina; it held the ghost gifts delivered to her. Her father's letter box, a vessel that held scraps of paper—the many ghost gifts left in his care. And now, before her, a box meant for the victim of brutal crime. The sight of the coffin took on an unnerving presence—the most enigmatic ghost gift. "It's not possible. There's no way . . ."

"Pete." She whispered her son's name. When he found Aubrey and Zeke together in the bedroom, she'd perceived it as an awkward meeting. She'd read Pete's reaction as anger. Aubrey drew her hand to her mouth.

But that wasn't it, not even close. Not her son, a boy who shared an unde-fined manifestation of the Ellis family gift. The day Pete saw Zeke, Aubrey hadn't witnessed adolescent anger. She'd witnessed shock and awe. Twelve-year-old Pete was the same age as Aubrey the first time she'd encountered a physical specter. Pete's reaction wasn't about finding a strange man in his mother's bedroom. His reaction was about seeing—*a ghost.*

Aubrey staggered backward, her body quaking like tremoring earth. On carnival air, from a place she associated with safety and the emotions soothed by a singular man, came a voice.

"You once told Levi it's an incredible opportunity, to be able to com-municate with someone you loved. Someone you'd never thought you'd see again. That's all I was doing, sweetheart." The candle on the other side of the casket extinguished, and Aubrey turned toward it. She refused to face the voice. "You've always felt slighted, the burden of your gift compared to the benefits. Never a visit from your parents . . . your mother or father."

Consumed by dread and knowing, Aubrey pivoted. Standing mid-way in the aisle, between the rows of empty chairs, was Zeke. Neon lights, the kind that blinked from the Ferris wheel, flashed in Aubrey's peripheral vision. It told her that despite the dark, despite reality, Zeke Dublin's ghost stood before her.

Then it registered—he was ageless, precisely the picture in her mind's eye. His clothes, jeans, and a green flannel shirt, cotton so soft she could feel it without touching it. They were the same clothes Zeke wore years ago, the sleeves rolled up and the tattoo visible. The same tattoo found on the body in the casket behind her. The steady steps with which she'd approached the coffin eluded her. Aubrey stumbled to a chair and clamped her hand around the back. "Zeke . . ."

"I'd say in the flesh, but my best carnie bit couldn't sell you on that. Not anymore." In a lazy motion, just as she would have envisioned, just as her mind would have fabricated, he shoved his hands in his front pockets. Zeke's grin, an enigmatic thing, took on an eerie essence. "I wanted to be *here* for you. I know how upset you've been . . . Levi leaving, then Pete." His shoulders appeared to shrug. "I was never any more than this, Aubrey—a ghost in your life, even when I was that flesh-and-blood man. It made it easy, if not natural, for you to perceive me as part of the here and now." He grinned wider. "It's your gift protecting you. Really not that difficult to imagine. Not for you."

"It's why Levi hasn't seen you, why Charley hasn't heard from you since California." Rash thoughts seized her: praying, bargaining, clawing at the macabre image before her. A wad of pain gathered at the base of her throat, and her breathing matched his—nonexistent. Gravity lowered Aubrey into a chair. "How . . . how didn't I know?"

The grin vanished and stillness governed. "For as complex as your mind is, your heart won the battle, sweetheart. At least for a little while. You were in pain; you needed me in your present—not a murder victim. Not on top of everything else. But now it's time."

She pointed lamely at the casket. "All along . . . since Dan called, and Levi went to Maine . . . you. You're the body they've been chasing?"

"Wasn't the most pleasant exit. Just one last smoke before it all went black. But maybe a fitting end for a grifter. Not a great line of work, in case anybody asks."

"But you said . . . you admitted to wanting Jude Serino dead."

"Well, yes." A languid grin emerged, so anchored to reality it sent Aubrey's stomach into a topsy-turvy spin. "I did want him dead. And here's the really strange part . . ."

"Stranger than this?" Aubrey moved her hand through the air between them.

"Had I gone through with it, killing Jude, you wouldn't be in this spot. I'd have a hell of a lot to answer for, more than a grifter's soul should. But still . . . I would have done it . . . for you and for Nora. For my parents." His frame wavered, brightening and dimming, like a bulb about to die. "For all our sakes, I should have killed Jude Serino long before he had a chance to kill me."

Aubrey squeezed her eyes shut and opened them to the same sight.

"You're not dreaming, sweetheart."

"Charley's dream . . ."

"Did you show up in it last night?"

She nodded.

"I figured it might be the first step to . . ." He pointed at the casket. "Moving us on to this. But if I'm going to help you, really help you . . ."

Aubrey stood and shuffled forward, staring, never having seen a tear glisten in the eye of a specter.

"You needed to know about me. And it's okay."

"What . . . what's okay?"

"That you're glad it's me. You're glad Charley's dream and tonight didn't lead you to Pete."

"Yes, but I don't *want* it"—Aubrey nudged a shoulder at the casket— "to be you either."

His lifelike irises, so dark and real, edged away from hers. "Not much we can do about that now. And it's not all bad, baby. I finally understand my purpose in your life. It was always a good question." His gaze ticked back to hers. "Haven't you always wondered, Aubrey? We both know I was never *that guy*." Zeke thumbed gently over his shoulder. "Your hardheaded reporter. He won that lottery a long time ago—he was meant to. The one thing I predicted on my own." Laughter emanated, and Zeke reached up, running a hand through the dark locks of hair on his head. "Grifters tell so many lies. It's the truths we remember. I was never sure why I belonged in your life. And now I do."

"And that's . . . ?"

"*To help find your son.*"

"Pete? You know where Pete is? Tell me!" Her voice rose to a shouting demand. It penetrated the heavy doors, and Levi burst through.

"Enough, Aubrey. Are you all right? What about Pete?"

And on Levi's energetic entrance, Zeke vanished the way ghosts so often do.

CHAPTER THIRTY-THREE

"We've sent a Las Vegas team to collect a DNA sample from Nora Montague. We'll know in a few days if our John Doe is Zeke Dublin." Standing in the Ellis–St John living room, Dan Watney shook his head again. Levi thought that by now he must have developed a crick in his neck. Head shaking was Dan's physical response to the rare thing he could not grasp. "Look, you know I come down on the skeptical side of this whole *ghost* business, but—"

"Finding Trevor Beane, Liam Sheffield, that wasn't enough to convince you?" Piper stood in her usual spot near the fireplace, slightly away from the people in the room.

"I read your report." Dan's head no longer shook. "I have connections too. You cited a full confession from Suzanne Serino, Deputy Chief. There wasn't a single word about 'ghosts'"—Dan air quoted the word—"leading you to the suspect."

"And reactions like yours are the reason we don't stray from textbook tactics when it comes to reports. Catch up, Agent Watney. Zeke Dublin is how we're going to find Peter St John."

"I'm waiting to see, Piper. Can I call you Piper?"

"No. You may not."

Dan rolled his eyes at the deputy chief, who did outrank him, and held up his hands to Levi in a vague gesture. In turn, Levi was too drained to negotiate verbal sparring. "Let's just see what the DNA says. Or maybe . . ."

"What? See if Zeke Dublin *makes contact* again? If it's all the same to you, I'll keep a standard op going for now. Any objections?"

"No," Piper said. "But allow me to cut to the chase. Your people haven't turned up a thing on Zeke's whereabouts, have they?"

"Not yet. But we're backtracking to Dublin's last documented movements. Levi only hit me with this . . . what? Less than eight hours ago?"

"When your child is missing, Agent Watney, eight hours is a lifetime."

Levi looked at his watch. "And we're approaching seventy-two hours. What's the statistic, Piper? After forty-eight hours, what are the odds of getting your child back alive? The percentage, it drops dramatically, doesn't it?"

Piper's usual tough façade tapered. "Yes. The odds drop. But I'd hardly label this case as typical. Let's, um . . . let's not step off the ledge just yet, Levi. I've seen the results when Aubrey's involved. I can't imagine her gift would fail her when it comes to her own son."

"It's what I'm hanging on to." Levi looked toward the stairs. "Maybe I should go and get her. After we left the funeral home, spoke to both of you . . . I've never seen Aubrey behave that way. When we got here, she turned the place upside down."

Their collective gazes moved around the room—open drawers everywhere, the remnants of a rummaged-through closet, usual orderliness gone awry. It was a snapshot of their lives—total chaos.

"She was looking for a way to connect to Zeke." He pointed to Aubrey's box of ghost gifts, its contents scattered near the hearth.

"Touch," Piper said.

"What about it?" Dan asked.

"Touch often facilitates communication for Aubrey. That's what she was searching for. To be honest, I'm surprised she didn't insist on opening the casket."

Levi absorbed a chill that penetrated his bones. "She did."

Piper cupped a hand to her mouth. "Sweet Jesus. She didn't?"

"Damn." Dan sat again. "You didn't tell me that. I, um . . . I know the condition of those remains. That takes some serious nerve."

"If it will lead you to your own child, Agent Watney, it's not nerve. It's hope. And it doesn't require a second thought."

Dan's phone rang and he connected to the call. "Yeah, Jack." He listened; Levi and Piper watched. "So we can document a plane at Logan and passport ID, but nothing landing in the Serengeti? That is interesting." He glanced curiously at the two of them. "You're kidding. You did? I had no idea she was your suspect, that *you* interrogated Aubrey Ellis." As Dan stared at Piper, his head shaking resumed. "Yeah. I have Deputy Chief Sullivan right here." He listened for a few moments longer. "So I've been told . . . you too, huh?" A few moments later, he ended the call but continued to gaze blankly at his phone.

"And?" Levi finally prompted.

"That was Jack Hanlin. He was recently reassigned to my team." He looked at Piper. "You get around. Apparently, Hanlin is the agent who questioned Aubrey after the Prudential Tower explosion."

"Amazing how all you Velcro guys with your GI Joe gear find one another." Piper smirked in Dan's direction. "What else did he tell you?"

"Jack said it's not in his report either, but not only did Aubrey convince him of her *gift*, he, um . . ."

"He what?" Levi said.

"Jack said he had no rational explanation for her prior knowledge. That the deputy chief here is the one who vouched for Aubrey, cleared her in the end. Once the blast was traced to a faulty valve and not terrorism, he had no choice but to flush the pending charges."

Piper strode toward him, her arms folded. "You can add that to your need for proof list. Aubrey *did* foresee the explosion."

"Dan," Levi said. "Could we get to the point? Did this Jack Hanlin have anything to offer on Jude Serino?"

"Nothing definitive, like a location. A private plane was scheduled and did take off from Logan on the twenty-ninth. But FAA records show a last-minute change in flight plans; Serino's plane flew to Nova Scotia. Jack's tracking where it went after that. But with zero communication from Serino, we don't know—"

"If after killing Zeke Dublin, he went off to hunt big game or twelve-year-old boys—"

"Levi, I'm not ruling out theories," Dan said. "But until I have irrefutable proof that Jude Serino *isn't* our John Doe, he's a person of interest. No more."

"Thanks, but I have all the irrefutable proof I need." Levi stood and lingered at the bottom of the staircase.

"What I can't figure out," Piper said, "is why Zeke Dublin would offer Aubrey hope and then vanish. It doesn't make sense—not from what Aubrey's told me about him, their relationship."

"As theories go, I've got one there," Levi said. "I spooked him. If Zeke Dublin doesn't come back . . ." His flinty gaze avoided Piper and Dan. "Things weren't great between Aubrey and me before her past turned up—in whatever form. I'd hoped we'd work it out. That was my intention. But if Zeke is a no-show and it's my fault . . . if we don't get Pete back . . ." He looked toward the stairs again. "It will end us." Threads of stress pulled so tight, Levi thought he might have arrived at the thing that would rip him in two. "Our son . . . our relationship . . . I can't believe my life is going to come down to this."

"This what?" Piper asked.

His lost gaze moved toward hers. "A ghost of a chance."

◆ ◆ ◆

It seemed impossible that physical exhaustion could win out, but that's what the clock indicated. Aubrey blinked into bright blue numbers: 9:22 a.m. She jerked upright in the bed, swinging her legs over the side. Three hours. She'd been asleep for three hours. Voices filtered up the stairs. She knew them all: Piper, Dan, and, of course, Levi. Aubrey started for the bedroom door but stopped. Surely if there were anything new, he would have woken her. She looked toward the bathroom. A shower. She should take a shower; it might wake her up, clear her head.

After returning home, Aubrey had scavenged and scoured the house for a conduit, a connection to Zeke, but there was nothing. She'd gone on to beg and pray and promise, whatever combination it took to unlock a portal. She'd come up empty.

She inched her tired eyes around the room: a made but rumpled bed, scattering of discarded clothes, sunlight. Aubrey turned, dragging herself toward the bathroom. It wasn't touch or even a whisper. It was instinct that said to do an about-face. To hell with the shower. Aubrey hurried to the window seat. She looked out into the preserve behind their home, beyond the tire swing and picnic table where Zeke's ghost had sat across from her. The green reeds of summer had given way to a golden fall, and even at the distance, droplets of dew shimmered. A flock of grackles fluttered in unison, startling Aubrey as they rose in a turbulent cloud of black wings. The empty field rolled on until it met with dense forest. To her considerable disappointment, all Aubrey saw was earthbound nature. Wrapping her arms around herself, she wanted Levi to come upstairs. She needed him there—with her. But what she found herself wishing for more than anything was Zeke.

Aubrey bowed her head. "If wishes were horses, beggars would ride . . ." It was grifter code, something Zeke had said years ago—a winsome proverb or an excuse for his nomadic, broken life. While the wish wasn't granted, Zeke didn't appear, Aubrey's eye caught on the three drawers built into the window seat. The seat on which Zeke had sat—or appeared to sit.

She dropped to her knees and tugged on the first knob. The intention of the drawer space had been a linen chest. But the builder had mistakenly divvied one large drawer into three smaller compartments, rendering them useless for bulky storage. By default, they'd turned into junk drawers, the miscellaneous catch-all every home harbored, even Levi's.

The first drawer held his past—writing awards he'd won, retired from his desk, but the sort of thing you'd keep. There was an old camera, the digital kind most people discarded in the age of smartphones. About a year ago, Broderick St John had given his son his military medals. They were ultimately intended for Pete, who had bonded over war stories with his grandfather. It had been Levi's intention to have the medals framed, displayed on the wall—at least when his father visited. He'd never quite gotten around to it, and without touching the pile of medals, Aubrey closed the drawer.

The middle bin contained baby-Pete keepsakes. Reverently, Aubrey tugged it open. It only took a glimpse of bits of blue—a blanket, his baby book, and a monkey named Moe—to summon a fresh onslaught of tears. The muscles around her mouth wouldn't bow up from a frown, and Aubrey started to close the drawer before ending up in a puddle of despair. A worn ribbon and tarnished medal caught her eye. Instead of avoiding the memento, she was drawn to it, picking it up. It was an ornate thing, composed of three points of a star with raised swords crossed through the center. Attached to the heavy emblem was a faded rainbow-colored ribbon. Her first instinct said it belonged to Broderick. Maybe Pete had been into the memorabilia, so enamored by his grandfather's heroic past. She opened Levi's drawer again, only intending to put it with the other wartime keepsakes. The date stopped her. "What in the . . . *1918*? That's World War I." As far as she knew, Broderick St John hadn't collected medals beyond his own—the Falklands War, secret participation in US engagements, a variety of British covert operations.

She turned the medal over. On the back were the initials P.L.S. and the words *For eminent duty in Belleau Wood, France.* "P.L. . . . those are . . ." They were Pete's initials: *Peter Levi St John.* Aubrey closed her hand around the medal, drilling obvious explanations through her brain: it had to be a reproduction. Probably something Pete's grandfather had made for him. Aubrey and Levi didn't overly encourage their son's keen interest in Broderick's military past, but when Pete's dreams intensified, one of a few soothing measures seemed to be his grandfather's visits and battlefield chatter.

"Belleau Wood . . ." She yanked open the third drawer, snatching up the journals that noted Pete's dreams and random phrases he uttered. She flipped through, page after page. Then it began. For nearly two years, until Pete left to live with Levi, her son had said words she'd transcribed as "Blue Wood." Palm up, Aubrey stared at the World War I memento in her left hand, touching the words on the page with her right index finger. "That's what Pete was saying, Belleau Wood." Aubrey put down the notebook and closed her fingers around the medal.

Like a ghost gift, it radiated heat, but it was more than this as the coppery, aged keepsake began to elicit a vibration. Pete felt closer now than since the moment he'd gone missing. Aubrey concentrated harder, feeling like she somehow held a piece of Pete's past in her hand. Frustration mounted; she couldn't make it connect to the present situation and what might have become of her son.

With the medal still in hand, she looked in her own drawer—the notebook drawer. Typically, Aubrey "keepsakes" resided in her box of ghost gifts. But not everything. At the bottom of the drawer was a gold velvet pouch with a black silk drawstring. "Of course." In front of her was the thing she'd searched for all night—a physical connection to Zeke. She placed the medal on the window seat and opened the pouch. Into her hand spilled a necklace with a teardrop pearl. She held it up to dappled sunlight, where it spun with fascination, not unlike Zeke.

She remembered what he told her years ago: *"Look at the necklace and think of me."*

She did.

The scent of wandering and lure flooded the room like a wall of lilacs, full bloom. She could feel Zeke invade her life, not so different from all those years ago. "Zeke!" Aubrey leaped to her feet while holding tight to the necklace. His voice reverberated through her body and the surrounding space.

"You've found a piece of Pete's past. But it's not the puzzle piece you need, sweetheart. Not right now. Rummaging through those drawers, you're getting colder . . . not warmer. Come back to them later."

It was standard Zeke talk, his words almost a riddle. Aubrey heard footsteps, but they were wholly human: Levi thundering up the stairs. She held her hand up as he appeared in the doorway. Levi gripped the frame and stayed on the hallway side; he needed no further clarification to know Zeke had turned up.

"Please," she said. "Just tell me what you know about Pete. Where is he?" While Zeke's presence was strong, Levi was a natural threat. She turned toward the window. Aubrey could feel the flannel fabric, smell the singular scent of Zeke's skin. Coffee, so much coffee. The bitter, lingering taste of cigarettes clashing with the scent of the outdoors. Little electrical pulses forever tangled with her life burst through Aubrey and connected to Zeke. He'd come to finish what he'd promised, to help her. "Zeke?" She turned back to Levi. He remained silent and at a distance, an attempt to be a lesser presence than the man he was. Nothing moved, nothing the human eye could detect. Zeke stood behind Aubrey, the ghostly touch of his hands penetrating her shoulders, traveling through her body.

The connection they shared had found its purpose. With a gentle nudge, Zeke prodded her toward the dresser. Before moving, Aubrey closed her eyes and tipped her head, feeling the touch of his. Zeke whispered: *"The answer's in there. Like father, like daughter . . . you've known where to find Pete since you were five. You wrote it down yourself."*

No other message filtered in, but a massive pull of energy was evident, and Aubrey's eyes drew wide as her father's letter box glided steadily across the cherry dresser. She'd never seen anything like it, but she'd never encountered a spirit so connected to both her and the other side. Like the grifter he was, Zeke used every bit of his soul—whether man or ghost—to sustain survival. And now he was doing the same for Pete's.

The letter box moved like a fingertip pushed it. It was only inches, but as soon as it stopped, Zeke's presence began to wane. Aubrey felt it—as clearly as she could hear his voice, taste coffee and cigarettes, smell the outdoors, sense the feel of worn flannel. His presence transformed from a heavy shroud to a thin, gauzy curtain to naked, empty air. "Zeke?" Aubrey's voice shook, the force of her old friend, first love, spiraling into the distance, into a sense of loss.

Levi charged forward. It was as if he and Zeke traded both places and heartbeats. His hands were around Aubrey's shoulders now, firm and present, just like they'd been for the past dozen years.

"What did he tell you?" Levi's voice hushed through the silence. "What does he know about Pete that we don't?"

A trace of laughter gurgled from Aubrey—nerves and astonishment; she brushed at a tear. "Zeke said I've had the answer to where Pete is since I was five. How can that be? My father, until recently, he's the one who—"

"Had the gift of predicting the future."

Levi moved his hands from her shoulders to around her body. Her hands clasped over his. They stood like one person, staring at the letter box. "But is that what my father did—literally?" She broke from their unified hold and turned, making hard eye contact. "Think about it. Peter Ellis never really *predicted* the future."

"He wrote down information given to him." Levi looked past Aubrey's shoulder, to the box. "He was a conduit, a transcriber, a note taker." He stepped to the dresser and retrieved the letter box, delivering it to Aubrey. She opened the lid. Light penetrated clouds, a narrow, streaming line aimed at the letter box. "Aubrey, maybe he wasn't the only one."

Pieces of the past gathered in the present. Her fingertips rose to her mouth as she realized the box contained more than her father's ghost gifts. "Last night, do you remember me talking about a vague memory? My father and me, we were sitting at a little red table."

"You said this letter box was there too. It was the first time you recalled it being anywhere but the top of a closet."

She looked from the box to Levi. "But it was there, with us at the table. I'm sure of it." Aubrey plucked the pieces of green construction paper from the letter box, two of a few ghost gifts that differed. She could almost see the little hairs stand up on the back of Levi's neck. "Levi, if that's true, which one of us—my father or me—would have written a forecast about the future on construction paper?"

"I'm guessing the little girl. The one who already had glue . . . and scissors and crayons in her hand."

"I wrote these predictions, Levi. I drew the picture of Santa Claus . . . the stick houses . . . wrote the word 'Springfield' in crayon."

"And that would mean . . ."

"I captured the clues that led us to Piper's missing boys. Not my father. So if that's true, if I was the one who wrote on the green construction, it probably means I . . ."

Parental gazes clashed, and they spoke in unison. "Made the blue star!" Levi let go of the letter box, which thudded to the floor, ghost gifts wafting everywhere. Captured in his left hand was a five-pointed paper star. Drawn on it were ocean waves in the foreground, and on one point, a sticklike house with a red roof. A bright yellow sun sat center. The word "SUN" was spelled out. The word was underlined over and over—enough so a hole broke through when Levi handled it once again. It was just like the clue she'd captured regarding Lily North's whereabouts, drawing a line under the Edsel until the pressure pierced through the paper.

Aubrey felt as if her heart were beating outside her chest. She couldn't focus, grasping frantically for a connection between what was on the blue star and what had happened to Pete. She took the paper from Levi and closed her eyes, relying on self-preservation and cold wit. It was a battle—the urge to panic, scream, tear apart at the seams, the frustration and inability to decipher a ghost gift she'd written herself. The only thing that kept turning over in her mind was the advice a couple of ghosts had given: "Zeke . . . even Eli, they both indicated that finding Pete would take both of us. I thought it was metaphorical."

"You think it's literal?"

"I think it's both." She felt the paper slip from her fingers. Aubrey opened her eyes, her mind pounding and panicking. Levi's fingertips touched the paper. It went against instinct, but Aubrey had the urge to hand it to him, for him to hold it. "Levi, does the drawing mean anything to you?"

"No. I . . ." Then he was quiet, his stare so intense she thought it might light the paper on fire.

"Focus," she said, grappling to convey the mental stream of consciousness she used when connecting elements from this world to the next. "Think beyond what your eyes see. Think how an artist would view a scene and then interpret it onto a canvas."

He looked between her and the paper, his brow nearly twisting inside out. "This place. I've been here."

"You've been there?" Aubrey pointed to the drawing her five-year-old self had made decades before. "A sun-filled common stick drawing of a house from when I was five?" She started again, channeling Levi logic. "Break it down, just like you would any story. When . . . why were you *there*?"

Short breaths hustled in and out of Levi; Aubrey guessed he was mentally pursuing pieces of the biggest story he'd ever chased. Finally, he looked at Aubrey. "When I was with Dan. The swamp in Maine, the dead John Doe . . ."

"Zeke."

"Zeke," he said. "I was focused on what was in front of me. But the cove, it's formed from beryl rock. It has a blue hue. The cove also has edges . . . points . . ."

"Like a star? Like this piece of paper?"

"Not from eye level . . . or swamp level, but land definitely jutted out at several angles. It's this house, Aubrey, there's one with a red roof. I don't know who owns it, but—"

"Oh my God! The sun," she said, pointing to the arrow on the star. "I meant S-O-N."

"That's why it's crooked." Levi smiled. "It doesn't point to the sun you drew."

"It points to the house."

"Five Points at Blue Cove. The overall development belongs to the Serinos. It makes sense: if Jude Serino truly believed you possess your father's gift . . ."

"And Zeke swore he did."

"If he made enough enemies, was responsible for enough gambling losses, which Zeke also told you, Jude wouldn't come right at you. He'd go for leverage."

"He'd take the one thing that would guarantee my cooperation."

Aubrey's fingers flitted across her forehead. "A prediction." She looked down at the letter box, the ghost gifts that had come to pass scattered at their feet. "And while Jude could have taken Pete anywhere on earth . . ."

They each held a point of the blue star, an abstract thing on which their world suddenly balanced. "We have a map, thanks to you," Levi said.

CHAPTER
THIRTY-FOUR

It wasn't long before a caravan of agents was racing up Interstate 95. The team naturally included Piper, who'd accommodated Levi's request, asking Agent Watney and his team to assist. They assembled and were briefed as one unit on a singular mission.

Physical evidence had amassed, which included identifying the owner of the red-tin-roof house, perched on a point of blue beryl rock. As Levi predicted, it belonged to Jude Serino, and it was located not far from Dan Watney's John Doe. It ratcheted up intrigue, and evidence continued to fall in their favor: analysis on the cigar band had determined a partial fingerprint. It belonged to Jude Serino, whose prints were on file due to federal and state regulations regarding casino ownership. While it wasn't a direct connection to Pete's abduction, the house did make Jude a suspect in the quest for answers regarding Zeke Dublin's whereabouts. As for further earthly evidence regarding Pete, Dan's team struck gold with a traffic light camera about a block away from the defunct rubber factory. Footage revealed a dark van hurriedly exiting the area on the day Pete disappeared, the license plates registered to Serino Enterprises. It was more than enough to provide the entire entourage with probable cause.

As the procession of vehicles approached a staging area, Aubrey sat nervously in the back seat of a government SUV. Levi sat beside her, his hands knotted so tightly they were pure white. Clutched in her hands was a blue paper star with a drawing of a house, and an even clearer photograph. The photo had been taken hours before by the Coast Guard; it revealed a red-roofed house hidden from roadside passersby. The aerial view validated Levi and Aubrey's conclusion: the cove, indeed, looked like a five-pointed star—a shape that only could be seen from the heavens.

As cars came to a halt and doors opened, Aubrey was startled to find Jack Hanlin standing five feet away. Her former interrogator offered a steel-chin nod of respect. Interesting how circumstances could change.

The team took its final instructions from Piper, and it was Jack who volunteered to wait with Aubrey and Levi. Initially, he was all business, finally saying to her, "I don't claim to get everything that happened that day, back at the tower. Your, um . . . your communication with Shaun . . . Cairo . . . my canine . . ." Jack paused to listen to radio checkpoint reports. "Know that in the end, your bad day brought me peace—the kind I never thought I'd have again." He eyeballed Aubrey like he'd done in the basement interrogation room. "We'll get your son back. It's what *we* do. I'm thankful for the opportunity to pay it forward." He said nothing else, assuming a defensive position several yards in front of Aubrey and Levi.

It'd taken the collective convincing of the federal team players to keep Aubrey and Levi at bay, about a hundred yards from the house. When the wind gusted, tiny snips of the red roof were visible through a thicket of tall pines. Together, they stood on guard near the SUV. A half mile behind them was local law enforcement, an ambulance—any backup assistance that might be needed. A myriad of thoughts spun through Aubrey's head. She grabbed on to a comforting one, a long-ago connection that gave her hope, maybe the ability to cope in the moment. "I remember," she said to Levi, her breath hanging on chilly Maine air.

"Remember what?"

"That day." Aubrey spoke, knowing if the wedge in her throat grew any larger, talking would be impossible. "Sitting at the table with my father; it wasn't unusual. Maybe that's why it didn't stand out. He'd often sit with me. Sometimes he'd just be an adult at craft time with his daughter. But there were other times . . . his head would jolt up; his eyes would go wide . . ."

"Like he heard a voice?"

She nodded. "He'd bolt from the chair. You could see his discomfort—or I could, even at five. It was like he was trying to escape whatever he heard. He'd go away from the table. When he came back, he'd have a scrap of paper in his hand, a pen or pencil. Sometimes he'd pick up a crayon. Then he'd start writing furiously. He'd smile at me. *It's like medicine, Aubrey. The quicker I get it down, the faster it's done. For a little while, it'll be okay.*" Aubrey focused on the distance, but the memories wouldn't ease. "Sometimes he'd ask, *'Did you hear that?'*" She shrugged. "I'd say no and show him what I was making or drawing. I never thought anything of it. Most days it was so early, hours before my mother was up. I'd be in my pajamas—wide awake from the conversation I'd had with a specter in my bedroom.

"The morning I made that blue star . . . my father knew. I remember. He asked why I'd drawn it." Teary eyes blinked at Levi. "I said, *'Because she told me to . . .'*" Aubrey's jaw slacked; her next thought lit a dark corner of her mind. "It was a young woman . . . her name was . . . *Esmerelda.* She said I should keep the star safe until I needed it."

"Esmerelda?" Levi frowned. He inched forward and back. It was the nervous pacing of a parent caught between terror and finite space. He squinted in the direction of the house. "I don't suppose she confided to you how this whole thing turns out?"

"Unfortunately, the prognostication did not come with a postscript. At least none that I recall. But my father, he took the star from me. I imagine he put it in his letter box for safekeeping."

"It's why he sent it ahead, to Charley, before he and your mother died. He knew. He knew you were making a prognostication, just like him. Aubrey, you understand what this all means, right?"

"It means I've always had a gift like my father's." She pointed toward a house that they could see better in a stick drawing than through the trees. "I guess it just didn't make itself known until I needed it most."

"Exactly. And that part of his gift . . . your gift, it may very well get us our son back. So for all the turmoil it's caused . . ."

"It might end up being the most incredible gift ever."

"I'll go one prediction further. I don't believe it will ever do to you what it did to your father. You're too in control. You've proven it. Do you believe that?"

"For myself . . . yes." Forty-six years of immersion—while Aubrey could not account for every avenue of her gift, she did see herself as the more dominant force. "Assuming we get Pete—"

"*When* we get Pete back."

"When," she said, counting hard on Levi's own tenacious will. "I'm not worried about me, how this rebooted piece of my gift will affect my future. Not anymore. It's the unknowns in Pete's life."

"We'll handle them." He squeezed her hand. "Just like old Eli said—together."

The waiting and natural sounds—distant ocean moving and seagulls squawking from above—seemed to offer an opening. "Levi, early this morning, I was looking through the storage bins beneath the window seat. I found a World War I medal. I need . . . I think I should tell you about it, and how I believe it ties to Pete's dreams."

◆ ◆ ◆

Minutes moved at a glacial pace, and Aubrey was unable to hold her position any longer. Moments before that, she'd heard a fast exchange between Jack Hanlin and another agent, something about going radio silent until they'd breached the target. "Copy that" had been his only response.

Motherly instinct moved Aubrey in Agent Hanlin's direction. He didn't turn but simply held up an arm, impeding her forward charge. "I'm sure this is beyond difficult, the waiting. But if your son is in there, letting us do our job is in his best interest and yours." He made unlikely eye contact with Aubrey. "We're good at our jobs, Miss Ellis. Count on it."

And for whatever else Aubrey knew to be true, she understood this about Jack Hanlin, Dan, and Piper. "You are." She backpedaled to Levi.

"It'll be all right," he said. "Pete's going to be all right."

She nodded, but it was no more than trembling extremities. "I don't think I've ever felt so powerless."

"Why do you say that?"

She pointed toward the forest of trees and obscured house. "Isn't it obvious?"

"For an ordinary person, maybe." Levi put his arm around her, pulling her close. "I'm choosing to see it this way: Piper . . . Dan, they went in there to get our son back. Those are damn good odds all on their own. Imagine, on your behalf, the army of ghosts they took with them. They owe you, Aubrey. All of them. As capable as this team is"— Levi pointed toward the line of defense they could see—"Jude Serino should be more worried about ethereal wrath than the power of law enforcement."

Aubrey wanted to believe him. She wanted to think it was more than Levi spinning the best scenario he could envision. She tried to force a smile. It cracked and fell as the sound of gunfire shot through the air.

CHAPTER THIRTY-FIVE

The glacial wait morphed into a rapid meltdown. Aubrey's knees gave way as adrenaline spiked. The white of her knuckles showed as she gripped Levi's jacket, and his face was as pale as her hands. Her mind reeled back to the last time she'd seen Levi's color so ashen—also the result of gunfire. But Levi did not fall to the ground; blood didn't slowly saturate his white dress shirt. Instead, he plowed forward, almost dragging Aubrey along as Piper's voice cut through the tall pines and whipping ocean wind.

"We've got him! We've got Pete!"

Unnerving commotion followed. The whirl of noise was like the hottest of carnival days, clogged with strangers and uneven movement. Aubrey, Levi, and the extended detail surged toward the house. Team members dressed in full body armor, fortified with a variety of weapons, seemed to be everywhere. Other men and women clad in blue jackets and authority raced past, some running in and others running out. Someone shouted about an inbound ambulance, and Levi's hand gripped tighter to Aubrey's. Her heart felt like it was beating outside her body, almost trailing behind her and Levi.

The stretch of land leading to the house was rough, sloppy terrain; decaying leaves permeated the air with the smell of dying things. In her panic, Aubrey mentally grasped for the guide of a specter, opening her mind like a spigot, looking for the rush of her father, Zeke, even Brody. It was pure instinct, and until that moment, something Aubrey would not have viewed as comfort. Near the door, she stopped and assessed. She had to, for her own sake and Pete's. It wasn't a ghost but Levi who was right there—bordering on the same panicked breaths, the only person in this world, or the next, who felt the same things.

"Pete will be all right," Levi said.

And for all her gifts, Aubrey could only pray his iron will had the power to haul hope into reality.

The secluded house was a glass fortress with Levi and Aubrey stumbling up its modern steel steps, the sound of echoing metal clashing with dense forest. Piper met them at the door. "He's alive." Aubrey clamped a hand over her mouth; she could hear the breath expel from Levi's body, his hand so tangled with hers it felt as if he were breathing for both of them.

"Where is he?" she demanded. "Pete!" Aubrey pushed past Piper, her gaze bouncing from corner to corner in the vast interior. Her line of vision collided with a pool of blood, glistening as it streamed onto the floor. An adult male body lay beside it, agents pulling up close, surrounding him. "Pete! Where are you?"

There was no reply.

"Aubrey." She turned to the grave sound Piper's voice made. "He's alive, but he's not conscious. His pulse is weak but there," she said hurriedly. "They drugged him. Looks like they were holding him in an interior room with no egress." She pointed toward the next level, about six steps up. "He's unresponsive."

"Where is he, Piper?" Levi said. "Show me—now."

"Right here." Dan appeared in the upper-level hall. Lying limp in his arms was Pete. "His pulse slowed even more. Fuck waiting on the ambulance. Let's move."

Fortunately, sirens sounded as the medical cavalry met them outside the front doors. While Aubrey could get a glimpse, she could not get ahold of her son, cranking angst up another notch. A gurney sank a smidge as Dan laid Pete's supine body on it. Levi held fast to Aubrey's shoulders, keeping them both stationary as paramedics crowded around. Hovering over Pete, medical personnel forced open one eye, then the other. "Pupils are sluggish—constricted."

"BP eighty over fifty . . ." The second paramedic stared at an unconscious Pete. "Counting thirty-second periods of apnea." He turned Pete's arm, revealing multiple needle sticks.

"Any idea what they pumped in him?" Piper said.

"Opioid, anesthetic of some sort. But that's no more than a baseline guess."

"For sure, a whole lot of this." Jack Hanlin's voice came from behind them. In his gloved hand was a vial and syringe in a plastic bag. "Agent Donavan just handed it to me. It was in the room with the boy."

"That'll help—a lot." The paramedic took the evidence. He looked at Piper. "We'll know more when we get him to the hospital. How old is he? Do we have some parents en route or on the scene?" For the first time, the paramedic's attention deviated from Pete to the surrounding commotion.

Levi stepped forward. "We're his parents. He's twelve—Pete, his name is Peter St John."

"Let's move." The first paramedic secured some straps. "One of you can ride in the ambulance."

"Go ahead." Levi nudged Aubrey.

She was frozen—fear, responsibility, dread. A tremor that Aubrey thought might be permanent ripped through her, her head moving back and forth. "You go with him," Piper said to Levi. "I'll bring Aubrey in the car, right behind you." The gurney started bumping across the wooded yard. The abrupt departure was so sudden, Levi couldn't do anything but let go of Aubrey and grip his son's lifeless hand.

Levi and Pete vanished into the shroud of trees. Aubrey panicked; his breathing wasn't there to steady hers, and she started gasping for air.

"Aubrey, stop!" Piper grabbed both her hands, forcing her attention away from what were now exiting sirens. "He's alive. He's going to stay alive. But you've got to keep it together—for yourself, for Pete . . . for your family."

Aubrey understood terror; the deep bite marks in her forearm were visible as Piper held tight to her hands. More specifically, Aubrey thought she had a handle on the fear born out of the unknown. She moved toward the SUV, not sure how one foot was getting in front of the other and understanding that she'd never known a fear like this.

♦ ♦ ♦

Pete was already in a treatment room when Aubrey arrived. She found Levi pinned to a narrow slip of glass that was part of the door. "They asked me to wait outside. It's not a big space," he reported. "He was okay on the way here. Out cold, but breathing," He sidestepped a nurse as she went inside the room with an IV bag of something.

There was nothing to do but wait. Aubrey stood against a wall; Levi looked caged. If room allowed, he would be pacing, no doubt adding to his tight mental list of logical ways to navigate tragedy. After Brody, even after so many years, Aubrey didn't know how much space was left on the list. Piper and Dan took several calls, gathering facts as they unfolded. Jack Hanlin said he was going to question the man shot at the Serino residence and walked toward the other side of the ER. Having been on the receiving end of a Hanlin interrogation, Aubrey guessed he'd return with answers.

Still, in the moment, Aubrey was amazed how much she did not care. Levi appeared more engaged, and she thought this was a good thing. It would give him something to do besides wait and pace. When she got around to feeling anger, perhaps revenge, she might know where to find Jude Serino. Ten minutes hadn't passed when Jack Hanlin returned with a notepad of information. She didn't want to, not really, but Aubrey was compelled to listen, awed as Zeke's implications turned into facts. The man shot at the scene readily admitted to being employed by Jude. He was one of several men charged with kidnapping and holding Pete captive.

According to Jack, the man confirmed that for years Jude had parlayed eerie prognostications into his own personal and widespread gaming operation. Unfortunately, his clientele was the type who celebrated wins and came looking for you if they lost. When Zeke provided him with a string of losing bets, Jude ended up with a lengthy list of angry gamblers—people who lost huge amounts of money, others who felt Jude was holding out on them, perhaps looking to up his share of the take.

Dan Watney picked up the story from there. Since arriving at the hospital, his team had reported in with additional initial findings. "In the house, they discovered a detailed plot plan—apparently, Serino didn't want anybody missing a step. He should have taken a few cues from his sister-in-law; the plan wasn't terribly clever, just a basic ransom-for-payment operation."

"Except for the part where they shot my kid up with God knows what to keep him quiet," Levi said.

A chagrined look hung from Dan's face. "Right. Sorry. Of course there's that."

Jack interjected with more facts from his ER interrogation. "After I informed Jude's lackey of the penalty for kidnapping, he got real motivated, all before going into surgery." He nodded, his lips pursed. "Interesting what the threat of thirty years in prison and the desire for anesthesia will produce. Apparently, gunshots can be quite painful."

"Tell me about it," Levi said.

"Part one of the plan was to take Peter St John, a mission easily accomplished by abducting him from the back of the defunct rubber plant in Surrey. From there, they were told to wait several days."

"Enough time to instill the fear of God or the wrath of Jude Serino in us," Levi said.

"Correct. Duress and turning you into desperate parents seems to have been the immediate goal. That brings us to about now." He pointed his notebook at Aubrey. "That's where Serino's flunky got a little fuzzy. I don't think he had clear knowledge of the entire strategy. He said Jude Serino had instructed him to take the boy, then keep him sequestered."

"But why drug him?" Aubrey said. "Locking him in an interior room wasn't enough?"

"Apparently not. As it was, according to our squealer, your son was savvy enough to get ahold of a cell phone at one point. That's when they . . ."

"When they what?" Levi demanded.

"Upped the dosage on what they were pumping into him. The creep on his way into surgery, he tried to score military comradery points with me." Jack's shirtsleeves were rolled up, the Navy SEAL emblem obvious. "Said he was an army paramedic—four Middle East tours. From the track marks on him, I'd guess it was a drug-induced dishonorable discharge. Guy knows his medicine cabinet backwards and forwards. He copped to what he gave your kid, but the docs here won't take his word for it. Anyway, administering drugs *is* this guy's wheelhouse. Unfortunately, ex-junkies find it difficult to employ such a skill set. Made him a prime pick for Serino's op."

Levi drew the rest of the conclusion. "So the idea was to terrorize us, then use Pete as leverage, exchange him . . . or dangle him, betting on Aubrey's ability to provide him with future prognostications."

"And how would he even know to do that?" Piper asked.

"That, Piper," Levi said, "is the mother of all ghost stories."

Aubrey added more reverently, "A story that cost a grifter his soul."

Before Aubrey could go into specific details, the ER doctor came out of the treatment room. Aubrey and Levi whipped around to face her. "How is he? How's Pete?"

"His pulse is still thready. I don't have definitive answers yet."

Aubrey's heart thudded to a near standstill. Her response wasn't what she had anticipated. This was supposed to have a happy ending. The doctor was supposed to come out of the treatment room declaring that after some rest and time, Pete would be fine. "What is it you don't know? Is he awake . . . can we see him?"

"He's very groggy. The first labs show propofol in his system. It's an anesthetic. Whoever administered it knew what they were doing—the exact amounts to keep him under and alive. A person can wake up agitated, saying incoherent things. As far as that goes, it seems to be the case for Pete."

Aubrey and Levi exchanged a glance. "What, um . . . what sort of things is he saying?"

The doctor offered a befuddled look. "Ramblings, really . . . I'm sorry, I wasn't paying close attention to what your son was saying. I'm more interested in what's going on with Pete physically. He's also running a high fever."

"Because of the drugs?"

"Not likely," she said. "But we don't have concrete answers just yet, Mrs. St John."

Aubrey didn't bother to correct her. Levi interjected, "Did they do anything else to my son? I want to know."

"Not from what we've assessed so far. Nothing that will allow these good folks," she said, pointing to Piper and company, "to press additional charges. But there are significant bruises, scratches. They could have been a result of the initial abduction, Pete fighting them off, but . . ."

"But what?" Aubrey said.

"He's been gone three days, correct?"

360

"That's right."

"It's puzzling. The wounds I'm seeing are fresh. With the amount of propofol still in his system, I doubt your son's been conscious enough to put up a fight in recent days. He's dehydrated, which is also hard to explain. According to the paramedics at the scene and the initial findings, they had him hooked up to IV fluids. So while I'd like to blame the dehydration on Pete's fever . . . his treatment . . . it's not adding up from a medical perspective. As for his surface injuries, we can ask when he's fully conscious. There must be a logical explanation."

Aubrey traded a glance with Levi. "Can we go in, see him?"

The doctor's gaze moved around the tight waiting area, which was dotted in federal agents. It seemed to remind her that this wasn't an ordinary admission. "Yes. Of course you can go in. Just be mindful of the drugs in his system. If you're upset by his demeanor, it will likely only agitate him further. I'm sure none of us wants that." Aubrey nodded as she and Levi turned for the door. "I'll be back, hopefully with some more lab results."

Aubrey's attention was hyper-tuned to her son, not so different from the last time they were in a hospital together—the day Pete was born. She made brief eye contact with a nurse, who adjusted an IV. "Can, um . . . can we have a few minutes alone with him?"

The nurse looked tentatively between beeping monitors and her patient. "Dr. Eason didn't request a one-to-one. I guess it'll be okay. I'll be back in a few minutes."

Aubrey didn't say another word, watching from the corner of her eye until the nurse exited the room. She took a motherly inventory: one piece—her son was in one piece. This was despite scratches on his arms and face, bruises that did look fresh. Her chest moved with his—life-assuring breaths.

"Pete . . ." Levi stood closer than a shadow against Aubrey's frame. He repeated his son's name. The boy's eyes fluttered open.

"Mom?"

She smiled and gathered his hand in hers; it was mad hot. "I . . . we're right here, Pete. Both Pa and I. You're going to be fine. I'm so sorry this happened to you."

It appeared to be a fight for Pete to open his eyes. Long dark lashes that were Levi's fluttered as Pete's eyes rolled up into his head again and again. "Esme . . ."

"What?"

"I don't want to leave her . . . but I don't want to hurt her again. Esme."

Aubrey shook her head. "Pete, who's Esme? You're here . . . with us, at a hospital."

Levi moved to the opposite side of the bed, gripping the hand attached to an IV. "Pete . . . you're going to be okay. It's over. Everything's going to be fine."

Pete's head began to thrash from side to side, legs moving as if he were trying to gain traction, enough to raise himself out of the bed. "No! I don't want to be here. I have to go back! I have to fix it!" Using his parents' grasp as leverage, Pete managed to hoist himself upward. Levi let go of Pete's hand and held his son's shoulders, urging him flat onto the mattress. "Get your hands off me! I won't leave her, not like that!"

Aubrey and Levi looked at one another. It wasn't the out-of-sync words or the out-of-character actions, it was his voice. Pete's voice was deep, as if he'd passed through puberty in the three days he'd been gone. "Pete, stop," Aubrey said. "You won't leave who? Where are you, exactly?" She asked this, recognizing that her son wasn't in the same room or realm. Aubrey began to tally the clues—Pete's visions, his talk of war, the notes she'd taken, and his possible reality.

His head slammed back onto the pillow, and a violent cough overtook him. But he continued to fight, his bruised body reeling upward; Levi did everything he could to hold his son in place. This wasn't the fight of a twelve-year-old boy; this was the strength of a grown man. Monitors responded, chirping and beeping to mirror Pete's frenzied behavior. Then the tremendous force Pete thrust upon them began to wane. The coughing dominated, his chest heaving as his breathing labored into a desperate wheeze.

"Levi?" Aubrey said.

"Maybe it's the drugs . . . like the doctor said."

"I don't think so."

Pete's coughing intensified, so jarring it shook his entire body. But as a foamy trail of blood trickled from his nose and the same spouted out his mouth, Aubrey yelled Levi's name again. He bolted for the door, calling for help as their son's body went rigid and the heart monitor hit a flatline skid.

CHAPTER
THIRTY-SIX

The next ten days passed, and Aubrey waded through a blizzard of emotion. During that time, she and Levi asked questions, wanting to know precisely what had happened to their son. Piper answered some; Dan Watney took action when it came to others. Their joint investigation resulted in this: Jude Serino had purposely steered clear of the actual kidnapping, directing things from afar. Not from the Serengeti, where he was supposed to have been, but an off-site location in Nova Scotia. In the end, the CEO of Serino Enterprises could not thwart justice. Levi had relayed the most recent news early that morning: Dan and his team had located Jude. He'd been arrested without incident and was being returned to the States for prosecution, including the suspected murder of Zeke Dublin. Among Jude's possessions was Zeke's .22-caliber pistol. Adding to closure was a detailed inventory compiled from Jude's waterfront property. Before belonging to Jude, the house had served as a model home for the upscale community, perhaps at one time putting Suzanne Serino at the scene. It seemed even more likely when rolls of green tape were found in the garage.

The overall news was huge, but Aubrey could do little more than listen. She barely absorbed the information, her complete attention on Pete. Skilled medical personnel had saved him, shocking Pete's failing heart back to life. Yet amid the panic and chaos, Aubrey did not feel like she'd witnessed a resuscitation. It read more like an electrifying demand for Pete to stay in the here and now—his weakened body had obeyed on the second round of shocks. The thought solidified when Pete's attending physicians could not come up with a medical reason his heart would have stopped beating.

Once their son was stable, she and Levi went on to absorb a myriad of puzzling lab reports. They took in the results but offered no plausible explanation. Appearing clueless seemed like the most reasonable response, at least when it came to probing medical eyes.

Dr. Eason, the ER physician who treated Pete, was understandably baffled. Aside from the propofol, which she wholly expected to find, Pete also tested positive for influenza, a malady to which she attributed the bloody, foamy excretions. However, the knowledgeable doctor could not recall seeing a case quite like it in her tenure. She was further confounded by high levels of sodium and traces of other chemicals not immediately identifiable in Pete's bloodstream.

As Pete slowly recovered, he was unable to provide clarifying information. In fact, he recalled almost nothing after his captors cornered him at gunpoint behind the abandoned rubber factory. When asked about the fresh bruises, an agitated Pete only replied, "I don't know. I don't want to talk about it," and turned his head the other way.

While his recollections were foggy and lab results curious, Pete had made a full physical recovery. Once the medical team deemed him stable, he was scheduled for release. Aubrey prepared to head for the hospital, where she expected to meet up with Levi. During their last conversation outside Pete's hospital room, Levi indicated that he and their son would return to the condo. At the time, a disappointed Aubrey hadn't the wherewithal to argue.

Just as she reached for her purse and keys, a car pulled into the driveway. She peeked around the dining room curtain. Her heart leaped ahead as she sprinted onto the front porch. Levi was already out of his car, assisting Pete on the passenger side.

"I'm okay, Pa. I got it."

Levi let go of his son's arm and opened the back door of the vehicle, retrieving a gym bag. Together, they walked toward the porch.

"I was just . . ." Aubrey pointed toward her car, parked in front of Levi's. "I thought we were meeting at the hospital."

"Change of plan." Levi shadowed his son as they made a slow rise up, Pete having to grasp the handrail for support. Aubrey stepped forward, but he held out his free hand, warding her off. She fought every raging instinct and kept her distance. Instead, she held open the screen door. Pete's gaze met with hers as he walked by, Aubrey's stare tangling with eyes that looked so like her own.

Once inside, Pete hesitated, lingering near the leather chair that was Levi's.

"I don't understand," she said. "Yesterday, your father and I discussed . . ."

"Pete," Levi said. "Why don't you sit down?"

The boy nodded vaguely and eased himself onto the sofa.

"When I called before, I was already at the hospital. I've done a lot of thinking since this all happened, more so since Pete and I talked last night."

"You saw Pete again last night?"

"He called, asked me to come back to the hospital. Do you want to tell your mother what we talked about—the things you didn't share with Dr. Eason?"

A tender snicker rose from Pete. "Not unless I wanted to end up on their psych ward."

Aubrey heard the hint of the deeper voice, the same one they'd encountered at the hospital. Aside from Pete's peaked color, which would not wane, Aubrey thought he had both lost weight and grown several inches since his ordeal. That or there was something older about her son, a change she could not put her finger on.

"I wanted to talk to Pa first because . . ." He shrugged. "I think I needed to test it out on logic before . . . well, the illogical." Pete ran his blue-gray gaze over his mother. "No offense."

She shrugged.

"There's something you need to know—about me."

Gravity forced Aubrey into Levi's chair. It was the "about me" part. Aubrey recognized the tone. It was one she might use in rare instances when she explained her own psychic gift. "Go on, Pete. I'm listening."

Levi sat too, easing into a chair across from their son.

"My dreams, if that's what you want to call them. I have a better idea of what they're about. Like I told the doctors, I don't really remember anything after those guys came at me behind the old factory. I don't remember the house or the room I was in. Pa said it was in Maine."

"That's right. But it's not surprising you don't remember. Dr. Eason said there was enough propofol in your system—"

Pete held up a shaky hand. "The reason I don't remember anything, Mom, is because I think I was somewhere else."

Aubrey closed her eyes and shook her head. Her own speculation was one thing, validation from Pete was something else. She looked at her son—her troubled and gifted son—as Levi spoke.

"Your dreams," he said. "Isn't it possible that you were just wildly absorbed in them because of all the drugs?"

"They're not dreams. I don't think they ever were. I was somewhere else, Pa."

"Where?" Aubrey asked.

"A bunch of places . . . Europe, but a long time ago. And Coney Island—"

"Coney—"

"Island." Pete ran a hand through his thick dark hair. "Then a place called Camp Upton. It's on Long Island, a town called Yaphank."

"You've never been to Long . . ." Aubrey paused, perhaps experiencing some of the disbelief she'd been subject to over the years. "Not in this life, anyway."

"The drugs . . . whatever they gave me, it allowed me a . . . *portal* to the things we think I dream. I was there, Mom. I knew people and they knew me. Over the years, in all my dreams, it's like I was behind a piece of glass or a shadow I couldn't see around. But this time, while I was so out of it, I was right there—with a girl and in a war."

"A war?" she repeated.

"A battle. Somewhere called Belleau Wood."

Then, together, mother and son said, "It's in France."

Pete blinked at her; Aubrey sat erect in the chair. Then she gave in to the inevitable. "Hang on for a minute, Pete. I'll be right back." Quickly as she could, Aubrey scrambled up the stairs and past her unmade bed. She made a beeline for the window seat. Snatching the war medal off the seat, she raced back downstairs. It was all still a crazy, scattered mess, but the medal felt like the first tangible bit of help she could offer her son. Levi's curious gaze met hers as Aubrey gripped the faded ribbon between two fingers. She came around the back of the sofa, holding it up. "Do you recognize this, Pete?"

Pete's hand came forward and stopped. He was hesitant about touching the medal, the same way Aubrey often feared touching new ghost gifts. You couldn't be sure where they'd been or what they brought.

"Before we found you, I found this medal in one of the drawers in the window seat. Your, um . . . your past . . . your visions, it all started to add up for me."

Levi took the medal from Aubrey, turning it over, examining the other side. While she'd told Levi about her suspicions and the medal, they hadn't taken the conversation any further, not in the frenzy of Pete's near-death experience. Now he stared at the coppery medallion.

"My initials, they're on the back. Aren't they?" Pete said.

Levi nodded, a hard swallow rolling through his throat. "You, um . . . do you know where this came from, why you have it?"

"I earned it."

Levi and Aubrey stared at their son.

"In respect for meritorious duty and service to country . . ." Pete ran his hands through his hair again, this time grabbing knotted fistfuls at the crown, his body visibly trembling as he lowered his arms. "That's what they said to me when they pinned it on me, after the Battle of Belleau Wood . . . after I got sick . . . after Esme . . ." Pete shot to his feet, a spark of life he did not possess when dragging himself into the living room. In any other conversation—wearing a Thrasher T-shirt and worn jeans, the unlaced Doc Martens—Aubrey would have labeled his clothes as typical. Now they looked as if a stranger wore them.

"Wait. Let's slow this down, take it one piece at a time," she said. "We all agree you have a gift, Pete. I think part of it might be like mine."

"I think it might."

The willing admission surprised Aubrey. She didn't say any more, guessing Pete was referring to his Zeke sighting. Like she'd told him, one piece at a time. "But what you're suggesting . . ."

"From the things Pete conveyed to me last night, combined with his dreams . . . his visions over the years." Levi's voice stayed steady, pragmatic. "If I had to use gut instinct, which I am, it sounds like Pete's gift is tied to . . ." Aubrey watched as he visibly traded disbelief for conviction. *"Reincarnation."*

Aubrey inched back, blinking into Levi's staid expression. Her gaze traveled the living room, gliding over her box of ghost gifts, placed near the hearth, and on to her father's letter box, returned to the credenza near the dining room table. She thought of Charley and how her gift, while less powerful, connected the living to the dead. The Ellis family gift did appear to intensify with each generation, and enough facts were in evidence to drive Levi's theory.

"I've been thinking the same thing. Is it possible Pete could have lived another life and, because of his gift, carried the memories into this one?"

"You're not hearing me, Mom. They're not memories. I was there." His voice grew louder, sounding more like his father's. "In France . . . in someplace called Camp Upton . . . there's a girl . . . Esme. I can't leave her there. I can't leave her, because I . . ." He stopped, his breath visibly strained.

Aubrey shook her head, wanting to reply: *"You don't even like girls . . . yet . . ."* But this boy in front of her, intense emotions crowded his face—feelings that did not add up to her less-than-teenage son. "Pete, who is *Esme?*"

"She's . . ." He shook his head and closed his eyes. Aubrey saw it: Pete reaching for words to convey sentiment he could not grasp. Emotion that could not belong to a boy his age. Instead, he pointed to the medal, still in his father's hand. "I don't have to read the back, because I had it pinned on me then—I mean now!" A growl rose from his throat. Pete slapped his hands to the fireplace mantel and kept his back to his parents.

"Okay," Levi said, rising. "I think that's enough for now. We're not going to conclude anything in one conversation."

Aubrey stood as well and moved toward her son, who spun around from his stronghold on the fireplace mantel. "Do . . . do you believe me, or do you think I'm crazy? I need to know."

"Pete," Levi said. "I don't think it's a question of believing you. I think it's more about unraveling what it all means. That's going to take time."

"And for now? What happens right now? What's my life going to be like if it's all true?"

"Pete, calm down," Aubrey said. "Like your father said, we need time to explore the possibilities. My gift. It took years for me to get to here. Listen to me."

He made forced eye contact.

"When I was your age, I was terrified. Charley did the very best she could. But with my father gone for so long, my gift so intense, understanding it took time. To be honest . . ." She glanced at Levi. "It took your father for me to come full circle. Whatever your gift is, Pete, it's exactly what Pa just said: we're not going to answer all the questions in the next five minutes, probably not even five years."

"Which brings me to the other thing," Levi said. "The reason we're here."

"What's that?" Aubrey focused on Pete, who stood with his arms folded. He was nearly as tall as her. She shook her head vaguely. When had this happened?

"It's what Pete and I concluded before we left the hospital. We'll do a better job of figuring out his gift, handling it, if we're together."

Through the pain of what her son had endured, maybe what was yet to come, hope sparked. She whipped her head toward Levi.

"You were right, Aubrey. Trying to ignore or control Pete's environment isn't the answer. He needs you. I need you."

"We want to come home." The emotion whirling around Pete shifted, and glimmers of her son emerged. "Can we, Mom, come home? I . . . I'm sorry about the way I've behaved; the way I treated you. I . . . I need you to help me. It can't just be Pa; it has to be both of you. You're the only one who really has a chance of understanding this."

Aubrey's fingertips fluttered over her lips, her throat tightening. She wanted to rush forward, claim her son. She didn't. There was something surrounding Pete stopping her. Maybe not physically, but an aura indicating that this was not the same boy who had left her house months ago. She quietly replied, "Of course you can come home, Pete."

"I'm coming back worse, not better. I don't know how to do this or what to do with it. All I keep thinking is what if I'd told the doctors about what's in my head, the things I know. They would have shot me up with something else, dragged me off to the floor with all the other crazies. Just like . . ."

"My father . . . your grandfather."

Pete nodded, the flat of his fingers slapping at a tear, the way a boy might. Aubrey's heart broke a little. She didn't want this for her son. She didn't know how to stop it. She could only say what he needed to hear.

"That won't happen, Pete."

"We won't let it," Levi insisted.

"But the visions, they're so clear," Pete said. "I can smell gunfire . . . artillery. I smell blood and dirt . . ." He swallowed hard. "And death. I know exactly how much death stinks, the rot . . . the body parts that fall off, or they cut off."

Aubrey and Levi exchanged an alarmed glance.

"Every time I close my eyes, I see open fields and tiny bunks. Then, other times, there's a Ferris wheel." He shook his head. "It's not your Ferris wheel, Mom. It's a giant place—there's a sign." Pete's pale brow tightened. "A tiny room with a dirt floor. An Indian boy who wears city clothes, he lives there." Through his confusion and pain, he smiled. "But the girl. There's also the most beautiful girl . . ." Pete's expression grew murkier than his words. "I'm damned if I go back . . . I'm damned if I don't."

Aubrey wanted to press, ask Pete more about an Indian boy and especially Esme—who she was and why she was so important. Instead, she rushed forward and held on to her son. "One day at a time, Pete. We'll sort it out together. All your memories and the things that are happening to you right now."

He held on tight. "Promise me, Mom. Promise. Part of me doesn't want to go back . . . I . . . I'm scared. Scared about what will happen if I do."

Levi's phone rang. "It's the hospital. I'll, um . . . I'll get this out on the front porch."

Aubrey's grip didn't ease, and she knew that the last time they'd stood in this position, Pete's head had tucked under her chin. Now it wasn't close; he nearly surpassed her nose. Even so, the sudden height differential was not the thing that disturbed her most. "Pete," she said, not looking him in the eye, but counting on physical closeness. "Who . . . who is Esme? All of your past has become so vivid . . . detailed. Why are you so scared? I get the feeling it has more to do with Esme than any war."

His fingers nearly clawed at her back.

"Tell me. It's okay. Whatever it is, I'll understand."

"I . . . I, um . . . she's everything. Most of it is . . . good. I don't know how to say it. But it's the part that makes me want to go back."

Aubrey guessed whatever emotions her son was feeling, they were meant for a much older Pete. She stepped back from the tight hug. With separation came the melancholy notion that someday she would take second place as the woman in her son's life. For now, she grappled for middle ground. "And are you so afraid because you don't want to leave us for her?"

"No. It's not that . . . I don't think." He swiped a hand at his wet face. "Like I said, most of what I know about Esme . . . it's good. It's like . . ." He nudged a shoulder in the direction his father had gone. "It reminds me of you and Pa, before things got bad and he left. And then some of it . . ."

"Some of it what?"

Pete shoved his hands in his front pockets. He blinked into his mother's eyes. "Something happened between me and Esme. It was different . . . worse than the loudest argument you and Pa ever had. Uglier than the Battle of Belleau Wood."

"That's, um . . . that leaves quite a range, Pete. There's a lot of ground between a verbal argument and a battlefield. Can you be more specific?" She'd need to tread carefully. "I'd like to help if you'll let me."

"I don't know how to say it." He dropped his gaze to the unlaced Doc Martens. "I can't. Can't believe what I did." His hand trembled as he dragged a sleeve across his nose, and he drew a breath that shook.

"All right. We won't talk about her anymore. Not right now." As much as Aubrey wanted to know, her son's recently stopped heart was enough to end the query. "Why don't we go in the kitchen? Get something to drink."

A few minutes passed, Aubrey coaxing Pete into a bottle of Gatorade, getting him to sit at the kitchen table. Shaky breaths still moved in and out of him, the liquid sloshing about the bottle as it rose to his lips. Levi came back into the kitchen, his phone in hand. "That was Dr. Eason."

"And?" Aubrey said.

He looked at his son and hesitated. "Apparently, when the lab couldn't readily identify the strain of flu, they sent a sample off to the CDC in Atlanta."

"Why there, what's that?" Pete asked.

"It's the Centers for Disease Control, a place for people like Dr. Eason to go when they come across things they can't easily categorize."

"So what was so weird about my blood . . . or the flu I had?"

Levi glanced at Pete but spoke to Aubrey. "They finally matched it to a sample they have there. The strain of virus Pete had, they eradicated it in 1919, after the first pandemic. There haven't been any known cases in decades."

"In 1919?" As the year left her mouth, Aubrey physically inched forward.

"That's not all."

She looked between Levi and Pete.

"He should hear, Aubrey. It's his gift . . . his circumstance." Levi pocketed his phone and pushed his glasses up. "When they tested your blood, Pete, they found high levels of sodium. They also found another compound. After extensive testing, they identified it as coal."

"Coal? Like from working in a coal mine?" he said.

"Actually, that's what ran through my head when Dr. Eason said it. But she did some additional research. Apparently, during World War I, there were a number of trial-and-error vaccines for the flu, all of them futile. One of the most popular was concocted by a woman from Missouri. She managed to sell it to a Major General—"

"Bundy," Pete said.

Levi nodded vaguely; he and Aubrey were becoming, if not used to, more expectant about Pete's innate knowledge. "He was in charge of a Camp Upton and—"

"The Battle of Belleau Wood. A lot of soldiers died there—from tetanus. Muddy fields and cows."

"And for those who lived?" Aubrey asked.

Pete ran his fingers over the veins in his arm where needle marks from doses of propofol were still visible. Levi answered. "They received a crude but effective tetanus shot, of which the main components were salt and coal."

"They found that vaccine in me too, didn't they, Pa?"

"They did."

Pete looked from his mother to his father. "I don't know what's possible and what isn't. But I do know that no matter what, they don't find your dreams running through your blood. So what do you think it means, Mom? The things they saw in *my* blood?"

With a shaky landing, Aubrey placed her glass of iced tea in the sink. "Well, I think . . ." She mustered steadiness, Levi's logical thinking. "We should look at it this way. What showed up in your blood is proof." Her line of vision stayed on the sink. "We'll take it as the glass half full." She looked at Levi, who followed her lead and smiled at his son. "More proof than a box of ghost gifts or future predictions ever offered."

Aubrey pushed back her shoulders and made commanding use of her height. She faced her son. Acceptance would start now, today. Pete would own this gift. They would help him. It was more than Aubrey ever had.

"So what we know, what your blood proves, is that you lived a life long before this one. Maybe all of us have." She shifted her shoulders. "Who's to say? But in your case, you have to factor in an inherent gift that brings an even deeper connection. The good news is we know more about it than my father did. Than I did. That will help us, Pete—tremendously."

"And?" Pete waited for more. Aubrey was out of immediate answers. Fortunately, fatefully, Levi picked up the slack.

"Piece by piece, we'll sort it out, all the parts of your gift, Pete. I may not share in your gift or your mother's, but I'm pretty handy with order and reason. Together we'll figure out the how, maybe the why. Why your past life has gotten tangled so tightly with the one you're living."

CHAPTER
THIRTY-SEVEN

One Week Later

Sitting on the bedroom window seat, Aubrey stared into the nature preserve. It'd been a foggy Sunday morning, rolling puffs of mist moving like ghosts across the field. In her hand was the gold necklace with a teardrop pearl. She held it up to the window. A ray of sunlight broke through, catching on the chain. It swayed like a pendulum, almost as if a fingertip set it into a time-ticking motion. Aubrey turned her attention back to the preserve, a field where low fog roamed. In the millisecond of a brilliant flash—so much like his life—an image appeared. She saw a green flannel shirt and jeans, a mischievous grin that would forever hold a piece of her heart. Then it was gone.

She glanced fast at Levi as he came through the bedroom door. In his hands were a laptop and a screwdriver, wheels of some sort. "Hey. There you are."

"Here I am." She said it softly, turning back to the window, where she pressed her fingertips to the glass. Aubrey twisted back to Levi and cleared her throat. "How's the research coming?"

"Good. I now know as much about World War I as an Ivy League history professor. I'm not sure what good it will do us. But it can't hurt, having a solid knowledge of the past."

"I'm sure it'll come in handy. It's only been a week. And Pete seems better, doesn't he? At least improved from when he came home."

"He does." Levi put the laptop on the bed. "He even asked if I'd help him put new trucks on his favorite skateboard. If the fog lifts, maybe I can coax him into a ride over to the skate park." For now, Levi placed the skateboard parts on a desk. Aubrey drew her knees to her chest, and he sat beside her. "I wanted to talk about something else."

"What's that?" Life had been a whirlwind with Levi and Pete moving back home. They'd talked a great deal, mostly about Pete. But it all felt rushed, as if struggling for their footing in between conversations. The pace finally slowed as Levi rested his arm on her pulled-tight knees.

"We've spent a lot of time devoted to Pete, which makes sense. But I was wondering . . ." It was unusual for Levi to hesitate. "I think we also need to talk about us."

Aubrey brushed her hair behind her ear, her fingers running over the traffic jam of earrings that Levi did not love. A year ago, when she said she had been thinking about getting a small tattoo, something representative of a little mysticism, he didn't hide his objection. Maybe the months apart had highlighted their differences—the gypsy and the intellectual. She tensed; he smiled. His square jaw and dark eyes framed chiseled good looks that, if anything, were only enhanced by a touch of gray.

A futile thought ran through her brain: *Why is it women never come out on the winning side of age?* She sighed and focused. Levi removed his glasses, quickly polishing the lenses and readjusting them on his face. This tactic, Aubrey knew. He was stalling. "Levi . . . what? Just say it."

"You're not supposed to."

"Not supposed to what?"

"Just say things like this."

"Say things like what?" She laughed, but with a touch of nervousness. "You're being awfully cryptic for a straightforward man."

"Newness stirs my hesitant side."

"What's so new? You just moved back to the place you've called home for the past dozen years."

"For a lot of reasons . . . some pretty obvious, others that have recently occurred to me . . ." Air filled his lungs, and apprehension filled hers. "I think we should . . ."

She tipped her head forward, an attempt to will the words from his mouth.

"Aubrey, would you marry me?"

She jerked her head back, and it smacked hard into the alcove's beadboard wall. "Oww." She touched her hand to her head. "Would I . . ."

"I know there should be a ring, but that's something I'd want to give a lot of thought to." He shook his head. "Not buying one, just what kind you'd like. Or maybe you'd like to pick it out yourself. I know this seems kind of sudden."

"Uh, Levi, we've been living together since Pete was born."

"I know. We've been busy. And I know it's come up. Maybe not so much in recent years, but, at times, I'm aware that it's been the elephant in the room. Anyway, with everything that's happened recently, I've been thinking, and—"

She'd never seen him in such a fluster. Not when Aubrey and her ghosts took up residence in his life, not even when he was handed a red-faced, crying infant, quietly remarking, *"Huh. The book advice on crying varies greatly in terms of pacifying. I suspect we may have to try them all."*

"Levi." She scooted forward on the window seat, placing her hands around his unshaven Sunday-morning face. For all the turmoil of recent months, where they were only weeks ago, Aubrey had not imagined such a stunning turnaround. Oddly, she was suddenly wary of *rushing into* their future. "You're back. Pete's back. I have everything I want. I don't need a piece of paper."

His hands wrapped around hers, drawing them away from his face. "I want the piece of paper. I said 'together' to Pete." His wide shoulders shrugged. "I want us as together as we can be. In this life, and maybe the next one."

She smiled at the most faith-oriented statement she'd ever heard from Levi. "And you think being married guarantees that?"

"I have no idea. But the concept of *other lives* has suddenly taken on more meaning than a redolent book title. It's the right thing to do—for us, and for Pete." Levi reached for her, pulling Aubrey into a long, clarifying kiss. "Please. Marry me."

Before she could answer, Pete called from the bottom of the stairs. It was a tone absent from the past week; now it was fearful and tense. "Mom! There's somebody here to see you."

◆ ◆ ◆

At the bottom of the stairs, Aubrey came to a halt, Levi all but crashing into her.

"Nora." Zeke's sister stood in their living room, her frail frame swallowed by the space and palpable loss. Her tiny face was one large blotch of red as she pressed a wad of tissue to her nose.

"The official call came yesterday. I mean, I knew it was probable when you rang me. But the confirmation, it hit harder than I thought. Zeke, he . . ." Nora drew a trembling hand to her mouth, her shoulders shaking. Aubrey closed the gap and threw her arms around the sobbing woman. "What . . . what am I going to do without him? Zeke, he took care of everything. Even after I married Ian, Zeke was the person who . . . helped me live life." Gasps and tears choked her words. It didn't matter. Aubrey didn't need to hear them.

After her realization that the John Doe in the coffin was Zeke, she'd phoned Nora. It was the hardest call she'd ever had to make. Gently as possible, she relayed the news to his stunned sister. In the meantime, Levi had contacted Dan, whose team collected a DNA sample from Nora. Scientific testing officially concluded what Aubrey already knew—Zeke Dublin was dead. It was surreal for Aubrey. She couldn't imagine Nora's reaction. Nora, who'd counted on Zeke to be her protector and even her reason for continuing on in a life that at times had been more than cruel to her.

Minutes passed. Eventually, Nora let go of Aubrey and hurriedly brushed tears from her face. "He'd tell me stop this right now, wouldn't he?"

Aubrey blinked back her own tears and smiled. "Zeke wouldn't want you to grieve for him? I don't know about that. But he never liked to see you sad. Right now, I think both things are okay."

"You saw him . . . *afterward*. Will you tell me about it?" She didn't wait for Aubrey to answer. "Oh, could you? Would he visit with me? Can you do that for me, Aubrey?"

In so many ways, Nora remained the anxious, unsure girl who had followed her brother like he held her next breath. "He'd have to seek me out, Nora. You know that's how it works."

"Yes, but just this once. If I could tell him how much he meant to me, how much we'll miss him."

"Nora, you don't need to tell Zeke that. He knows."

She was quiet for a moment. "Then I should want to speak to him to tell him how sorry I am. How I wished he'd told me about the Serinos years ago, who they really were, what Jude did. As it is—"

"As it is, thanks to Zeke, the authorities are going to take a long hard look at the circumstances surrounding your parents' deaths. Jude Serino may end up paying for more than one murder."

"Well, I should hope so. But Zeke, he kept it all from me because . . . because I was weak. If I'd been stronger, able to hear such a thing."

"Nora," Aubrey said with the kind of command Zeke would have. "He wouldn't have done a single thing differently. Your happiness meant the world to him. It still does; I'm sure of it. A conversation with Zeke won't change any of that."

Aubrey wanted to fulfill Nora's request; she knew it was doubtful. Unless it suited him, you couldn't conjure up Zeke Dublin in life. And it was more than that. As much as Nora thought she wanted contact with her dead brother, communication would only leave her with a greater sense of loss. Closure would not be the result of an ethereal encounter. Zeke knew it too. The emptiness surrounding Aubrey was dense and telling. The glimpse she saw in the field wasn't an entity she could summon at will—it was a fleeting ghost gift.

Like carnie summers that were gone but not forgotten, Aubrey couldn't say if she'd ever see Zeke Dublin again. But that was the thing about a grifter's soul—you never knew when or where it might turn up.

After Nora caught her breath and Levi offered to make tea, she seemed to accept that there'd be no contact with her brother, at least not today. "I'm sorry. I didn't come here to make demands or have a breakdown in your living room."

"It's fine, Nora . . . really."

For the first time, she appeared to take in more than Aubrey, her gaze looping around the space. "This is your home."

Levi offered an odd look back, heading into the kitchen. Aubrey smiled at classic Nora behavior—not necessarily engaged with the facts in front of her. "This is our house. I'm glad you came. I wish you had called, though. I would have picked you up at the airport."

"It was fine. Ian, my husband, came with me."

"He's here . . . now?"

"Oh heavens, no. I left him back at the hotel with Kieran. You know boys and travel. They weren't interested in any more sitting."

"And Emerald?"

"Good gracious!" Nora flitted a hand across her tiny brow. "I left her on your front porch. Told her to have a seat on the swing. I did think ahead, suspected I'd be a mess when I saw you. She has her favorite doll with her. I'm sure she's fine."

"Pete." Aubrey cocked her chin toward the door. "Would you . . ." He'd been standing in the dining room alcove since his parents came downstairs, his hands tight around the back of a chair. He didn't move. "She's just a little girl, Pete. She won't bite you."

"Uh, sure. I'll go get her." He moved toward the door, though his pace was a reluctant drag.

"Pete!" Nora said. "I haven't seen you since you were a baby. I'm so sorry to crash in on your Sunday like this, in such a state."

"It's, um . . . it's okay." His steps quickened. There was something off in his reaction, like he didn't want to be near Nora or retrieve her daughter. In the end, he stood with his unlaced Doc Martens straddling either side of the threshold, gingerly opening the door. Pete's hand was gripped around the knob, his knuckles going white.

"Pete?" Aubrey stepped away from Nora. Levi came back through the kitchen. A glance moved between them; it was all that was necessary to put Levi on alert. In two steps, he was next to his son. But Pete let go of the knob, his leg bracing the partially open door. He held up a hand to his father, warding him off. Levi retreated.

Pete's jaw slacked. It was as if he were mustering the courage to lick his lips; Aubrey could tell his throat had gone dry. "Your, um . . . your mother wants you to come inside."

A breeze accompanied her, enough to blow back Pete's hair and lift his overdue homework off the coffee table. A girl brushed past—several years younger than Pete, her hands clutched around a china-faced doll.

"Zeke gave the doll to Emerald a year or so ago. Said he bought it here, an antique shop in Boston. Such a sweet gift." Nora said. "She fell in love with it, old as it is. Oh!" She giggled, which might have been odd for the circumstance, but not if you knew Nora. "I'm going on about a doll when you haven't met my sweet Emerald. This is her; this my daughter—Zeke's favorite niece."

She was an exquisite child. Wavy hair like her mother, but the color far more red. Her skin was as chinalike as the doll she held. Aubrey could see a little of Zeke, all of him when she smiled, saying, "Hello." But Aubrey's attention was drawn back to Pete, who closed the front door with a thud, his back pinned against it. Emerald turned. Her entire being appeared wildly self-possessed for a girl her age, perhaps with Nora as her mother. "You're Phin."

"No, darling. His name is Pete," Nora said. "He's Aubrey's son." She looked to her hostess. "Do you have a powder room I could use?"

Levi answered. "This way." He guided Nora toward the kitchen, glancing back at Aubrey and Pete.

Pete remained pinned to the door, his skin surpassing ghostly white. "Pete?" Aubrey moved toward him. "What's going on?" He never took his eyes off the girl, who was absorbed in her china-faced doll. Only briefly did she glance at mother and son, her smile quick and curious as a secret.

Like a rigid wire, breaths plucked from her son's chest.

"Pete." Aubrey said it louder, a demand that his heart keep beating, that he put into words the terror on his face.

"In the war, the girl . . . Esme. I felt . . . it's, um . . . it's hard to explain."

Aubrey's cheeks warmed. "We kind of understand how you felt about her."

"What I couldn't say was, in that other life, I loved her. What I couldn't tell you is . . ." Pete's horrified gaze ticked toward his mother. "I also killed her."

And as he spoke, as her son confessed to murder, Aubrey felt the world tilt a little harder on its axis.

ACKNOWLEDGMENTS

Truthfully, I think about the acknowledgment page of a book long before I've earned one. *Foretold* is no exception. I had my running list while crashing into the prologue and delivering the draft of this book to my agent, Susan Ginsburg. Her opinion as a reader is as important to me as everything she does as a literary agent. Thank you, Susan, for being fabulous at both. Thanks to Stacy Testa as well; it continues to be my privilege to be a part of Writers House.

This is my third novel with editor Alison Dasho. Her enthusiasm is contagious, and she was on board with this story from the moment I said the name Zeke Dublin to her. Thanks, Alison, for your many efforts throughout the book publication process. This is also my third book with developmental editor Charlotte Herscher. If a good editor is worth their weight in gold, Charlotte is the whole treasure chest. She has become the perfect ear to my words, and I am appreciative of the opportunity she affords me: the chance to write a better book. Much gratitude to everyone at Montlake Romance, in particular Anh Schluep and Jessica Poore.

Write about ghosts long enough, and eventually you end up talking to the undertaker. Fortunately, one of the friendliest, most genuine people in my little New England town happens to be one. Funeral director Jim Ginley possesses a wealth of curious knowledge. It might not be everyday conversation, but it sure comes in handy if your story necessitates facts inherent to the dead. I am truly grateful to have had such an accessible resource. Also, thank you to Walt Sosnowski, retired NYPD sergeant, for verifying facts from his expert point of view. Many thanks to Dr. Melisa Holmes, who, when not serving as "the ear most likely to listen to me whine," assisted with a variety of medical details. Many thanks to my sister, Christine Lemp. She's good at many things that I am not and was quick to come up with the early research needed to develop Peter St John's story—plot points I had to get right in this book before even beginning to pen the final installment of the Ghost Gifts trilogy.

I wrote *Foretold* on a tight timeline. I could not have accomplished this without the dedicated effort of my critique partner, Karin Gillespie. She kept me focused, on schedule, and rooted for me the entire way. Thanks also to authors Kendra Elliot, Kristina McMorris, and Barbara Claypole White. In past books, I've noted the Wednesday-night critique group. I'd like to thank them by name on this go-round, a fine group of writers who have become good friends: Margo Ball, Jocelyn Bates, Kathy Ginley, Cheryl Martin, and Sheri Oppe.

Ghost Gifts was a Kindle First. It gave my book the chance to connect with readers who otherwise might never have crossed paths with Aubrey, Levi, and company. When I wrote the book, I never imagined it would receive such a positive response; I never thought I'd write about ghosts again. I suppose *Foretold* proves that you never really can tell the future. Thank you, wonderful readers, for wanting more of Aubrey Ellis's story. I am thrilled, excited, and humbled to bring it to you. Over the years, from *Beautiful Disaster* to *Unstrung* and now on to *Foretold*, I've gained a gracious and willing range of first readers whose encouragement is critical and friendship invaluable. I am most grateful for their continued support.

Lastly, writers spend a lot of time wringing their hands—over plots, over deadlines, over reviews and book sales, over the fact that there's been no milk in the house for three days. It's a short list of people that

I can drop a dime or line to when these things become overwhelming: Melisa Holmes, Karin Gillespie, Barbara Claypole White, and Steve Bennett. You're all awesome.

I always end my acknowledgment page with the people at home—Matt, Megan, Jamie, and Grant—because they also do the things noted above, without malice, plus they have to run out for the milk.

ABOUT THE AUTHOR

Laura Spinella is the author of the #1 Kindle bestseller *Ghost Gifts*, as well as the highly acclaimed *Unstrung* and award-winning novel *Beautiful Disaster*. She also writes the Clairmont Series novels under the pen name L.J. Wilson. She consistently receives reader and industry praise for her multifaceted characters, emotional complexity, and intriguing story lines. *Foretold* is the second book in her Ghost Gifts trilogy; the third and final installment is slated for release in 2018.

Spinella lives with her family near Boston, where she can always be found writing her next novel. She enjoys hearing from readers and chatting with book clubs. Visit her at www.lauraspinella.net.